Unanimous acclaim for

Silk Road

"Fascinating. . . . An immensely satisfying new world. . . . It's not easy, even 50 years afterward, to write about China without following the steps of Nobel Prize winner Pearl Buck, whose novels of China have set a standard with which any other writer is bound to be compared. I think Larsen has managed it."

The Washington Post

"Lively and entertaining. . . . It passes back and forth easily and frequently between the real world of old China and the fantasy world of Chinese myth." *The Milwaukee Journal*

"A Homeric novel. . . . Larsen breaks many of the 'rules' or traditions of conventional narrative fiction. . . . An astonishingly rich novel, filled with vivid descriptions and unpredictable turns of plot." *Roanoke Times & World-News*

"Enchanting, ingeniously constructed. . . . Historical and cultural details illuminate the era with brilliant clarity. . . . Larsen has used a dazzling diversity of prose styles to adroitly demonstrate how history is transmuted through the centuries into something not quite true, yet not entirely false. In the process, she treats readers to an illuminating and absorbing story."

Publishers Weekly

"Fairy tale and myth entwine in this gently humorous fantasy. . . . A translator of Chinese verse has cleverly blended feminism, Chinese history and myth, and beautiful language in an enjoyable, exotic fantasy." *Library Journal*

"Larsen has created a joyful blend of scholarship and fancy and an appreciation of the simple, strong, lyrical line of Chinese verse."

The Kirkus Reviews

Silk Road

A NOVEL

JEANNE LARSEN

Fawcett Columbine • New York

The author wishes to thank Hollins College and the Virginia Center for the Creative Arts for making the writing of this book possible. She also extends heartfelt thanks to Amy Hertz for her superb editing.

A Fawcett Columbine Book
Published by Ballantine Books
Copyright © 1989 by Jeanne Larsen

Library of Congress Catalog Card Number: 89-91512

ISBN: 0-449-90523-3

This edition published by arrangement with Henry Holt and Company.

Cover design by James R. Harris

Cover illustration by Jim Barkley

Manufactured in the United States of America

First Ballantine Books Edition: July 1990

10 9 8 7 6 5 4 3 2 1

for Tom,
though the Lady Guan-yin knows he deserves better

Preface

Early in the eighth century, a great dynasty flourished in China. While the Angles and the Saxons disputed the borders of minor kingdoms on the patchwork map of England, and the Mound Builders in North America carried baskets of dirt to raise their effigies, the mighty Tang reached a golden age. A powerful emperor ruled lands that stretched from the deserts of Central Asia to the jungle-covered ranges of northern Vietnam. Staffed by educated men, the government maintained a prosperous tranquillity at home, while the emperor's glittering armies warded off attacks by Tibetans or nomads from the northern steppes. Travelers from Persia, India, Southeast Asia, Japan, Korea, and the Iranian city-states of Soghdiana in Central Asia traded their goods for tokens of China's wealth. More than anything else, they came for a fine-spun luxury: the supple fabric called silk.

These travelers found a culture rich in its arts. Painting, sculpture, calligraphy, architecture, and music flowered. Worldly wise poets gathered at banquets, reciting lines that continue to move readers today. Talented women of the winehouses tossed off charming song lyrics and danced with heart-catching grace. What's more, idle scholars, Buddhist monks with a message to spread, and, perhaps, the first few marketplace storytellers spun tales to teach and to delight. As you travel the Silk Road to Great Tang you'll find stories and poems and scraps of old books that echo in English the forms and rhythms of these Chinese texts.

"All under heaven" was Great Tang. But people knew that this was only the human realm. They lived in a multilevel cosmos that included paradises in the sky, palaces of divinities on faerie islands or beneath great lakes, and a fearful underworld. Their own realm corresponded to a heaven ruled by the Jade Emperor and administered by a celestial bureaucracy of lesser gods and spirits. To distinguish native Chinese beliefs from the Buddhism that had come from India some centuries before the Tang, the old beliefs are called Taoism, though they're a far cry from the mystical philosophy of the Taoist sages.

Most of the women and men of Great Tang looked at various religions with open minds. They paid homage to the heavenly hierarchy of folk Taoism. They worshiped the goddess of the moon or the tigerish Western Motherqueen who dwelt somewhere in the wild Himalayas. They respected ancient local deities—among them, the dragons of the rivers and seas. They revered the whole new pantheon that had arrived in China along with the Buddha's teachings, including the merciful bodhisattva Lady Guan-yin and King Yama, who judges the dead in Buddhist hell. Even skeptical intellectuals honored the spirits of deceased ancestors, sometimes catching glimpses of terrifying ghosts from the corners of their eyes.

The people of the Tang understood that all things known through the senses, the ten thousand things, manifest the endless alternation of two essential forces: darkness and light, inaction and action, yin and yang. As followers of the Buddha, they also recognized that the phenomenal world is the senses' trick. And all the while they lived in an enchanting multiplex world where events on one plane of reality resonated with those of other realms.

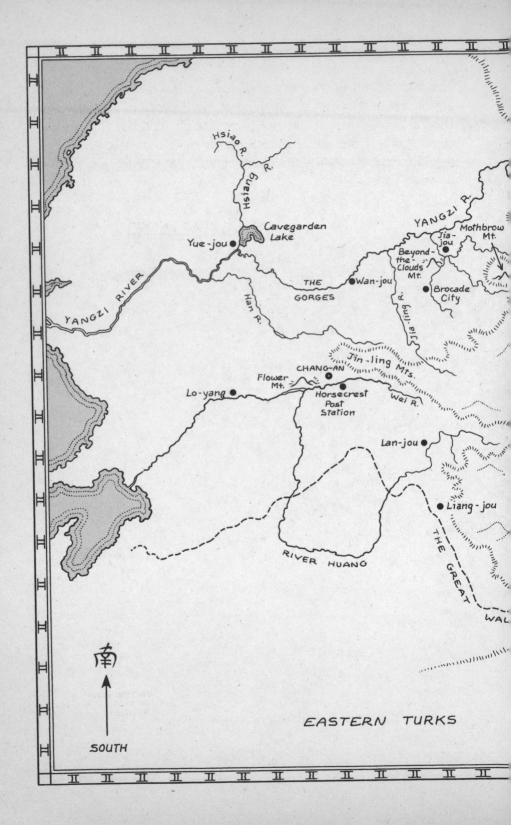

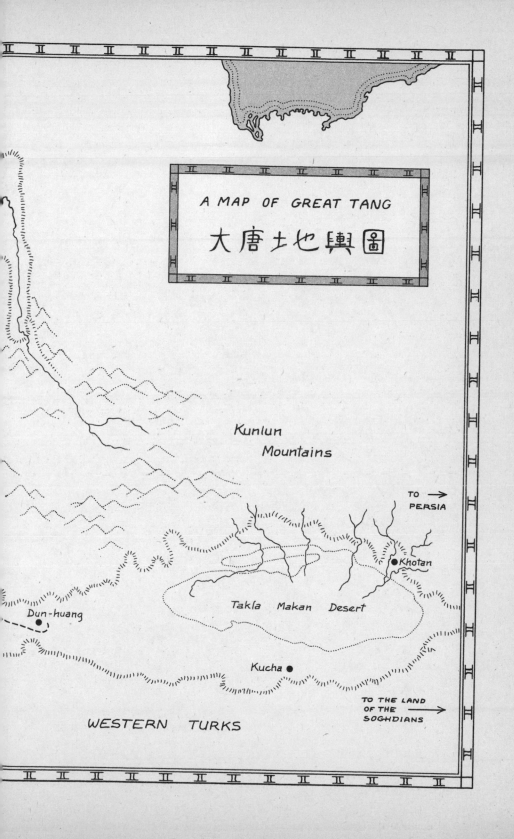

A MAP OF GREAT TANG

大唐土地輿圖

Kunlun Mountains

TO → PERSIA

●Khotan

Takla Makan Desert

Dun-huang

Kucha ●

WESTERN TURKS

TO THE LAND OF THE SOGHDIANS →

PART I

Nu Wa's Grotto

Before the beginning, blanker than an eggshell, blanker than the blankest scroll, blanker than all the hungry wordless pages in the hungry word-filled dynasties of what will someday be the future, is the uncarved block.

And then there is Nu Wa. Who gets bored.

She twitches her divine and snaky tail. She hums a tune, sweet and nasal as the flutings of reed pipes. Heaven and Earth, and the ten thousand things that litter them, have now been born from that watery womby uncarved block, but none of this is quite amusing enough for Nu Wa. She has just finished repairing the cracks in the sky-dome and is resting in her Snail Grotto Mansion far beneath the Yangzi River, grooming her long hair and polishing up her scales. After such a wearisome task, Nu Wa, tugging petulantly at a knot in one of her cloudy sidelocks, feels she deserves a treat.

A small water dragon slithers up beside her, and she absent-mindedly reaches out a hand to scratch the tender plates beneath the hinge of its jaw. The water dragon grunts in contentment. Then a tiny gleam of light from a moonpearl lamp strikes the pupil of its eye. The water dragon, who is very young, twitches its head, and the dot of light dances in the black sea of its eye and splits in two. "That's it!" cries Nu Wa. "I shall make a creature that will see one thing as two. It will look at moon as moon, and pearls as pearls, and it won't see that moon and pearl are the same thing. In fact"—and here she becomes so excited that she drops her tortoiseshell comb and cracks it, which makes her peevish again—"it will see only the ten thousand things and not the One."

The small water dragon, wishing to remind Nu Wa that she has stopped scratching its jaw, nudges her hand with its damp nose, and gazes at her with pitiable eyes. Nu Wa, who is not peevish by nature, relents. "It won't be so bad, little one," she murmurs. "Some of them may learn how to see properly. Who knows?" She looks down at the cracked comb. "If a crack in a tortoiseshell is not just a crack, if they take it to have some other meaning, what might they do with it?" So she takes a bit of yellow mud, and pats it, and pokes it, and prods it into life.

She makes one creature, and then another, and their antics are so comical that she soon feels better, so much so that she begins thinking of summoning her consort Fu Hsi for a bit of rest and recreation. "Brother," she will say, sliding her silken-scaled tail over to entwine itself around his, "look at these curious scatterbrained creatures I have pinched together out of a little yellow mud." Fu Hsi, no doubt, will titter as his tail begins to coil.

The water dragon has been waiting for some time for Nu Wa to resume the scratching. It nudges her hand again.

"Patience, darling," the goddess says. "Look! They're running about on their hind legs now. Be a dear and go summon Fu Hsi for me. I'll tell you both a story if you do."

Parrot Speaks: 1

My name is, for the moment, Parrot, though it has been by turns Little Imp and Dragonfly and Bordermoon and Skywhistle and Heavenglaive and Greenpearl and more. I'll tell you the story of how I got each of those names, though that is rather a forward thing for a woman of Tang to do. Or a man (and I was that too, for a little while). But no matter. Here the rules are different, are whatever you and I can agree for them to be.

But to proceed: I was born in the Tang garrison town of Khotan, on the edge of the dry wastelands of the Takla Makan, far out along the Silk Road that stretches west from China across the desert toward Samarqand and Persia and the fabled empire of H'rom. My father was the garrison commander and I his only child and so prized (foolishly, Baba always said as he dandled me on his brocaded knee) even though I was a girl. He himself took little concern with my upbringing, caring only that I was dressed well and learned to play the wild sad music of the frontier lands; those barbarian melodies were sweeping through the banquet halls and winehouses of the Chinese empire, and he thought himself a connoisseur. Perhaps he would have taken a stricter interest in me had I been his son.

I remember clearly one evening when the notion came to him that I should be brought in to play a song. He'd dined with an important visitor—an emissary from the military governor in Kucha, I believe—and the two of them were laughing and arguing over bow hunting when my nannie led me in.

"Truly your daughter?" exclaimed the visitor, who must have had a bit too much to drink. "With those deep-set Iranian witch's eyes?"

I stood hang-faced while Baba rose to the occasion with a joke about how no man could be absolutely certain of paternity with the wanton women of Khotan; the governor's emissary was not to be offended, after all. But he added in a growl that I was surely his, and quickly bade me play.

Nannie placed my bent-necked lute in my hands, giving my shoulder a squeeze. At the end of the song, the emissary made haste to praise my skill, and the blackness of my hair. Baba took me into his broad lap and chucked me underneath my chin. His left sleeve fell back as he raised his arm; I saw the tiger tattooed on the hard muscle above his elbow.

"What's that?" I asked, for I had not yet learned caution with my tongue. But immediately, I saw that my asking was wrong. Frowning, Baba dismissed me. Later, Nannie explained that the tiger was the sign of a military brotherhood not to be spoken of, especially in front of an aristocrat who was bound to look on such marking of the body as not properly Chinese. She found this attitude amusing, but in my mind my shame at having said something that irritated Baba mingled with the embarrassment of the emissary's comment on my eyes. In my other memories of Baba, he rides past me, tall upon his mount, the eagle's head on his helmet-mask stern as his face when I displeased him.

What my mother felt about me I could not have told you. I knew that she was living in my grandfather's house in Chang-an, capital of the empire, and the hometown I'd never seen. She had, quite properly, stayed there when my father and his troops were posted to the uncouth lands of the far northwest before my birth. And so we never met.

The woman who bore me was a concubine of my father's. "Auntie" I would have called her, had she survived my birth, since Baba's formal wife was my true mother. My nurse always told me that the concubine had been a pretty, fair-skinned thing, mostly of Iranian blood, as Nannie was herself. My father's own mother, I heard Nannie whisper to Second Cook one afternoon in the servants' courtyard, had been Grandfather's Turkish concubine; these outlandish foremothers (as Second Cook murmured back to her) explained my odd-shaped green-flecked eyes. "Barbarian eyes," Second Cook called them, with all the smug pride of a full-blooded illiterate from the home provinces, quite forgetting Nannie's origins. Leaning across the table by the cistern he poured himself another cup of my father's best tea.

"No!" I cried out, as children will, reaching to my full height and beating Second Cook about his stringy thighs. Whoever I am, I am no barbarian. I knew my family name was Li, the same clan name as the Sons of Heaven, the very rulers of Great Tang. But Second Cook only drained his cup and laughed, picking me up and swinging me around by my arms, like a dragonfly tied to a leash of thread.

My legs kicked the air. I screamed. What came after this, I cannot say; I was surely no more than five at the time, or four, as Nannie, with her determinedly non-Chinese ways, would have reckoned. I remember only the sour face of Second Cook leaving in a huff and Nannie's promise to take me out to the bazaar, if only I would hush.

I realize now I had a childhood freedom there in Khotan that I would not have had growing up in Chang-an. The only woman in that soldier's household, besides Nannie and a few servant

7

girls, was my father's newest concubine, a gloomy thing of fifteen or so, with wide-set eyes and a flat, flaring nose. She mostly kept to her apartments, except when Baba let her come hawking with him or take part in a game of polo with the other officers and their girls. At least she bore me no ill will.

In any case, Nannie took me out often to the bazaars. As general over all the garrison troops, Baba had a splendid house, more elegant even than the gaudy painted mansion of the puppet who still called himself king of Khotan and the villages round about. But I preferred the byways of the city, shadowed over by the five fortresses that guarded the trade route and Chinese sovereignty. I loved to look at the fine silks and the intricate patterned rugs of knotted wool. The merchants haggled in half a dozen languages, but mostly in Soghdian, which every trader knew; it was Nannie's mother tongue, and so my own, though I spoke Khotanese with the lower servants and, with Baba and his personal staff, chattered freely in Chinese.

Best of all was the gem bazaar. In the booths there, raw stones jostled against gorgeously worked bracelets, goblets, boxes, and pipes—gleaming bits of lapis lazuli, and pomegranate-red agate, and blue-green *lang-gan* from the jeweled world tree, and moonstone and malachite, and the rock crystal that some call watersperm, and amber and coral and jet. What I loved most, though, was the jade, the famous jade of Khotan: pale chunks from the stream bed of the Yurung Kash, deep green from the Kara Kash. Nannie told me they were gifts from the earth goddess to her best-loved city, whose first king she herself had suckled. These precious pebbles washed down with the melting snows from the Kunlun range to the graveled incline where the piedmont meets the sands. Here the two rivers marry to form the River Khotan, which flows out to dusty nothing among the dunes. Here the oasis waters the thirsty irrigation ditches of the farmers, and the troopers' hardy ponies, and the camels of the caravans. Here stands the gem bazaar in the city of my birth.

I remember how I cried and kicked because Nannie would

not take me to the bazaar one particular spring morning, the morning that the raiders came. So much of that day is blurred by fear and chaos and time that I can't be certain of all that happened. But in the clear, distant vision of memory I can see a girl of nearly seven in the outer courtyard, clinging to her nurse's full trousers and wailing like a younger child. Nannie would not indulge me that day; she had other plans. She rolled her large eyes and lifted me up to my usual seat in front of her on the black mare. Her mind must have been on her appointment, though she could not know just who else she would meet.

My mood changed quickly as we rode through the crowded streets, past the flat-roofed houses, and out the city's eastern gate. By the time the mare trotted over the bridge across the first of the countryside canals, I was staring eagerly at the farmers and pilgrims traveling with us, southward along the road to a tiny village on the bank of the Yurung Kash. At first we passed through irrigated fields. Seeing a stand of mulberry trees, I asked Nannie to tell me again about the long-ago Chinese princess who smuggled mulberry seeds and silkworm eggs in her elaborate hairdo when she was sent out to marry a king of Khotan. Though I knew the story by heart, I always thrilled at the princess's defiance of the centuries-long ban on letting the secrets of silk out into the barbarian world. Nannie smiled, and sighed, and pushed her hidden thoughts aside, and began to spin the tale. Listening, I half watched two or three vultures idling overhead.

The croplands yielded to a sparse, sandy grassland. Then we drew close to the great river, and the land grew green again. The full heat of the spring forenoon had not yet risen when we reached the Buddhist temple that was our ostensible destination. We'd come before, more than once, but the gold leaf on its walls still dazzled me. Nannie made her offerings to Lady Guanyin, to Vaisravana, and to the Buddha Sakyamuni, who they say once came to Khotan when he was in the world, enveloping all the city in rays of liquid light. While she prayed, I slipped round a corner, and spied on a monk with a sloping forehead, who copied out a holy text in some Indic script. Later, I half convinced myself that all that day's pain had been sent as punishment for my flighty curiosity. Could it have been avoided if I'd paid attention to Nannie's sincere, if slightly hurried, devotions, rather than to those meaningless scratchings of a wooden pen?

We left the temple in peace. Nannie had finished what she'd asked Baba's leave to do; now she would do what she pleased. After our pilgrimages, Nannie always took me to the same shabby inn just beyond the temple, for a griddle cake or a drink of cool fruit juice. This was all so matter of course that I never wondered why we didn't rest at the monks' guesthouse instead. Matter of course, too, was Nannie's disappearance for an hour or so, while a cross-eyed old woman in the kitchen taught me Khotanese songs until Nannie returned smiling with a tall man who, if time allowed and the day was pleasant, would walk beside us to the shade of the poplars by the river.

Nannie, the tall man, and I were on such a walk when it happened. I don't know what manner of men they were—they spoke some gibberish foreign to my ears—but I suppose their veins held the dogs' blood of Tibet. This was in a troubled time, early in the second decade of the Brilliant Emperor's reign, when the mountaineers came down from the peaks of the Kunlun and leagued with the Turgesh tribes to steal Chinese grain, and cattle and horses, and slaves, dashing into the outskirts of the settlements that ringed the Takla Makan, and out again to the safe, twisting valleys of the foothills before armies like my father's could set off after them.

We wandered beside the riverbank, Nannie laughing at some story the man was telling, until my legs tired. So we squatted by a clump of tamarisks, and I sang my new song for them. When I finished, Nannie praised my singing, and the tall man reached out to pat my shoulder and told me that from now on he was going to call me Crystallized Moonlight, as people call the white jade of Khotan, because my face was so fair and my voice so pure. I suppose now that they were putting me in a good temper for the long walk back to the black mare waiting at the inn. But at that moment I was simply and flawlessly happy, for I had always loved to sing.

The man winked at Nannie and opened his mouth to say something more. His eyes widened and his jaw worked. Yet his tongue lay still. He leaned forward toward me as if to share a secret.

He leaned farther, still silent, the arm around Nannie's shoulders drawing her with him. Her full breasts rose once, quickly. A faint breeze slid up the riverbank and, it seemed, set the feathers of the arrow in his back to quivering. I think I saw every barb in every vane of the fletching. Nannie made a strangled sound as the blood burst from his mouth to splotch the drab hemp cloth of his pants and spatter my silken peachblow trousers.

Her head whirled to look behind her. I could see nothing beyond the hump of the tall man's body except a trail of dust in the wheatfield and perhaps a column of smoke rising above the farmhouse on the horizon. "Run, Little Imp," Nannie said. "Go hide in the reeds, and whatever happens be as quiet as a froggie in the mud."

What of the tall man? I wondered, but only said, "Come with me."

It wasn't often that Nannie wouldn't do what I asked of her. But she had to go hide somewhere else, she said, until the silly game was over. "Then"—and she fixed her eyes on mine as she waved her hands to shoo me off—"I promise I'll come back to you. I promise. Now go."

I scampered toward the reeds. Usually the laundrymaid would grumble when I dirtied my clothes, and Nannie would frown and say that soon I'd have to put aside my childish running about and learn how to be a young lady. But this time, I could do what I liked. I burrowed down in a marshy spot at the edge of the river. Three or four shallow channels meandered through the broad stony bed; the high water wouldn't come for some months, when the snowmelt from the great peaks reached the plain in midsummer. Looking back up the bank through the reeds, I could see that Nannie wasn't playing the game properly: instead of running to find her own hiding place she crouched beside the tall man's body, as if the scanty tamarisks could hide her. Then she lifted her face from her hands, glanced sharply in my direction, tucked up her skirts, and ran back the way we had come.

She didn't get far. A broad-chested man rode after her, caught her by the thick knot of her hair, and threw her to the ground. I almost jumped up from my hiding place, but she screamed to me—in Chinese, for safety's sake—"Stay away, Little Imp! Be still."

The raider clearly did not understand her words, but in any case he paid no attention when she begged him in Soghdian to stop, nor indeed to whatever noises she made. He jumped from his pony and, holding Nannie down simply by placing one foot on her stomach, slung his belt free of his pants. After he hit her once across the face with it, she was silent. Then he let his pants fall loose around his knees.

Of course I understood now what happened next. Then I just felt bewildered and dirty and cramped in my little hollow in the mud. Or perhaps I have invented those emotions afterward. What I am sure that I remember is the sound of tearing cloth and the awkward rhythm of his naked buttocks' rise and fall.

Before he had finished, two others rode up, laughing. At first, Nannie didn't seem to notice them, but when the broad-chested man stood and hitched his pants, and the older of the others stepped forward, she threw her body over and scrambled up to run away. Broad Chest stooped to catch her arm. The young one bent and grasped a rounded river stone to stun her with.

Nannie spun around and hit him, hard, between his legs. I do know that I was surprised at this, at least—this angry blow from a gentle woman like Nannie, who generally got her way with men by quiet wit or easy smiles. The blow must have been painful; the young raider doubled over, while Broad Chest and the older man roared with laughter. Then the young one straightened and hit the back of Nannie's head, twice, with the stone. She fell.

The two made quick use of her. Broad Chest jerked the earrings from her ears and all three mounted, wheeling their ponies back toward the plume of smoke. At last I could run up to her. I think I started crying then.

Is it only my imagination that paints that deadly river stone the dark green of the jade called "black jade," *kara kesh?* In any case, it was better to look at it than at Nannie's blood-streaked legs, or the way the red forward thrust of her brains had pushed one eye from its socket.

I didn't look for long, though. One of the three raiders must have glanced back toward Nannie and seen me standing there, stunned and muddy and useless. Pony hooves thudded, Broad Chest leaned from his saddle while his mount pivoted without breaking stride, and I was flung facedown across sweaty withers, the air knocked from my lungs.

The rest of the band of raiders milled about the farmyard, jabbering and shouting with elation. The smell of burnt timbers hung in my nostrils. Some other child sobbed. Goats bleated their distress. I felt the pony brace as Broad Chest heaved a heavy sack up to balance upon the tops of his thighs. There was hardly room for my body between the rough-woven sack and the pony's neck, but wedged in as I was, I couldn't fall—or jump away. Broad Chest yelled and the others followed us, splashing through the lazy channels in the wide riverbed, then swinging right, toward the secret canyons at the foot of the Kunlun range.

Song by the River's Edge

The White Jade River rushes,
The Black Jade River flows:
Two streams of lifeblood, mingling, wet the sands.

A fire in the Chinese watchtower
Signals, *The pass holds firm*.
But the desert folk and the tribes of the West roam free.

The bent-necked lute of Kucha
Plays songs of walled Khotan.
Chill as the winds blown down from the Kunlun range,
Sorrowing like a bird swept off its course,
It thrills to a tale that like all things must end.

The Jade Emperor's Celestial Palace

Once above a time, deep within the rosy cloudbanks of the morning sky, in the great Yang-Purple Palace of the supreme Taoist deity, the Jade Emperor Himself, the Assistant Undersecretary of Baubles humbly presents a newly arrived gift of tribute to His Divine Majesty. All the spirits, sylphs, and sages of the court gather round to see it: a board for playing Go, made of rhinoceros horn inlaid in squares, and two bowls of Go stones, each bowl studded with violet cowrie shells. The courtiers draw in their breaths and move closer.

The Undersecretary slides his eyes sideways to savor the attentive faces of the immortals crowding round him. He has never before approached the Jade Emperor directly and is only able to do so now because the Chief Secretary drank far too much Liquid Sunset at last night's banquet and lies at home in his bedchamber pressing a silver cup of ice to his head. "This," says the Undersecretary with only a tiny tremor in his voice, "is offered to Your Divine Majesty by his loyal vassal, the Tutelary Deity of Pearlshore. Allow me to show you the Go stones, if you will."

The Jade Emperor nods, and the Undersecretary removes the first lid with a flourish. Within the bowl rest nearly two hundred perfectly matched black pearls, each just the size to fit the tiny depressions where the corners of the squares meet. The crowd of heavenly courtiers gasps.

Allowing his lips to curve just the slightest bit upward, the Undersecretary removes the second lid. Instead of the white pearls one would expect to complete this stunning Go set, the bowl holds pearls in a multitude of tints: pale peach, and creamy gold, and powder pink, and the faint blue of the sky seen through thin wisps of fog. The courtiers are still now. The Jade Emperor's face glows with pleasure, and he reaches forth a gracious hand and runs it through the bowl of colored pearls. "We are pleased with the gift," he says, "and you, Undersecretary, will write a letter to the Tutelary Deity of Pearlshore, informing him of his promotion to Illustrious Pearl Baron of the Southern Sea. But first"—the Undersecretary's heart quickens—"first, you will join me in a game of Go."

A buzz runs through the court, and the courtiers settle down on their cloud couches to watch the game. The Undersecretary, who is no fool, chooses the plain black pearls, and they begin to play.

The board is nearly half filled with pearls when the Jade Emperor reaches absently into his bowl. His eyes are on the board, for he is thinking that on his next move he can complete a dragon's eye, surrounding and thus capturing one of the Undersecretary's pieces. So he hardly notices that the pearl he takes up is oddly shaped, and a bit smaller than the rest. Just then the Undersecretary lays down a black pearl, encircling eight of the Emperor's and removing them from the board.

The hot breath of anger rises in the Jade Emperor's breast.

His dark eyes flash like lightning, and the sound of thunder rolls round the celestial audience hall. But the Emperor says nothing, and bends his lips into a smile, and clears his throat. "Well played," he says. "I like a man who gives his, ah, his *all* to the game."

The Undersecretary's head swims with relief. "The game is far from over, Sire," he mutters, not daring to raise his face.

"Indeed," says the Jade Emperor, tossing and catching the lumpy pearl he is holding. "Indeed."

The Undersecretary looks up, fixing his gaze on the pearl. He is just opening his mouth to speak when a tiny voice says, "Far from over. Indeed, indeed."

The spirits, sylphs, and sages crane their necks and look about to see who is the source of this impertinence. The Undersecretary jumps to his feet and glares, hoping in this way to make it clear that it is not he who has irreverently echoed the words of His Divine Majesty. He pulls his eyebrows down as far as they will go, and tugs sternly at his rather scrawny beard. "Who presumes to—" he begins in a fierce voice, but before he reaches the fatal word *mock*, a heaven-shaking laugh rings out.

"Ha," says the Jade Emperor. "Ha, ha. Far from over. Indeed. Indeed."

"Ha," say the courtiers. "Ha, ha. Far from over. Indeed."

The Undersecretary's eyebrows float upward, turning as they rise from youthful blue-black to gray. "Ha," he says. "Ha, ha, ha, ha, ha."

"Ha," says the same tiny voice.

"Who speaks?" asks the Jade Emperor in a terrible roar, though his eyes still spark with merriment.

"Who, Sire? Speaks?" the voice squeaks. "Who indeed?"

The Jade Emperor holds his sides and laughs some more. "Speak!" he cries out. "I command you to speak."

"It is I," says the voice. "In the palm of your hand." It pauses and adds, "Sire."

The Undersecretary and the Jade Emperor stare, and the pearl in the Emperor's palm trembles, as if with excitement. They see how small and greenish it is, and how irregularly shaped. "Is it you who speaks, pearl?" asks the Jade Emperor, screwing up one divinely lustrous eye.

"Yes, Sire," replies the pearl. "Now that you have commanded me, I do the thing I have long desired: I speak."

"How odd," says the Jade Emperor in a musing voice. "An odd desire from an odd-looking pearl."

The courtiers wave their fans and whisper, "Odd."

"Because you have made me laugh, on an otherwise boring day," the Jade Emperor says, with a meaningful sidelong glance at the Undersecretary, who smiles and nods agreeably, "I shall call you my Luminous Emerald-Green Lunar Essence Sprite and keep you beside me in my Yang-Purple Audience Hall to make me laugh, and I shall grant you any boon."

"Oh, if you please, Sire," says the pearl, "there is only one thing I want, and that is to learn to speak the speech of human beings. I first heard it when the divers of Pearlshore pulled me from the depths of the Southern Sea. When they wrenched my shell open and their chattering swirled around me, I felt a great desire and swore a holy vow that I should have no rest until I could speak as they do. Guan-yin the Compassionate heard me and took pity. The blessed Lady kindly slipped me into the pale-pearl bowl of the Go set. That is why I am here."

"Ungrateful wretch!" The Jade Emperor stamps his foot, and down in the human realm a mighty river breaks through its dikes, ravaging two townships. "Guan-yin the Meddling Bodhisattva is more like it. She doesn't want the karmic responsibility, so she passes you on to me. And you! You'd rather suffer through the dusty moils of human existence than enjoy the pleasures of Our court?"

The Undersecretary twists his face in what he hopes is the correct mixture of shock and disdain and amazement and righteous rage. But the Jade Emperor leans back in his star-sprinkled throne and composes himself. "I am a deity of my word," he

says, drawing out each syllable, "and you will have your wish."
He waves his Magic Mushroom Scepter toward the Undersecretary. "This foolish game of Go is ended. You, my lad, are transferred to the office of the Acting Assistant Controller of the
Ministry of Babble. Effective *now*. Your duties will be to watch
over this silly thing you brought me, and to report to me of its
adventures. I sentence you, green pearl, to a lifetime in the human realm. I daresay you will learn to speak." With that, the
green pearl vanishes. "And," the Emperor's voice rings out after
it, "I believe you'll have a tale to tell."

Parrot Speaks: 2

In the long morning shadows of a valley in the foothills, I awoke to a snarling and growling of curs: the words of the Tibetans clashed in the chilly air. Broad Chest, and the young man who had crushed Nannie's skull, and three other raiders strutted near a meager cookfire. A one-eared man hunkered down across from them. He spoke from the side of his mouth, first snapping at Broad Chest, then turning to the clot of dirty nomads behind him for confirmation of whatever it was he said.

Some say that upon waking in a strange place they are lost at first, and forgetful of how they came there, but that morning I knew instantly where I was and all that had happened. Jolted, filthy, barely able to draw breath, I had watched the trampled grain and pebbles fly beneath the hooves of Broad Chest's pony as his band met up with a larger group and we left the last outlying farm village for the raiders' camp. The ride was hard and long. It was nearly dark when he jumped from his mount, tied my ankles carelessly, and pushed me over, half stunned and exhausted, to huddle with five other children. A thick-lipped farmboy of some eight years began to howl as we approached. Perhaps I reminded him of someone; perhaps Broad Chest did. An indifferent cuff silenced him. None of the rest spoke or acknowledged my arrival with more than a blinkless gaze.

After that, the Tibetans built a fire, and feasted and drank and sang, not fearing—or pretending not to fear—pursuit. They were safe enough. Some say the troops of Tang, men like my father's, stationed there in the far frontier had grown weak, their administration sloppy, their discipline slack, too many of the soldiers not Chinese. Yet my father was a good general; he must have been. Who could maintain perfect watch over a desert basin ringed by a maze of mountain hiding holes for barbarians who refused to recognize the commands of the Son of Heaven? In their hidden camp, the raiders celebrated freely.

In the early morning, surely no more than a few hours after the last roistering had slurred into silence, the men around the cookfire quarreled. Broad Chest and One Ear gestured toward where we lay. One or two of the raiders, ignoring the skirmish of words, slung booty into saddlebags and rounded up the stolen goats and cattle. An old man, toothless and almost too bent to ride, brought us a leftover haunch of half-cooked kid. None of us would reach to take it from him; he grunted and tossed it at our feet. The farmboy picked it up and began to eat with energy and greed, then passed it to an older girl who looked to be his sister. When it came my turn, I stared at the greasy, blood-pink thing and thought I could not choke down even a bite of it. But soon enough I did.

My stomach held all it would take when the growling of the quarrel burst into open shouts. One Ear stood now, with the angry air of a commander defied; he pounded the black-lacquered scales of his leather armor. Those who had been gathering up the loot sat astride their restless ponies on his side of the cookfire. The old man who fed us waited near the flock of stolen animals, his mouth distorted with repressed nervousness. Broad Chest stepped forward, closer to the embers that still lay between him and the leader.

One Ear barked an order and jerked his chin toward the mountains. Broad Chest folded his arms and stood his ground. Nannie's killer began to kick dirt over the embers, edging round to One Ear's side as he did so, but at a word from Broad Chest, he melted back and took the same pose, defiance painted on his face. Off in the hills, a marmot whistled, but no one seemed to hear it.

One Ear waved a hand toward us children. He shrugged. Turning his head halfway—but no more—from Broad Chest, he called for his pony, snatched the reins from the youth who brought it, and mounted. Those beside him made way. A grimace like a smile tore his lips apart. His white teeth shone as he uttered what seemed to be a rough joke and, deliberately, turned his back. His pony began picking its way over the rocky ground toward the upper end of the valley and the knife-edged ridge beyond. The others, except the few with Broad Chest, fell in behind. Goats bleated as the old man switched their rumps and prepared to follow the band. Broad Chest stood unmoved.

Then, with a shrill whoop, One Ear wheeled his mount and bore down on us at full gallop. The raiders behind him drew to a halt. What Broad Chest did in that moment I cannot say, for my eyes were fixed on the pony hurtling toward me. One Ear passed so close to where I stood that—I remember it clearly—I could feel the heat of the pony's body in the chilly air. He leaned from his saddle, snatched up the farmboy's older sister, and threw her facedown across the pony's withers. On his way back to the head of the loose column of raiders, he tore through the last of the cookfire, his pony's hooves kicking up a cloud of hot coals and ash.

The farmboy took up his howling again, and no one stopped him. I and the others remained dumb. Two of the four men behind Broad Chest muttered to one another until he turned and spat in the settling ashy dust. At a word from Broad Chest, the young raider hustled to fill water bags from a stagnant pool beneath a cleft in the rockwall and loaded them on the few pack ponies that had been left behind. Then each rider mounted and pulled a child up to sit behind him; only Broad Chest rode alone.

We rode downvalley. Some distance behind me the farmboy sniveled and blubbered, though I count myself no braver for my silence. Hours later, as we left the dry grasslands of the piedmont for the gray-brown soil of the desert's edge, I heard a small flurry up ahead and saw that one of the other girls, the one I'd soon learn to call Nephrite, now lay prone across the withers of the pony just ahead of me. She had evidently tried to slip off and escape, though even I could see that escape in this unmarked stony wilderness meant a slow, dry death. My head slumped and I stared only at the uncurried fur on the pony's flanks. I had never ridden a horse this far before; my thighs and buttocks and back burned.

Once out of the valley we had turned more or less east, paralleling the distant line of mountains. We rode straight through the hot part of the day, and I prayed, as Nannie would have had me do, a prayer of thanks to the compassionate Lady Guan-yin, Bodhisattva of Mercy: Had it been summer, and not the height of spring, I surely would have died of thirst, if not that day, then the next. Had it been earlier in the year, I would have died another way, curled blanketless among the other captives, during the cold nights.

It was on the second afternoon that we saw the monk. We'd angled down to strike the Silk Road well to the east of Khotan. I still did not know what Broad Chest and the others planned to do; I had learned in two days a good deal about understanding their meaning without understanding their words, but I could tell only that they were looking for something and that they were anxious to be rid of us.

The monk seemed at first to be no more than a glimmer on

the far horizon, not moving toward us at all. The Road ran very close to the dunes just there, squeezing past the last few struggling steppe plants by a huge outcropping of rock. Waves of heat danced above the hot earth. Then the glimmer grew a little larger and began to coalesce into bodily form. The Tibetans drew up their ponies' reins, and waited.

Incredibly, the monk traveled with only three disciples and four puny camels that slouched along the trail worn into the loose earth. Other travelers might have stopped at the sight of Broad Chest sitting tall astride his pony, or might have turned and fled, however fruitlessly. But the monk came on at a steady pace, eyes fixed on the back of his camel's head, droning his prayers. When he came to the impassive Tibetan, he merely nodded and sketched a blessing with one hand. "The peace of The Enlightened One be upon you, good sir," he said, in the pure Chinese of Chang-an, and began to lead his little caravan around Broad Chest and his pony. I noticed that he did attempt to pass on the side of the loose sands, away from where the rest of the warriors clustered. The plumpest of his disciples squinted his piggish eyes and prodded his camel to hurry after.

"Stop," said Broad Chest, first in what I suppose was Tibetan, and then in Soghdian.

The monk blinked his mild eyes and smiled a benign smile. "I go India," he said in Soghdian. "I go fetch holy scriptures. Lady Guan-yin watches me. Peace." Again, he made as if to pass. "Farewell."

"Trader?" asked Broad Chest, leaning forward, every muscle tensed. Then, jerking his chin in my direction, he added, "We sell slaves. Good slaves." Another disciple began to twitch, screwing up his face like an angry monkey's. But at a glance from his master, he grimaced, clutched his head, and was still.

"I no trader," the monk said with a patient sigh. "I go fetch holy scrolls. Farewell."

Evidently "scrolls" meant no more to Broad Chest than "scriptures" had, but the man I rode behind called out something and Broad Chest shrugged. "Trader where?" he growled at the frail-looking monk. "Trader that way"—he pointed in the direction from which the monk had come—"you go."

The monk nodded as if conceding a treat to a demanding child. All human wants were to be met in the same fashion, with detachment even from the desire to do good. "Trader there," he said, turning to point behind him. "Persian trader go Dun-huang. I meet one hour before. Farewell."

"Eee-yah," yelled Broad Chest, standing triumphantly in his stirrups and releasing two days' frustration with his yell. He scarcely looked as the monk, his three quaking disciples, and their camels began to pass them by. But before he could spur his pony on, the young raider who had killed Nannie pushed the farmboy from his seat behind him, drew his long knife, and headed for the monk. What wealth he thought the holy man might carry, I cannot say, but he was evidently prepared to slaughter him and the disciples for their rosaries and begging bowls.

The monk, who had already passed some way beyond, turned slowly back to fix the murderer with a severe father's look. "Guan-yin watches," he said in warning tones. "Peace."

The other ignored him. Brandishing his bright blade, the young Tibetan rushed past the disciples, evidently reckoning them easy prey once their master fell to his knife.

And then it happened. I have told this tale to more than one, swearing its truth to them as I swear it to you. Some have spoken to me at great length of the treacherous undertow of wind-driven sand. One old scholar, who loved yellow wine and arcane lore far more than Confucian texts, claimed that certain wizards can put people into a light sleep and tell them what to do, or see. But I believe that it all took place just as you will read it: The galloping pony seemed to slip, or turn its ankle on a loose stone. It heaved over on its side, pitching its rider into the sand beyond the trail. The first encroaching dune rose up, and roiled, and rushed toward him like a wave of meltwater when a river crests. The young Tibetan, screaming threats or curses, sank beneath the steep leeward slope of the sand. One of his brothers began to ride up to pull him out, but his mount stopped, unnaturally still, remaining unmoved by kicks or blows from his whip.

The sand surged from the murderer's chest up to his neck, his mouth, his nose, and he was gone. When I looked in their direction, the monk and his caravan were once again a shimmering on the horizon, as if they had been no more than a mirage.

The Yellow Springs

Now a soul arrives at the gates of the underworld. Its hair streams down thick, wavy, disheveled. It is weeping, but what soul doesn't weep when it comes at last to the Yellow Springs?

This soul has come wailing alone through the empty fields and desolate wildlands. It goes to judgment before Yama, great King of the Realm of Darkness, who will decide what fate it has earned by its actions in the life just gone by: perhaps a term in purgatory, to await release through the prayers of the faithful; perhaps rebirth as the lowest of beasts; perhaps an eternity of torment—tongue flayed, guts ripped out again and again by red-hot hooks—in an icy pool of pus and shit; perhaps another human life with its feet set at last on the way to paradise.

First, though, it must cross the River of Futility. It hovers on the bank, uncertain. It sees on the far shore ox-faced demons jabbing hordes of sinners, driving them down to the Eighteen

Hells. It hears all around it the piteous lamentations of other poor souls, who have hung their gaudy rags of silk upon the branches of trees made leafless by the noxious fumes. These creatures cannot cross the river; they gnash their teeth and moan, striding back and forth, endlessly back and forth along the riverbank. This new soul knows what it must do. It crosses over.

Reaching the far shore, it approaches, all atremble, the triple gate to King Yama's realm. Ten thousand guardians, armed with iron swords and staffs of bronze, bar the way. Air rushes out through the portal, heavy with the sobbing of those grown rich on the griefs of others, of those who lived in heedless luxury or sowed wild words with no regard for truth, of those who took pleasure in falsity and deceit. The Gatekeeper steps forward, sneers at the new soul's buxom form. His teeth are jagged spears; his mouth is a midwife's bowl of blood.

Leering, the Gatekeeper conducts the soul to the tribunal of the implacable judge of the netherworld. Twin torches blaze in the gloom; regal jade belt-pendants ring as King Yama bends to look down upon the sinner. The soul approaches the bench. Yama orders the General of the Five Ways to read the record of its actions in the Book of Life and Death. The General kowtows and complies.

This soul's sins, though not few, are merely venial: the vain admiration of its own rotting flesh, a love of taste and smell and the beautiful appearance of what is only illusion, a sweet indulgence of the body's laziness, and lust. This lust it fulfilled at the cost of distraction from its duties, and from contemplation of the One True Way. The soul hangs its head and feels its heart wrench with remorse as the list is read.

"And to the good?" King Yama asks.

"Sire," says the General, unrolling the scroll a bit farther, "though this soul had no child of its own, it was as a mother to a child who knew no mother. It gave alms to mendicant priests. It regularly burned incense at the altar of Guan-yin." For the first time, hope begins to rise within the soul, but it dares not raise its head. "Still," the General continues, "it raised the child for money, and carelessly at times. The alms never stood at more than it might have spent for a bit of ribbon. And its devotions never postponed its pleasures for long."

King Yama nods. The story rings familiarly in his divine ears: a fortunate soul, born where it could hear the Teachings of the Law, so that it had the chance to see beyond the false veil of the senses' lying signals and thus draw closer to enlightenment; a soul choosing instead to take fiction as truth and to tread the way of the body and its flimsy delights. He clears his throat and prepares to pass sentence. It will not be endless torment, but the next rebirth will not be a pleasant one.

Like a woman casting herself in despair after a heedless departing lover, the soul throws itself forward at the foot of the judge's ebony bench. "Mercy!" it cries. "In the name of Lady Guan-yin the Compassionate, in the name of Kshitigarbha the Deliverer of the Lost from Hell, I beg for mercy."

Yama frowns. "What is written—" he begins.

There is a disturbance at the door. King Yama, the General of the Five Ways, the guardian horseheaded demons beside the bench, even at last the lost soul itself all turn and stare. A young man with an old man's eyebrows shakes a sealed scroll at the ferocious soldier there, demanding to be let in. The General barks out a command, and the young man bustles up to the bench, hastily brushing sand from the sleeves of his official's gown. He wears silk robes fashioned in the style worn by the Taoist Immortals of the Heaven of Upper Purity.

The General rolls his eyes. He has little patience with the Taoists and their seeking after long life. But King Yama smiles an ecumenical smile and bids the newcomer speak.

"Permit me to introduce myself, Your Most Buddhistic Highness," says the Taoist, bowing to the precise angle demanded by correctness, and no more. "I am the Undersecretary—" He coughs. "That is, I am a factotum in the office of the Acting

Assistant Controller of the Jade Emperor's Ministry of Babble. I bring you greetings from the Ruler of the Taoist Heavens and Monarch of the Ten Thousand Things." One hand glides to the back of his neck; he brushes at a few more grains of sand, wriggling as they slide along his spine.

The General scowls, but King Yama airily waves a hand in his direction and smiles even more broadly. "Yes?" he says.

"I also bring word from the gracious bodhisattva Guan-yin, whom I have recently assisted by protecting a certain traveling monk." He flicks one last stray grain of sand from his collar. "The good Lady has brought it to my, that is to say, our attention that the soul who stands presently before you is bound to earth by a death promise. One that may even change the weighing of the balance. I—or, well, the Jade Emperor has, ah, taken a special interest in the case." He glances slyly in the direction of the General.

Yama bids him tell more, so the Taoist relates how, in its last moments of life in the human realm, the soul now before the tribunal promised to return to a certain child. "What's more, it would seem that it sealed that promise with an act of self-sacrifice, for the sake of the child's life."

The soul straightens up and begins to speak, but appears to think better of it. Its breasts heave as it sighs.

"Nonsense!" cries the General of the Five Ways, thumping the reading stand that holds the Book of Life and Death. "There's nothing of that written here!"

"One would not wish to accuse the karma recorders of inefficiency," the Taoist says with another little cough, "but the situation seems to have been rather confused just then. There were a number of sudden deaths. Such an omission would certainly be nothing if not understandable, don't you think? And"— he makes haste to continue, for one of the guardian horsehead demons has stepped forward and is looking to the General for instructions—"it is not *altogether* certain that the soul intended to make the sacrifice."

King Yama nods thoughtfully. "Still, the teachings of The Enlightened One are clear; the merciful course is to give it benefit of the doubt. And at very least, its business in the human world stands unfinished." The soul takes a small step, almost a skip, forward, then prostrates itself again before him. "It has been here in the Yellow Springs for some time now, however, so its body may very well no longer exist for it to attach itself to." The General leans over and whispers in the King's ear.

"Ah, yes," says Yama. "Well, a return to life in its body certainly is out of the question." He turns his terrible divine face to the soul. "You would have to go back as a ghost to finish up. Then we shall see where things stand. Are you willing to return under that condition?"

"Oh, yes, Sire," says the soul, aquiver with eagerness. "Yes, Your Highness. Ghost or flesh, it doesn't matter. I'm more than willing to go back."

The Taoist looks relieved. A sour expression spreads across the countenance of the General.

"Of course," says King Yama with a long exhalation. "They always are. Next case."

Parrot Speaks: 3

Now, when I recall the Takla Makan, or the crescent of dry, rock-strewn steppe edging that sandy basin, I think not of the lands around Khotan, but of the weeks of my journey toward Dun-huang with the Persian trader Ghalib, who bought me and the other children from the Tibetan raiders. As the carelessly pampered daughter of the commander of the Chinese garrison, I had ventured beyond the outlying settlements before—I remember my father's good-humored consent the time I begged to go out and wait with his field cook and the wine servers while he rode through the grasslands to hunt wild pigs. And then there were those trips to the village temple with Nannie, and the not quite licit walks along the river with her tall friend. But most of my early days were spent in the thick-walled rooms and garden courtyards of my father's house, or at least within the ring the five fortresses made about the city.

Passed from the Tibetans to Ghalib, certain only that wherever I was going, it was not of my own will, I nevertheless came to see the beauty of the countryside, despite the scanty supply of water and a gale of sand that turned the sun dark red and kept us huddled for hours, half smothered beneath our felt tent-cloths. The first few nights after the Tibetans sold us, the sky blazed starry-clear. Then the moon was born again and grew until half its disk blazed like frost. By the time it reached fullness I had toughened, and in the long weeks that followed I grew stronger still, though I was always tired, even after we had rested several days in one of the oasis towns.

The future hardly mattered to someone of my years. It was the walking that was difficult, mile after mile, gray-brown dust puffing up around my feet, sliding into my nose and throat. I envied the camels their double eyelids and the way they could close their nostrils to mere slits when they sensed the rising of a storm. There must have been fifty of the beasts in the caravan—and at that it was not a large one—but each was loaded heavily with goods, and all the traders walked.

But when the Silk Road led us onto high ground and I could turn my head to see the mica-sparkling realm of sand to the north, I felt peace. The unresting dunes sometimes revealed the broken corner of a long-dead home, or the pitted stump of a tree, yet I never felt that empty landscape to be lonely. It was as if the desert's colorless world were the only true one, and all the water-bound scraps of green life possessed a reality no greater than that of the dreams that plagued me when I slept.

High ranges of dunes ran along beside us, out of the west; lower transverse chains rose up parallel to one another, north to south. Something in me—something that loved the designing dance of the senses—took comfort from this wind-worked patterning. Mornings we wakened well before sunup and set off toward the mother-of-pearl of the early sky. East, I had been taught, was the direction of home; I was the daughter of a good family of Chang-an, reached by traveling east, east, east: Baba told me that more than once, tickling me and making a game of it, question and answer. Perhaps he'd seen other soldiers' children, born to frontier concubines and raised by foreign nannies, wander from the Chinese way.

Soon after Ghalib bought us from Broad Chest, we stopped to dicker for more water bags at the insignificant settlement on the Keriya River. Umar, Ghalib's lanky nephew, took great care to bar us from any chance to talk with people, there and in the other oases we came to. "You talk, I hurt," Umar had told us in his clumsy Soghdian as we drew near the Keriya. He leered then at Blackie, the farmboy whose sister had been taken off by the Tibetans' one-eared leader. Umar took pleasure in teasing Blackie, stroking his head with a heavy hand or flicking at his thighs with a camel crop, but Ghalib had quite clearly warned him to do nothing more. Us girls they generally ignored.

The winds blew strong out of the northeast the day after the full moon that marked our first half-month on the Silk Road. Ghalib and Umar and the other traders seemed not to mind them, but we slumped thirsty, weary, and now sand-stung as we walked. I could hear the demonic howls and whistles of the desert winds that lure travelers from the track, out into the wastes where directions have no meaning. The stretch of the Road we passed over worsened hourly: too many days yet from the easternmost section of the Takla Makan. There, water—welcome even when it was brackish—might be dug out where the camels stamped on the ground, in old stream channels and depressions that had been the lake bed of Lop Nor. Hares and an occasional fox roamed closer to Khotan and Keriya; eastward, we'd spot a few wild camels and a drift of gazelles. Here, though, nothing lived. I'd seen the skull of a horse that morning, beside a jumble of bones I chose not to examine too closely as we passed by.

At last, we halted for the night, near a low sandhill covered with tamarisk bushes. Each day took us through four seasons, and by now we were stopping for a few hours every afternoon to hide from the sun in the shade of our tents. Yet we never traveled straight through the night, as so many do. The caravan master must have wanted to avoid steering by the stars; the full heat of summer would force them to that later, on the return trip from Dun-huang. Now, in the fading light, I felt the evening's coming chill.

Umar fed us: first a shared cup of camel's milk, which soured as always in my stomach but wet my throat, then jerky and sweet dried apricots. When he came to the boy, he pretended to hand him a share, then snatched his hand away when the boy reached out for it. Blackie's eyes filled, Ghalib called out something in an irritated tone, and Umar dropped the food in the grayish dirt. After he'd moved on, Nephrite, oldest among us, moved to put her arm round Blackie; still he wept. The second-oldest girl, whose name I've lost, fixed her eyes upon him, but kept eating, too tired—as I was—to do more.

I didn't know the fifth child's name. The only one younger than I, yet still well beyond the age of speech, she did not talk. She must have seen things, when the raiders struck her village, that pushed her back to the time before words persuade us to speak. Or perhaps her soul had entered this world mute. None of the children knew her. Because we had no other name for her, we called her Baby.

Baby gnawed her jerky as greedily as I at first, but when Blackie's sobs continued, she walked over to him and held out her apricots. As he took one and stuck it in his mouth, she clutched the rest in one hand and flung her other arm half crooked above her hair. Her chubby legs cut capers and she turned her head from side to side in rhythm with her feet. Blackie's wellspring of tears dried up, and then he smiled, and then he laughed.

Soon all of us laughed with him, and Baby took a bow. Grit and sweat vanished, for the moment. Ghalib was bent over a camel's foot, examining a cut; it must have hurt her when he touched it, for she arched her shaggy neck and groaned in protest. The other traders remained by their own tents, eating and talking. But Umar strode over, giving off an air of importance disturbed. He stood, arms akimbo, before Blackie and Baby, asking in Soghdian, "What you do?"

Baby's dancing ceased. She squatted. Blackie, showing what in him came closest to bravery, shrugged and sucked at his teeth, looking only at the ground. Umar grasped him by the shoulders and shook.

The boy howled. I could see Ghalib's obliviousness snap. He dropped the camel's foot, slapped her flank, and turned our way. Before he reached us, though, I decided that what Baby had done, I should do. But I had words with which to help Blackie: I shouted to Umar to stop.

I suppose I half realized that the effect of Persian on Umar would surpass that of anything I could say in Soghdian. I seized on the sound the men made to stop the camels; in fact, I must have used the Persian word for "whoa!" It worked.

Ghalib yelled out too, a stream of phrases that left Umar as limp as he had been proud. He slunk away, not even looking back. His uncle glanced cursorily at Blackie and Baby; Umar's flight had cheered them greatly, though they took pains not to smile. Then he turned to me, his handsome face alive with amused intelligence. "Say it again, girl."

I drew in my breath. "Whoa!" I blurted out.

Ghalib laughed till his eyes watered nearly as much as Blackie's had. "Splendid!" he said. Over his shoulder, he yelled "Whoa, Umar! Whoa!" Umar pretended not to notice. "Say more, girl," Ghalib commanded gently, "not in Soghdian. Say what you know in my tongue."

What could I say? "Gee-yap!" I mumbled. "Camel's milk. Time to get up. Hurry, brats. Shut up." Then I added a name Umar often used for Blackie, which set Ghalib to laughing again.

"Can you others speak in Persian?" Ghalib asked, scratching at his dense, curly beard. But they all stood mute as Baby. "Come then, Little Parrot," he said to me, and led me to his tent, waving me over to squat on a corner of the rug now spread before his doorway. "Take a piece of this," he said, reaching in a sad-dlebag and pulling out something sweet and fine. I nibbled at the candy and then—so strongly had Baby's actions struck me—tucked it inside my sleeve, intending to share a bit with her later.

The hawk-nosed merchant asked what else I could say in his language. Some of the words sounded like the Khotanese I'd spoken with most of the servants at home, or Nannie's Soghdian, but I'd only picked up a few more. "Can you say interesting things in Soghdian, then?" he asked, leaning back on the rug, one elbow propped on the saddle at its end. His baggy trousers fell in graceful folds as he bent one leg upward at the knee. Looking at the embroidered facing on the lapels and cuffs of his round-necked tunic, I thought for the first time how he resembled a younger version of my father: a man of some elegance, when time allowed.

Something interesting, he'd said. I took a deep breath, and recited a poem that Nannie taught me. Ghalib grunted softly. "Not bad," he said. "Do you sing?"

"Water?" I said, careful to use the Persian word.

"A trader!" Ghalib's smile pushed his cheeks up like two round fruits on either side of his long arched nose. He handed me a green-glazed earthenware pilgrim's bottle. I drank deeply, and sang:

> We said good-bye
>   when buds first swelled on the poplar trees.
> I sigh alone:
>   the fall's last reeds go white with frost.
> You wind your way
>   upon long roads across the sands.
> I drop my head
>   to think of lovers' time-bound vows.

Ghalib clapped loudly, the sound echoing through the empty desert air. Several of the traders had looked over as I sang; now one of them said something that made the others laugh and turn away. Umar fussed with another of the camels, his sulky back toward us. I saw in that moment Ghalib's separateness; he was kept apart from unpolished Umar by age and temperament, and from the others in this caravan by his origins and by what I'd now call his sensibilities, although I then thought of it only as a difference that reminded me of Baba talking with his Khotanese sergeants.

Ghalib gave me another bit of candy—but no more extra water—and sent me back to the other children. After that, he paid little attention to me, except that now and then when camp was made, he'd call me over to sing. As for me, I grew closer daily to Nephrite and Baby, and watched the desert as we rode. I think it fair to say I know it far better than the courtesans and gallants of Chang-an, who compose their fashionable poems and songs of the borderlands and have never been within a thousand miles of Jade Gate Pass. Yet even the desert, and whatever wordless comfort the sight of it gave to me, did not relieve me of my terrible dreams at night.

Midnight in the Desert

The ghost's hair streams down unkempt about its shoulders. Its eyes glitter with a hunger that cannot be sated, the hunger for flesh: not to devour it, but merely to live again within it, or failing that, to know its feel. The ghost stumbles over to the sleeping child. A hand of colorless bone reaches out to touch a peachblush cheek.

The child rolls over and opens her eyes. They do not blink; they gaze unfocused like the eyes of someone who sits up with a shriek when a nightmare becomes too terrifying to bear. And yet she shows no sign of terror. Watching her, you would know that she has met this fleshless visitor before: the child bears an air of weary resignation. Night after night the hungry ghost comes, trying to break through the silence that divides a shade's existence from the chatter-filled human realm.

The ghost squats beside the rug on which the child slept.

The others curled together in the little tent sleep on, unaware. A faint whisper, like the rustle of sand trickling down the steep leeward slope of a dune, like the scrape of a flake of gesso falling from a mural to the floor of a cave, drifts from a mouth that works with anguish. A word comes through at last: *Promised.* Or is it *promise?* A history, or a command?

The child's gaze breaks, and she casts her eyes downward in avoidance. What is demanded of her? What is it she must know?

Promise, the ghost hisses. *Mother. Greenpearl. Silence.* An aura of pale flame flickers into being around it, the shadow of the flame auras around the Blessed Ones painted on scrolls, or in temple caves.

Now the child looks up, startled. She has not seen this barely perceptible halo before: night after night the ghost has waxed stronger, clearer. At first it was only a pair of large, blood-ravaged eyes in the dark hollows of a mouthless face. Now the completed outlines of a body waver in the desert air, lighted by this emanation of weak fire. "Greenpearl?" she says. "Greenpearl is me."

The ghost shudders. *Silence! Promise. Greenpearl must bear another name.*

The bewildered child can do nothing but nod her head in agreement. She does not know if she must promise to use another name, or if the ghost is telling her the consequences of some promise—kept or broken?—in the past. And if she is to hide her true name, Greenpearl, what name is she to use, and why?

Gasping like one who has not tasted water for days, the ghost stretches to its full height and the flames grow ever so slightly stronger. *Find the mother,* it sighs. *Find her and seek the meaning of the words.* It is compelled to say these things, compelled to further the working-out of karma. *Find the words, their meaning, and seek the gem beneath the waters.*

As the faltering image flares briefly brighter, the child leaves off her wondering (Is my mother not safe at home in Chang-an?

What are the words whose meaning I must seek?). She cries out, finally understanding one thing: "Nannie!"

The ghost emits a terrible moan. *Greenpearl! Ah, my Little Imp!* Its lips wrench and work, even as its body begins to fade away. *Seagem. Find her. Lady Guan-yin would have it so.* Now the body vanishes, and then the mouth, and then the red-riddled weeping eyes. The child collapses, and only a kick and a curse, in the morning, bring her round.

The Two Daughters

Sometime during the Ming Dynasty (say 1500-something, some eight hundred years after the height of the Tang), in a city marketplace, a storyteller clears his throat to still the crowd and begins to chant a poem:

> Greedy parents send daughters to ill fates,
> But a filial child can save a mother's life.
> A promise made before your birth still binds you,
> And ghostly visions outlive idle talk.

He continues:
This poem tells us that love of right action, not love of riches, should guide us in life, and that filial piety is every child's duty to its parents. Thus Old Lai-zi played like a toddler, and dressed in toddler's clothes, to lighten the hearts of his parents when

42

they feared they were getting too old. But why, you ask, should this storyteller be talking of such things? Well, today I will tell you about two young women (step right up there, you in the back—plenty of room in the audience for all), each loyal in her own way to her parents. One of them paid a terrible price for following her parents' will, yet in the end rewards were heaped upon her head, while the other, daughter to the first, set forth on a quest to rescue her mother from a living death beneath the waters of Cavegarden Lake. As the saying goes:

> If even hens know Virtue's Way,
> Then surely cocks must Law obey.

Today's story relates how, long ago in the Great Tang Dynasty, in the glorious reign of the Brilliant Emperor, there lived in the capital city of Chang-an a certain merchant, a seller of coffins. This merchant, whose name was Jiang Guang-lang, loved nothing so much as unusual savory dishes, and so was called Greedygut Jiang. His wife, a sharp-faced, sharp-boned woman, despised her husband's gluttony and cared only for jewelry. Because of her appearance, and because she thought nothing of haggling furiously with each grieving relative who came into the coffin shop, and each oldster planning ahead, everyone referred to her as The Needle.

Now, The Needle would have preferred to spend all their money on fine bracelets and hairpins for herself. Yet she knew that if she fed her husband well, and kept him in a good temper, he would allow her to buy at least some of the things she desired. As for Greedygut, he didn't care one whit about managing their finances, as long as his dinner arrived at the table on time. So every penny that came into the household flew quickly out again. If it wasn't sea-pine seeds imported from Korea, it was lichee fruits rushed up from the southland. If it wasn't a ring of russet jade, it was a wavering kingfisher hair ornament worked in fine gold.

One day, not many years after Greedygut and The Needle married, Greedygut left the shop in his wife's charge and rode out into an outlying district in search of a rare and tasty mushroom he'd heard about. He was looking in a clump of trees beside the river when he heard a strange voice calling, "Help!"

Greedygut looked all about him, but he saw no one. "Here," the voice gasped, "beside the riverbank." There, flapping on a slab of stone, a giant red-gold carp heaved its gills and struggled mightily, to no avail. "I am the younger brother of the Dragon Monarch," the carp said. "Throw me back into the river and I will reward you handsomely." Greedygut considered briefly how tasty such a fish might be but decided he'd better not take the risk. Puffing and sweating, he threw the great carp up and out, so that it landed with a mighty splash in the river.

The carp danced and played among the waves for several minutes. Finally, he stopped and swam up close to the bank. "You have saved my life," he said. "I was leaping high above the water when an ill wind buffeted me over to the stone. Come to me here tomorrow at this time and I will tell you what your reward will be." Greedygut wondered if he'd been tricked, but he merely agreed to meet the carp and continued his search for the mushrooms.

Greedygut failed to find the mushrooms, but the next day, when he arrived—a bit late—at the stone on the riverbank, the brother of the Dragon Monarch was waiting. The carp broke from the surface of the water, twisting in midair to catch a dazzling ray of light on its ruddy scales. "I bring you greetings, Master Jiang, from my august sibling, who has suggested a suitable reward. A son has just been born to the Dragon Monarch, and your new wife will bear a daughter in eight months' time. Why not ally your family with mine in marriage? As my nephew's wife, your daughter will live in luxury in our Mother-of-Pearl Villa beneath the waters, and we will send her to visit you as often as she wishes. Should you accept, I am empowered to present you with a few trivial betrothal gifts."

Greedygut considered briefly. The whole thing struck him as rather farfetched, since as far as he knew his wife wasn't pregnant. Still, it would never do to offend the Dragon Monarch, and if such a marriage did come to pass, it might prove fortunate for him. So he clasped his hands together and bowed deeply toward the carp. "You honor me greatly," he said in oily tones. "Let the match be made."

The carp presented Greedygut with splendid gifts: a sack of gold coins, a chest of pink coral, and another chest of black. Each chest was filled with fabulous riches dredged from ships sunken on the ocean floor. But the thing that pleased Greedygut most was a tortoiseshell tureen filled with a tasty soup made of rare mollusks from the Southern Sea. No sooner had the carp departed than Greedygut sat down and devoured every drop of the soup. The rest of the gifts he took home. The betrothal still seemed unlikely to him, and he feared the scolding he'd get from The Needle for not demanding even greater riches from one as fabulously wealthy as the Dragon Monarch. So he merely told his wife that the chests and coins had been brought to him by a courier, the bequest of his long-lost cousin, a sailor who'd recently died in his home on the shore of the Southern Sea. The carp had said that a necklace from the coral chests—a simple chain holding a small, oddly colored pearl—was to be given to the daughter, but Greedygut wanted no awkward questions, so he quietly put it away in a corner somewhere and soon forgot all about it.

With their new wealth, Greedygut and The Needle bought a fine new house and began a mad whirl of banquets and jewelry buying. Soon enough, The Needle told her husband she was expecting a child, but even then he kept silent about his meeting with the younger brother of the Dragon Monarch, knowing all too well what a tongue-lashing he'd get if she found out he'd lied about the long-lost cousin. The whole thing came to seem to him no more than a story he'd been told long ago, or a half-remembered dream.

So lavish were the betrothal gifts that even Greedygut and The Needle lived well for many years. Their daughter grew up to be a beauty, as generous as her parents were grasping, remaining always dutiful and good-natured. She wove and embroidered beautifully and kept herself busy sewing fine things for the household and for her dowry. Raised as she was by a coffin merchant, she naturally had many chances to hear the sayings of the Buddhist priests who officiate at funeral services, and her devotions to the compassionate Lady Guan-yin were frequent and heartfelt.

The Needle, thinking of the jewelry she loved so greatly, and of the seafaring cousin who—she believed—had sent them such wealth, had named her daughter Seagem. One day, when the girl was fourteen or so, The Needle came in to her husband, her face alight with expectation. "Good news, old man!" she said. "We have received a wonderful marriage offer for our Seagem. Goodwife Hsueh has come to us with a proposal from the Li family of the Yong-ning Ward. They have a fine son, a childless widower who is looking for a young wife, and it seems that one day he passed by our gate and happened to glance in and see Seagem at her embroidery. In short, he will have no other."

Truly, members of the audience, is it not the case that

> for beauty, strong men lose their heads:
> a single glimpse will snare a heart?

Greedygut's stomach swelled with happiness. These Lis were a military family with aristocratic pretensions, only remotely related to the imperial clan but rather well-to-do. That even so distant a relative of the Brilliant Emperor should want their Seagem as his second wife amazed the merchant; her beauty had captivated him indeed. Greedygut and The Needle had spent so extravagantly that they soon would come to the end of the wealth the carp had given him, so the proposal was timely enough. By now, Greedygut had come to think of the money—

when he thought of its source at all—as his reward for the rescue, pure and simple. Still, he cared for Seagem in his way and asked his wife if the intended bridegroom was a suitable match.

"More than suitable, old man!" The Needle snorted, pursing her lips and stopping to polish a jade bracelet on the sleeve of her jacket. "True, Goodwife Hsueh tells me he's actually the son of his father's Turkish concubine, but there's no shame in that, and having no other offspring, the father dotes upon him. As for his present career, he's an important officer in the Palace Guard, and they say he's bound to move up quickly."

Seagem herself bowed to her parents' wishes, of course. She had grasped something of their financial straits, and it pleased her that she would be serving them so well in this marriage. But deep in her heart, she hoped her husband would be an understanding and gentle man and that her parents-in-law would be kind. Every morning she lit incense to Lady Guan-yin, praying that this might be so.

Indeed, it all came about as any bride might wish. Her wedding night went well enough, and her husband cared as much for her as for any woman. More important, Seagem's parents-in-law treated her kindly and the fortunes of Greedygut and The Needle were secured.

The days and nights flew past with an arrow's flickering speed. Seagem and her husband regretted only that she had not yet conceived a child, not even a daughter who might call forth a younger brother. Then the husband—who was General Li by now—received orders posting him to a desert garrison town in the far northwest frontier. Bidding farewell to his young wife and his parents, he set off at the head of the column of troops. Seagem climbed a tower to watch him go.

Look, members of the audience!

> Twin banners flutter gay before
> a thousand prancing mounts,

47

as the warrior-husband leads them down
the road out of the east.

By day he traveled and by night he rested, as the saying goes, and so he reached his destination. But let us speak no more of him, but rather tell of Greedygut, who one rainy afternoon about six years after his son-in-law's departure heard a heavy knocking at his door.

The stranger that the little maidservant showed in turned to Greedygut with a fishy smile. "Good day, good friend. I have come to fetch the betrothed bride of my nephew and take her to the Dragon Monarch's realm for the wedding. I trust that she and you and the honored lady your wife have all been well?"

Greedygut hemmed and hawed, but eventually the truth came out: Seagem was already married.

The stranger's eyes bulged, and his skin reddened with rage. He demanded the return of the betrothal gifts, but alas, Greedygut told him, that too was quite impossible. The stranger rolled his red-rimmed eyes, and his sides heaved as he drew in great breaths. "Very well, then," he said, flinging a few drops of water from a vermilion sleeve as he turned sharply to go, "we shall make the arrangements in our own way." And he left.

Greedygut pondered the situation that night after dinner, but he saw nothing he could do except hope for the best. It was a year later to the day that a messenger came from the Li household to tell him that Seagem had been seized by a mysterious illness and lay in a deep sleep, neither alive nor dead. This troubled Greedygut greatly, and even The Needle sorrowed.

Seagem's kindly parents-in-law did not wish to disturb their faraway son with the worrisome news, but they summoned every Taoist Practitioner and Master of Medicine who claimed to know a cure. All failed. The young woman lay as if entranced, not talking and not moving, neither wasting away nor growing well. Finally, during a great storm, a foreign doctor dressed all in red came to the Lis' mansion, promising to save their daughter-in-law from what ailed her.

The foreign doctor took her wrist and felt the yin and yang pulses of her body. "She is the victim of a broken pledge," he said, rolling his bulging eyes, "though there is no blame to her. Clear the room, please, and I will set things to rights."

Seagem's mother-in-law and the maids left the bedroom with some reluctance, but so eager were they to have the smiling, compliant Seagem back with them that they would have done almost anything the doctor requested. Soon wisps of incense drifted under the door, bringing with them an odor of lotus blossoms and watercress. The incense dissipated, the members of the household waited, but the doctor never came forth.

Finally, Seagem's mother-in-law could wait no longer. She broke into the room and found it empty. When Greedygut heard the news, and the description of the foreign doctor, he sobbed bitterly. His neglect of a promise had sent his only child off to languish in the Dragon Monarch's watery realm. Under the circumstances, they would certainly never let her return. After thinking over all that had happened, he remembered the little pearl necklace he'd tucked away so long ago, and went to look for it. But it had vanished, though he could not say when.

Our story forks here. Let us say no more of Greedygut, but rather tell of the daughter of General Li, born to an Iranian concubine in the jade-rich city of Khotan, soon after he was stationed there. The concubine died giving birth, and the girl was raised to honor her mother in Chang-an. When word had reached Seagem of the child, her open heart had rejoiced, wishing only that—since it was impossible for her husband to return to her just then—he might also sire a son. Indeed, one night Lady Guanyin had appeared to Seagem in a dream, smiling and praising her for bearing the proper generous attitude toward a concubine's child.

General Li, wishing to honor his good wife Seagem and at the same time commemorate the child's birth in the city famous for its rich green jade, named her Greenpearl. But such a name seemed too fancy, so he called her simply "Little Imp," as so many doting papas do. Her Iranian nursemaid, a devout Buddhist from Soghdiana, hoped to protect the little girl from jealous demons and did the same.

Greenpearl grew apace during the years that Seagem awaited her husband's—and her daughter's—return to Chang-an. But on the very day that the mysterious doctor carried Seagem away, Tibetan raiders captured Greenpearl and her nursemaid outside the walls of Khotan. The nursemaid they murdered, and the child they sold into slavery.

A sad tale, members of the audience, yet we learn from it the importance of promises. For the nursemaid, just before she died, vowed to Greenpearl that she would return to her, so Yama, King of the Underworld, bade her do just that. Meanwhile, the good bodhisattva Guan-yin had taken note of Seagem's plight, and charged the nursemaid with encouraging Greenpearl to rescue her mother from beneath the waters.

But how, you ask, could a little slave girl rescue a woman held in the Mother-of-Pearl Villa in the aqueous realm of the Dragon Monarch? How, indeed, could any mortal enter that place? Alas, my time today is ended (thank you, sir, a fine gratuity), so if you want to know what happens (thank you, thank you, most kind), you will have to listen tomorrow when I tell of the ghostly workings of the nursemaid and the adventures of Greenpearl (thank you), a maiden as dedicated to her filial quest as any knight-errant.

Dun-huang

Balanced on the acute, shifting angle between the city of yesterday and the city of tomorrow stands the rank, fragrant, bustling, dusty oasis of Dun-huang—its caravansaries crowded with camel dealers and curly haired traders from across the desert, its markets rich with conjurers and fruit flies and hawkers and duck squawks and priests telling instructive tales. Or perhaps the city is balanced not upon an apex but at a particular notch on a sixty-year cogwheel, a notch named for one of the ten celestial stems and one of the twelve earthly branches, in a cycle that has rolled round since the long-ago reign of the Yellow Emperor. Or again, the city may be sliding downward through time, as if down a chronos-firehouse pole, forenoon to after, the past month above this one, the next month below. It is, in any case, certainly not riding on a line shot, arrowlike, one way, irredeemably, left to right across the page.

Outside the city wait the caves. Carved deep into the sandy bluffs, they hold a honeycomb of temples, dizzying the traveler with a thousand Buddhas and more. Painted in niches, on the walls and overhead, plump, delicate disciples cluster round their master. Bodhisattvas, male and female, float on lotus thrones beside The World-Honored One. Fingers and palms curve into mudras signifying the peace of contemplation, or a radiance within, or comfort, or awe. Satin valences adorned with rosettes of pink and blue-gray and white cast deeper shadows on the frescoes; deer batiked in indigo on silken banners caper in any breath of air.

And in some of the caves rest the fruits of that other human effort to render in two dimensions a universe made up of four: not paintings, but written words. Some are in Sanskrit, some in Chinese. Others reveal—if the eye desires, and knows the script—words in Tibetan or Uighur or Nepalese. There's even a letter or two written in Persian with Hebrew letters. This welter of words marks silk. It marks leather. It marks palm leaves from the very homeland of the Buddha. It marks paper made of bamboo pulp and mulberry bark, or the fibers of less trustworthy plants, swamp ivy and kudzu and hemp.

These things will last for centuries in their arid tombs. The flamboyant colors will fade. Bits of the intricate patternings of flame auras and petals and jewels and clouds will slip into dust as a mural flakes and crumbles. Scrolls will rot, and morsels of palm leaf chip off, falling away from between the Indic boards that bind them into books. Here a graceful forearm disappears; there a text grows lacy with lacunae. Still, the desert air can keep them awhile, and in some of the caves—their mouths blocked for protection—documents and stories, contracts and sutras will remain walled up and safe for some time yet, as human reckonings go.

Look then to the city itself, at this moment when the caves and libraries swell toward fullness, lavish with signs of knowledge and beauty, but growing still, not yet sealed shut. Here a

Turgesh envoy glares at an Arab caravan master. Here hook-nosed Nestorian Christians from Syria jostle usurious, wine-loving Uighurs, followers of the teachings of the prophet Manes. Here well-to-do Iranian merchants from the city-states of the Soghdians bargain with Tang citizens of Indian descent. Each is well enough accustomed to the other; each to the other is utterly strange.

And here the slave market prospers. Most of the Chinese empire's slaves come from the far south, but, though poets and emperors decry the trade, the good people of Tang prize more highly the slaves brought in from Central Asia along the Silk Road. On this particular day (whether apex or cog tooth or slide), a bearded Persian trader named Ghalib strolls through the marketplace with his lank-limbed nephew, who idly switches at the heels of four girls and a boy. Ghalib's camels carried mostly loads of pepper and gemstones and myrrh, of healing thorn honey, and blue kohl and Persian brass. These thirsty, wide-eyed children he acquired more recently. Most of them look to be offspring of the nomads of the north and west, their bloodlines mingled with those of the Iranians of Soghdiana, or the Western Turks. In any case they are not, it seems, Chinese, so selling them is legal enough.

The boy's dough face crumples easily; he blubbers. Small chance that he will fetch much of a price. Although no one may want him as a houseboy, his sturdiness signals a decent potential groom. Ghalib hopes better for the girls. They'll look exotic enough once they pass on to the Chinese heartland, and one of the younger ones bears even now, beneath her cloak of fatigue and watchful silence, a snap of pride, the mark, perhaps, of a captivating *artiste*. Her green-flecked eyes will surely sweeten the exchange. In any case, he acquired them cheaply enough, and they've cost him less in food than if he'd bought them farther west.

Ghalib's assistant ambles forward and twitches his uncle's sleeve. An old man is rushing from his shop to greet them. "You have returned!" he cries out, as if Ghalib stands in a brother's place within his heart. "Come in, come in. Sit down, if you please. Perhaps a cup of tea?"

Ghalib smiles a smile to match the other's. His nephew grins and moves back where he can keep an eye on the children. The girls stand warily; the boy hangs his head. "A pleasure indeed to see you again, Master Ma," Ghalib says.

"Master Ma!" The old man clucks his tongue. "I tell you again, you must call me just Old Ma, as everybody does. I am ordinary, a simple man."

Ghalib demurs, as well he might, and accepts an offer of refreshments. "The lad stays well enough outside," he says. Neither trader mentions the children. As the tea and sweetmeats are brought to them, Ghalib asks Old Ma for news of his children and of the town. "As for myself," he says, "I am anxious to return—a new young wife, you see." He winks.

The Chinese dealer laughs and shakes his head. "Felicitations. But I fear the skin of my face has been too thick. I cannot bear my rudeness any longer. The noble youth, your assistant, wearies himself with waiting. Let him come inside and drink a bit of this tea. It is certainly poor, but on a day like this one, thirst adds savor to such tasteless stuff."

"Hardly poor!" Ghalib says, pleased that Old Ma has been the one to open the negotiations. "He cannot refuse your bounteous kindness. A moment—" He draws aside the curtain of the shop door and steps outside.

And frowns. The lad has wandered across the lane to where a professional storyteller lures a crowd with some foolish tale. Well, at least he's kept an eye on the children; they squat beside him in the dust. Ghalib calls and the little group hurries over.

Once inside, the children squat again, with the patience of the powerless. After a suitable interval of chitchat, Old Ma inquires, offhandedly, about them.

"These?" Ghalib replies. "I picked this lot up in Kashgar, from an Iranian out of Samarqand. They're just nomad folk, he told me, but take a look at this one, with the pretty green eyes. She's thin now, from the Road, but she'll grow up a beauty, I warrant. Sings well, too." He reaches out, and raises the girl's chin with one hand. Ghalib has been kind enough to her on the passage to Dun-huang; she lifts her head easily. Then, as she looks squarely at Old Ma's eyes for the first time, her face flashes with surprise. Her back straightens.

"Huh!" says Old Ma, wondering what it is about his looks that makes her respond so. No good to show too much interest at this point. "I'll grant you, she's got something of an air about her. Young, though. Take a lot of training. That boy now, would you be so good as to have him stand up?"

The discussion continues over a fresh pot of tea, Ghalib insisting that he wants to give his good friend the best possible price but equally insistent that the children be purchased as a group. "As I told you," he says with a smirk, "I've traded off the rest of my cargo, and I'm in somewhat of a hurry to complete my business and get back home."

Finally, Old Ma turns again to the green-eyed girl. She, he thinks, is the pearl among these pebbles; if she learns well, she alone will be worth more than the price he'll have to give Ghalib for the lot. "What's your name, young one?" he asks. He speaks, as he and Ghalib have been speaking, in traders' Soghdian.

To Old Ma's complete surprise, she answers in his own language, Chinese. "My family name is Li."

Old Ma shoots a glance toward the doorway. The curtain hangs unmoved. Ghalib reaches up to scratch his beard. "And your own name?" Ma asks, his eyes intent.

"I mustn't—" The girl takes a deep breath. "They always called me Little Imp," she says at last.

"Sorry, I hardly speak any Chinese. You're asking her name?" Ghalib is quick to shift the conversation back to Soghdian. "The Iranian fellow I got her from called her Parrot. Said she was a wonderful mimic. Shouldn't wonder if she was his own daughter, by the look of her. You know us Persians and our cousins in Samarqand: anything to get rich." He chuckles, and scratches his beard again.

Old Ma throws back his head and laughs dismissively. But he stops short as he takes a sip of lukewarm tea. "Funny, though. She says they called her a Chinese nickname"—and he says Little Imp in Soghdian—"as if she were any Chinese child."

Ghalib whirls and stares down at the girl. "What's your name?" he barks. "Your other name, not Parrot."

"Parrot?" she says. "My family name is *Li*. I can't, I can't remember the rest." Her voice trails off. She bites her lower lip.

Ghalib's shoulders loosen and he smiles. "Li," he says. "Well, that explains things. Half those would-be Chinese families out there claim the name of Li. A strange kind of homage to the Son of Heaven, isn't it?" His smile broadens. "I suppose she saw your face and decided to put on airs." That, he thinks, should take care of Old Ma's doubts, at least if he wants to have them taken care of. "She really is a fine mimic, you'll have to grant her that."

Old Ma's eyes narrow as he considers. "Parrot! She's the kind of mimic that gets an honest slave dealer into trouble. I'm afraid I don't see how I can pay the price you're asking for a liar. A girl like this is nothing but a nuisance. Pity you won't break up the group. I had taken something of a fancy to the boy." There. If Ghalib acquired these children honestly, he'll take his business elsewhere. If not, he'll come down on the price.

Ghalib jokes again about his new wife, offers a discount of twenty percent—for friendship's sake—closes the deal, and leaves. In an awe-inspiring grotto on the edge of the city, a novice monk working on a mural applies the last flake of gold leaf to a halo, and begins to pray. And just so, as the city moves to the next moment in time, the storyteller finishes off another text, seals the entrance to the cave, and so protects the tales within.

Parrot Speaks: 4

Old Ma raised his hand again and I fell silent. "So you will remember, Parrot, that you are not Chinese?" My throat choked and my mouth swelled salty where a tooth had cut my lip when the back of his hand came down. I nodded yes. He grunted with a detached satisfaction. No ill will had lain behind his blows; he simply ensured that I would receive the message in a language any slave was bound to understand. But he also ensured, unknowing, that what I could not say, I would remember: I was a Chinese general's daughter, from a good family of Chang-an.

Ghalib had left us in Old Ma's shop in the bazaar an hour before. In the doorway, he paused long enough to catch my eye and incline his head in a brief, oddly formal farewell. His alert, strong-featured face went grave. Then he was gone. The Chinese merchant brought us to the elaborate clay-brick complex of hallways and courtyards where he lived and took me off to the little room where he set my memory. After he left, a young woman of sixteen or so, his daughter, walked in, bearing soup and steamed rolls on a tray. Baby, Nephrite, and the other girl from Khotan trotted in after her. We sat and ate, at last, our fill. Blackie never appeared again; Old Ma must have sold him off right away.

Old Ma's daughter, Beauty, treated us well enough, as might a shepherd's daughter who'd been given charge of some orphaned lambs. She spoke to us—and to the eight other girls living in the tiny back rooms of Old Ma's family compound—in a mixture of Soghdian and Chinese. Gradually, Nephrite picked up the Chinese words, though she never lost her foreign lisp. I pretended to understand no more than she but pronounced the language as I always had. No one commented on my Chang-an accent. Baby's sweet desire to please kept her alert to what Beauty wanted, but she never spoke.

So for some days we rested from the hardships of the Road. Nephrite, having been judged old enough, helped Beauty and some of the others sew new clothes to replace our travel-worn rags. I remained rather thin, but Baby grew plump again, and the shadows passed away from under Nephrite's eyes. We talked only of things in the present: Beauty's green-painted eyebrows (a fashion new to Nephrite), the short temper of the laundress who sometimes oversaw us, or how cunning Baby would look in her new crimson pantaloons and her boots with the turned-up toes. The other girls had been living there a little longer than we but seemed no more knowledgeable, or no more inclined to speak, of the future. No one mentioned her earlier life at all.

It was not an unhappy time at first. The horrific dreams that plagued me through the desert journey had climaxed on the last night before Dun-huang and came no more. Sometimes I pondered Nannie's warning to me, then, helpless and uncertain, let it fall away from my thoughts, holding only to what I finally took her command to be: that I not reveal my given name and that I make my way to Chang-an, where my mother waited. In the evenings, after every dish in the kitchen shone and the lamps had been made ready, we girls would sit in the courtyard to catch the first coolness, singing together while Baby danced a comic dance. Others might dance beside her, but none so well. It was as if she had been granted a special language of the body to compensate for losing the speech of the tongue. Her fingers snapped as she skipped and spun. Still the youngest of the group, she soon became a general favorite.

Things were different with me. Though I'd never spoken directly of my father's position, Nephrite and the other older Khotanese girl had sensed long before that I was no farmchild. Nephrite kept by nature a certain reserve about her, treating everyone with sisterly care but maintaining some part of herself safe within. Still, she was the closest thing I had to a friend, and it hurt me when she drew away, as a villager might at the approach of a sedan chair carrying the daughter of a lord. Perhaps the other girls imitated her unknowingly, treating me like someone to be kept at a distance. Sometimes I did things that made matters worse.

One hot afternoon, when I had been in Dun-huang only a few days, the laundress came for a few slave girls to help her bring in and sort the wash. She blustered into the room where six of us took our afternoon naps, rousing me from an unusually deep sleep. Her red face reminded me of one of our serving maids at home; still drowsy, I ordered her to run and fetch me a cup of cool barley tea.

Her face grew redder than any I'd ever seen. "Fetch you what, you arrogant little snippet? I'll show you what I'll fetch you." With that, her meaty hands boxed my ears until they rang. At first the other girls watched stupefied, then one by one they began to giggle, until all but Nephrite laughed while the laundress dragged me off to bring in the laundry by myself. After that, she found fault with me whenever she could, and though the others had reason to dislike her, they grew wary of me, as children are of one a powerful adult has marked as different.

59

Not twenty days later I set myself apart from the others again. In twos and fives, young slaves from the north and west joined us at Old Ma's. Beauty grew busier, though she'd trained Nephrite and the older girls to help her get the new ones into shape. We continued to gather in the courtyard near day's end to sing, and even Old Ma came out to listen to us, watching with the remote pride of a landlord observing the peasants bring in a healthy harvest.

Until now, our only accompaniment had been Beauty playing on her bent-necked lute. But one of the new girls, a gray-eyed Kuchean, arrived with an oboe, and another in that lot could play a little lacquered drum. The music of Kucha is said to be modeled on the sound of rainfall and tumbling waters; listening to them, I felt the truth of that. I saw, too, how Old Ma seemed to favor them and how Beauty treated them like friends. I'd found the language that would win me a place in the group, I thought. I could be one of the musicians, and the others would be pleased. "Miss Beauty!" I called out. "Let me use your lute. I can play three songs."

In my excitement I'd spoken too loudly, and just at one of those moments when the various conversations in a group come all at once to a pause. The laundress snickered, Beauty raised a willow-leaf eyebrow, and all the faces in the courtyard turned toward me. "Let her try," Old Ma said, his voice dispassionate.

Of course I failed. Now I realize that Beauty—who had neither sisters nor a living mother—must have been as lonely as I among the transient slave girls and that she may have hoped to learn something from these exotic musicians before they passed onward to the east. Then I saw only her glare as she handed me the lute, daring me to succeed. The earth of the courtyard retained the day's heat long after the air cooled; now its hot smell wrapped itself around me. My fingers cramped and stumbled. The lessons I'd had in Khotan seemed the events of a former lifetime, remembered only in a fevered dream. I limped through one melody as best I could, broke a string—earning another snicker from the laundress—and, shamefaced, handed the instrument back to Beauty.

"Perhaps you'll honor us with your other two melodies another day," Beauty said in a tone too loud to be quite a murmur. She glanced over to the musicians from Kucha, inviting them to join her in a sisterhood of *artistes* condemning the inept. The other children whispered to one another that they hadn't liked me from the start. Old Ma's face displayed a quiet satisfaction, but whether he was glad to see a potential source of trouble put into her place, or whether he sensed some talent despite my clumsy fingering, I cannot say.

After another song, when everyone's attention had returned to the new musicians, I slipped into the dusty hallway leading to the room where I slept. But in my distress I turned instead toward Beauty's bedchamber. I was looking for a place where no one would see me cry, though I realized as I stepped inside her doorway that I couldn't stay.

Just as I turned to go, a high-pitched voice rasped, "Good girl! Good girl! Come to Mama!" My belly wrenched with sorrow, while curiosity filled my heart. Mama? No one was in the room, only Beauty's parakeet, cocking its bright head and peering at me from its perch. I'd seen the bird before, but I'd had no idea that it could speak. I stopped dead, openmouthed.

"Little Parrot! Come to Mama," it rasped, and I took a step closer. The bird preened the lavender feathers of its breast and looked at me as if for praise. By now, I've seen a dazzling five-colored parrot from the Indies, and rose-crested tropical cockatoos, and splendid scarlet lories with tongues like writing brushes. But even then I knew that this bird, small yet brilliantly green on its head and back and wings, came from northern China. It must have been brought west from the Loong Mountains, where the Silk Road crosses them on the last stage of the journey to Chang-an. "Good girl!" it squawked. "Good girl!"

I knew I should leave. But the little parrot crooned, "Come

to Mama," and again I stepped forward. The bird fluttered awk-
wardly from its perch to an old wooden trunk near where I stood.
As one entranced, I heard it say, "Take this, Little Parrot. Good
girl!" Did the lid of the trunk open by itself, or did I reach out
to lift it? I know my hand glided into the trunk, brushing aside
the folded silks and cottons, burrowing past the old papers in
the corner. "Take this," the parakeet squawked again, as if it
offered me a meal of millet grains. My hand folded around a
tiny, tight-rolled scroll just as I heard the footsteps in the hall.

Praise to Lady Guan-yin that the trunk lid was oiled and
closed without a bang. Praise to Lady Guan-yin that though there
was no time to escape the room, or hide, I stepped back three
paces and half sat, half fell to a cross-legged pose on the floor.
My hand thrust the little scroll inside my sash, and the bird
fluttered back to its perch, so that I seemed to be staring at it
when the laundress rushed into the room.

"You sneaking child of a foreign turtle!" With a roar she was
on me, slapping me about the head. She bent and thrust her fat
red face into mine. "What are you doing in the Young Mistress's
room, eh?" She slapped me again. "Young Mistress!" she
screeched. "Come quickly, please. To your bedchamber."

In a moment, Beauty arrived, still grasping her lute. Old Ma
showed up behind her, with a crowd of others eager for excitement. "She was sitting right here," the laundress cried. "The
little barbarian sneak. I wondered where she'd gone off to, but
who would think she'd dare to enter Young Mistress's bedchamber? Thieving brat!" The last she addressed to me, punctuated
with a final slap.

The servants gabbled, Beauty lifted an ironic brow, and then
even the laundress hushed as Old Ma stepped forward. "Here?"
he said, fixing his puffy-lidded eyes on mine. "Sitting in the
middle of the floor? Curious behavior for a thief." He lifted my
chin. "So, Little Parrot," he said, "tell me what you did here."

I was crying too hard to speak. "Look at her," the laundress
huffed. "Her tears speak lies." A stern look from Old Ma silenced her; I'd seen before that the woman irritated him.

The trader knew how to act the master to a frightened slave. Every line of his large body spoke of authority. "Tell me," he said, tightening his grip on my chin and pulling upward. "Stand up and tell me what you did."

I stood up and swallowed my tears. "The bird," I said. "I listened to the bird." The parakeet squawked as if in affirmation. Beauty stepped over to the perch, and the bird hopped onto her forefinger. She lifted it gingerly to her face and made little kissing noises, which the parakeet repeated.

"And why were you here?" Old Ma asked.

"I came in here—" Shame flooded through my body. Already singled out from the others, I was now marked as one inevitably alone. "I came in here to cry, and the bird, the bird said, 'Come to Mama.' I want to find my mama, and I can't." The tears returned. I could say nothing more.

A shade passed across Beauty's face. Old Ma said, "Little slave girls have no mamas," but even his voice lost some of its commanding tone.

"A pack of lies!" the laundress said. "A pack of foreigner's lies."

Old Ma didn't bother to look at her this time, but when the parakeet squawked, "Good girl!" he shot a glance in its direction. A babel broke out among the crowd. Everyone knows the stories of how talking birds report on unfaithful wives and disobedient servants. "Come to Mama," it said, confirming my claim. "Good girl!"

After that, the laundress hushed. Old Ma warned me never to wander into the family's rooms again and ordered all of us off to bed. As I left Beauty's bedchamber, walking alone behind the chattering crowd of servants and slave girls, I looked back. The parakeet fanned out its wings, skipping from side to side on its perch. Beauty leaned over it, her face turned down. Old Ma clapped one awkward hand on her shoulder. I hurried away to my bed.

The other girls had settled down. I was thinking that in only a few more minutes everyone would be asleep and I could finally release my loneliness in tears, when Nephrite slipped over to crouch beside my bed. "Little Parrot," she said, for everyone called me by the name Ghalib had given me, "are you sad?"

I lifted my head and nodded glumly. Then, looking at her face, I remembered that she too, and Baby, and all the rest, had lost both mother and father. It is not easy for a child as young as I was to imagine another's grief; perhaps I only think I did. But in any case, the tears that had been crowding my throat vanished. I would find my mother, that was all. I didn't need to weep.

"I have something for you, Little Parrot," whispered Nephrite with a soft half-smile. In the moonlight, I could see that she held out toward me a pair of embroidered shoes and a small bundle of cloth. I sat up and took them. The cloth unfolded into a shimmering, tight-sleeved tunic. "You know Beauty is having us older girls sew a special outfit for everyone. You're not to wear this yet, but I thought you might want to see it early. I picked the best bit of fabric for yours. And look." Her large round eyes brightened. "Inside the collar. Do you see the little Chinese word embroidered there? It's a secret, just for you and me. It means 'jade.' I asked Beauty how to write it. So when you see it, you can remember the beautiful jade of Khotan."

The tunic hung dark gray in the dim light, but the next day I would see it glimmer a deep rich green that brightened the green cast of my eyes. I rubbed its softness—so different from the hemp cloth I'd worn since Ghalib had replaced my stained silk trousers and tunic from home—against my cheek. "And you, Nephrite. It will make me think of the older sister who sewed it for me."

Nephrite squeezed my hand. "It's time to sleep now. Put them in the chest beside your bed, little sister. Good night."

I whispered good night to her and lay down on my back, the tunic draped across my torso. For a long time I thought about Nephrite, and Nannie, and how Beauty's bird said "Come to Mama." At last I remembered the tiny scroll, still tucked inside my sash, for I'd thrown myself into bed fully dressed. Drowsily, I pulled the thing out and slid it into one of the shoes; it fit, barely. I put the shoes in the little chest, covered them with the tunic, and fell at once to sleep.

In the morning the other children regarded me curiously at first, but nothing changed, except that Nephrite gave me a special smile and Beauty avoided meeting my eyes. That afternoon, she called us all together and told us that in a few days her second brother would take us with him, east to Liang-jou; Old Ma had gathered enough little slaves to make his son's journey worthwhile. We were caught up in a final flurry of stitching and packing that kept us too busy to wonder much about what was to come. I mostly thought, *Chang-an!*—for Liang-jou was the next major city on the Road toward the capital—and tried as always to keep out of the laundress's way.

The day before our last in Dun-huang, as I was packing my new shoes and tunic into a saddlebag, I came across the scroll. Looking as busy as possible, I carried the bag into the shadows of a storage room and slipped the scroll from its hiding place.

Its fine silk, tightly wrapped around a thin roller, gave off a ghostly whiff of sandalwood. Tiny words brushed in vertical lines covered every inch of the cloth. What they said, of course, I had no idea. The scroll was as out of place in my world as I had come to be in the world of the other children. I didn't dare return it to Beauty's room. Yet if found, the thing might bring me trouble. Why didn't I just toss those meaningless swipes of ink into the back corner of the storage room for the mice to gnaw?

But I didn't. The parakeet had said, "Take this." The scroll resembled my dreams of Nannie: obscure but compelling nonetheless. The lively brushstrokes seemed to promise something. Maybe I kept it because it was beautiful. Or maybe I just kept it because I had nothing else.

Heavy footsteps sounded in the hallway. I dived behind three big grain sacks. The laundress's peevish voice sounded through the stuffy room: "Where is she, then?" I held my breath.

She left. After waiting as long as a young child could, I took up the scroll. But its slick silk wrenched itself from my fingers, or seemed to, and the whole length of the writing unrolled itself before me, a white road marked with black signs through the dusk of the room.

Beneath Cavegarden Lake

Cavegarden Lake, richly fed by myriad vassal streams, spreads its vast waters in the distant, not-quite-Chinese lands south of the Yangzi River. The lake, it is said, serves as an entryway to the subterrene circuitry of mystical caverns and Taoist grotto heavens that honeycomb a world beneath the one we know. Here, sudden squalls spring up and sink the boats of unwary fisherfolk. Here, the occasional poet, perhaps a government magistrate of unusual sensibility, comes to the moss-covered shrine of the Hsiang River Ladies to pay homage with fragrant pepperwort and the innermost longings of his heart. Here, mystical islands bearing springs of sweet wine rise up and disappear among the waves. And here, a mortal woman married to the son of the Dragon Monarch roams the watery Mother-of-Pearl Villa, longing for news of the human realm.

The woman, Seagem, wanders beneath rainbow rafters,

through cockleshell gates. Her mind turns again and again to the husband and the unknown child she was forced to leave behind. Just now, she must go to a family birthday party for her uncle-in-law, the impetuous younger brother of the Monarch. Sighing, she takes her place among the others gathered in Misty Daybreak Pavilion.

The celebration is a merry one: the members of the family feast and drink and watch the sinuous dancing of the eels and starfish come to entertain them. Only Seagem sits quietly, with downcast eyes. Her new uncle notices.

"What's this?" he roars, shrugging his shoulders and changing from human form into his true aspect as a gigantic vermilion dragon with lightning eyes and thunder breath. Most of the guests, familiar with his quick shifts of mood, continue talking and joking, but a school of catfish cousins seated at the lower end of the pavilion dart under their amber tables to hide. "The new bride's too modest!" he says. "Let's see a smile for your husband's uncle." A bit of flame flickers, beardlike, upon his chin.

But at the word *husband*, Seagem can bear no more, and bursts into tears. She wants to please this fearsome creature, just as she has wanted to please everyone she's come across in life. Yet here she is, she who was always chaste and virtuous, she who always did what she was told, married to two men. She buries her face in her sleeve and sobs.

The Hsiao River Princeling, Seagem's recent bridegroom, hurries over to comfort his wife. In truth, he is quite besotted with love for her, enamored as he is of her compliant ways. He does wish that she would cry a little less often, not realizing that it is the very quality he cherishes, her desire to do what others would have her do, that brings on her tears. Ignoring his uncle's scowl and the amused glances of some of the older members of the company, he puts one arm around Seagem and with the other hand offers her a sip of wine from a cup made of narwhale ivory. But though Seagem has responded warmly and willingly to his touch at night, when they sport like Mandarin duck and drake within the cloudy curtains of their bed, now she only tenses and sobs all the more.

For the worst of her dilemma is this: It is the Hsiao River Princeling, not General Li, that she really loves. And the teachings of generations of pious Confucian scholars tell her that, kidnapped and given to another man, she should kill herself to preserve her virtue, or at the very least should pine away. But how can she choose to die when she is, at last, so happy? The general treated her well, and to a sensitive woman such as Seagem, life in his parents' household was infinitely superior to the vulgar ways—may she be forgiven the thought—of her grasping, quarrelsome parents. But the general was far older than she and chiefly interested in military strategy and the music of barbarian *musiciennes*. It was duty that bound her to him, while what binds her to the Dragon Monarch's son is true affection and the warmth of their secret flesh.

The vermilion dragon snorts; murky winds gust in, bearing pellets of snow and waves of sleet. The guests begin to grumble. The Princeling glares at his uncle. The Monarch looks annoyed. And Seagem finally breaks her lifelong observance of feminine decorum and wails aloud for everyone to hear, "How can I be good if I'm married to two men?"

Silence falls upon the pavilion. A few members of the more promiscuous scaly tribes cock amused eyebrows at one another, but most of the company are touched by her simplicity.

Not so the vermilion dragon. "So you'd spoil my birthday feast with *that?*" he asks with a sound like the booming of a great bronze basin. "You humans are altogether too pathetic. Mustn't make clouds and rain with one man while the other's still alive, eh? Well, I'll fix things up for you, Madame Chastity!"

The Hsiao River Princeling wants to explain that all this is hardly Seagem's fault, although he's a bit miffed that her passion for him hasn't led her to cast all her conventional training to the winds. But before he can say something to placate his temperamental uncle, the vermilion dragon has departed in a flash of brilliance and a crash of clouds.

Seagem, having been raised to cultivate her embroidery skills rather than her mind, is not the first to deduce what her new uncle's mission must be, but when she does, she collapses, facedown, in the Princeling's lap. A rather awkward expression spreads across his countenance, an eel dancer snickers audibly, and the Dragon Monarch hastily orders the musicians to play something lively on their barnacle-covered pipes.

Fortunately, the vermilion dragon soon returns, clutching the supernatural pearl that embodies his whirlwind of power and looking pleased. With a shake of his reptilian body, he becomes once again a human figure clad in bright red brocade. "Well, that was easier than I expected," he announces, taking his place of honor at the table. "My naughty niece need not worry about her virtue. Now, how about a nice hot cup of yellow wine for the birthday boy?"

Seagem's eyes meet the Princeling's. His look of tender concern mingled with a rising passion stirs similar feelings within her. His hand strokes the delicate high chignon that he himself decked with tiny starfish after their midday rest. But then Seagem thinks of how General Li has been cruelly murdered because of her and of how her life story will doubtless be recorded in the official history of the dynasty, in the section titled "Biographies of Pernicious and Depraved Women." The combination of desire and anguish and shame is too much for her. What, she wonders, is a proper lady to do in such a situation? But the Empress Chang-sun's *Selected Rules for Women* certainly never covered anything like this. There's only one solution: she swoons.

Parrot Speaks: 5

The morning I learned of my father's death, Beauty sat weaving at her loom. The outermost courtyard was awhirl: Old Ma and his son called out orders, servants loaded bundles of provisions, and the ponies that would carry us east and south on the long road to Liang-jou shook their shaggy heads. We little slave girls scurried back and forth, arms filled with whatever we were told to carry. I felt excited: Beauty's second brother was taking us closer to Chang-an, where I was sure to find my mother.

I knew that I could never make my way back to Khotan, across the wastes of the Takla Makan. Besides, all my life I'd been taught to regard that frontier city as at best a temporary home; Chang-an was where I belonged. And now, amid shouts and whinnyings and the stamping of hooves, I would soon be on my way.

Only Beauty remained apart. From her shadowed seat at the

loom, she could oversee the bustle in the courtyard, and occasionally she would rise, with an air of patience sorely tried, to remind one of the household servants of some forgotten task. The stoop of her shoulders as she bent close to the gaily figured cloth proclaimed that her responsibilities toward the rest of us had ended.

Before we had half finished the loading of the ponies, a friend of hers came to call; I wonder now if Beauty might not have deliberately invited her for that morning, to show that she had other business to attend to. She seldom had visitors from outside the household.

This other merchant's daughter was fashionably plump, but her small eyes and mouth seemed lost in her broad face. She sat fanning herself, admiring the design of Beauty's cloth and insisting that she not stop weaving. "Go on, go on," I heard her say as I passed by with a rolled-up felt blanket almost too heavy for me to lift. "I know how *busy* you are." Her fan wavered and she sighed. "Aiya. Will autumn never come?"

"You!" Beauty called out, bringing me to an instant halt. "Finish with that and run to the kitchen to fetch a cup of grape juice for Miss Honeymelon. Quickly now." She turned to Honeymelon. "It would frustrate anyone. I barely get them trained and then they're off."

I left with Honeymelon's polite protestations hanging in the heated air. When I got back, she had picked up an ivory statuette of a goddess that Beauty kept near the loom and was admiring the roundness and the easy stance of the figure. "Quite nice, actually," she said. "Is it the Western Motherqueen? No, no, of course not. She doesn't have the headdress, and you'd never see the Motherqueen suckling a baby like that. It's—what's that silly Indian name?—Hariti, *isn't* it?" A giggle broke from her lips. "Do you think we'll be married ladies with children at our breasts like that someday soon now?"

Beauty did not seem at all inclined to discuss motherhood. "Yes, it's Hariti," she said. "You can tell, can't you, by the foreign look about the carving? From Khotan, maybe, or somewhere farther out." Then she noticed that I'd returned. I was proud that I'd thought to bring two cups of juice, but she only frowned and signaled with her eyes that I was to offer the tray to Miss Honeymelon first.

Honeymelon ignored me. Her voice forgot its cultivated languor and grew shrill as she told a story the mention of Khotan had brought to mind: the vassal king of the city-state had forsworn his oath of loyalty to the Tang and risen in rebellion against the Chinese forces—Baba's army!—garrisoned there. "The khan of the Turgesh Turks sent forces down from the north to help the rebels. Can you imagine the nerve of the man? He was given a Chinese princess in marriage years ago." Her fan waved briskly in indignation, then slowed. "Well, not real Chinese like us, but the daughter of a loyal Turk, which should be good enough. Though I hear he's *also* joined himself in marriage to the Tibetans *and* some of those awful unpacified Turks in the northeast." At last she deigned to notice me and reached out diffidently for her cup of juice. I stood unmoving as she took a deep slurp.

Beauty's eyes had locked back onto her weaving as Honeymelon's talk slid from the uprising to marriage. "What happened?" she prompted. "In Khotan?"

Honeymelon slurped again, finishing off her cup. "Oh, the rebellion didn't last long." She plunked it down on my tray. "They killed the general in command, though, and three other important officers. And a fair number of troopers, of course. But they were only *soldiers*, after all." She went on to express her opinion of disloyal foreign kings and, more heatedly, of men like the Turgesh khan who forget the obligations that marriage entails. Eventually, Beauty looked up and snapped at me to set the other cup of juice on the little table near her loom and get back to work.

I suppose I did. I suppose I did whatever else was required of me, mounted my pony, and left with the caravan. I don't remember. For weeks we traveled the Silk Road between Dun-huang and Liang-jou, along a narrow plateau that formed a kind of corridor within the bitterly bought safety of the Great Wall. To the north lay the A-la Shan desert and beyond that, the cold, dry Gobi; to the south rose terrible mountains where Tibetans waited to prey upon Chinese travelers.

Riding felt like a luxury after walking to Dun-huang with Ghalib's caravan; Old Ma didn't want us to look worn out when his son sold us in Liang-jou. But the nights grew steadily colder, and some mornings the rocks and scrubby grasses of the plain bore a white dust of frost.

As my pony plodded toward the next outpost town one forenoon, my head bobbed and I stared unseeing into the chilly air. A dance of sparks showered into my field of vision, struck from the cobalt hooves of a mighty chestnut horse as it flew across the great ravine we were skirting. My mother rode astride its gleaming saddle, bold and joyful, come to rescue me. Her mount—a dragon in disguise—could outrace any caravan pony. Its nostrils flared; it sweated drops of blood. We would dash past Liang-jou without stopping, on to Chang-an. Then she would laugh out loud and cuddle me and sing as Nannie used to do.

This waking vision kept me company day after day. I no longer tried to befriend the other girls, who still kept their distance from me. Nephrite always had a calm smile for me and made sure I had a warm place to sleep. But she remained wrapped in silence, more inclined to sit by herself, well away from Beauty's second brother and the other traders in the caravan. Even Baby was subdued. Still, the other girls took pleasure in gathering for a bit of music when they could, or simply in sitting together exhausted for a few moments before they slept.

I can remember only one other thing from the journey. The day I left Dun-huang, passing the last of the willow-lined fields outside the city, I started back to awareness when my eye caught the white-tailed flash of deer sprinting off into a gully. Then I felt it with the shock of an unexpected slap. Baba was dead, and nothing in the world was sure.

Seagem's Soul Journey

Sometime earlier, while her daughter still walks the sands of the Takla Makan, Seagem lies in her swoon upon her pearly nuptial bed. The Hsiao River Princeling watches over her, bending once—when the servants aren't watching—to loosen the neck of her gown and kiss a golden breast.

But only her fleshly self remains at rest in the Mother-of-Pearl Villa. Her soul has risen, as if on a chariot pulled by sea serpents, to travel to the farthest reaches of the cosmos. It soars, it hovers, it roams through emptiness. The Confucian teachings that ordered her earthly life as filial daughter and faithful wife have failed her. She bears the guilty weight of causing her unruly dragon-uncle to murder her husband, the first of her husbands. And perhaps she will never meet the daughter she has longed so to greet someday in Chang-an, for all that another woman bore her.

Only Guan-yin can calm this turbulence. At last that compassionate Lady glides into the vision of the troubled soul. The Wheel of the Dharma-law hangs from a silk cord about the bodhisattva's neck; she confirms for the human woman General Li's death in the uprising at Khotan. With a sweet severity, Guan-yin reminds Seagem that all mortal beings must let go of earthly existence in the end and that to mourn them merely gives rise to a foolish attachment to the unreal. Chastened and comforted, Seagem hangs her head, vowing that she will pray—but will not weep—for the man who has died a fitting soldier's death, just as the Lady has told her to do.

"But what of my daughter?" asks Seagem. She can't release herself from mother love, even for this child she's never seen. "Did she too die there in Khotan?"

Lady Guan-yin smiles. The tiny bells of her headdress tinkle. She tells Seagem of the girl's capture and that just now a Persian trader is taking her on the Silk Road toward the city of Dunhuang, where she will stay awhile in the household of a slave dealer named Old Ma. "So you see," the bodhisattva concludes with divine indifference, "what you might have regretted, her enslavement, was in fact a blessing, for it freed her from the vanities of a wealthy child's life."

Seagem takes the news with less detachment than Guan-yin might have hoped. Her daughter, the little girl she has, in years of daydreams, played with, crooned to, and petted, has been sold into slavery! But the Lady has other souls to comfort, and turns to go.

"Wait!" Seagem calls out. "Compassionate Lady, can you rescue her?"

"Ah," says Guan-yin. "It is not I who binds her to this fate, child, but the desires of her own soul, which before her birth set her feet upon the road she travels." She pauses to consider. "But perhaps you could get some kind of message through to her. A letter, maybe. Or a scroll. I'll see. Now really, I must go. I'll arrange for you to meet someone who can explain the child's situation to you, dear." And trailing vaporous ribbons of cloud, she takes her leave.

The turmoil that is Seagem jerks and reels. It dashes east and west of the sun. It thrashes and shudders and hurls itself against the portal of the utmost Taoist heaven. A rather cranky-looking transcendent with a youthful face and old man's eyebrows bustles out to meet her.

"Now, now, my good woman," he says, "this really will not do, you know. Quiet yourself." Tapping one brocade-slippered foot, he waits while Seagem's soul settles into a subdued quivering, taking on the semblance of her bodily form. "Tell me," he asks in an officious tone, "what is so important that I must be roused from my duties—from my *many* duties—by the will of a, of that, of a bodhisattva?"

Seagem stammers out the story of her concern for her daughter. The Taoist official nods sagely. "I see," he says. "As a matter of fact I am familiar with the case, having been transferred— more or less promoted, actually—to a supervisory position over it by His Divine Majesty, the Jade Emperor. But I must say, for once that Buddhist—that is to say, the good Lady Guan-yin— was right. Before her birth your daughter chose a life of exile, and for—" He begins to titter, then remembers that he must convey the dignity of the Celestial Administration to this mortal woman. "Well, shall we simply say she's chosen it for a reason that *some* might regard as a bit peculiar?"

There's one thing Seagem's upbringing has taught her well. Her long eyelashes tremble, her ripe mouth purses, a dainty sigh lifts the breasts that both her husbands have so admired. "And is there no one who can help me get some word to her?" she asks in a musical, plaintive tone.

The official's eyes grow wide. He chokes. No one watches. No one hears. Does he dare?

He does not. Except for this: "There is one chance," he whispers. "If." He pauses to swallow and to still the yang essence that rises within, all too eager to spill itself into the consuming

yin of the creature before him. "If you go to the Western Motherqueen. She has ways of sending messages to the human realm,
so— Perhaps."

Now Seagem's limpid eyes widen with genuine awe. The turbulence in her soul begins to swell again. Even during her dutiful life in the household of her father and the mansion of her
father-in-law she heard of this mighty deity who dwells in the
heights of the Kunlun range: the Metal Mother, the Amah,
the Western Motherqueen. But how is a poor mortal to persuade
the tigerish goddess to send word? Seagem inquires soft-voiced,
as a shivery, quivery, shimmy shakes her soul.

"Don't ask me," the official says, pulling his gaze at last
away from her rounded hips and picking irritably at a loose
thread on his purple robe. "You're a woman. You should know."

In the Palace of
the Western Motherqueen

In the peaks of the Kunlun Mountains,
  heaven looks like earth:
A soul flies west to the Amah
  in Her palace by Malachite Pond.

It waits, a supplicant,
  before the rose-gem gates,
And is received, no adept,
  in an outer court.

Astride a milk-white tigress,
  the Metal Mother comes.
Blue-black hair coiffed high,
  attendant maidens play.

Canopied with feathers—
  jade chimes ring the air;
Among immortal-peach trees—
  pipes waft tremulous tunes.

It begs the Queen to free
    a girl in the human realm.
Headdress strings of dawncloud
    shake: the boon's refused.

But She grants to the mortal seeker
    secrets of the Way:
On silk made of moon hare's fur,
    a scroll with pine-black words.

PART II

New Year's in Liang-jou

Here's another city. Liang-jou. Back up and take a look.

Late Pleistocene: Glaciers grip the heart of the continent that someone someday will call Asia. Cold, dry winds blow outward toward the Pacific, heavy with a fine calcareous dust that will give to the River Huang its tawny yellow color, and hence a further boon, its name. Great sheets of soil are laid down, a hundred feet thick, or two, or more, covering tens upon tens of thousands of square miles where China is to be. A few scrawny bipeds scrabble out a living despite the fearsome storms. The soil cleaves vertically, forming fissures that will be a traveler's bane, but it's rather nice for carving out cool and dusky cavern homes. When the scrabblers have figured out agriculture, they'll find the undulating landscape fertile. Some while later, other roaming bipeds will assign the stuff a name in their twisting Schweizer German: *Loesch,* "loose." You'll call it "loess."

The Recent Holocene: That naming hasn't happened yet. Right now the city governs the northwesternmost prefecture of a mighty empire, always keeping a nervous eye on the neighboring barbarians and on the frontier lands farther to the north and west that slip in and out of China's hands. At this particular moment, the twenty-fourth day of the last month of the thirteenth year of the golden reign of the Brilliant Emperor (may he live ten thousand years)—that's A.D. 725 to you—the West is pacified by Tang troops, and Liang-jou's sitting easy. Looked at from the east, it seems exotic, though it has been safely tucked behind the Great Wall since perhaps 112 B.C. From the west, it's China, sure enough.

Just at this moment, although the city takes a certain pride in its touch of foreignness—secure in the knowledge that it *really* is Chinese and not some mongrel colony town as, say, Dunhuang is—the people are preparing feasts for the Kitchen God in the proper Chinese way. And within the entertainment district, in the Lutegarden House of a retired courtesan called Mama Chen, the servants have been sent home for a few hours with their families. Mama Chen and her girls are also gathered to celebrate the festival. It's a bit early, but the house will be busy tonight, consoling men whose homes lie far away.

Outside, drumbeats fill the air, driving off the baneful spirits. From his niche above Mama Chen's stove, the Kitchen God gazes sternly as she plys him with food and candy and prayers. He's about to leave for heaven to make his annual report, and she wants to be certain that he'll say nice things about her—no need to mention a slip or two in her reckoning of her customers' accounts, no need to bring up the occasional curse or the beatings some of her more willful girls bring on themselves. She's decent to them once they fall in line with what's expected, and she's a busy woman, with a major establishment to keep up, no time to mollycoddle anyone. She knows that they'll need an inner toughness if they are to survive their youth.

So Mama Chen places the soybeans and the vegetables before

him. Her soft neck creases as she turns her head to urge the girls to join their prayers with hers. The older ones, Bellring and Saffron and Glory, do just as they're told. Little Pink chants out the loudest and most melodiously of all; she'll make her debut over New Year's, and she's more than ready. Nephrite, one of the new apprentices, joins right in, despite her thickish foreign accent. But the other new one, that Parrot, just stands there stupidly, off in one of her daydreams, until Nephrite reaches out to touch her arm.

In the months since Mama Chen chose the two as having the right combination of talent and looks and cheap price, she has wondered more than once if she made a mistake. Generally she has a good eye for hidden ability and gets her girls for considerably less than if she went for those already partly trained; the mistakes she can always sell off at a profit once they've learned enough to get through a decent performance of at least a song or two. Somehow, though, these two haven't quite fit in. She sighs. At least Nephrite tries, though Mama Chen is beginning to think she'll never have the stage presence of a star performer. But Parrot! She could be good, quite good; that much is clear enough. Yet she's always off somewhere with her head in the clouds.

The drums boom again, and Mama Chen's eyes snap up to look at the paper image of the Kitchen God. She can swear she just heard him clear his throat in annoyance, as if to remind her of the proper focus for her thoughts. She reaches out to light another stick of incense and place it in the bowl of sand before the niche. Then it's time for the Kitchen God to go, literally, *up* in flames. The paper bearing his image burns; the god ascends.

Upon his arrival at the heavenly court of the Jade Emperor, Mama Chen's Kitchen God gathers with his peers to wait his turn to inform His Divine Majesty of the doings of the household. He holds his back erect while exchanging dignified nods with those around him.

Mama Chen has had a good year. Yet her Kitchen God is

feeling rather grumpy. He's still ranked unconscionably low, stuck in that provincial town out in the boonies, so it's quite a while before he can make his report. It's little comfort that down in the human realm Mama Chen has scurried about all morning directing the cook and the kitchen maids and the girls as they cleaned for New Year's, and put up poles before the gate, hanging banners from them to proclaim good fortune to come. What's all that to him, after all?

Finally he is ushered into the Audience Hall. And then, one slight piles upon another: His Divine Majesty, for some reason, is less concerned with the excellent job the Kitchen God has done in increasing the prosperity of Mama Chen's than in the conduct and circumstances of a little apprentice musician who has been there only since the fall. Worse, some flunky from a minor department hovers nearby, practically breathing down the Kitchen God's neck as he tries to give a smooth account of the household's debits and credits through the year.

The young flunky actually has the audacity to interrupt. "About this Greenpearl, ah, that is, this Parrot. Has there been any sign . . . ? That is to say"—his old man's eyebrows twitch compulsively up into his young man's forehead as he sneaks a nervous glance toward the Jade Emperor—"have you noted any interference in her affairs on the part of Lady Guan-yin, or any other Buddhist, or even Buddhistically inclined, deity?"

The Jade Emperor himself leans forward, but the Kitchen God answers, as curtly as decorum will allow, that there has been none. He finishes up his report, in no mood to hint at the suitability of a promotion in recognition of his more-than-capable performance, and hastens to make his final kowtows and go. But even that is not the worst. In the Starry Antechamber to the Jade Emperor's Yang-Purple Palace, the same anxious flunky bustles up to him and clutches him by the arm. "A word, good sir?" he asks, *sotto voce.*

What's the Kitchen God to do? Flunky or not, this fellow is a member of the Celestial Administration. "Yes?" he says.

The divine official draws him over to stand in the shadow of a cumulus pillar. "One more thing. One hesitates to ask it in the Divine Presence." His grayed eyebrows jump and he glances over one shoulder. "A matter of tact, you know. About this matter of interference from, ah, other deities. You have affirmed that the Lady Guan-yin has not intervened?"

The Kitchen God looks at him coolly, refusing to acknowledge that this last has been put to him as a question. Is his word actually to be doubted by this bureaucrat?

"Well, yes, of course you have. But, ah, one wonders if there might not have been some tampering in the case by anyone—or any One—else?" He pauses in what is meant to be a significant fashion, but the Kitchen God makes no reply. "More precisely, by, perhaps, the Western Motherqueen?"

The Kitchen God snorts, and shrugs, and flicks back to Mama Chen's, just in time for a somewhat perfunctory offering of steamed kohlrabi. Today the whole cosmos is in a tizzy, and the humans pay less attention than, in his opinion, they should to kitchen gods. The souls down in the Yellow Springs move restlessly. The yang principle begins to grow toward fullness (a matter, granted, that is not viewed in the same way by all the gods and goddesses). And on earth, monasteries sponsor public lectures for the more pious folk, chickens and goats are sacrificed, bonfires are laid in the courtyards to be ignited when night falls, and people gather with their relatives to celebrate the renewal of the year.

There's an undertone of gloom at the Lutegarden House on this family holiday, not at all what the Kitchen God needs to cheer him up. Bellring, as eldest "daughter" of the household, has served the dried-peach soup, and now she pours out cups of pepper wine from a silver ewer in the Persian style. But even she feels a pang when she thinks of her own parents, with whom she feasted long ago, before their need for money sent her off to be adopted by Mama Chen. "Have a bit more wine," Bellring says to Saffron, a thin-faced flutist with Indian features who is next to Bellring in age and her closest friend.

"Oooo. *I'll* have another cup!" says Little Pink. "Pepper

wine's good for you. Keeps a person's body light and active." Her cheeks have already turned from pink to brilliant red, and it's still barely afternoon. They're celebrating early at Mama Chen's, since they'll have to keep their minds on business tonight.

"You'll get your turn," snaps Mama Chen. The girl has been the pet of the household for too long; she's gotten rather spoiled. "You know the wine's served to the youngest first at New Year's." She nods toward Bellring. "Number One, when you've finished pouring this round, rest a bit and then you may each have one more cup. Parrot first. After that, it's time for naps and makeup. It's going to be a busy night." The military governor himself has summoned the four older girls to entertain at his banquet; this means a fat purse and a lot of prestige for Lutegarden House. Mama Chen rubs her thumb over one of the raised figures of Soghdian musicians that decorate her silver cup.

Little Pink scowls openly at Parrot, then begins to hum "Barbarian Enchantress," the song she'll open with tonight. Perhaps, thinks Mama Chen, this private celebration was a sentimental mistake. But she, too, was once the "daughter" of a house like this one, in Chang-an, until a young officer brought her to Liangjou with him and then left her here to make her own way in this hick town. She's been remarkably successful and much prefers her independence to the life she'd have had if she'd wound up as someone's aging household entertainer, or a petty merchant's wife. Still, at times like this she feels a bit lonely herself. Never mind—she drains the cup that Bellring has filled brimful for her—business is good, and watching Little Pink she thinks of the splash that she herself made among the gallants of the capital in her springtime years.

Which reminds her: "Little Pink!" she says, and the girl looks over, though she continues her sulky humming. "Don't forget to keep yourself a bit aloof from the men this evening, do you hear? I don't want you to throw yourself at the first pretty-boy junior officer you meet."

"I know, I know," says Little Pink. " 'A person's got plenty of time to find a patron. A person's held to be more desirable if she maintains her modesty. The girls of Lutegarden House are skilled performers, and any gentlemen who want to be their intimate friends will have to earn the privilege with a long' "— she hiccups, and her pouty mouth slides into a grin—" 'a long and *profitable* courtship.' "

Glory laughs her throaty laugh. Honestly, thinks Mama Chen, and not for the first time, that one's nothing but a voice and a pair of fluttering eyelashes; she never once stops to think of the effect of what she does. Mama Chen prefers Little Pink's liveliness to Glory's simpers, but that doesn't stop her from turning a stream of scolding onto either of them. "You'll never hold a man if you laugh at every foolish thing that rings inside your empty head, I'll tell you that much. And then where will you end your days? In some filthy public wineshop, selling smiles to every customer who'll have you, that's where."

Glory's lashes dampen in the way that several minor officials have already found enchanting. Little Pink sulks in silence. Saffron tosses a knowing look at Bellring, while Nephrite stares uncomfortably into her untouched cup. Parrot continues to gaze, oblivious, into the embers of the stove, where the pepper wine has been left to warm.

The tomfoolery of the humans and this attention to the hearth lighten the Kitchen God's mood just a bit. But at the same time he's irked that the only one to pay the stovefire any mind is that new apprentice they were so worked up about in the Jade Emperor's court. What's more, if he takes a special interest in any member of the household, it's in Little Pink, who's fond of incense and lights a stick each morning before his niche. And now this new one's upsetting her on an important day. A bit of unburned wood within the charcoal of the fire pops and flares.

Just then the gateboy of a neighboring house sets off a string of firecrackers in the courtyard just across the Lutegarden wall. Mama Chen laughs to break the gloomy mood—so unsuitable for a holiday, these girls have no sense of how to behave, no sense at all—and the others look relieved. Except for Parrot. Off somewhere in her dreamland, she sees the flash of light in the stove, hears the hollow bamboo of the firecracker split and shatter as the gunpowder inside it ignites, and she jumps up with a shriek.

"Ba-ba-ba-ba-baaaah!" she cries. Nephrite reaches out a cool white hand to touch the younger girl's arm. Little Pink seizes the moment, scoops up Nephrite's cup, and drinks it down. No one notices. Then she giggles. "An evil sprite!" she says. "Parrot's afraid of the New Year's firecrackers—she must be one of the demons Neighbor Tian is trying to scare away!"

Glory's eyes grow large, and she edges over closer to Saffron, away from where Parrot sits. "Nonsense," says Mama Chen, though everyone knows that evil spirits in disguise reveal themselves by their fear when the firecrackers explode. Nephrite offers a soothing sip of wine to Parrot, only to discover that her cup has mysteriously emptied itself. The Kitchen God feels pleased.

Parrot is unable to find any words to say that would ease the situation. A moment ago she was walking by the river back in Khotan with her nannie; now she's been jerked back bereft to this new and complex city, and to this new and complex life. She wants Little Pink and Glory and the older girls to like her, but even if she knew how, she doesn't want to act with men as Little Pink and Glory do. Parrot knows that her lips will not bend to that teasing, lying smile.

"Nephrite . . ." she begins, falling into the Khotanese the two of them now use only when they are alone together.

Mama Chen grunts in irritation and sends them all off to nap. "You little apprentices, too," she says to Nephrite and Parrot. "You'll be up late tonight at His Excellency's—the party's bound to go on well past dawn—and I want you to look lively when you come in from the waiting room to help your elder sisters put on their wraps and get the instruments home."

Later, Parrot will hold the circular bronze mirror for Little Pink while the older girl applies her rouge, and a delicate oval of palest yellow to the center of her forehead. "Keep it still, clumsy demon!" Little Pink will scold when the mirror jiggles as she fixes a gold filigree hairpin borrowed from Glory. But mostly she'll ignore Parrot, thinking only of the performance to come. Then, when Little Pink sweeps off to light another stick of incense to the Kitchen God, Parrot will trace the pairs of lions and phoenixes on the back of the highly polished disk, return it to its carved stand, and stare into its depths. Perhaps, she'll think, practicing a dainty simper, I can learn to speak this language after all.

At that very moment, Seagem in the Dragon Monarch's villa will be whitening her face with powder from a mollusk-shaped box. *Her* mirror will be ringed with eight petal lobes, backed with gold, and ornamented with a pair of dragons. Suddenly, both reflections will cloud, as if with a mist of exhaled breath, and mother and daughter will each behold an instant's apparition of the other. "Who's this?" Seagem will cry out, and Parrot will echo, "Who?" But a second later, the images will return to their proper places, the flickering red candle on Little Pink's dressing table will once again burn straight and bright, and Parrot will rub her eyes and run off in answer to a resonant command from Glory's room. Little Pink's mirror will never again reveal a sight into another world. But in rare, erratic moments, Seagem's will.

Decades later, an emperor forced into abdication, the man named Li Long-ji (also Hsuan-zong and the Brilliant Emperor), will gaze brokenly into yet another mirror, longing for a glimpse of his Precious Consort Yang, to whose unjust execution he consented when his mutinous troops demanded her life for his freedom. But he'll catch no reflection of the seductive smiles the soldiers blamed for the destruction of the state, and in the sixth year of his son's reign (nearly forty years after the New Year's Eve you've just read about, in A.D. 761), he'll die within his guarded quarters in a back wing of the grand imperial palace: nine thousand, nine hundred, and twenty-three years short of what he might have wished. On that spring day, unseasonably cold winds will rise up and swirl through the streets of Liang-jou, Chang-an, Dun-huang, through the cities of his lost empire, scattering their throat-tightening loads of yellow dust.

A Record of the
Music of Liang-Jou

by Lan Jen-yi *(style name,* Jing-yun)

(A.D. 669?—c. 768)

It is only now, looking back at the profligate expenditure of
my youth among the byways of the willows and flowers, that I
realize the need of leaving a warning for future generations. And
so, I take up my pen and jot down these random notes concerning the music of the northwestern city of Liang-jou in the days
of its glory.

I have become an old man, and the empire has fallen on evil
times. The traitorous general An Lu-shan has been assassinated,
and I have heard that the last of the rebels were defeated some
three months ago outside Lo-yang [*early in* A.D. *763*], but lawlessness and disorder have taken their toll. It was not so in the
splendid reign of Hsuan-zong the Brilliant, grandfather of our
present emperor. In those days, though the barbarians pressed at
the gates of the empire, yet they were pacified or held at bay.
The rule of the Great Tang stretched then far past Dun-huang

to the desert cities of Khotan, Kucha, and beyond. Today even Liang-jou and all the provinces around it have fallen into Tibetan hands.

Often I think deeply on the winsome singers and skillful instrumentalists of bygone days, and my breast heaves with sighs. Alas! The city had perhaps two ten-thousands of households; some say more. All of them, being persons of the west, had a certain firmness of personality. This is not, however, to deny the charm of the women of the entertainment district.

Many of the people, both householders and musicians, came from Soghdiana or India, and the music too was a mingling of Chinese and foreign. They played the classical instruments of antiquity together with those of the far west; thus the respectable stone chimes of long ago strangely harmonized with the alien lute of Kucha. Some of the music was nothing more than barbarian modes. In this, I daresay the music of Liang-jou resembled the music of the empire today.

In the entertainment district of the city, songs of the streets mixed with exotic melodies. The players cannot be said to have had the stately decorum of those of the Ministry of Confucian Rites and Music in the capital, nor the dazzling skill of the performers from the Brilliant Emperor's vanished Pear Garden Conservatory, nor even the alluring polish of the *musiciennes* of the Teaching Quarters in Chang-an. Yet their performances were not without charm.

Like the talented courtesans who specialized in singing or dancing, most of the musicians were the daughters of poor families. In other cases, some member of the clan had committed a crime and had their relatives consigned to slavery as a part of the punishment. Still others were the offspring of western tribes, purchased or captured, and brought into the music schools of Liang-jou to be trained.

Their study began at an early age; five or six years was not considered too young and they continued until they reached puberty or beyond. They were not the same as the mere prostitutes of the marketplace brothels. Indeed, although their origins were lowly, they interacted with the most brilliant lights of the age, vying with scholars and officials in the composition of lyrics. Of many, it can be said that, while they did not follow the ways of the daughters of good families, they were rather elegant creatures of deep feeling.

In closing, I record the titles of some of their songs.

Pliant Willows in the Wind
Tying Loveknots
Floating Dragonboats
Midnight Glee
Looking at the Lunar Palace
Farewell to a Traveler
Overheard Beyond Heaven
This Parrot-Shaped Goblet
Broken Bowstring
Mistress As-You-Will
The Foreign Monk's Ruin

Shamanka Mountain Girl
Scattered Golden Sands
Spring Pervades the Garden
Seven-Star Flute
Lamplit Meeting
In the Land of the Queen
Bamboo in the Southern Skies
Song of the Grotto Spirits
Lady of the Tao
The Flower Monarch Blooms
A Dipper of Salt

Parrot Speaks: 6

I must have been eleven when I saw Baby again, the first time in the three years and more since Mama Chen chose Nephrite and me from among the little slaves offered her by Old Ma's son. It happened four days after the end of the Festival of Lanterns, the gaudy climax to the two weeks of New Year's. I've heard that long ago, in the Han Dynasty, people stayed up the whole night through to worship the gods; now of course they mostly wander through the streets, buying snacks and flirting and gazing at the year's first full moon.

Those three days are the busiest of all the year in the entertainment district: much of the time the dancers and musicians are dashing about from party to party, jostling through lanes filled with peddlers and vendors and strollers. Crowds gather before the most splendidly lighted households, sometimes blocking the way of the entertainers who've been invited to

96

brighten a soiree. The chance of spying a popular beauty on her way in to sing or exchange poems with the gentlemen guests only leads the curious common folk to pack the area before a noble lord's crimson gates more tightly than ever. That year, Little Pink's career had reached full flower, and her name was on everyone's lips: "There she is!" some oaf would say, too loudly. "There's the governor's favorite courtesan, Little Pink." She'd pretend to ignore him, but it made her only more difficult to deal with back at Lutegarden House.

Evenings when no one from the house had been asked out were no better. The whole place might be booked by some officer eager to throw a bigger banquet than his quarters in Liangjou would allow. Or we would simply have our usual open house, the customers going and coming in a tizzy of food and wine and conversation. On these nights Mama Chen never knew who would show up or whose feelings were going to require her delicate management, so they were the worst of all. Things would have been less hectic if she had been willing to keep a full staff of maids, but she couldn't bear to part with the money.

The last night of the festival had been like that. The governor himself had come with a couple of his friends to call on Little Pink, which necessitated the clearing of the best public rooms, which in turn meant that Nephrite—who was no longer an apprentice—and Bellring and Glory had had to entertain a group of slightly put-out officials in the common reception room downstairs. In springtime, the situation could easily have been saved by a wistful suggestion from Nephrite of flower viewing in the garden, or in summer by Bellring calling for a game of Floating Wine Cups in the little pond. But though the blazing lanterns proclaimed the growth of the brilliant yang, the fact remained that it was cold. Even indoors, the guests wore their sable-trimmed hats and jackets until they were well warmed with drink, and Little Pink's famous cheeks glowed pomegranate red with the snap of the weather.

The next morning most of us had gathered as we usually did

in the reception room, near the kitchen, when Little Pink made her solution to the problem clear. Bellring, who as eldest had the best set of rooms in the house, should give them up to Little Pink. "Then," she said, toying with a lock of her hair as she leaned back on the new rosewood couch, "His Excellency might be entertained as suits a man of his rank."

Mama Chen was quick to point out that although the governor was obviously enjoying the flirtation, he had as yet shown no inclination to spend the night. "That's the worst thing you could do, you little empty head, is rush him." She waved a bit of fried turnip cake to underline her words. "I'd have to keep Parrot in there waiting on you the whole time to avoid any indication of impropriety—or overeagerness. And until I can find another decent apprentice at a reasonable price I need her helping out the other girls as well as you."

"Anyway, wouldn't people be more impressed if you let His Excellency summon you to serve him at his residence?" asked Glory, who then looked puzzled by the glare her friend shot in her direction. "I mean, surely he will, sooner or later," she added, looking down at her plate.

But Bellring's position in the house was safe whatever Glory said or didn't say in her thoughtless attempts to please Little Pink. It was true that Bellring had had no special protector for some time now, but the liveliness of her fashionable tunes on the lute and the subtle technique with which she plucked melodies on the classical chyn still drew eager customers. And as Mama Chen's famous fingers stiffened with arthritis, she'd come to depend more and more on Bellring to help with the music lessons she gave to us and to the girls from lesser houses who were sent to study with her.

Just then Saffron came in, sleepy and a little sad-faced. Everyone, even Little Pink, turned toward her. "Oh, Emissary Gao's gone," she said. "Saw him off before daybreak. I suppose the governor will have me over to keep Gao company at the official farewell dinner tonight, but that's it. Back to Chang-an tomorrow. Parrot, *would* you be so good as to run and fetch some fresher tea?"

I thought how happy I'd be when Mama Chen did take on a new apprentice, who could share the errands with me, and how miffed—and how funny—Little Pink had looked at Saffron's casual mention of the governor. Perhaps Saffron had overheard Little Pink's attempt to replace Bellring.

By the time I got back with the tea, Saffron's usual brighter spirits had returned. I was glad. Bellring kept a teacher's distance from me, Glory in her silly way had never quite forgotten a distrust of me she'd acquired my first New Year's at Lutegarden, and Little Pink was absorbed in Little Pink. Nephrite remained my one true friend and quiet protector, but we had less time together now that she was no longer an apprentice and had a little room of her own; even when she was free, as like as not I'd find her meditating there. But Saffron and I had something in common, a taste for poetry. When the calligraphy teacher came, the two of us would laugh and race our brushes down the page as we copied out the latest poems and lyrics we'd picked up. I was still just a beginner, of course, but I learned quickly. Only the day before I'd suggested a change in wording in a farewell poem that Saffron was composing for her lover from Changan, Imperial Emissary Gao.

"You know, Parrot," she told me as she drained her second cup, "that line you altered still seems better to me. I'm going to write the poem out that way when I give it to him tonight." Her narrow face lost the fresh look the tea had brought to it. "That way, at least he'll remember me for a little while." She turned and poured another cup of tea for me. "You really do have a knack for words."

"Then she ought to learn to write them better," snapped Little Pink. She could barely scrawl her name but fancied herself a connoisseur of calligraphy these days; the governor was noted for his elegant hand. Mama Chen had, I'd heard, ended Little Pink's writing lessons years ago, telling her to concentrate on the oboe, and conversation, and memorizing the words to other people's songs.

"Perhaps someday she'll manage to write as prettily as you," murmured Bellring, and everybody except Little Pink—even Nephrite—laughed.

"Enough, enough," said Mama Chen, reaching for the last sticky piece of turnip cake. "The festival may be over, but I don't give you girls a home so you can lie about and scratch at one another with your hairpins. Saffron, you'll want to look especially pretty tonight for the farewell dinner. Apply your rouge with a light touch, though. You'd best appear wan." Saffron turned her gaze from Mama Chen's. I saw that though she was resigned to what she could not change, she couldn't look at this visiting dignitary's departure as calculatingly as Mama Chen did. It wasn't until much later that it occurred to me Mama Chen might have been offering her, in artifice and coolness, the only balm she could.

"Bellring," Mama Chen continued, "get Parrot started right away on that new song for her lute. Then go over the part for the chyn again with Glory. I want us to be ready in ten days, for Colonel Duan's party, and I don't know if she can get it learned in time. *Try*, will you, Glory? Little Pink, you've been coming nicely with your bit." Little Pink's plum-blossom face didn't move, but her eyes revealed that the simple flattery had restored her mood. "Saffron, Nephrite, find a quiet corner and practice your flutes. And Nephrite, I want you to eat a bite of breakfast first. Don't think I haven't noticed that you've sat here all this time without eating a crumb."

Nephrite protested that one of the customers had made her share a whole bowl of greasy noodles with him late last night and that she was still full. But Mama Chen refused to listen.

"You're too skinny, child. You'll start looking like a hungry ghost and then what will the guests think of Lutegarden's kitchen service? Run and have Cook fix you something hot if you like, but eat." Nephrite nodded, though I doubted she'd comply. "Do you all know what you're to do? Good. I want you junior girls—Parrot and Nephrite and Little Pink and Glory—back here after noon, when the drum sounds for the tenth watch. You're about to start on something new."

"Something new" turned out to be a lesson in a dance called Whirling Sashes. The holiday season had exhausted our repertoire, and Mama Chen knew we had to work up some novel performances if Lutegarden House was to maintain its fashionable standing in the city. She herself was no dancer, so two years ago she'd acquired an accomplished young Turkish dancer and renamed her Grapevine. But unfortunately Grapevine had been such a success that the governor had insisted on buying her contract—at a nice profit, to be sure—and had sent her as a gift to the president of the Imperial Tribunal of Censors in Chang-an. Mama Chen still grumbled about it.

Whirling Sashes, she told the four of us as we sat in the reception room waiting for the teacher to arrive, was in the gentler Gan-jou style. "If the gentlemen guests want tricky things like Sword Dance or The Barbarian Egret, they'll simply have to go someplace else. But there's no reason you four can't learn a few of this sort."

Then the teacher walked in: an Iranian with only one eye. The other socket puckered grotesquely about an ugly knife scar that jagged from above his eyebrows to the middle of one cheek. It must have been the embittering end of his career as a performer. He grunted his commands, and his every gesture let us know that none of us was worth a second of his time. When Mama Chen left us while she fetched Bellring to relieve her aching fingers at the lute, he pulled Glory over to him and stood behind her to reposition her arms. "Like this, Miss Sweet and Foolish," he said. But when he finished posing her, instead of stepping back, he thrust himself against her buttocks and one hand snaked inside the deeply V'd neckline of her dress.

Of course Glory knew how to twirl about and step away in

quick evasion, though the nervous tone of her laugh told me that she was as surprised as I that such a move would be necessary from a teacher invited as a professional into the house. And then she gasped. His hand had remained an instant longer, pulling the dress open, and I saw his long-nailed fingers deliberately catch the nipple of one breast. Little Pink had paid no attention to the whole thing—and it was over in a moment—but Nephrite paled as if her own flesh felt the sharp pinch.

Then Mama Chen bustled back with Bellring, and the music was struck up at once. I saw Nephrite whisper something into Glory's ear, but she just blushed and hung her head and shook it "no." Had it been a boorish drunken guest who'd hurt her, I'm certain that she would have embarrassed him with laughter, or complained to one of his companions, or had a quiet talk with Mama Chen, who'd set him straight in the way best suited to his rank. But the looks the man gave her now, his single eye speaking not of impetuous admiration or honest need but of his superiority and her defilement, seemed to silence her. I thought how he, who should regard her with the benevolent sternness of a teacher for a pupil, did not even regard her with desire, but only with the will to hurt. Glory's lashes dampened, her feet stumbled, the lesson went on. Then I wondered how it was he'd chosen the one out of the four of us who was the slowest-witted and the least likely to take action on her own.

Three days later the dancing teacher returned. Glory tried to excuse herself from the lesson, claiming a headache, but Mama Chen simply scolded her. "You've got a headache. Nephrite's stomach hurts. Both of you are lazy, that's all. Of course you'll have to join the lesson. I don't pay him good money because I don't know what else to do with it, you know."

This time he came with an apprentice, a young girl in a western dancer's trousers. She followed him in, head down, squatted in the farthest corner, and pulled her little lacquered wether drum from its hemp-cloth bag. My attention was all on the teacher, and on Glory, but Mama Chen stayed with us that day, content at times to rest her fingers and let the drummer carry us through the steps.

It was a certain quality of sorrow in the drumming that first caught my notice. Whirling Sashes was in the "soft style," yet it had a sprightliness about it. But though the drummer kept the variable rhythms remarkably well for one so young, somehow the beating told of humiliation and fear.

We paused to rest a moment, and Nephrite rushed to settle on the cushion next to mine. "Have you noticed the drummer?" she asked me in her usual low tone.

"Yes," I said. "She sounds sad."

"Oh, but more than that." Her eyes brightened. "It's Baby!"

And in an instant I saw that Nephrite spoke the truth. Taller, slender-waisted now, her cheerful round Khotanese face subdued, still the little drummer was clearly the child who'd been the darling at Old Ma's, and the only tie, besides each other, that Nephrite and I had to Khotan. I thought of the time Baby had made poor Blackie laugh after Umar tormented him.

"What are we going to do?" I whispered to Nephrite in Khotanese.

She shook her head. "I'll pray to the Western Motherqueen to help her, of course, but what else is there you and I can do, Parrot? Remember who we are."

Did her acceptance reveal the difference in being raised a poor farmer's daughter, rather than the indulged child of a powerful commander? Was it that her soul had come into this lifetime to learn how to control its desires for action, while mine had some other charge? I know only that I wanted to retort that even little entertainers could do something, just as Baby's dancing had once helped sobbing Blackie forget Umar's bullying.

But Mama Chen's sharp voice cut off our conversation. "You two! Stop that foreign gabbling and stand up. Teacher's ready to begin again."

Glancing at the one-eyed man, I thought of Nannie, and how she'd use sweet words to get her way. "We're having trouble with the second turn, Mama Chen," I said in a placating voice. "We can't seem to get it as smooth as Teacher does and still keep together. Do you suppose Teacher and his apprentice might run through it together, so we all can watch?"

Mama Chen pursed her lips. The man's face acknowledged our incompetence and his superior skill. He grunted to Baby to stand up. Mama Chen's stiff fingers grasped her plectrum and she struck up the tune.

Baby had lost her gaiety, but her talent for dancing had bloomed into a remarkable skill. When the two completed the second turn and the teacher barked at her to stop, Nephrite and I clapped in nearly spontaneous applause. Even Mama Chen smiled. "Now, that little dancer," she said, "is what I want the four of you to look like by the time General Jao's party comes around."

By luck, that night was a busy one at Lutegarden. At last the governor had asked Little Pink if he might visit her in her rooms alone. A rich merchant who'd lately taken quite a fancy to Glory had made an appointment to come by with a guest from out of town. Mama Chen was not supposed to let anyone into Lutegarden except scholars and officials. But sometimes rules could be bent, Liang-jou being a provincial town, and the clerk responsible for the entertainment quarter being as eager for bribes as Mama Chen was for traders' wealth.

She sent Nephrite in along with Glory to wait on them, in keeping with her theory that it wouldn't do to let the merchant spend time alone with Glory too soon. Then a whole group of young bravos dropped in to eat and drink, asking Mama Chen to let them hear some of her "famous musicians, especially someone skilled at playing the flute." The old woman knew what that meant: word was out of Saffron's brief attachment to Imperial Emissary Gao; there'd be a flurry of interest in her now. I couldn't yet play more than a few songs on the lute well enough for guests, so most of the time Bellring played, or sang while Saffron piped. I struck the gong and the great drum when I wasn't

running for more wine. Mama Chen beat the wether drum herself. But then her hands tired, and she needed to check things
in the kitchen, and someone had to keep popping in to "assist"
Glory and Nephrite, and Little Pink, in order to keep an eye on
both those situations. It was altogether an exhausting evening.

It was nearly dawn before the big group wore themselves out
and left, and the weary kitchenmaids hurried in to clear out the
room. The merchant and his friend had given up and gone home
only a short while earlier, though Mama Chen had allowed Glory
and Nephrite to walk with them through our little garden to
the front gate to say good-bye.

I sighed, and made my hundredth trip to the kitchen, where
Cook was draining the last drops from the ewers into her own
cup. When I returned with a final pot of tea, Nephrite, Saffron,
and Glory were chattering in the lively way that entertainers do
when the guests have left at last. Mama Chen was telling them
about checking Glory and Nephrite's party only to discover that
they were completely out of wine, and the merchant and his
friend were bellowing in the general direction of the kitchen,
rather than letting the girls go together for some more. "Not
wanting to be separated, they'd told the men that they were a
bit afraid to go out through the passageway to the kitchen
alone!" she chuckled. "Fortunately I got there before the merchants disturbed the other parties. Men of that class really are
completely unrefined."

An idea struck me. "I should have gone down to see them
sooner, Mama Chen, instead of making you do it," I said, placing
a marbled pottery cup in front of her. "But Little Pink had rung
for me to go fetch a few cloves for His Excellency to chew, to
clear the wine fumes from his head." I poured her tea. "I feel
ashamed that you should have to do apprentice work after all
these years. Forgive me, Lady, please."

She chuckled again, leaning on her armrest while the tea
cooled enough for her to drink it. " '*Old* Lady' is more like it,"
she said, but I could tell that she was pleased. "No, the problem

is clear. We need another apprentice. Nephrite's been out for months now, and there's too much for you to do alone. Besides"—she glanced slyly at Saffron and Bellring—"sooner or later *someone* is going to leave us."

The two older girls laughed tipsily, and I said, "It really is too bad that we lost Grapevine. Saffron and Glory dance nicely enough, but none of us can attract guests with our dancing like she did. But Mama Chen, how can a person tell an apprentice's dancing skill before taking her on?"

Mama Chen conceded that, though she had the ear to discern talent in an untrained singer or musician, the real gift of dancing—something beyond a general grace—wasn't as easy for her to pick out. "Perhaps I should just say farewell to this difficult life, retire to some quiet place outside the city, and take the veil of a Lady of the Tao," she said, in a voice that made it clear that in fact she at least was one ex-courtesan with no such plans.

The subject was shifting in the wrong direction. I hastily agreed that she was indeed overworked, and admitted that I feared I'd been so tired I came close to angering Glory's friend with my carelessness. Before she could begin to scold, though, I added, "What we need, then, isn't it, is to find a little girl with the skill of the Iranian teacher's apprentice. But surely Mama Chen's eye can pick out such a child."

There. The seed had been planted. We had another dancing lesson in two days. Tomorrow I'd mention the expense of bringing in a teacher from outside the house; I was certain that Baby knew enough to train us. Maybe I *could* save her with my words.

Seagem's Bedchamber

For years now, as mortals reckon time, this hungry ghost has roamed the human realm. Most nights, it haunts the riverbank where its soul was torn from flesh. Once it was called against its will to a back room in a shabby inn, where two lovers lay together in a bed the ghost had known. And at times it has trailed along the Silk Road, keeping an invisible, longing watch over the child to whom it is bound. It roams desirous. It remains unfulfilled.

Now another chain of wanting tugs it to where it has not been before. The woman Seagem, residing with her otherworldly husband in the fabulous villa of the Dragon Monarch, has prayed repeatedly for some word of her daughter, to whose fate this roaming soul's is linked. Good Lady Guan-yin, who keeps the ghost in her charge, is pleased to grant Seagem's petitions. Guan-yin's ways are a mystery, but whatever her reasons, she allows this interview.

Seagem has seen so many strange things since the fishy, vermilion robed doctor—her husband's hot-blooded uncle—took her away from the house of the Lis in Chang-an. Even so, she's startled when the ghost appears. Seagem is lying with her head on a coral pillow, her body sweet with the recent touch of her husband, asleep beside her. She breathes out her quiet supplication to the Lady once again. And then the apparition rises before her, more solid than if she'd met it up on earth, but quivering, flickering, all the same.

Where is this? Why do you summon me? And who are you to call? The ghost's unkempt hair flies wild as tumbleweed, or kelp washed by subsurface tides.

Eventually they work the story out: each of them mother in her own way to the same child; the granting of the scroll by the Western Motherqueen at Seagem's request; the hungry ghost's confirmation that the girl received it at the bidding of a talking bird, though it seems that Greenpearl has forgotten it this long while; their fruitless guesses at what text its silk might bear. All this while—as the women feel now the blood tie of true sisters, now the aching jealousy of rivals for one daughter's heart—Seagem's husband sleeps.

"And now?" asks Seagem quietly. "How is the girl living, so far from home and family, her father dead, and me kept here underneath the waves?"

So the ghost tells of Greenpearl's present life: she's a little apprentice in the Entertainment Quarter of Liang-jou, ready soon for womanhood as a skilled musician whose talents and way with words will win the hearts of men. To the spirit's great surprise, Seagem begins to weep.

"My daughter ruined!" she says between her tears. "Good Lady Guan-yin, is this your punishment for the delight I've taken in illicit love?" Her husband stirs and mutters in his sleep; she reaches out and smoothes his fine black hair. "Oh, husband!" she whispers. She always thought, At least we are bound in marriage. We must have been joined before birth by the red thread that ties those destined to become husband and wife. But her beloved daughter will lose her chastity as an entertainer. Shame tingles across her shoulders. "Is it retribution for my two husbands that she'll have none?" Seagem sighs.

Softly, the ghost moans. She shudders, she fades from sight for a moment, but she cannot leave.

"Don't go!" says Seagem. She is afraid of losing this only link to the satisfaction of a hunger she has nourished within herself for years. So she listens in silence while the ghost stammers out the reasons a woman might choose to lie with a man to whom she is not wed. *Love*, it says. *Or an empty stomach. As a gift of comforting, or as comfort taken. For the sake of foolish laughter. Anger. Spite. Because she'll soon grow old. In a moment of hot joy, or a long cool hour of ease. Loneliness, or fear. For the honey taste of someone unknown. Contempt. To feel the dizzy pulse-race of adventure. To hear him praise her beauty. Pure unreckoning desire.*

"But what will we do?" asks Seagem, as soon as she can turn the talk back to her daughter. "Is there no way we can send some further word to the child, to bring her here to me? Surely that will let you find your rest."

The soul moans its agreement: If the girl can complete the search for Seagem, as—following Lady Guan-yin's command—it bid her to on the desert night when it summoned all its longing and uttered a few words audible to Greenpearl's mortal ears, then the Lady will release the ghost from the death promise. Then it may end this aimless wandering, perhaps may set its feet again upon the wheeling way of rebirth, in hopes of reaching enlightenment, and peace.

Yet how *will* they get a message to the girl? Her heart is closed, by the doors fear closes over memory, against any appearance of the hungry ghost. Is there not someone else then, Seagem asks, who might give guidance to her daughter? Some person who might make a link between the realms?

Perhaps there is someone. Hissing and shaking, the ghost

describes a mortal different from other mortals: a round-faced, slender-waisted child, with a dancer's nimble feet, and bruises scattered on the insides of her thighs, and a scar like a knife wound near the nipple of one budding breast. She is mute, and so not fully bound to the labyrinth of lies that is the human world. Perhaps she can get a message through.

Parrot Speaks: 7

Baby had been with us at Lutegarden for two years—it was the beginning of spring and the plum trees were in bloom—when I "broke the melon" and the moon-ruled coursing of my blood marked me as a woman. Even then, I remained slender, but Baby had grown plump again. Mama Chen beamed when Baby danced and the guests applauded; she beamed more broadly when the rest of us learned the steps that Baby showed us without a teacher's fee. That the little dancer never spoke didn't seem to matter much just then, though of course it had been a useful bargaining point when Mama Chen and the Iranian dancing teacher negotiated her price.

Not long after Baby moved in to share the apprentices' room with me, I told her—hoping to make her smile—the story of how I had persuaded Mama Chen that we needed a new little apprentice who could already dance. Baby knelt before me, threw her arms around my legs, and began to weep.

I felt ashamed: of course I'd wanted to get her away from the casual viciousness of the dancing teacher, but I'd also been moved by my desire to share the apprentice work, and mostly by a need to have someone else around me from Khotan. When I felt homesick for the city of jade where I was born, Nephrite would only say, "The past is past"; then she'd turn back to the latest scroll lent her by the Taoist holy woman she'd begun to study with. My homesickness grew worse every time I heard Little Pink's "barbarian this" and "uncultured foreign that," and Glory's murmurs of agreement, even though Bellring—whose looks were as fully Chinese as theirs—would tell them they were being tiresome. In Khotan I'd been held apart from people by being a daughter of Chang-an, yet visitors to Lutegarden would look at my Turkish cheekbones and Iranian eyes and call me "exotic" or "outlandish" as they pleased.

So I pulled Baby up to stand before me and put my arms around her. I did this shyly. Sometimes, walking in the garden before the guests arrived, I'd see Little Pink and Glory holding hands in friendship, and I'd envy them. Or a guest, his spirit eased with wine, would throw an arm about the neck of the companion come to drink with him, and I'd feel more than ever a loneliness of the flesh. But of course, when that same guest brushed against my leg, it meant his thoughts were elsewhere, and a little apprentice girl must smile bashfully and turn away.

Baby's tears stopped, but she held her body stiff and cold, waiting for me to drop my arms. I did. Even Baby finds me strange, I thought, and almost began to weep myself. She must have seen that idea within me, for she explained herself without speech. Sitting on the wide platform bed we shared, she opened her skirt to show me the last greenish bruises on her thighs. Then she held up a hand to silence me, and let me see a scar torn across one small breast.

Poor thing, my heart said, but there was no need to utter that aloud. I asked if it had been the Iranian who'd done it, knowing as I asked that she'd nod yes. Reaching toward her, I traced the scar line with one finger, as if a touch could smooth it from existence. Then she covered her body again with her clothing, and waved one arm in a gesture that took in the room, all Lutegarden, and her new life. She smiled and, as she waved, shifted her body a fraction farther from me.

Still, in the years that followed, Baby did begin to take my hand on those garden walks, or in our bed at night. At times I longed for something more, but never asked for it. I was afraid of what the Iranian had done to her trusting nature, afraid of driving her away.

Nephrite took an elder sister's care to see that all went well for Baby in the early days at Lutegarden. Yet Nephrite's mind was elsewhere. The summer before Baby came, when Nephrite was ready to step from her apprentice life to that of a full-grown courtesan, Mama Chen sent her off by sedan chair to stay a few days with a certain Lady of the Tao who lived with other Taoist holy women at Darkdazzle Vista, on a hilltop outside town. This woman had been an "elder sister" of Mama Chen's years ago and, on retirement from the Entertainment Quarter, had taken on the cap and robes of holy orders. She'd studied the boudoir techniques for nourishing the body's vital energy and was skilled in the methods for attaining long life through the fivefold joyful struggle of woman and man. When it came my turn to be sent to her, she lectured me on the importance of maintaining a tranquil spirit while uniting with a man. She told me, too, how to use the ten movements and the nine essences to increase my pleasure and my partner's.

During Nephrite's stay with this Lady of the Tao, she fell one afternoon into a conversation with a Purified Teacher, the holiest of the women at Darkdazzle Vista. The Purified Teacher, whose austere devotions and skillful practice of alchemy had transformed her into a transcendent spirit on earth, told Nephrite of her visionary travels to the palace of the Western Motherqueen. After that, Nephrite wanted nothing else but to become a Lady of the Tao herself, though Mama Chen declined to be of any help.

So Nephrite studied, saving every coin that came to her in

hopes of buying her freedom from Mama Chen, while Baby and I worked and laughed together by day, sleeping at night together in our little room. But things could not remain so: I broke the melon, went to Darkdazzle to be instructed, and returned to enter into the life for which I'd been trained.

The first day, I was nervous. I made my courtesy calls to the other houses in the entertainment district that afternoon, bowing to Mama Yuan and Mama Bai and the rest, asking formally for their favor in my new career. Their daughters gathered round to greet me, some solemn, most merry-eyed, a few quite openly appraising my looks and my new clothes. Saffron had helped me pile my hair up in a high loop, rather than a musician girl's two simple knots. Then she'd dotted a glittering beauty mark, a "yellow star dimple," on my cheek. When I returned to Lutegarden, she called Bellring and the kitchen maids to come and admire my new look.

The two kitchen maids joked and chattered. Bellring brought her lute in with her—a beautiful thing, its pear-shaped body made of red sandalwood inlaid with flowers of tortoiseshell— and lent it to me for the evening. Tilting her graceful neck, she told me I'd play well. Her kindness, and Saffron's, eased my mood a bit.

Of course I'd played for guests before. I often helped serve the wine and dishes I brought up from the kitchen, and once or twice, late in the evening, I'd been allowed to join in a party game. I'd even gone along on several pleasure trips to the countryside when some gentleman decided to appreciate nature with his friends. But Mama Chen had always been careful to keep me in the background. "Men desire more to pick the flower they haven't seen a hundred times before," she'd say, calling me away.

I can't even remember who it was we played for that first night, Saffron and Glory and I. Glory was put out at first, because Mama Chen had told her not to play her chyn but to accompany me on the wether drum while I played and sang. But just before we went into the best room to meet the gentlemen, Saffron scolded Glory for sulking. "The emperor himself is famous for his skill at beating the wether drum, silly Glory. How can you look down on it?" Glory brightened then.

I do recall that the guests were five old men, who teased me when I spilled a bit of tea. Toward midnight, one of them asked his friends who would be "the one to enrich his virility by returning some night to join with the little virgin," but just then another old gentleman broke out with a snore and all of us laughed. Nephrite had urged me to store up vital energy the way some Taoist adepts do, taking as many lovers as Mama Chen's notions of profitable elusiveness would allow—provided I kept my own emotions under firm control. But I was in no hurry to enter into that part of my new life.

What I'd been most worried about, keeping up an entertaining conversation, turned out to be easy enough. One old scholar took me aside and recited an ancient poem from the *Book of Odes*. He praised me extravagantly when I recited it back. But most guests preferred a courtesan as young as I to smile, and listen, and nod.

A few weeks later, a minor government assistant named Fan began to visit Lutegarden regularly, and to ask for me to keep him company. He gave me a finely carved ivory plectrum for the old lute I played, something I valued much more than the hairpins or earrings he might have chosen. His high smooth forehead reminded me of that gleaming ivory and although he drank heavily, he took great care about his person, always bathing in water scented with aloeswood. The crab apple in the garden blossomed luxuriantly that year, just when he presented Mama Chen with a gift of silk and asked me if he might stay with me one night.

On the advice of the older girls, I refused at first, hanging my head and blushing, which was not at all difficult to do. But when he sent me a poem on a slip of deep crimson paper, it moved me.

I still slept in the apprentices' room, because there was no other free, but Nephrite changed with me for a night, helping me to fill the incense brazier with cassia and patchouli and musk before young Fan arrived. Baby waited on us, slipping into the room with hot wine and dishes, for Mama Chen was careful to send up plenty of food, not only to increase the bill, but in order that he might not sink too far into intoxication. Even then, my heart beating with nervousness and anticipation, I noticed how subdued Baby was, though I supposed she was taking pains not to break the mood.

After a while, his face flushed but his eyes still clear, Fan led me toward Nephrite's gauze-curtained bed. Baby loosened my hair and helped me undress, but then left quickly, though I would have preferred to have her stay a while longer. Mama Chen had given me powdered cuttlefish bone and hyssop dissolved in wine that afternoon, to protect me from pain or undue bleeding; indeed, although I normally drank little, that night I had gone cup for cup with Fan, until I grew quite tipsy. At first he sat on my left and then spread his legs out and took me onto his lap, wrapping his arms around me. We kissed and touched one another, all in the proper way. But he lost his restraint and hurriedly pushed me onto my back, so that I might be the rising phoenix and he, the dragon overturned. In that moment, I thought of Nannie by the riverbank and saw the river-polished stone of dark green jade that brought her to her violent end.

The vision of the stone, its coolness and gloss, stayed in the air above me. Soon Fan cried out and lay snoring beside me on the bed. The next day, Nephrite told me I should be pleased: though his male essence had been nourished by my virginity, in his greed for exhilaration, he had enriched me by the prodigal wastage of his vital force. I too had been taught this at Dark-dazzle Vista, but I felt less certain. A new hunger had been stirred up in me, and it remained unsatisfied.

That very afternoon, Mama Chen heard that Fan's gambling debts already rose around him like a floodtide and that he had failed to pay several large bills in the Entertainment Quarter when he left Lo-yang the previous fall. The next three times he came to visit, she told him curtly I was previously engaged. The weeks passed and I sometimes thought of him. But so many things were different now that I was no longer an apprentice. I came to pride myself in my growing facility at the word games our guests played as we ate and drank, and at playing that other game of banter with both word and glance.

After Baby danced, or when she slipped into a party to refill the ewers, she would roll her eyes comically to show how overworked she was, but we both knew there'd be another apprentice soon. In fact, it looked as if Saffron was about to be taken off to the south by a well-to-do officer of advanced years. I think she still longed sometimes for that visiting Emissary Gao from Chang-an, though I never heard her speak of him; in any case, this older officer found her flute music and her Indian good looks enchanting, and he seemed the sort who, whatever happened, would not leave her destitute.

Finally, it was late spring, and the peonies bloomed. Saffron's officer was transferred and she did go with him to the south, just when the heavy crimson flowers scattered their petals to the ground. Taking her leave of us, she threw her arms around me for the first and only time, and we both wept. I never learned what became of her, but afterward I would remember Saffron, as people think of absent lovers, when the peonies bloomed. I don't know what circumstance of life had cast her into Lutegarden House—none of us talked about that—but I did know that her family, though arrived three generations back from India, had come to be fully people of Tang. Little Pink and Glory had kept their remarks about barbarians to themselves in Saffron's presence, and the combination of her Chinese ways with her narrow foreign face had comforted me when I gazed into my mirror.

So Little Pink took Saffron's rooms, having persuaded Glory—who should have moved up into them by right of seniority—that it wasn't worth the bother of moving, and I switched into Little Pink's old room, which was no bigger than Nephrite's. In midsummer, a new apprentice named Jujube came to help Baby, and Mama Chen let me know it was time I found a patron.

Secrets of
the Jade Terrace

by Ji Ni-lu
Lars Jensen, translator

BOOK SIX: THE TEACHINGS
OF THE WOMAN INCOGNITA

. . . Thus the seeker, having heard of the arcane mysteries of the
Western Motherqueen, went to inquire of [her devotee] the
Woman Incognita. She answered his many questions, saying, "It
has long been taught [that] the union of man and woman is no
other than the struggle of air and blood, each seeking to subdue
[the other] by stifling [his or her own] joyfulness [i.e., orgasm]
and gaining [the other's] vital essence [i.e., the vaginal secretions
or the semen of the sexual partner]."

Then [he] asked [her], saying, "But is it not so that [in this
way] the hundred illnesses are banished and [a lifespan of] ten
thousand years is achieved?"

Forthwith [she] replied, saying, "[They] say it is so. Yet is this not a foolish thing? For after ten thousand [years] must come [the] ten thousand and first, and on earth even a lifetime free of illness must end. How much better it is, then, to put aside this business of stifling [one's own] excitement and preying on the passion [of the unsuspecting or undisciplined partner]! How much better to celebrate the rites with joy and so become a transcendent, if only [for a] brief [span of time]!"

Then [he] asked again, saying, "I see. To do otherwise [than what you recommend] is merely to grasp after vanities. But how is the celebration to be accomplished?"

Again the woman answered, saying, "I have the form of a woman, while your body is [that of] a man. Let us observe how, when the Jade Stalk is first brought into contact with the Lute Strings and the Crimson Seed . . ."

[text ends]

This previously unknown esoteric text, recently discovered in the Un-u-ji Temple in Nara, Japan, is unique among Taoistic sexological writings in its advocacy of sexual pleasure as an end in itself, provided of course that the Woman's teachings are offered in earnest and not for her own purposes. The fragment has been tentatively identified as a Heian era copy of a seventh- or eighth-century Chinese original; words appear to be garbled or missing in several places, suggesting that the copyist's knowledge of Chinese was less than perfect.

The translator most gratefully acknowledges the extraordinary generosity of the abbess of the temple, and the contributions of Ms. Rose Edo, without whose expertise the technical terms would, perforce, have remained untranslated.

Parrot Speaks: 8

It was the middle of the eighth month: the his-face lilies were budding on the Lutegarden pond. I stared at them as Little Pink told me my yearlong liaison with Collator Wu had come to an end. He hadn't visited or written in two weeks, so I supposed that something was amiss, but it was Little Pink who gave herself the pleasure of telling me just what. She'd been called out to a banquet and had seen him there with a singer from another house, a woman named Whitecaps. Little Pink quickly got the whole tale from an acquaintance of his: Wu was said to be deeply infatuated with her and had been seen at breakfast time that very day, eating fried sesame cakes at a little stand across from the lane where Whitecaps lived. "I'm sorry," Little Pink said, eyes adance, "to be the one to let you know. But I thought you might be wondering why he dropped you without a word."

"Oh, so that's it," I replied; it wasn't really so difficult to keep my voice calm. There was one thing I wanted to know—whether she looked foreign. Little Pink informed me soon enough: rumor had it that Whitecaps's father had been a government minister executed for treason. "I've seen this Whitecaps," Little Pink added with an air of innocent chatter, "and she certainly *looks* like a proper Chinese lady." She stopped, as if embarrassed, and added hastily, "Strange, isn't it? I always thought Collator Wu preferred your *special* kind of prettiness."

Baby was sitting with us, and she reached an arm around my shoulders to console me. Yet watching the pond water glint as a huge red-gold carp broke through into the late summer sunlight, I truly didn't feel a great loss. I'd liked Wu; he was spendthrift enough to keep Mama Chen happy and to allow me to put a little by. He hadn't demanded all my time, and—except for his cowardice in leaving me without a farewell—hadn't been unkind. His genuine interest in poetry far surpassed that of the officials who learn only how to turn out acceptable set pieces for examinations and social occasions; he didn't know it, but in the early weeks of our flirtation, he'd won me by his willingness to discuss his poems with me seriously and to polish the wording or correct the tone pattern of my own attempts.

Wu's attentions had flattered me. But a few days before Little Pink gleefully informed me of his new romance, I'd realized that he wasn't going to come to Lutegarden again. I spent several hours hidden in my bedroom, staining my nails with Persian henna flower while tears washed the powder from my face. Then my thoughts had turned to the nights he'd stayed within the curtains of that very bed: he took no particular care for me, though I knew enough to shake my head and moan when he did; Mama Chen's instructions on that point were strict and clear. In truth though, I would only close my eyes to keep his face away, and in the darkness the image of the stone with which the Tibetan raider murdered Nannie would rise up again. Sometimes it was darkened by dried blood. Sometimes it glowed with an unearthly greenish luminescence, like an odd misshapen pearl. Looking at it then, while Wu's steamy breath struck my shoulder or my neck, I felt somehow I saw my true self, solitary and inviolate.

If this makes me sound unfeeling, I can only tell you that my ideas about many things were soon to change. And even then, my life was not untouched by the passions. The night after Little Pink dangled her toes in the lily pond and triumphantly passed on her news, Baby slipped into my room once again.

How she managed, in a house where stealthy feet wandered the corridors at any hour and Mama Chen made it her business to know who was where, I don't know. But although the gate-keeper's duties included keeping a special watch over the place late at night, his ears had dimmed with age. Even Mama Chen sometimes had to sleep, and Baby could move with the grace of beings not of this world. Evenings when Wu stayed over, she'd avoid me, waiting on the others if it could be managed, and letting Jujube serve as my little maid. Now she came, when all the house was quiet, to lie beside me in the darkness. Hearing her draw aside the bed-curtain, I sat up to light a candle. She made a wry face and picked up from the table by my bed a tiny glass sash ornament Wu had given me. She held it so it glittered in the candlelight; a faithful Mandarin duck and drake amor-ously entwined their gleaming necks. What could I do but laugh? Soundlessly, she joined in.

Then, as she'd done more than once these past few months, she leaned forward to kiss my lips. And I, as if groping after some unspoken language, kissed her back, softly, careful not to frighten her away. By the light of that candle she let me touch her scarred breast, as I'd done just after she came to Lutegarden. "Don't be angry," I whispered, and bent my head to kiss that poor torn nipple, and then as quickly as I could, the other one.

She jerked away and out of my bed in an instant, snuffing the candle as she stood. "Wait!" I hissed, too loudly. But her feet pattered swiftly over the floor and out into the hallway, and I knew that nothing I might have said would have made her stay.

I slept little that night, and in the morning, when I whispered that I wanted to talk to her alone, she shook her head and walked off.

Mama Chen and the others assumed my pale face and heavy eyes spoke of my longing for Wu. They treated me gently, or left me to myself, each in her own way, and Mama Chen told us at breakfast several of her favorite warning tales about the high cost of love.

About ten days later she sent me in to the reception room with Little Pink to entertain a party of foreign traders. "Take your lute," she said, turning me about to see that my gown hung well, "and give them songs from the west, but don't let them get rowdy. They're merchants and foreigners and their manners are none too good. Little Pink, one of them's from Kucha. Show him how well a Chinese girl can play the oboe." Little Pink looked smug, and Mama Chen continued. "They can manage a little pidgin Chinese, but they mostly speak Soghdian—and some other foreign babble, I suppose—so Dragonfly, you'll have to keep up the chatter. Little Pink, join in when you can."

"Dragonfly" meant me. When I was enrolled in the official government register of entertainers, Mama Chen gave me a new, more decorative name. She'd insisted that the others call me Dragonfly as well. Only Nephrite still said Parrot, in Khotanese, and Baby signified me by linking her thumbs and flapping her hands like wings in a way that could indicate an insect or a bird. I used Mama Chen's surname as my own; all of us at Lutegarden House did. No one knew that deep inside I clung to Li, my own true family name.

Four foreign merchants waited in the reception room, grinning and obviously too ignorant of Chinese ways to know that it was kept for the lowest-ranking guests. Little Pink and I entered in modest silence, and one of their number, the fattest by far, let out a great shout. "Ah, *musiciennes*," he called in heavy accents. "Come in, girls. Come in. We've been on the road for months!"

Two of his companions roared with laughter. The third, a man with a long arched nose, leaned back on his couch, pulling himself slightly away from the others. He lay on his side, and bent one leg upward at the knee. His trousers fell in graceful folds: Ghalib. I knew then what song to sing.

Jujube scampered in to fill their wine cups, and I used the moment to tell Little Pink that I wanted to go first. Normally, she'd have hurried to make the strongest possible impression, but these were only merchants, and outlanders besides. She shrugged.

The strings thrummed as I sang a song in Khotanese, an autumn song sung by a woman whose lover departed when the poplar leaf buds opened in the spring. "You wind your way," I finished, "upon long roads across the sands. I drop my head, to think of lovers' time-bound vows." I hadn't let myself remember Collator Wu for days, but somehow that old song stirred feelings that surprised me. My eyes dampened and I quickly put my lute aside and knelt to pour the guests another round of wine.

Little Pink cleared her throat, preparing to play her first melody, but the largest and loudest of the foreigners beat his palms together and insisted I come sit next to him and drink a cup. "I want you to explain those words to me in Soghdian, you little deva. What language was that? Not Persian, and not quite Soghdian, and *certainly* not Chinese." He laughed at his own wit, and the two beside him joined in.

"I'll tell you, sir," I murmured, giving him the kind of look that quiets with promises for some future time. "Only first I really ought to pour for the other gentleman, and then perhaps after she has played a song you'd like my friend to sit with us as well? She's quite talented."

The fat man chuckled. "Now, she's a Chinese girl, by the look of her. Yes, yes, let's hear her play."

I eased over to the fourth man, refilled his cup, and saw that it really was the Persian trader who had brought me over the sands of the Takla Makan. He caught my wrist. "Tell me *your* name," he said quietly, "and where it is I know you from." I gave him the same promise-look, though perhaps not as well, for I could only think: *So. He doesn't remember me,* forgetting entirely how much I'd changed during the six years that had passed. He looked no older to me, though a few gray hairs now curled through his beard.

Little Pink, for all my care to draw the attention onto her, frowned briefly in our direction before she began to play. It was easy enough to stay then, kneeling at the little table by Ghalib's couch, and when Little Pink had finished, to tell her that the first guest wanted to speak with her. She'd already seen that he seemed the leader, and so presumably the richest, of the group. In a few minutes, she and the three men were chattering in a broken mixture of Chinese and Soghdian, and playing a finger-guessing game.

"Here," I told Ghalib, "I'm known as Dragonfly. But my few friends call me a name you gave me one evening between the Keriya River and Dun-huang, when I was a child who'd learned to speak a Persian word or two."

"Parrot!" he said. "The little girl who could outtalk Umar." To keep from discussing my life at Lutegarden, which the thought of Wu had suddenly made sad to me, I asked him how he came to Liang-jou.

"And how I came to travel with these louts?" He laughed. "More than once I've crossed the Pamirs and that awful desert, only to turn around at Dun-huang. It seemed an interesting idea—and a profitable one—to travel farther on the Road this time. I'm bound for Chang-an, to see the capital of the Tang. So quickly, Little Parrot, give me another cupful and teach me more Chinese!"

His smile broadened, pushing up his round cheeks. I bent my head as I poured, to hide my face. Here was a man who liked me, a man who perhaps needed someone to instruct him in Chinese, a man bound for Chang-an. When next I played, I chose another song of love; I kept my eyes downcast until the final line, when I swept them up to join with his.

I was deep in conversation with Ghalib when Mama Chen

returned. The other three visitors clustered round Little Pink, who was laughing and showing off her soft, pretty hands by spinning a top that kept whirling off the little table. Mama Chen asked them if they'd like to meet another of the talented musicians of the house, who also spoke a bit of Soghdian. Yes, yes, of course, they said, and send in more wine with her. So she left to dispatch Nephrite with her flute and to mark the hour on their bill. It was after candle-lighting time now; the fee would double.

Ghalib drank heartily, but less so than the others, and remained clearheaded when my own vision began to swirl. "Here," he said. "You'd better take a cup of tea now, girl." Soon the fat man grunted and heaved himself to his feet. I heard Nephrite and Little Pink making it very clear that the gentlemen could not stay the night—Mama Chen would not allow it—and the three, disgruntled, made ready to leave.

"Let's go, Ghalib," one of the other traders said, with a hiccup. "This is a high-class place. Afraid you'll have to leave that child you've been talking to all evening."

Mama Chen glided to meet them at the door of the reception room and to take care of the bill. One of the fat man's friends looked shocked, but the leader only turned to him and said, "I told you this house was something special." I signaled to Mama Chen in the usual quiet way that I wished to accompany the guests through the lamplit garden to the street. Her eyes flickered with surprise, but she nodded assent, and said aloud that all of us should walk out to the gate to say good-bye. Little Pink's face showed her annoyance, but soon she basked in the admiring cries of the traders over the strange rock that stood like a miniature mountain range beside the lily pond.

"Will you come back to see me?" I asked Ghalib in an undertone.

Perhaps he would, he said. If he had time. He was leaving for Chang-an in two days and had a lot to do. I suggested that surely his friends could take care of things and he could slip away for a few hours at least. "Oh yes, Little Parrot," he said, and his eyes laughed at me like the eyes of a father amused by the transparent deceptions of a child, "I know what you mean. If I come, I'll come alone. And bring a gift for your mama here."

He left with the others. My heart sank. I'd panicked when I learned how quickly he was leaving—why hadn't he told me sooner?—and done the worst possible thing, suggested a private meeting before he could think that it was his idea.

The next day he didn't come. Nephrite and Little Pink were summoned to a country outing, but no one at all, except Glory's latest patron, visited Lutegarden, and no one sent for me. I went to bed early with a headache and thought of how I'd have to build up a regular clientele again now that Wu had left me. Then I thought of Nannie's easy ways with men. Wondering what wordless persuasions she would have used on Ghalib, I mumbled her name and began to cry. I was still awake when the first light broke.

Collator Wu Suffers
the Fate of the Faithless

*T**he Ming Dynasty marketplace again, a time closer to your own than to that of the Tang: The storyteller spreads his mat and strikes a gong three times. A gang of urchins gathers. Soon a crowd begins to form.*

> The feng-huang bird once only takes a mate;
> The duck and drake together spend their days.
> Let the betrayer of his lover's faith
> Beware the voice that calls beyond the grave.

This poem tells us of the fidelity of the feng-huang bird and of the Mandarin duck and drake, who mate for life, and even when the mate dies, take no other. As for humans, The Old Man in the Moon ties a thread between a man and a woman who are fated to wed, and no one should attempt to deny it. This is why the virtuous widow does not wish to remarry and why an upright man does not desert a wife unless she's guilty of one of the seven legal grounds for divorce. Indeed, even in the case of irregular liaisons, if fidelity is pledged, a certain obligation is incurred. Thus we are taught that heaven holds us to our promises. It is just as the following verse says:

> A vow unkept is like a broken branch;
> A false-tongued lover's a chameleon.
> Justice comes in this life or the next,
> Good for good, and bad with bad repaid.

It is told how during the Great Tang a certain courtesan took in her former lover after he had been reduced to a sore-covered beggar and nursed him back to health. Encouraging him to study, she spent all her money on his education. The young gentleman placed first in the Imperial Examination, and the courtesan fulfilled destiny by becoming his proper wife. Their sons became great officials, too, none ranking lower than prefect of Tai-yuan. All this from the loyalty of a prostitute! If one for whom the six marriage rites of welcome have not been performed can be so faithful, how much the moreso ought men and women united by formal vows.

Members of the audience, listen today while I tell the story-with-poems entitled "Collator Wu Suffers the Fate of the Faithless." In this story, we will, at first, present only one person, whose name was Wu Jiao-shou. It is told how, in the seventh month of a particular year in the Kai-yuan reign period of the Tang Dynasty's Brilliant Emperor, this young man arrived in Liang-jou, having been posted there from Lo-yang. Followed by his groom, he rode into that northwestern city on his fine roan gelding, and the eyes of all who saw turned to follow the noble-looking youth. How would you say he was dressed?

Supple leather boots clasp graceful calves.
A satin gown enfolds a strong, straight chest.
On one slim finger, a gleaming red-jade ring;
Above a proud dark eye, a black silk cap.
He brushes road dust settled on his sleeve,
Waves an undyed fan pulled from his sash.
Indeed the scion of a learned house,
He's what they call "blue-green more deep than blue."

Now, this Mr. Wu was indeed an example of "blue-green deeper than blue," a pupil who surpasses his masters. From his childhood he had been praised for his accomplishments by all around him, especially for the technical perfection and the emotional refinement of his poetry. He was the youngest child of an old couple who already had five daughters. Consequently, he had always had his will and had come to have one weakness: he thought that other people existed only to serve his needs. After he had settled in his lodgings in Liang-jou, and had made the customary salutations to his superiors in the government, he began at once the execution of his duties.

But even an upright young man like Wu Jiao-shou must rest, and eventually he began to wish for some relaxation. Some of his co-workers invited him to join them at a gambling party, but this virtuous fellow never indulged in such spendthrift pastimes. Then another group carried him off with them to an establishment in the Entertainment Quarter, a place called Lutegarden House, run by one Mama Chen.

When this avaricious old woman saw the fresh face of the young man, she knew he was just the naive sort of youth who could add greatly to her hoard of treasure. Coming into the room where the men were eating and listening to an ancient ode played upon the classical chyn, she hurried up behind him and exclaimed, "Imperial Emissary Gao! How delightful to see you again after these many months! Why didn't that dolt of a gatekeeper tell me it was you come back to see us again? Surely you have returned to renew your friendship with the beautiful Miss

Saffron! I'll send her in immediately to entertain you with her flute."

Wu quickly turned, and answered, his neck flushing a dull purple. "Is the good dame addressing me? I am not named Gao, and I could never presume to become an imperial emissary. I am a mere collator of texts, and my humble surname is Wu."

"Oh, a thousand pardons, exalted Master Wu! I am an old woman and my eyes grow poor. You resemble a noble lord who recently—I am ashamed to say it—carried on a bit of a romance with one of my ill-disciplined girls. But now that I see your fine, broad brow and flashing eyes, I see that you could never be that elderly gentleman. Ai yo! How embarrassed this foolish old woman is!"

"Really, my good dame, think nothing of it," Wu replied.

"No, you must let me make up for this rudeness in some way," she said. "Let me make a gift of a ewer of wine for you and your party. This is a poor place, but we do have a rather special jug or two tucked away. And perhaps you'd like to hear some music that's a bit livelier? We've a girl here who's an absolute enchantress when she plays barbarian music on the lute."

Perhaps you are wondering how that old woman could be so forward. Now, wouldn't you agree that

> Like a creeping weasel intent upon a bird's egg,
> The avaricious owner of a winehouse seeks out gold.

These unprincipled creatures will stop at almost nothing, if they can gain in the matter.

Wu protested, but the shameless woman insisted on presenting the party with wine, and sure enough the lute player arrived carrying it. The young gentleman could hardly send the girl away, and indeed her downcast eyes and maidenly modesty marked her as someone different from the usual run of courtesans.

Soon, the wine's heat warmed Wu beyond the hotness of the

summer evening. He loosened the collar of his robe, and rested his usually erect head on one hand. The *musiciennes* joined the party, and the chyn player, who was rather bold, told anecdotes of several gay blades and flower-fair ladies of the quarter.

"I don't object to such goings-on," young Wu said as the group began another round of toasts, "but I fear I may never find a young woman suitable to accompany me." Just then, the lute player raised her eyes to meet his, and Wu's hot blood stirred as the seeds planted by the romantic music and the risqué stories began to sprout.

Let us not become too wordy but rather tell of this young player on the lute. Her father, a brave and noble general, had been cruelly murdered in an uprising on the far frontier, and her mother, a most dutiful young woman, had been stolen away to be wed against her will to the Dragon Monarch's son. So although she came of a good family, the girl—whose name was Dragonfly—had fallen into the profession and had no way to rescue herself. Yet she was still quite young and so far had managed to resist the pressure of greedy Mama Chen to take a lover. Her music was her great passion, and she worked hard at learning and composing lyrics to accompany the songs she played so bewitchingly on her lute.

Now, on the evening of the first day of the ninth month, when autumn coolness had at last freshened the hot air of the city, young Wu felt drawn to visit Dragonfly in private at the Lutegarden House. In part this was the work of loneliness and bad companions, and in part, the natural response of a spirited young man to the girl's refinement and her beauty. Do not forget, good members of the audience, that the clever and artistic courtesans of the Great Tang were a different thing from the singsong girls and prostitutes of our own depraved times.

Yet there was another force at work on the heartstrings of Collator Wu. As if Mama Chen's sly tricks were not enough, a hungry ghost, the restless spirit of Dragonfly's former nannie, had taken a fancy to him. This hussy had been condemned, as

punishment for her lustful ways, to roam this world in disembodied form. At night it sent disturbing visions of "making
clouds and rain" with Dragonfly to haunt the young man's
dreams. It was through such stimulation of lewd thoughts in
innocent young folk that the ghost consoled itself for having lost
its ability for sensual gratification. Indeed, in its perversity, this
hungry ghost sent similar scandalous visions into the bedchamber where Dragonfly lay mourning her lowly position in society
and wondering how she might retain her purity. So one thing
led to another, and soon, with the connivance of Mama Chen,
the scholar and the beauty became lovers. Wu pledged himself
to rescue Dragonfly from her life as an entertainer and to marry
her properly as soon as he had amassed the necessary funds. One
evening in Dragonfly's room she ground some ink, and he took
up her writing brush and wrote out on a piece of white silk his
promise of marriage.

But alas for those who make hasty vows! Nearly a year after
the start of young Wu's affair with Dragonfly, as he pored over
some ancient scholarly texts one evening, he heard a strange
pounding at the door of his lodgings. He opened it, and a ragged
old man with eyes that protruded like those of a great fish burst
into the room, hobbling with amazing speed on a crooked crutch.

"Ah, Master Wu! Forgive my impolite entrance, but I have
some words for you." So saying, he closed his bulging red eyes,
and throwing back his head, chanted:

> Tie not the knot you wish not to untie!
> The white-silk vow becomes, I trow, silk-white.
> The Fairy Maiden now a fair-made ghost,
> The Turtle-Husband huddles in the night.

Having finished, the strange old man struck his crutch three
times on the floor of Collator Wu's room, and disappeared. The
young man rubbed his eyes and stared. After much thought, he
could make nothing of it at all and returned to his studies. Thus,

good members of the audience, do mortals ignore at their own peril warnings sent from the supernatural world.

Let us put down one strand and tell again of the mother of Dragonfly, now the wife of the Dragon Monarch's son. Gathering her courage and her womanly wiles, she asked her husband's uncle to take on the form of a giant carp and spy upon the happenings near the pond in the garden of Lutegarden House. And so she learned of the irregular relationship into which circumstance and the lasciviousness of the nannie's hungry ghost had forced her daughter. She decided that since it was not within her power to put a stop to the affair, she'd do the next best thing: test the faithfulness of her daughter's lover.

So Dragonfly's mother persuaded the vermilion dragon-carp to disguise itself, first as the queer-eyed beggar who gave warning to young Wu, and then as a beautiful woman, a singer. In this latter guise, the scaly creature took up life in the Entertainment Quarter of Liang-jou. Soon enough, young Wu encountered the otherworldly warbler, who called itself Whitecaps, at an official banquet, and fell under the spell of its unnatural charms.

In this, Dragonfly's mother's plans went awry, for what she thought would be the final strengthening test of the young man's honor became instead a seduction. This was nothing other than the work of the troublemaking hungry ghost of Dragonfly's nannie: Having learned by eavesdropping on the mother's conversations with the carp that she hoped to make a good marriage out of her daughter's shameful affair, the jealous ghost had immediately begun to seek a second mistress for the attractive young Wu. It also cast about for another possible lover for poor Dragonfly. And so, in order to stimulate itself with prurient sights, it turned the young man's carnal interests to the singer Whitecaps. More must be said later of these things.

As for Wu, in Whitecaps he'd been given a test that no mortal man could pass. He failed to notice that the lake-born monster of whom he was now so enamored cast no shadow, even on the brightest day. The spiteful ghost egged him on, willingly letting Dragonfly's heart be broken, that it might enjoy the lust-provoking sight of Wu's meetings with the fishy seductress. And Wu, fallen under this enchantment, quite forgot his beloved, and pledged to take Whitecaps with him when he departed Liang-jou for Chang-an, as he had recently received orders to do.

When Dragonfly's mother learned what had happened, she chided her husband's uncle, as boldly as she dared, for seducing her daughter's lover. But the willful creature protested that she had told it to give the young man a proper test and that Wu had responded so readily it seemed almost as if he were under the spell of some malevolent spirit—as indeed, good listeners, he was. When his new mistress disappeared, poor Wu was far too ashamed to return to Dragonfly at Lutegarden, for he knew that word of the affair had surely reached her, and so, traveling by day and stopping at night, he went on to Chang-an by himself.

Members of the audience, when you hear of Wu's behavior, perhaps you will remember the old proverb,

> Heedless of oaths and heaven's destiny,
> The rake runs off, and leaves the girl to pine.

And yet, when you look at it, you will see that such actions are not entirely blameworthy in a spirited young man who was spoiled by his parents and five elder sisters, and who had to contend with the interference both of Mama Chen on earth and of the misguided mother and the licentious ghost from another realm.

Now, keep your ears clean while I tell how the mother of Dragonfly, heedless of Wu's virtues, took a terrible revenge on the young man who had made a fallen woman of her daughter. The days and nights passed like an arrow, and Collator Wu's family arranged his marriage to a young lady of Chang-an, whose name—just as the vermilion dragon-carp in its guise as a crippled old man had foretold—was none other than Fairy Maid. But, alas, Wu had forgotten all about the strange warning he'd received that long-ago night in Liang-jou.

One morning, Wu was walking near his fishpond in Chang-an with his new bride when a large ruddy carp leapt up among the lotus leaves. Of course it was the spy of Dragonfly's mother, come to the human world to report on the doings of the young man. When the mother learned that Wu had married Fairy Maid despite the vow he wrote out for Dragonfly on that length of white silk, she begged the dragon-carp to disguise itself again, and that night it appeared in Wu's garden, in the form of a comely youth who crouched outside the bedroom window and called Fairy Maid's name in the piercing whisper of a clandestine lover.

In a frenzy, Wu ran into the courtyard, but the vermilion-clad youth had changed back into a fish and leapt into the pond. Returning to Fairy Maid, Wu interrogated her, but of course even when he slapped her, she could not explain the presence of the youth. This happened night after night, with the dragon-carp taking many different guises, until Wu hovered on the brink of madness. The servants gossiped, spreading the tales of his jealousy, until the people of the neighborhood began to figure,

> If there's chaff in the courtyard,
> Someone's been threshing grain.

Taking him for a cuckold, they called him Turtle Wu. This only convinced him all the more that his beautiful young wife had broken her marriage vows. Soon his friends stopped visiting him, so unpleasant were his jealous fits, and he deserted his official duties altogether, that he might stay home and keep watch over her.

When the dragon-carp reported all this to Dragonfly's mother, she rested content and told the creature to leave Wu alone. But when the youths stopped beckoning at the window, Wu only decided that the lovers had become more secretive. His grip on Fairy Maid grew tighter, and his questionings grew more brutal, until one night, sleepless and crazed, he beat her to death.

Now, all actions have their consequences, and the ghost of the unjustly murdered Fairy Maid returned to haunt Wu. As for him, he was already wracked with remorse over killing his wife, and this stirred up once again the guilty remembrance of breaking his vow to Dragonfly. Every time he closed his eyes to sleep, Wu was greeted by the appearance now of Fairy Maid, now of Dragonfly, moving slowly through the bed-curtains toward him, gaze fixed beyond his shoulder, looking through him as if *he* were only an apparition. Sometimes the two of them merged into one figure, whose preternatural beauty was even greater than that of either woman. This doubled being had the unearthly paleness of one whose heart has long ago left this common world. Except for the hectic flush on her cheekbones, this strange blend of Fairy Maid and Dragonfly had a skin so fine it was nearly translucent. Wu stared and called out first one woman's name and then the other's, but she refused to meet his eyes, and all he saw was:

> Willow brows arched fine over glittering eyes;
> Clammy shadows soft in cavelike cheeks.
> A drifting fairy, a hovering dragonfly,
> Her hands silk-white as summer's deserted fan.

And so, as the sun and moon flew like a weaver's shuttle, Wu fell into a decline and died. But let us leave such talk at rest and tell instead how back in Liang-jou, Dragonfly languished desolate as any forgotten woman still faithful to her man. Her one remaining desire was to take the veil, becoming a Lady of the Tao, and so retire in solitude to a place outside the city.

But if you want to know whether she accomplished this (my young assistant is passing among you now, should you feel inclined to make a contribution), or what became of the enmity between the girl's chaste mother, held beneath Cavegarden Lake (my gratitude, madam, for your generosity), and the wandering lascivious ghost of her nannie (ah, even the little urchin has contributed his mite! thanks, my lad), you will have to return to listen when I continue the tale.

Parrot Speaks: 9

H ave a bit more tea, Parrot," said Nephrite, pouring me another warming cup before I could refuse. We sat in the garden, the afternoon following my sleepless night of longing for Ghalib, and Wu—and Nannie, too, I suppose. Clouds blanketed the sky; it was the end of the eighth month, and the dark yin principle, ruler of the cold months, rose daily in ascendance over the sunny yang. Nephrite liked this sort of weather, but she'd sensed my low mood and took pains to cheer me as best she could. I told her who Ghalib was: she merely shrugged off the coincidence of meeting when I suggested there might be some strange sort of reason for it. "What land route would a Persian trader take into China, Parrot, if not the Silk Road?" she said. "And what caravan doesn't stop a while in Liang-jou? Anyway, put your mind on other things. The Amah will look after you, if you devote yourself to her."

She lectured me like that often, reminding me of the powerful Western Motherqueen, who watches over her worshipers as a faithful amah watches over a child and doesn't know the subservience of good daughters and wives. I never knew what to say when Nephrite talked about those things; the ideas seemed dangerous, and yet somehow attractive.

This time Bellring arrived and saved me from making an answer. "Bellring," Nephrite said, switching out of Khotanese, "come have some chrysanthemum tea. I was just discussing a poem of Tao Chien's with Dragonfly. My guest last night taught it to me. It's a lovely thing for an autumn day."

"And I suppose it's all about the peace of life in retirement from the world," said Bellring, laughing as she sat beside me. "Just the thing for you, Nephrite. And Dragonfly, if it's like the Tao Chien poems I've heard, it reminds us of the virtues of endurance. Not bad advice, though I don't suppose Old Tao ever suffered from a broken heart." She sipped her tea. "Delicious! Too bad we can't all be brave as chrysanthemums in the autumn frosts. Well, I'd like to hear it, please."

So Nephrite recited the poem, and Bellring teased her gently about last night's guest. "I'd never have known to see you with him that you wanted him to stay the night. However do you keep yourself so uninvolved, dear one? And how can you give Dragonfly a bit of your forbearance?" She tilted her head in her slow way and turned to face me. "You really mustn't mind about that fellow Wu, you know. One's first real lover is rarely the only one. Besides"—her voice changed to a more playful tone—"who knows? Perhaps someday you'll be the heroine of a story like one of Mama Chen's—a virtuous *musicienne* betrayed by a man driven by demons into faithlessness!"

We all three laughed then, and Nephrite added, "And in the end of course she'll give up her musician's life, and take the veil, and the man will come to some suitably awful end."

It was a rare moment, sitting there with Nephrite and Bellring treating me more like an equal than a younger sister or a student. My throat warmed with the tea and the laughter. I said that I wondered what else such a story would distort, adding, "At least it's true that Whitecaps woman is some kind of monster," which made them laugh again, and so warmed me more.

Whoever tells of the women of the entertainment districts, I thought then, lies unless it is acknowledged that beside every conniving Little Pink and flighty Glory there stands a Saffron who must hide genuine feeling beneath glittering poetic wit, a Bellring caring for her unfortunate sisters, and a Nephrite who only protects herself as she can from the onslaughts of this dusty world. Perhaps I should have added that behind every Dragonfly hard at work to learn the silent language of enticement lingers a Parrot who would like only to speak the truth.

But Bellring broke into my brooding, taking me into the house and showing me how to twist up my hair in a new style from Chang-an. By the time the kitchen maids had lighted the red gauze lanterns outside our gate, I was playing happily at Double Sixes with Baby in my room.

Then Mama Chen bustled in. "Are you presentable, Dragonfly?" she asked, as if I hadn't spent much of the morning bathing and making up as always; that day I'd dotted a blue floret beauty mark on each cheek, just to fill a few moments more. "Baby, clear these things away," she said, "and tidy up the room. Quickly now! A gentleman's come to call on Miss Dragonfly, and she'll be dining with him here."

Baby's face showed no feeling at all, not even a natural annoyance at the abrupt end to our game. Mama Chen hurried off to keep the man entertained in the reception room while we made ready, leaving me to wonder who had come that she would show him directly to my room.

"Do you think it's Wu?" I said to Baby. But she only shrugged, swept the pieces off the game board, and rubbed the fingers of her free hand together, signifying money.

So. Wu if he'd been generous enough to get back in Mama Chen's good graces. But when Mama Chen returned, the man behind her was taller than Wu, and his nose arched too high for any Chinese man's. Mama Chen would let someone skip the preliminary courtship before a private meeting, if she knew he was bound to leave town soon—and if he made it worth her while.

"Why the silly girl's forgotten to light incense, sir!" she exclaimed in Soghdian, snatching up the golden-duck brazier by my bed. "Please do sit down. I'm off to the kitchen to oversee your supper—I'll order some specialties of the town, if you like, sir—and the little apprentice here will bring it up. Well, don't just stand there gawking, Dragonfly. Ask the gentleman if he'd like to hear you play a song. Baby, come along!" With that, the two of them departed, and I stood alone before Ghalib.

"You said you'd be off for Chang-an by now," I said. Had he only meant to tease me?

"Umar's taken sick. They're looking after him at the caravansary, but I'll have to stay in Liang-jou for a while. Shall I sit over there by the little table?" He looked as if it amused him to remind me of my duties as a hostess.

The truth was that I felt this outsider saw much too easily beyond the subtle dance of word and gesture we stepped through with our guests at Lutegarden House. Yet his nature—unaccustomed though he was to Chinese ways, he was still refined—prevented his taking me for a whore, as his companions seemed to do. Still, his amusement angered me; did he suppose my life allowed sincerity?

Mama Chen rushed in with the fragrant burner wafting long trails of smoke and looked askance at me. I asked him, in a shy tone that I knew she would approve of, what song he'd like for me to play. On her way out, she nodded, satisfied.

"No worn-out words about true love that you sing to every stranger," he replied. My cheeks blazed, though I could only swallow my anger. He was, after all, a guest.

"Perhaps that's all I know," I said, fixing my eyes and watching as he reclined on a cushion and made that graceful bend of his leg.

Then he apologized, saying he'd been rude. "I've a clumsy

tongue in Soghdian, Little Parrot," he said. "Not everyone has your gift with foreign words."

Simple flattery, perhaps, but in that moment it reminded me of the times when Baba had praised me for saying something childishly clever. I felt the anger dissipate like incense from the brazier. I asked again, meaning it, if he wanted me to play.

He said he did, adding, "Can you give me a song with words you wrote yourself? I've heard you're quite talented." His cheeks rose as he smiled. "It doesn't matter about the language. Later you can tell me what it means."

LOVE-LONGING TARRIES

Leafless willow withes,
Silken threads of rain—
She lifts the blind to watch
   gray twilight shade into the night.
A west wind rises, scatters heavy clouds.

Incense floats up slowly
Toward a jade-hook moon.
After midnight's watch is struck:
   on fall's last flowers, frost.
Alone, she waits to see them in dawn's light.

Within the Incense Vapors

And so the dizzying vapors rise from their brief burning on the coals in the metal brazier. The strings of the lute, one for each season of the year, cease their melancholy twanging. Autumn swells toward fullness; the damp, womanly yin principle reigns over human emotions as well as over the weather now. A hawk-nosed traveler sits up and takes a singer barely more than girl onto his lap, as a father might his child. At first she holds herself apart, fearing his scorn, a thought she never had with earlier lovers. He feels weary with the long months over dry lands and lonely in the way of men nearly always alone. He has sensed that same fastidious loneliness within her and begins to touch her very slowly, like a tribesman of the mountains come to tame a wild, exotic bird. There is, of course, a purpose to that taming, but sometimes that is also what the bird desires.

They make a game of it, teaching one another words in their

differing tongues: *and this means "throat" and this is "breast"
and these are "waist" and "hip" and "thigh."* Then language
fails, or is cast aside, and they move through fragrant smoke to
the wide low bed. He takes uncommon pleasure in their joining,
but not a pleasure he has never known. For her, though, the long
night holds something new: not the urgent wanting—her mouth
has tasted that—but its fruition. Blood suffuses her delicate skin,
her body seems to deliquesce, soft sounds lift from her throat.
For a moment, hearing her, he supposes this last is merely acted
out, another of the songs she's been taught to sing. Then he
decides, correctly, that he's wrong.

In the morning, he'll wake quickly, and she'll already be
awake, watching him like one struck dumb, unable to be charming, or witty, or bright. Passion will have wiped away the languages she has so carefully learned, or if not passion, then some
deep impulse toward self-protection; his power to move her, for
all that she wants to be moved, is the power to hurt. Perhaps
he'll take her silence for dullness, or indifference. In any case,
he'll feel the coldness of the little dancer come to bring the
lovers tea and air the room. He'll rise and leave at once.

But now, in the night, the ghost of the woman's nannie
comes, drawn helplessly by the fumes of musk. The ghost takes
no perverse pleasure in its disembodied hovering over the lovers'
bed, though it feels a kind of happiness that the child has at last
grown enough to brave those fleeting carnal joys. Indeed, the
ghost suffers a great anguish for what it has lost. And the mother
of the woman is drawn, too, to gaze into a mirror cloudy with
aromatic smoke and see the two, and know. Her heart divides:
she believes she should feel shame at the unwed shamelessness;
she fears for her daughter's future sorrow in a world where
women are said to fall; she wants for her the free-breathing ten-
derness of her own unlawful bed.

The ghost and the mother both wish one thing, the one thing
impossible. They want to give the girl now woman some account of what they have learned of passion, its rewards and price.

Compelled to watch, each thinks of the white silk scroll given by the Amah. Might its words let her know what experience teaches? And yet, whatever it says, it waits forgotten, and if some teller of stories—anxious as always for a sensational tale— were to read from it to an audience of voyeurs, would it not be transformed into a pallid cloth of lies, as empty of truth as a false lover's vows?

As the two in the wide bed sigh and tremble, and the other two watch and sigh, up in the distant mountain palace of the Western Motherqueen, a jade woman—star-souled attendant on the Amah herself—stirs and wraps herself close in her indigo cloak and without knowing why, breathes deep, and deeply sighs.

Parrot Speaks: 10

After staying the night with me, Ghalib left, and I slept until early afternoon. A west wind blew in fresh, cold air; I woke to a clear sky and a mixture of apprehension and languor and sleepy excitement. I had no idea whether he would come again or not.

I'd eaten little the previous day, but I wanted only tea, so I drank the rest of the cold, bitterish potful by my bed. Then I ground my inkstick on the stone, patiently mixing the powder with a little water until it pooled smooth and black in the well. Half in a trance, I took up a scrap of paper, an old practice sheet still clean on the other side, and wrote out new lyrics to the melody I'd played last night for Ghalib. My brush flowed down the page as if of its own accord, the words released as my body had been the night before.

Reading over what I'd written, I wondered what to make of

it. The old gentleman who first taught me a poem from the *Book of Odes* lectured me that same evening on the moral importance of poetry, on how it teaches the ruler how to rule, and the people how to live. I've heard other scholars—their spirits elevated by wine, their thoughts running on to high things—bemoan the vulgar verse of this fallen age, even while I played them the women's songs in everyday language that they had come to Lutegarden to hear. And one spring evening by the lily pond, a friend of Collator Wu's had argued with him that in composing poetry one's deep thoughts accord with the cosmos itself, as a lute string will resonate when one plucks another tuned to the same note.

Perhaps that last idea was right, for that sleepy, nerve-tingling afternoon, my brush glided freely, as if it harmonized with the natural workings of the Tao itself. But I think the truth is something less grand. Wu had quoted to his friend a few sentences from some famous essay, and I never forgot them: "Feelings move within, and take form in speech. If speech will not suffice, one sighs. If sighs will not suffice, one sings them out."

The others awoke from their midday naps, and I rushed with the poem to Nephrite's room, to read it to her. She was kind in her praise as always, though I knew from her voice she thought I might better have chosen a different sort of subject: a wandering journey in the mountains, say, in search of immortal sylphs. What's more, her comments almost seemed comments on another set of words, as though the lyrics I'd brushed out on that scrap of paper differed somehow from the ones she heard. In any case, I knew enough to tuck the paper away where Baby wouldn't see it and read however much she could. It would distress her to be reminded that Ghalib had stayed the night. In fact, Baby was beyond such jealousy just then, though I didn't know it yet.

Nephrite smiled and asked me to help her pack up a few things. At last she'd wheedled permission from Mama Chen to stay two nights with the Purified Teacher at Darkdazzle Vista. "Don't tell, dear Parrot," Nephrite said as I walked her to the gate to see her off, "but—I might be able to wear the cap of a Taoist Lady sooner than I'd hoped." Then she set her lips firmly and climbed into the waiting sedan chair.

Absorbed in helping Nephrite, and in preparing myself in case Ghalib should visit again, it didn't occur to me to look for Baby until nearly evening. In fact, Mama Chen sent me off rather sharply to find her, muttering something about what a trouble Baby's muteness and moodiness had turned out to be. "The girl dances well enough," she said, "but what possessed me to think she could amuse a gentleman caller properly when it's time to sit and gossip or play games, I'll never know. And now she's turned so sullen! Well, run and fetch her, Dragonfly, and tell her she'd better look livelier tonight than last."

I would have defended my friend if I dared, but walking back toward the apprentices' room, I realized that the cheerful, capering Baby of long ago had vanished behind a thickening veil of sulkiness. Some of the fault lay with the twisted cruelties of the Iranian dancing teacher. Yet just before I stepped into her doorway, it came to me that another reason rested somehow on my shoulders. The half-hidden pleasure she'd taken in knowing that I only tolerated Collator Wu; her loverlike overtures at night, so quickly taken back, her ill humor when any guest took too much interest in my music or my words: if she had let me, I would have been hers, but though she denied us that, she both loved me and resented me as any betrayed woman might.

I found her flat on her back on the apprentices' bed. Her head tossed from side to side. A low moan slid from her lips. She made no response when I said her name, but a touch to her heated forehead let me know that the reason wasn't sulkiness. I rushed to report to Mama Chen.

Her manner was more one of annoyance than concern over Baby's illness, though I knew some of that was only show. "I'll look after her, child. We needn't call for a doctor yet—just send in one of the kitchen maids to help. Then go tell Bellring she's to keep an eye on things tonight. I'll want her to come in here for instructions." She paused to loosen Baby's clothing. "Ai, what a trouble this one has turned out to be, poor thing. Have little Jujube wait on you if your barbarian gentleman returns, unless Glory's patron drops by. She's your senior, so in that case you'll have to manage him on your own." She looked up from Baby to cock an eye in my direction. "You will manage him, won't you, dear?" She cackled when I hung my head and blushed.

Ghalib did come back. He said it was against his better judgment, but he'd been bewitched by my eyes. Then he smiled benignly, in a way that meant I was to understand his words as a compliment. It pleased me to do so; I found it hard to believe anyone, even a foreigner, valued my looks. The night stretched as long as the one before. He liked best the way called Cranes Entwine Their Necks, when he sat upright and I knelt astride his thighs. He was so tall that I had to reach up to throw my arms around his neck. I liked the safe feeling I had then.

Again we parted early, but this time Ghalib stayed a while, and told me that Umar's strange illness seemed a little better, though he couldn't travel yet. "A lucky chance, my Parrot," he said, "or perhaps the intervention of some god?" I laughed aloud at the idea, and because he thought it fortunate.

After he left, I hurried to dress, feeling guilty that I hadn't stayed by Baby rather than with Ghalib. But of course it was understood that a guest had first claim on my time and my attention. Perhaps, I think now, part of Baby's anger grew from her own acceptance of that idea.

Mama Chen's head jerked up from her drowse when I stepped into Baby's room. "The girl's still sick, hotter even than last night," she said as she laid her palm on Baby's forehead. "I'll have a doctor in when it's full day."

"Baby!" I said, as if to call her wandering spirit back to its place among us. I don't know if that was the reason, but suddenly she sat upright, eyes staring blank before her, and began to shake. Tremors wracked her whole body. A voice escaped her mouth. It was the voice of a full-grown woman, and did not sound as if it could be hers.

"The two," it said, "the two, two girls must go, must go to Chang-an. The two must go together to Chang-an."

Neither Mama Chen nor I moved, but I felt the chilly rise of hair across my scalp. Baby's face, wiped clean of any sign of recognition or awareness, turned toward me. "Greenpearl," she said. "Go." Then the twitching grew so great she could not sit upright but fell back, neck arched, head flailing again from side to side.

Celestial Audience Rooms

And that's all you have to tell me?" the Jade Emperor asks, a terrible look in his glorious eyes.

The former Undersecretary gazes downward, abashed. "That's all at the moment, Sire," he says. The Luminous Emerald-Green Lunar Essence Sprite has not yet received the little dancer's message. The former undersecretary considers throwing himself onto his face at the foot of the astral throne, but at times like this that only seems to annoy His Divine Majesty. Somewhere in a grassy glade down in the subcelestial realm, a group of Taoist holy women are pacing out the sacred steps that send the cloud-soul of an initiate dancing among the stars. It's not so bad when they're summoning a divine lover, but the adept at the center of this ceremony wants to travel to the Western Halls of Jade, the palace of the Western Motherqueen. The atmosphere at the Emperor's court always grows a bit edgy when this particular rite takes place.

"Well, I must say the creature doesn't seem to be learning much, or at least not much of the right things. She's forgotten her quest entirely, she's become far too attached to the way that foreign fellow makes her feel, and the only real spiritual seeker she knows is more interested in—in the Amah than in *me*."

The former Undersecretary murmurs a categorical denial of that last, even as a wild possibility. Simultaneously, he shakes his head in disgust at the seeker's lack of taste. Still, he can feel how, far away in the Western Mothcrqueen's fastness beyond the ramparts of the Kunlun Mountains, her attendant jade women make ready to receive a guest.

His Divine Majesty leans forward to impart a confidence. "Now listen well, my lad. She *is* picking up a bit of human chatter, so Lady Guan-yin should be satisfied on that count. But it's just as well we do all we can to keep up good relations in that quarter, and for some reason the Buddhists are holding me responsible for sending her to the human realm. You know what sticklers they are about the working out of karma. And there's that whole complicated matter of her nannie's death vow, not to mention the girl's filial obligation to rescue her mother and the broken promise to the Dragon Monarch's son—" He waves a hand as if tossing away a hopeless snarl of silken threads.

The former Undersecretary's face expresses great sympathy at the woes that beset a heavenly monarch, woes that one of his mean ability could never hope to bear.

"Really," the Jade Emperor continues, "ever since you brought me that silly Go set, and then let Guan-yin send you traipsing off to some sand dune to rescue that traveling monk, and down to King Yama's court . . . well, things are getting out of hand. I want you to do what you can to get her back on track and get the whole business over with. It would be a pleasure to see you promoted back to your old position, or even something a bit better." He leans back and his belly shakes as he booms out, "But you're not to interfere with the workings of her karma." His voice drops. "You realize, lad, that if you're caught, we'll be forced to deny any knowledge of what you've done."

The celestial bureaucrat stutters, stammers, and submits. He hurries off to his office to ponder the problem that's been dumped in his gorgeously robed lap. That troublesome Luminous Emerald-Green Lunar Essence Sprite needs to hurry on before His Divine Majesty gets stuck with more karmic consequences. But any obvious interference with Greenpearl's sojourn on earth by a member of the Taoist Celestial Administration will only bring new responsibility onto the Jade Emperor's head. Oh, the problem's clear enough. It's only the solution that eludes him.

The former Undersecretary, now a mere factotum in a minor ministry, calls for a soothing cup of Jade Sap and—when the heavenly servant boy has left the room—slouches in his chair. Who might serve as a go-between to the human realm, delivering a message that will get the unruly pearl back on the Road? Then the answer comes to him. He summons, and explains.

". . . so you see, mademoiselle, some sort of action simply must be taken." The meek ex-Undersecretary of Baubles now has the air of a respectable and important member of the office of the Acting Assistant Controller of the Ministry of Babble. He looks down along his nose at the diaphanous, full-breasted figure wavering before his desk. "So I—that is, we—thought you might wish to take advantage of this unusual opportunity to repay some part at least of your debt to His Divine Majesty for your rescue from the fire and ice of hell. Your link to the human world allows you, you see, to travel between the realms, ah, shall we say less *conspicuously* than I?"

The shapely, wavy-haired ghost cocks its head and stares directly into the Taoist official's eyes. It learned rather early in its time in the flesh to recognize when a man was leading it toward some end of his own; it learned, too, that a saucy stare could sometimes turn the situation to its own advantage.

The official forces a cough. "Now. I have already taken it upon myself to effect a brief delay of the foreign trader." He looks away. "The Persian trader, one might better say, mademoiselle." He can't afford to offend this potential agent. Things have not gone well for him recently, not at all, and he thinks he can sense another group of those libidinous, uppity Taoist women preparing for some rite: he feels a headache coming on.

But the ghost, busy smoothing its wild tresses and running its tongue over its dry lips, barely listens. It remains half bound to the human world, half barred from it; even in the villa of the Dragon Monarch beneath Cavegarden Lake it can barely coalesce into the semblance of a bodily form. But here in the ethereal domains of the Taoist heavenly hierarchy, something is happening. Like a stream of warm moist air breathed out on a cold day, it—or better now, she—has begun to take on the pure solidity of a cloud.

The official, having noticed the ghost's transformation, rushes on into his speech. "What's needed, mademoiselle," he says, "is some way to, ah, encourage the girl to get on about her business, before things get bogged down altogether." He starts to explain about the displeasure, the extreme displeasure, that the Jade Emperor would display, should the being in question follow her friend Nephrite on the path toward the Western Motherqueen's court. But the ghost grows more womanly by the second, and he decides to let that aspect of the problem remain unspoken. "Do you suppose you might—that is, I think it would be best for you if you arranged some way to help the girl get on the road to the east again. Some ghostly pressure on her mama—" He looks away again. "Her false mama, that is to say, the woman Chen. Or perhaps an extremely strong attachment on the part of the Persian man." The ghost drifts toward him. "Yes, that's a thought," he says hastily. "I'm certain your, ah, ability to charm could manage that."

The ghost at first thought this official who summoned her so abruptly both irritating and pompous; now she finds within herself the desire to undo the knotted fastener at the stiff collar of his sumptuous robe. She has always seen something rather touching in the boyish self-importance of certain men, and she has rarely perceived any reason to stifle such desires.

"One thing, though." The official holds up a hand, palm toward her, as if to fend her off. "We may need to send word to her again, so you'd best keep channels of communication open in some way. But, I remind you, nothing clearly traceable to this office." He smiles ingratiatingly. "I'm certain you'll handle things effectively."

LADY OF THE TAO

1. Lotus crown and feather cloak—
   Shimmering wisps of cloudy skirt float free.
   Starshine on sacred altar:
   In fragrant mists she steps a stately pace
   Through grassy precincts, through the starry void.

   Her girl attendant plays on reedy pipes,
   Longing for the day she'll don such robes.
   The Lady's wish? To call a spirit lover,
   Drawn there by her dance.

2. Morning's dew descends to earth,
   Gemlike drops deck hair disheveled in the night,
   The Lady's tears greet dawn.
   For hours she heard his faint, sweet, birdlike words
   And, earthly passions muted, made a tryst.

   At last he left, celestial mating ended.
   Now she yearns to fly with him again.
   Useless to wait, and yet she waits, and sighs,
   In case some word should come.

Parrot Speaks: 11

Baby seemed quite recovered by the afternoon Nephrite returned from Darkdazzle Vista, though the little dancer was under orders to spend one more night at rest. The doctor Mama Chen had summoned the day before checked her various pulses and prescribed a regimen of blended herbs, but the fever had already broken, right after her strange fit, and by the time he arrived she was sleeping normally.

After the doctor left, Mama Chen sent one of the kitchen maids out to the herbalist's to fetch the medicine. Still feeling guilty over leaving Baby for Ghalib the night before, I begged to be allowed to make the infusion myself. "Do it if you want to, Dragonfly," said Mama Chen, "but leave me in peace. I've hardly slept, and heaven knows I've other business to attend to. A certain official—a curse on his stinking mother!—is putting the squeeze on me. Some nonsense about an irregularity in Baby's registration. Claims I owe a small fortune in fines and back taxes." She passed a hand over her eyes. "Ai! Up all night, a girl in the house who's taken to speaking in tongues, and bribe money to be found. You'd *best* keep watch over this ghost-ridden bundle of troubles. I'm off to catch a wink of sleep. Tell Bellring to handle whatever needs to be done." With that, she left.

Soon the maid arrived with the packet of herbs. Impatient though I was, I managed to wait until Baby sat up to drink the herb infusion before I began to quiz her on what had happened. At first I expected her to answer me with speech, but when I told her that she'd talked and what she'd said, she only looked blank—nearly as blank as she had in her trance—and, finally, shrugged. I was still worrying at her, saying, "But you spoke then, Baby! Just try!" when Bellring came in to check on the patient.

She must have seen how things were: Baby's eyes abrim with a convalescent's weak frustration, me flapping my arms as if about to grasp her shoulders and shake the speech from a willfully silent mouth. "Lie back and rest now, dear," she said to Baby and signaled with her eyes for me to step outside. In the hallway, she told me how when ghosts slip within a human body and speak their messages, the medium has no awareness of what has passed. Such tales had always slid past my ears like unwanted memories. But in the shadowy hallway, the weeping blood-ravaged eyes of Nannie's ghost fixed themselves upon me. I blinked in shock, and they vanished, yet I knew then that the human realm was not the only one.

So I let Baby gather her strength in peace and cosseted her with treats wheedled from the cook. When Nephrite returned and heard about the fit, she flew into the room to see how Baby was. Even as she encouraged our younger sister to rest, I saw a rare excitement in Nephrite's eyes. Soon we left Baby napping, and Nephrite tugged my arm to hurry me off to her room to talk. Was this, I wondered, the same Nephrite, usually so pale and cool, whose cheeks flushed as she laid her hand on me?

"Oh, Parrot," she said. "So much has happened. They let

me—even though I'm not ordained, they let me play the pipes one night. For a holy ritual. The Purified Teacher—oh, I'm not supposed to tell you much, but I'm learning to walk the star-walker's walk, and some of the ways to recognize the Pure Ones, and what can happen if you truly enter in the Tao." She threw herself back on her bed. Her face still glowed. "The sisters are so kind. They're going to help me buy out my contract from Mama Chen." She sat up. "Do you realize what that means, Parrot? I can study all the secret writings. I'll be a novice, capped, a Lady of the Tao!"

"You're leaving?" I asked. I knew that in taking up a religious life at Darkdazzle, she'd be able to do as she pleased. Yet like a child who wants her nurse to stay with her until she falls asleep, no matter what the nurse's other duties or desires, I was ready to weep with anguish and rage.

"Yes, silly, as soon as I can, though it may not happen for a year or two. What good does Lutegarden do us? The Ladies of the Tao teach a better sort of music, and they say if I still want to pursue long life by gathering the vital energy of men, I needn't do it here. Did you ever hear about a rite they call The Conjunction of Breaths?"

Her words tumbled out with uncharacteristic joyful haste. My "elder sister," for years the closest I'd had to a mother watching over me, couldn't even see my unhappiness. I sat dumb with surprise: this rapturous absorption in her own plans was something new. I shook my head no.

"That's just as well, really," she said. "Officially it's forbidden, and people tell such terrible lies about it, as if it were some filthy orgy. Never mind, dear one. Just tell me, are you coming with me?"

"With you?" My voice shook. So I needn't be deserted once again. "But what about the money?"

"That's the best thing I have to tell you. They're willing to help out with your contract too!" Nephrite explained that several well-to-do older courtesans had recently taken holy orders at Darkdazzle, as well as a wealthy merchant's daughter, all of them bringing substantial "dowries." If the contributions of the pious were generous, the Ladies of the Tao would have enough to take in some novices with no funds of their own. The Purified Teacher felt it important that Nephrite join the sisterhood as soon as possible, and when Nephrite told her that she didn't want to leave me behind at Lutegarden, the Ladies had put their heads together and agreed to give Mama Chen the necessary funds as soon as their reserves built up a bit. "I'm sure you've noticed cash has been a bit tight here at Lutegarden lately, dear; she'll be reasonable. I told the Ladies how good you are with words, Parrot, and how you've helped me read the holy texts. In fact, I said you'd begged me to let you come with me. I know you really want to study more—" She broke off and looked at me, her face revealing her pride that she'd arranged things for the best.

Something within me shifted. I didn't want to be separated from Nephrite, but I didn't want her to dictate the path I'd walk, either. I understood the filial obligations that morality demands we keep. Yet surely it wasn't my duty to follow Nephrite's plans for me.

But another thought rose up strong inside me. What better path could I walk than devoting myself to deciphering sacred writings, holy mysteries, and poem exchanges with other Ladies of the Tao? I needed time to think. "What about Baby?" I asked.

Nephrite shrugged. "You know she wouldn't come. And, Parrot, she was a sweet thing when we first knew her, but except for you she treats people pretty badly these days. I suppose it's not her fault—that awful Iranian dance teacher hurt her—but I think it's best to leave her to her dancing and her jealousy and her sulks." She leaned forward to catch my arms with both hands. "Oh, we'll have her up to Darkdazzle to visit. Perhaps when she's older she'll be ready to set her feet on the Way."

So Baby had somehow driven off even Nephrite's generous goodwill. Suddenly I thought of another person who tied me to the world, one I was less certain of, yet oddly, all the more compelling for that reason. I didn't even know if I would see him again; surely only a fool would give up the life of a Taoist Lady for some brief affair. But then what of Baby's feverish oracular demand that I go on to Chang-an?

"Dragonfly!" Jujube burst into the room, her feet adance with the importance of her message. "I've been looking everywhere. You have a caller, and he's quite impatient. Hurry!"

For a moment I simply stared at her. Nephrite and I had been speaking Khotanese of course, and in my confusion, Jujube's Chinese seemed a language I'd never heard. She could only have called me Dragonfly, yet for an instant I thought I heard her use the name I'd hidden so long it lay almost forgotten, the name that Baby had called out in her trance. "Greenpearl," I thought she said. "You must hurry!"

Ghalib lounged in the reception room, his heavy eyebrows half frowning as he tried to follow Little Pink's mixture of Chinese and broken Soghdian. He said something and her laugh tinkled her delight at his cleverness. My stomach shrank as I thought how plump and pretty she was—far more attractive than a skinny odd-faced thing like me. Then I scolded myself for my silliness. She had plenty of admirers and would hardly waste herself on a foreigner passing through. I should be grateful, I thought, that she's kept him entertained.

"Ah, there you are, Dragonfly!" she called lightly. "I must say you've kept your handsome friend cooling his heels long enough. Come try to make it up to him, dear. I'm afraid I've got to run." Though she addressed me, she spoke unusually slowly and distinctly. Turning back to Ghalib, she said, "I wish I didn't have to go, sir. I feel we've more to say to one another. But I'm sure you'll be happy with little Dragonfly. So many of the guests are." With that, she swept out of the room, leaving Ghalib to stare after her, bemused.

I set my lips, waiting to hear what he had to say. If he preferred a common flirt like Little Pink to the daughter of a general, I wasn't going to throw myself at his feet.

"So you're here," he said, turning back to stare at me, his face impassive. "I've brought you a present, for some reason. Do you want it now?"

"Only if you want to give it to me," I said. "I suppose you'd like to go up to my room?"

And he said just, "Perhaps. Not right now, I think."

The small coldness in my stomach grew. I wouldn't let him see the effect of his indifference, though. "I'll fetch some wine first—we're a bit shorthanded right now—and then I'll see the present, if that's all right." If nothing else, I could sell the thing and present the money to the sisters at Darkdazzle. I could be as practical as any courtesan. I left the room in a rush.

When I returned from the kitchen, Ghalib was standing in the opened doorway, looking out at the garden. "Quite a lovely place you live in. Everything designed to allure and please."

"So it is," I said, coming up behind him with the tray. "But my favorite thing is that strange rock by the pond there. Because of its delicate pattern of streaks, someone uprooted it and brought it here, and yet it keeps its simplicity unchanged. Certainly it never asked to be here." I took a breath. "Sometimes I wonder what it would tell us if only we could read the signs nature's written on it."

He faced me then, a softer look in his eyes, though his mouth stayed a straight line. "Difficult to know the heart of such a thing from its surface," he said. "Sit with me, Little Parrot, and pour us some wine, and then I'll give you the present."

We raised our cups and drained them, and Ghalib reached under the rosewood couch where he reclined. I knew what it was when I saw the shape of the bag protecting it. He held it out to me, and seeing my expression, smiled for the first time.

"I thought you'd be happy with it. You've given me real pleasure, and this seemed the best thing for you. Open it, now. Carefully."

He spoke like a father to a pampered child. And, child that I still was, I didn't hear the farewell behind those words. I drew the lute from the damask bag.

Any lute of my own would have made me happy. I'd used Mama Chen's plain practice lute so long. But this one was truly lovely: made of the sandalwood called "purple rosewood" and inlaid with figures of mother-of-pearl. I looked up at him, speechless. He might have given me any sort of expensive gift, or a number of trinkets, but he'd thought to choose the one thing I wanted most. I took that as a sign of some bond between us, though perhaps what he was trying to do by the extravagance was make things up, somehow, to all the little slaves who'd passed through his hands.

"Here, girl," he said. "Look at this." He pointed out one of the inlaid figures and I saw it was a parrot, gleaming iridescent blue-green and pink and creamy white.

Then the words poured from my lips quick as lively music, and I thanked him and began to tell him everything I knew about lutes. "And do you know," I babbled, "they say that since the inside of the instrument is empty, though what we see on the outside looks substantial enough, that it resembles heaven and earth themselves? And, look, the neck stands strong while the body yields in curves—a perfect expression of yang and yin."

I had to explain those last words as best I could in Soghdian—I'd fallen into Chinese—and then I poured more wine and began to play for him. The tone of the instrument was rich and full. Soon one of us suggested we go to my room for more songs and wine; suddenly it no longer mattered who took the risk of asking for what we both wanted. We left the reception room for a more private place.

In front of my door I glanced back at him. He frowned and I asked him what was wrong. "Nothing," he said. "Nothing. I was just thinking about the light way you walk and those bewitching green glints in your eyes. Perhaps I should call you Dragonfly after all."

FROM *The Thousand-Insect Classic*

by Jin Luo-sun

DRAGONFLIES

I. Interpretation of Names

Dragonflies are known as Carmine Turquoises, or Ol' Blue-greens. Those that are large and green are: Vertpavilion, Greengarden, Glaucous-tinkle, and Lonelyverdure. Those that are small and yellowish are Foreignpears. Those that are small and red are: Crimsontiger, Red-robed Messenger, Maroon Lepidopteron, and Scarletbanner.

II. Assorted References

1. "If, on the fifth day of the fifth month, one buries a dragonfly's head in a doorway facing west, and does not eat for three

days, then it will change into a precious green pearl. Others say one should bury it beneath the main gate."

2. "Dragonflies drink dew. They have six legs and four wings. Their pinions are delicate like those of a cicada. In rainy times, one encounters many of them."

3. "The *Jun-nan-zi* states, 'As for toads becoming quail, and water scorpions becoming dragonflies, both are born of that which is not their species. Only holy persons understand these transformations. Those who don't understand are surprised; those who understand don't consider it strange.' Thus it is pretended that this kind of change is not at all surprising.

"In fact, anyone who studies can understand this; one need not wait for a holy person. Since water scorpions become dragonflies, dragonflies accordingly return to the surface of the stream and scatter their eggs. Hatching, these in turn become water scorpions and water scorpions, in turn, become dragonflies."

III. Essential Pharmacopoeia

Introducing Names   In some places they are called Goldenheifers, or Silkywethers, in others, Childsflag, Riverfowl, or Mulberryroots. Some call the red-and-yellow ones Tawnykids. Some call the black ones with white spots Springcattle. Another common name is Gauzeox, because the wings are like gauze.

Fragrance   Slightly cool, not at all noxious.

Major Pharmaceutical Functions   The Alternative Record says, "Being strongly yin, it stops the semen." The Solar Efflorescence says, "Being vigorously yang, it warms the liver."

IV. Assorted Sayings

1. From *The Forest of Changes*

> When dragonflies form clouds,
> The cities bar their gates,
> The country's ruler guards,
> The people fear ill fates.

2. From *Proverbs Ancient and Modern*

> When dragonflies go high, the grain will parch and die;
> When dragonflies go low, the levees overflow.

V. Recorded Events

1. From *The Record of the Pure and Marvelous*. In the Latter Tang, some palace women caught dragonflies in nets. Loving their halcyon-flashing tenuity, they used a gilding brush to paint them with tiny flowering boughs, and kept them in gold-wire cages as pets.

2. From *Miscellaneous Transcriptions of Wu-chen*. A great dragon rose from the shore of Lake Tai in the southland as from a cocoon. Larvae emerged from among its crocodile-like scales; they quickly turned into crimson dragonflies. Those who caught them contracted malaria. Today, people who see crimson dragonflies call them "dragon scales" or "dragon-descendants" and do not dare to harm them.

The above is a selection from a spurious scroll sold to that remarkable figure (explorer, imperialist, archaeologist, thief, as you will) Sir M. Aurel Stein. Purportedly a relic of one of the cave libraries at Dun-huang, the text has now been discovered to be a pastiche based chiefly on a corrupt version of the splendid eighteenth-century collectaneus, the Gu-jin tu-shu ji-cheng.

The Crystalline Palace
of the Moon

In the crystalline palace of the moon, the Moon Lady sits near the great cinnamon tree in her garden, breathing its subtle fragrance and reading a letter from the Shamanka Star. Sighing, she lets it fall to her white jade desk. Just beside the study pavilion where the Lady sits, the albino moonhare impassively pounds a great pestle in his alabastrine mortar. The seven moonmaids, her students, play ethereal melodies upon their flutes. Their music wafts among the pillars and roofbeams of the pavilion like opalescent filaments unwound from silk cocoons, but the Lady remains lost in thought.

It is the sixth day of the month: outside the palace walls, beneath mountains of phosphorescent pearl, the people of the moon smelt silver and refine mercury over fires of frost, releasing a radiance like the glow of ancient sea ice. The moon's newborn whitesoul—the womanly yin essence of the cosmos—

hangs, a slender hook, above the human realm. On the sixteenth day of the past month, the people of the moon began as usual to gather pallid flowers from the shadows of the forest called Wanewood, using them to wipe away the dwindling effulgence. The palace faded then from human view as if occulted by the ashes of a funereal sacrifice. But now the crescent grows again. And, wax or wane, the moonhare pounds tirelessly, preparing the catalyst for these alchemical transformations of light and dark.

It pleases the Moon Lady to hear from her dear friend Dame Shamanka Star, who dwells now as the tail of the constellation Dragon. Long ago, the Shamanka Star served as Lady Adviser to the legendary monarchs of the Shang Dynasty; since her ascent into the heavens, she has ruled the mediums and sybils who say sooth below. Consequently, she can most charitably be described as rather moody.

Sister! (the Shamanka Star has written) *I commend you on the splendor of this year's harvest moon. And yet, busy as you must be with the Mid-autumn Festival soon upon us, I must respond to your last letter at once and ask, where are they now, the literary women of the terrestial realm? You wrote to me that they flourish in this Great Tang. Outrageous self-deception!*

Sorry dear! But who among the subjects of the so-called Brilliant Emperor can match the Han Dynasty's Tsai Yen or Juo Wen-jun? Do the women of the modern aristocracy possess the wit and abstruse learning of a Hsieh Dao-yun? Do the chanteuses of today's Entertainment Quarters display the creativity and amatory exuberance of a Midnight?

Oh, I'll admit it—even today the courtesans compose their lyrics, the princesses their rhapsodies, the palace women their plaints, the boatgirls and farmwives their songs, the Ladies of the Tao their transcendent odes. Yet for male poets, this is the Golden Age, while for every female poet, a hundred others languish, mute. What is to be done?

The Moon Lady purses her lips and brushes a nebular wisp from her diaphanous robe. She herself is, after all, the renegade wife who snatched the Herb of Immortality from her selfish husband and ran off to live forever in this sky palace of candlelit quartz. I'll grant, she thinks, that my fitful astral sister may not yet have foreseen the flourishing of the perspicacious courtesan Xue Tao or poor Yu Hsuan-ji. But why such gloom? Young Li Ji-lan is already showing signs of her remarkable talent. And how can Sister have forgotten in mere decades the galaxy of feminine ability gathered in Chang-an under the Empress Wu?

Images flurry like new-hatched moths into the Moon Lady's thoughts: a Buddhist nun; a peasant woman; Madame Sun, who burned her own poems; Ladies of the Tao; empresses; consorts; more. True, many of their poems will be lost, as will other talented women's very names—Jang Li-ben's daughter, Liu Yuan-tsai's wife—but who could deny that, despite the strictures, voices alive with the yin force can be heard? The Moon Lady shakes her head.

"Is something wrong, Lady?" The moonmaids have put aside their flutes and one of their number, White Aureole, has drifted over to the goddess's side. "Shall I fetch you a cup of dew?"

The Lady assures her that all is well, except that Dame Shamanka Star is in one of her glum moods and wants some cheering up. "If she weren't beyond such things, I'd swear she was premenstrual." The Moon Lady pauses to chide herself for the thought. "Well, the poor dear has a right to be a bit eccentric, I suppose. Imagine having the responsibility for all those twitching, moaning mediums and ecstaticas when you know how many of the messages are going to be misread or ignored."

White Aureole murmurs sympathetically and floats off toward the Lady's study to fetch paper, writing brush, inkstick, and the concave stone on which to grind the solid ink and mix it with water.

"Bring my Hyaline Cloud Inkstone this time please, dear," the Moon Lady calls softly after her. "The ink I grind on it always seems to give the brush a special flow." As she waits, she returns to the letter. The albino moonhare flicks one ear but never breaks the rhythm of his pounding.

The letter continues in an erratic welter of emotions: . . . *so that's the last time I invite that tiresome Clerkstar over to tea— she insists on bringing up the conquest of the Shang by her wonderful Zhou Dynasty. As if that wasn't a major calamity for all the yin-ruled!*

Possessed too many times by too many voices, sometimes the Shamanka Star loses her own. A hasty note at the end adds: *Sorry, dear Sister, to have babbled on like this. You know how I am. And just now—a most distressing piece of news. A blue raven has come from the Motherqueen herself—some little chit has taken to speaking in tongues without even a by-your-leave! I could just nova! Apologies. S.*

The Moon Lady places the letter to the side of her writing desk. She considers retiring to a chamber in her vast underground library to work on her reply, but the scent of the cinnamon tree urges her to linger in the garden pavilion. Two of the moonmaids take up huge peacock-feather fans on poles of silver and wave them above her head. The frog carved into the ivory of the pavilion's main rafter wriggles contentedly in the chilly breeze.

When White Aureole finally returns, her eyes are wide with distress. On a tray of translucent nephrite, she bears rice paper, an heirloom stick of ink, and a writing brush with a handle made of a fine bamboo spotted by the tears of the Two Ladies of the Hsiang River. There is no inkstone. The Moon Lady raises her eyebrows inquisitively.

The Hyaline Cloud Inkstone, says White Aureole, has vanished. She looked everywhere. None of the household staff has seen it for days. The cloth of nimbus in which the stone is usually wrapped lies crumpled in a corner of the storage chest. Shall she bring one of the everyday inkstones? Has the Lady any instructions for a further search?

The Lady and her students look through every chamber and courtyard. Finally, Oyster, the youngest of the moonmaids, spies an unusual nebular glow spilling from the moonhare's mortar. She cries out, and the others gather round. The hare continues to pound out time's passage. He embodies the insensible germ of the yang force in the moon, as the three-legged crow—dark as a sunspot—is the grain of yin within the distant solar palace.

There, in the curve of the mortar, shine the last powdery fragments of the Hyaline Cloud Inkstone. No need to look further. No hope of repair.

The Moon Lady smiles with a tranquil irony. A certain handsome visitor who passed a night within the moon palace once gave her that stone, before his sky raft took him back down to the human realm. It was carved, he told her as they bid one another farewell, of a rare rock found only on Mothbrow Mountain in his native province. In exchange, she had given him an inkstone made of a petrified star, such as those that sometimes fall to earth. But in later days, the man's great-grandson dropped that stone, and smashed it, and now hers too is gone.

The seven moonmaids exclaim in shock and futile outrage. The Lady is an incomparable calligrapher, but surely the graceful "silver hooks" she inscribes upon the page will suffer from the loss! How can another such rock be brought to their lunar dwelling place? No dweller on the moon may violate cosmic decorum by taking one from earth. Some human must be induced to offer one at once!

The Moon Lady smiles her cool but charming smile. "That," she says, "is exactly what will happen. Oyster, you may bring me my Wateressence Stone; it will do for now. I must advise Dame Shamanka Star to look into this business of an unauthorized medium. No doubt that's what's bothering the poor thing. All those energies released without any sort of regulation! It's enough to throw anybody out of kilter." She glances ruefully at the albino hare. "And now, girls, I want each of you to write me a poem on the sun crow, in heptasyllabic regulated verse. The exercise will help you calm yourselves. The word to rhyme with is *rays.*"

Oyster leaves, and the six other young scholars glide off after her toward their studios, chastened by the Lady's serenity. After her letter's written, she decides, she'll look into a report of a general's runaway wife that has reached her, slowly but inevitably, through the celestial grapevine. She pauses to gaze at her own frost-white face in the silver-washed disk hanging from one of the posts of the pavilion. The moonhare's monotonous pounding reverberates. The cinnamon twigs rustle. A sliver of hoarshine hangs above the pellucid air of the frontier wastelands, the autumnal loessclouds over Liang-jou and Chang-an, the argentine waters of Cavegarden Lake.

Parrot Speaks: 12

I sat inside the curtains of my bed, my knees pulled up to my chest. The ninth night of the ninth moon, Mid-autumn Festival, and I was passing the evening alone. Ghalib had come by earlier for a hasty meal and hastier lovemaking. Then he rushed back to his inn to oversee the last preparations: Umar had passed through some kind of feverish crisis, and tomorrow we would join a caravan leaving for Chang-an. I had told Ghalib I wanted only to go to the capital, that I knew he wouldn't take me back with him to Persia. Now I realize it was just this that fanned his feeling for me; had I vowed eternal love and pleaded to stay with him, he'd have stroked my cheek and left me as quietly as he could. But as long as he thought me ambitious for the opportunities of the imperial city, he came, frowning, to Lutegarden, striding to my room with the air of a man who catches himself attending to some trivial matter better left to a servant.

Yet in my bedroom, after music, and food and wine, he changed. "You've made me a greedy man, Little Parrot," he'd said three nights ago, scratching his beard, "but I'll take you with me. If this Mama Chen of yours will accept a reasonable offer."

She'd accept. I knew how badly she needed some extra cash right now—she'd grumbled about it most of the day—yet as soon as he gave me what I desired, my mouth went dry with loss. Though I returned often to Khotan in dream, and reminded myself at every mention of the capital that I was the daughter of a good Chang-an family, Liang-jou was the home I'd known for years. While I lived there, I felt I was an outsider. But when I learned I'd leave, I thought only of the smell of Liang-jou mutton pastries, and the melodies that came there first from the west, and the pond in Lutegarden, and Baby and Nephrite left behind.

So I told Ghalib that Mama Chen would be more willing to arrange my transfer to the Chang-an registry of entertainers if he asked for both of us, Baby and me, together. "She's ready to get rid of Baby, and buying two girls' contracts will convince her it's trade, not personal attachment." I lay on my stomach and traced the incised pattern of leaves and flowers atop my white ceramic pillow. "She'll drive a harder bargain if she thinks you want me because of some feeling, and not for business." The last sentence disappeared into the air between us.

He said nothing then, but the next day Mama Chen agreed to negotiate on Ghalib's behalf with the city clerk in charge of transferring entertainers' official registrations. The silver Ghalib gave her more than paid the bribe to have whatever problem there was with Baby's papers overlooked. That night Umar's illness grew suddenly worse and then suddenly better, and all was arranged so quickly that it did not yet seem real to me. The morning of the Mid-autumn Festival, when Mama Chen told Baby that she was to go to Chang-an with me, the little dancer broke two days of gloom with a leap and full twist in midair. Now she was out with Bellring, Glory, Little Pink, and young

Jujube. They were joining entertainers from other houses at the governor's big mid-autumn banquet. Mama Chen had drunk herself to sleep on chrysanthemum wine after seeing them off and Ghalib safely escorted from my room.

As for Nephrite, she'd left Lutegarden early in the afternoon, decked out in Mid-autumn Festival style, a spray of crimson dogwood leaves hanging from her sash and a tiny embroidered bag of the scarlet berries attached to one sleeve. A new young man had asked her to join him on a mountain picnic for the holiday.

I had just pulled myself from my bed and walked through the dark room to raise the window blind and gaze at the gibbous Ninthnight moon when I heard a thump and a giggle behind me. I whirled about and by the watery light saw Nephrite leaning in my doorway. I lighted a new candle, she threw herself laughing on my bed, and I sat down beside her. Usually her fastidious restraint extended to alcohol, but tonight she was as drunk as I'd ever seen her, her pale face flushed to beauty with the festival wine.

"Oh!" she said. "Oh, Parrot, what happened tonight! A perfect Ninthnight. I wore the long-life dogwood, I drank the long-life wine, oh and one other thing—" She sat up with a jerk and threw her arms around me. "Oh, Parrot, you may be leaving, and it may be months and months before the Ladies at Darkdazzle Vista can buy my contract, but I can still follow the disciplines and achieve transcendence." Her head hung down and she spoke with her warm face pressed against my breasts. "And, oh, he was so, so—"

Her shoulders shook and I thought she was crying. I smoothed her hair with my hand. Then she raised her laughing face and brought it so close to mine I could smell the spicy wine on her breath.

"Oh, Parrot, he was almost a virgin, and half drunk, and got so excited when I asked him if he wanted to slip away from the group and walk in the moonlight. When I lay down he opened my skirt and called me a frostfaery and said he'd never made clouds and rain out among the greenery before."

I asked her only if she hadn't been cold.

"Cold? I almost froze to death. Thank the Amah that it's warmer than last week! But that helped me keep control—not easy, Parrot, with the moon and the wine. I'm a little tipsy, you know. Anyway, sister, his male essence has fed my spirit. He almost fell asleep on his horse on the way home, and I feel so alive I must have added years to my longevity." She sighed and held my gaze with hers. "And tomorrow you leave me."

The candle burned brightly, and Nephrite asked if she might touch me, and first I said no, because I was afraid, and then I said yes, because I wanted her to. Sometimes it seemed strange to make love to a body that mirrored my own. Sometimes it seemed the same as with a man, and sometimes it seemed different but exactly right. Her fingers drew new patterns across the skin of my back. I called her names I've said to no one else. We had no book of secret teachings, no words for the ways our bodies fit together, and no struggle to see who might win what from the other.

At last she slept. The moon had sailed on past my window. I lay awake, thinking of what had happened, and how Nephrite had called me "little sister" the first time at Old Ma's back in Dun-huang, and how I had to leave her now because Baby had told me in a fever to go to Chang-an where my mother was. It was too late to stop it; I had made it happen.

Nephrite was still dozing beneath my quilts when I heard the others return at last from the governor's banquet. Baby hurried ahead of the rest, and burst into my room. But when she saw Nephrite roll over in her sleep so that the light of the guttering candle struck her white breasts, Baby's face distorted and she ran.

The next day is a jumble. I remember far more clearly the weeks of the journey to the capital: through scrub-covered hills of sandstone and shale where pheasants rose up crying, then down again to pastures and terraced croplands, the yellowish earth still riddled with the deep fissures that the Road must twist around and twist around again. Dust hung heavy about us, except when we hit the autumn rains as we neared Chang-an, and made our way afterward through thick mud.

The first six or seven days we traveled slowly, so that Umar might rest, and we lingered awhile in the city of Lan-jou, its yellow-brown walls set where yellow-brown hills close in toward the great River Huang. One miserable morning we crossed the pass over the Liuban range, a sleetstorm out of the west driving hard at our backs as we topped the divide.

There was more water than in the far west, though the first ten days out of Liang-jou most of it tasted brackish. And there were far more inns. Travelers' tales grow with the telling, I know, but one day we heard that the roof and flooring of an inn we'd stopped at the night before had burned, and its walls collapsed, and half the people died. Still, the Silk Road carried us on, east and south and east, while the soft, ceaseless plodding of the camels took me back to the peace I'd known along the Road before.

Baby treated me as if she knew nothing of what had passed between Nephrite and me—and as if nothing had ever been possible between the two of us. One day early on, as we picked our way among the loose stones of the plain just outside Liang-jou, I realized I could do nothing but accept this. Evenings, Ghalib and I taught each other what we'd learned, in our different worlds, about the ways of passion. Sometimes he told me stories of his travels, or I played my lute for him, but often we held to the silence of the day's long ride. I heard him say to Umar more than once that the cold was closing in and that he hoped we'd make good time, but when he and I were alone together he seemed to be in no hurry to end the journey.

Huddled within layers of clothing, I dreamed as I had on the journey from Dun-huang. This time, though, my mother came for me by night, and not in daytime reveries. Her gleaming chestnut steed still danced on hooves of cobalt gray. Once the swift rider had Baby's round cheeks and slender waist. Often she was Nephrite, pale and remote and beautiful as the moon. And on the last night that we made camp in the wild lands, I saw a queen's face, splendid, with tiger's teeth, and in her disheveled hair, a crown of stars shaped like a loom.

On my final morning at Lutegarden House, tired though I was, I woke early. Nephrite had slipped off to her own room. I walked out into the garden, to see it one last time alone in the first light. Then Baby walked up to where I stood beside the lily pond, something small and white held in her two fists. It was the strange scroll that the parakeet had led me to at Old Ma's. When I packed my things to take with me to Chang-an, I couldn't find it; in fact, I hadn't seen it for years. Now here was Baby, clutching the scroll with an air of triumphant scorn. Before I could ask how she had it, or where it had been, she threw it at me, hard.

When the scroll flew toward me, I tried to catch it. It slipped from my fingers and tumbled to my feet. The cord that bound it loosened and it fell open, so that I could see the first column of the writing. I knew how to read now, and the words still looked as if they were Chinese, yet they did not quite make sense. When I glanced up, Baby had marched off again, into the house. I picked up the scroll for a closer look. Word after word, column after column, the black signs hung on the silk like dark stars collapsing in on themselves. I shrugged, glad to have the curious thing again after all, and turned to take it to my room. Rerolling it as I walked, I passed through a patch of morning sunlight reflected off the garden pond. A long ray fell on one of the first words and I saw that it was, and was not, a word I knew: in pictographic, antique form, the ink made a human figure, her breasts large with milk for her child.

Seagem's Chamber

In a coral chamber of the Dragon Monarch's Mother-of-Pearl Villa, Seagem grinds a stick of ink upon a stone. A black lake forms and she sets the inkstick aside, breathing easily, feeling her body relaxed and alert. Raised to be a good wife, Seagem learned sewing and courtesy and how to keep accounts in her head and how to hold her tongue. She never unwound a scroll, never held a writing brush. Now, at the Dragon Monarch's suggestion, she reads, slowly, and practices the quiet discipline of calligraphy every morning. It has become another of the guilty joys of her new life, though she remembers, still, that her happiness in this unearthly realm violates the laws of man.

She dips the brush into the dark pool. She traces upon the untouched page a pattern held clearly in her mind. A sudden ray of light breaks from the nearby moonpearl lamp, startling her. The hand slips, the fickle ink twists, the word appears transmuted. No longer is it in the stylized form declared standard by that book-burning autocrat, the builder of the Great Wall. It has become again a true pictograph, the very image of *mother*. The brilliant runaway beam strikes the page and is refracted off, toward the human realm.

FROM *Esoteric Transmitted Records of the Bizarre*

by Lha Er-sun

I t is difficult indeed to distinguish the orthodox from the eccentric and the true from the false. Yet the Grand Historian of the great Han Dynasty, Si-ma Chian, having undertaken to record the strange lives and occult doings of magicians and diviners, charlatans and raconteurs—how can I feel shame in doing the same? What in these accounts of ghosts, spirits, swordswomen, and prophetic dreams are lies pretending to be veracity, what is self-deluding humbuggery, and what is merely degenerate and garbled history, I cannot say. Yet it is to be hoped that the narration is not without truth, and that some learning, or some pleasure, may come of it.

STRANGE PREGNANCY

A daughter-in-law of the Li clan, previously a virtuous and chaste young woman, began to dream of having intimate relations with a giant red-gold carp. Her husband was away on military duty in the borderlands. Night after night she fell into these dreams, until she began to waste away. A doctor of arcane arts was summoned, who exorcised the fish-monster.

More than a year later it became obvious that the woman was pregnant. She said that this time she had been visited at night by the dream spirit of her distant husband. The family, fearing the scandal that would arise when a wife whose husband had been absent so long gave birth, consulted the doctor again.

"Destiny has mated her to the giant carp," the doctor said. "This time he assumed the guise of her husband and crept into her room at night. He is the father of the girlchild she carries." On his advice, they took the woman to the shores of Cavegarden Lake and, dressing her in bridal clothes, set her on a flower-decked raft and floated her out into the mists of the great waters.

THE TALKING BIRD

Ma Lao-tou of Dun-huang purchased an unusual parrot from the far west. Its wit was keen and its words flowed eloquently; it stood far above the usual run of talking birds. One day he overheard it in conversation with a Chinese parakeet from the Loong Mountains that belonged to his daughter. "Alas," the parrot said. "I am in truth the daughter of a Chinese general, changed into the form of a bird. How can I ever return to the home of my parents?" At first, Ma Lao-tou did not believe the bird, but the parakeet spoke up and confirmed its words. Shortly thereafter, the parrot disappeared.

HAUNTING A MADAM

In the Kai-yuan reign period of the Great Tang, there was a certain dancing girl of foreign origins who was possessed by a ghost.

The ghost sent her into a fit, speaking through the girl's mouth and demanding that she and another entertainer be sent off to the imperial capital. But the mistress of the household where the girls lived refused. The girls were afraid to defy the ghost's command, and begged, but to no avail. Soon, however, the ghost began to haunt the madam's dreams, wailing and moaning, until she was half dead of fatigue. So she allowed the two to go, and the ghost never bothered her again.

THE GREEDY DEMON

Once, in the city of Liang-jou, a government clerk summoned an old woman named Chen. He threatened to have her arrested for nonpayment of taxes, so she was forced to sell her two daughters to a trader in order to pay the necessary fees. With great weeping, they separated, and the trader took the girls away to the east. When this Chen approached the official to make payment, he received the silver and suddenly transformed himself into a wild-haired female demon with bloody eyes and vanished. As to why the demon wanted the silver, no one knows.

A PERSIAN MERCHANT'S
SPIRIT-JOURNEY

During the reign of the Brilliant Emperor, a wealthy Persian merchant was traveling to Chang-an. Along the way he met a young musician, who became so enamored of the Persian that she courted him with enchanting songs upon her lute. He, in turn, was pleased by the musician's beauty, and soon they were intimate. When it came time for the Persian to leave the young woman and travel on, she begged him to take her with him to Chang-an. He told her it was impossible and returned to his inn, where he began his preparations for departure. The musician's lute fell silent, and she stayed alone in her room and wept.

No sooner had he begun to pack, however, than his companion, a younger Persian gentleman, fell deathly ill. His soul left his body and in the wink of an eye, it found itself before the tribunal of an important celestial official in the service of the Jade Emperor.

"I have a message to be delivered to your friend," the august official commanded. "The lute player is a spirit banished from heaven, and it is necessary for her to go to Chang-an. If he takes her with him, he will have good fortune and will acquire great riches. However, if he fails to do this, all his trade goods will be confiscated, and he will be imprisoned."

Now, the younger Persian, being a foreigner, did not know he should respect the words of the heavenly official. To show his indifference, he yawned, whereupon the guards beside the tribunal took him into the courtyard and flogged him. After they opened three great wounds upon his back, the Persian youth fainted.

When he opened his eyes, he found himself back at the inn, his friend standing over his bed and watching him with concern. The youth related what had happened, but the older man did not believe him until he turned over, revealing three faint scars down the length of his back. The scars had not been there before, so, fearing that the musician was no ordinary mortal, they took her to Chang-an, where they acquired considerable wealth, just as the celestial official had said.

THE PRESCIENT MUTE

Gao Li-bo was traveling with a companion and several slaves. One of them, a young girl named Bao-bei, was mute. Very early one morning, as the party lay sleeping in a small inn in Loong-yo, not far from Tibetan-held territory, the mute began to shake the shoulders of the slave beside her. The second slave awoke, and the mute began to signify with her hands that the entire party should depart as quickly as possible. Not knowing what to do, the second slave wakened the master. So urgent were the mute's signals and the other slave's pleas that the party arose and, with some grumbling, quit the inn. The next day they learned that soon after they left, a party of Tibetan raiders had swept down from the mountains, burned the inn, and murdered everyone within.

A PROPHECY

A certain young woman called Chen Yu was accepted as a novice in the Taoist retreat of Darkdazzle Vista. Because her name meant "nephrite," she was given the religious name Jade Clarity. After donning the cap and robes of holy orders, she began to collect numinous fungi and rare herbs, hoping to discover an elixir of immortality. Ignoring her teacher's warning of caution, she roamed the wild lands, trying every mysterious new plant she found.

Not long after Jade Clarity began her experiments, she came across a cluster of thin whitish mushrooms growing in a clump of cow dung. Not disdaining them, she mixed them with other efficacious substances and swallowed the potion. Another Lady of the Tao found her laughing wildly and wandering through the sacred precincts and wrote down her words. It is not known whether they came true or not, but they remain preserved at Darkdazzle Vista today:

> When the ice horse plunges to the river,
> The silent shell shall spread its lips and speak.
> When pearl and jade have met beneath the waves,
> The child of wood shall weave a heavenly web.

*These tales are from a collection compiled by Lha Er-sun
(?–A.D. 946), a courtier of the short-lived Later Jin Dynasty
(A.D. 936–946), during the period of political turmoil following
the fall of the Tang. Lha's literary work demonstrates once again
the fertility of the disputed territory along the border between
history and fiction.*

*Little is recorded concerning the compiler's career, except
that Lha encouraged the founder of the Later Jin to reward his
Mongol allies with lands located between the two nations. Unfortunately, after Lha persuaded the next emperor that tribute
no longer need be paid to those same bellicose neighbors, they
destroyed the Later Jin.*

Chang-an

And so, spread across a plain abundant with crops and tumuli, *the* city, eastern terminus of the Silk Road, center of the empire, residence of the Son of Heaven. *Chang-an*, they call it, Everlasting Peace, though it will not be spared destruction, and it is far from peaceful. Quite the contrary, it is alive; in every alley, in every courtyard, eyes hungry or gluttonous cast about for more—food or pleasure or power or fame—just as your eyes consume this page. A hundred ten-thousands, a million pairs of eyes are gathered within the city walls, and nearly as many just outside. The Imperial Palace stands properly centered within the great north wall, where the emperor can look southward (as the compass needle points always south) over the huge block of government offices, over the rolling mass of the city, over all the Great Tang, all Under Heaven.

You, too, can take a look. The saying goes: Chang-an is like a giant board for chess, its orderly layout reflecting the order of an empire, and a cosmos, ruled with righteousness. Nine broad boulevards run through it north and south; twelve wide avenues range east and west. They help stop the spread of fires, dividing the city into wards, each walled and gated and closed at night. Within these walls of pounded earth twist labyrinths of lanes, smudged with cooking-smoke and the fumes of nightsoil and the human passions. Each ward bears its own proud and hopeful name: Golden Walls, Lustrous Virtue, Gleaming Cottages, Eternal Tranquillity. The glimmering waters of the artful Serpentine wind through the great park in the city's southeast corner. To walk across the giant square within the walls would take two brisk hours, if there were no crowds.

Do you suppose that this city cares only for its wealth and worldly power? See: It has four Zoroastrian fire tabernacles, a Nestorian church and a Manichaean one, nearly twenty Taoist vistas, and close to a hundred Buddhist temples. Above the temple rooftops—roofs of chapels, of meditation chambers, of bell and drum towers, of walkways leading from the dormitories to great halls where statues of stone or gold stare down at worshipers—rise pagodas housing cherished relics.

Come closer. Over here is the precious ancient tower, *bao-guta*, called Great Wildgoose Pagoda, of the Gentle Mercy Temple; every three years, the forty or fifty scholars who pass the national examination flourish their names upon its bricks in the light of the springtime sun. Thousands have come to the capital to take the exam, and for these few, the way has been opened to success as government officials. The tower rises impassively into the clouds, delicate bells hanging from the tawny brick eaves of story after story, its cylindrical spire encircling the whole cosmic round. From the upper windows even your mundane eye can make out the steep rise of the blue Jin-ling Mountains guarding the city on the south.

Down in the southwest quadrant huddle the single-storied houses of the poor. Gaze northward instead, to the fashionable wards east of the great central boulevard. In one of them, a spinach peddler rambles door to door. He spies through one crimson gate a garden pavilion by an artificial lake, its pillars brightly painted, the brackets supporting its roof splendidly carved. An old gentleman in fine robes plays chess there with a crony, and a sweeper shoos the peddler off. Next door he sees an empty courtyard and a heap of sun-dried bricks that was once a proud ancestral shrine; they'll be used again soon to build a prince's archery hall, or a grand tomb outside the city for the father of an official whose star is on the rise. The peddler doesn't stop. In the adjoining lane he passes a neighborhood apothecary's shop. At a Buddhist convent that was once the mansion of a devout princess, the old nun who supervises the refectory smiles distantly at the peddler. After a little dickering, she purchases half his load.

The bright welcoming flags of a few cafés sprinkle the busiest areas. Has one of them caught your eye? Observe how, in a tea shop near a city gate, a painter and an architect argue happily with a civil engineer, while a scabby child squats outside the tea shop door, begging with his one arm. Remember this and look to the two Teaching Quarters close to the Imperial Palace, training schools for stunning dancers and musicians favored by the Brilliant Emperor himself.

Would you like to see the shops? A sign marks the entrance to each market lane: ironmongers, jewelers, butchers, dealers in bridles and saddles, sellers of scales. Here the flower vendors gather, and here is the bazaar of the silk merchants, where your fingers might slide over rosy-soft "dawnclouds tussah" from Korea, or nubbly pongee, or bombazine made of the short threads left when wild moths break free of their cocoons, or even the chilly icesilk spun by frostmoths amid the unmelting whiteness of the mountain at the center of the world. In the two great marketplaces—the east and the west—you can gawk at a contortionist bending round till his elbows rest against the backs of his knees, smell the rich oniony oil of wheat cakes frying, laugh at a dancing bear called Blackplum, buy rice shipped a thousand miles north along the Grand Canal, toss a copper to a kinky-haired juggler from the barbarous tribes south of Viet, or listen to the warning stories of a pious Buddhist monk whose master has returned with new Teachings of the Law from the birthland of The Thus-Come-One, far to the west. A Scholar of the Tao struts past, pausing only to crack a ribald joke to his stooped assistant, trotting along behind. Some other holy man, a foreigner with a bulbous nose who worships fire or brings tales of an outlandish murdered god, moves slowly through the jostling crowd, gaping: newly arrived.

Here's another new arrival, someone (you may think) rather more like yourself, educated, sensitive, a lover of literature and rather more given to contemplation than to action, but no doubt a bit worldly nonetheless. His eyebrows are long and fine; he has a scholar's hands. His tousle-haired manservant follows him on a donkey, but he himself rides a big roan horse of excellent bloodlines, though a few years past its prime; his mother pawned a fine old necklace to buy that horse, and the glittering tassele[d] saddle.

Young Feng—Feng Literary Victor, his parents call [him]—knows that, about his mother pawning her necklace, b[ut] [gue]ssing now his mind is on other things. His narrow squeak [i]d hard, the province-level civil service exam, for one. He s[tudied] so badly, fairly hard anyway, never expecting to come off g[..] caught out and feels now like an impostor who's bound to [..] to try to pass sooner or later. He has come north to Chang[..] stige and income the national exam, his one chance to get the [..] But he'll be competing accorded a government official and his fam[ily]. [t]he empire, and some peting against the best young men of al[l] [w]ho've been memorizing not young at all, dogged graybeards [..] pony-ribbed Top Scholar texts by moonlight for years. Only t[he] [..] splendid seat in the Great Star, flourishing his inkbrush up in [his] Dipper, knows who will succeed.

Feng's in no hurry to make his attempt. First, he'll settle into

Chang-an and recover from his long journey. He plans to take advantage of the months left before the exam is given to review the classics, and maybe write up a story or two that could catch the attention of a patron, some old scholar-official who'll see that a man of imagination deserves a good position.

Stories are, in fact, what young Feng really likes, far more than poetry or essays; the problem is how to find that patron. His family has no connections in the capital. Even the rich clan back home that his father serves as tutor are (he sees it clearly now, as he pulls his horse aside to make way for a shouting runner followed by two pages on matched black mares and a scarlet palanquin) provincials, rubes. Where might a young scholar with limited means and a taste for the less elevating sort of literature get to know an official who would put in a good word for him when the right time comes?

Where indeed? Feng and his mirthful servant have ridden about the city for hours now, eyes wide. The young scholar is too excited to seek out just yet the lodgings his father recommended. He's passing along the wall that closes off the Imperial City and the palace to its north and east. Within lies (he knows) a great audience room where the Son of Heaven holds morning [court,] and within lies a web of halls and walkways and bedchambers and pavilions, within lies a succession of hidden gardens. Sitting [in] the smallest pavilion, beside a clump of rustling bamboo, the [girl who] might be (he thinks) the newest of the palace ladies, her face exquisitely and pointlessly made up (for with so many in the imperial harem no lover will see her), wisps of hair trailing as she leans over the rail to stare into a smooth pond and sigh. She would be [a] girl—still virgin of course—of distinguished family, though not too distinguished, a girl of refined sensibilities and unawakened desire. She might pluck a leaf from the bamboo and drop it into the pond, watching it drift toward the weir-dam and over and down into the culvert beneath the garden wall. Then she might pluck another leaf, and another, and begin to write on them brief melancholic poems, and drop these leaves too into the water. And Feng would find them, up there, just ahead, where the water pours out from under the wall, and he would snatch them up and marvel at the delicacy of the tiny handwriting, and read the poems, and weep.

At the corner, where the water flows into the gutter, Feng peruses it carefully, but what floats in it is not bamboo leaves, only fish scales and a few shreds of vegetable skins from a kitchen floor someone has scoured. Another text better left unread. He kicks his heels into the flanks of the roan horse, guiding it around a farmer with a wen on his neck, stooped under two baskets filled with wild-eyed outraged hens. The servant, who has a slight potbelly, laughs and clucks at one of the hens, but Feng pays him no mind. He has come to the north gate of the Pingkang Ward. Tales of the winehouses here, the talented women and the merry roistering during the night watches, have made their way as far as his provincial home. Now the stories whisper to him, with a sound like tears dropping into a pool, like a writing brush sighing words onto a leaf. He has studied hard since he was five years old. He did pass the provincial exam, after all. A meeting with a discerning and powerful official in the reception room of a winehouse is not impossible. Perhaps he will just stop and take a cup.

The History of Dreamdragon Feng: A Tang "Transmitted Marvels" Tale

During the Kai-yuan reign period of the Brilliant Emperor, in the town of Jia-jou in southern Shu, lived a poor but honest scholar called Tutor Feng. His personal name I will not sully with my brush. Now, this man had one son, Feng Literary Victor, known to his friends as Dreamdragon Feng. Since early childhood, young Feng had studied the classics, gathering fireflies in the summer evenings so that he might read late into the night and yet spare his parents the cost of lamp oil.

Young Feng distinguished himself in the local and province-level examinations, placing first among all who competed. Consequently, he set off for the capital to take the national exam, taking with him his manservant—a slave named Sparker—all his parents' hopes, and most of their money.

Upon arriving in Chang-an, young Feng grew confused amid the hurly-burly of the capital and wandered by mistake into the lanes of the Pingkang Ward. The young scholar could hear the distant melancholy twanging of someone practicing an air on the barbarian lute. He passed a courtyard with an open gate; leaning in the doorway of the house within, a young woman dressed in willow green gazed out at him with heart-stopping charm. Feng's horse came to a standstill, and his riding crop slipped from numbed fingers. Beside him, Sparker sat just as still and just as silent.

The scarlet lanterns before the gate glowed in the first lengthening shadows of late afternoon, though it was yet some time before the sunset curfew drum would sound. A shabby gatekeeper emerged from the courtyard, picked up the riding crop, and respectfully held it up to the young man. Feng took the crop and handed the gatekeeper a handful of coins, hoping to impress the woman in the doorway. With a word to Sparker, Feng slid from his horse. Leaving his cap on the saddle, he stepped into the garden, toward the doorway where the beautiful young woman waited. Water trickled from a tube of bamboo into a rock-lined pond, making a hollow sound. Feng glanced at it for no more than the wink of an eye, but when he looked up again, the woman in the willow-green robe had disappeared.

A fattish old lady with a squint bustled out into the garden. "Greetings, Young Master!" she called, bending her body downward at the waist and her lips upward at the corners. "I see you have traveled a great distance. Will you come and rest awhile?" She waved Sparker toward the kitchen and led Feng into a reception room where two little maids brought him sweet warm wine. Introducing them as Catkin and Floss, the old lady excused herself and hurried off.

After Feng had drunk a cup or two, he asked Floss to bring him paper and writing materials. The little maid complied, Feng quickly downed another cup, and his brush flew down the page. This is the quatrain he composed:

A lovely willow wavers in spring's wind.
The passerby is drawn, as bees to flowers.

A melancholy lute song fills the air.
For whom do fine white hands pluck high-strung notes?

No sooner had the ink dried than Feng bade Floss take the poem to the beauty in the willow-green robe. Meanwhile, Catkin brought in fresh hot wine, and before Feng had finished his next cup, Floss returned, bearing another poem. The paper she presented to young Feng read:

> Alas, no lute rings from my empty room.
> My fingers only play the flute of jade.
> Suppressing longing, pressing parted lips,
> I make it rise, and make its small mouth sing.

With trembling fingers, Feng took up his pen once more. He was racking his brain for suitable words when the squint-eyed old woman returned, leading the beauty in the gauzy green robe. "Allow me to introduce my eldest daughter, Young Master. Her name is Willow, and though she is not without accomplishments, I fear I have mishandled her upbringing, for I discover she is a forward thing. Having glimpsed you from the doorway, nothing will do but that she have the chance to converse with you awhile." Willow hung her head.

Soon, however, the couple was chatting merrily, and Catkin and Floss hurried back and forth with more wine and spicy snacks and warm scented cloths for refreshing one's face. When the curfew drum sounded, the old woman—who had told young Feng to call her Granny Squint—returned to the reception room and, full of apologies, advised him that he'd better hurry home before the gates of Pingkang Ward were locked for the night.

"Alas!" said Feng. "I have no place to stay in Chang-an. All day my manservant and I have searched for the town home of a dear friend of my father's, but to no avail. I have a good bit of money with me and am rather afraid to lodge in a common inn. Can you recommend someplace for us to pass the night?"

Granny Squint knit her eyebrows into a dark line above her wrinkled eyes. "I'm not sure that anyplace one could find in the short time before the gates close would be suitable for a gentleman such as Young Master. Our little house is rough, but if you could stand simple fare and plain accommodations, you and your valet are more than welcome here."

A thrill raced through young Feng's blood. He thanked her warmly, and bade little Catkin find Sparker and have him fetch several bolts of fine silk from the goods his parents had given him for his expenses in Chang-an. Granny Squint refused to hear of payment, and it was only after much talk that Feng persuaded her to accept them as a gift. "Back in Jia-jou, my family has warehouses full of such stuff," he told her. "You would give me pleasure by taking some of it off my hands."

The rest of the evening passed like a fireside reverie on a winter's night, or a youth's daydream on a sultry afternoon. Sparker was given a bed in the servants' hall. Feng and Willow moved to a quiet apartment on the upper floor of the building and retired within the curtains of her bed. The joy of their union knew no bounds. Blissfully they sank among brocade cushions, tenderly they embraced beneath embroidered quilts, passionately they stammered words of affection, lightly their hearts floated on the springwinds of love.

The dream continued through the whole winter. Every day, Feng gave Willow some keepsake, or showed his gratitude to Granny Squint, or tipped the gatekeeper and the other girls of the house. When he wasn't with his beloved in her room, he was hosting little dinners for the gamblers and roisterers and honeybees who hovered about Willow and her younger sisters Fascination and Patchouli and Lilyskiff. Feng learned how to move his counters on the *liubo* board, how to bet heavily on the fall of the bamboo sticks, and how to shout with a charming anger when his luck was bad. He slept little and studied less, growing steadily thinner; his skin lost its pure glow and his hair its blue-black luster. The spark of poetic genius left his eye, though his words ran wild with wine and his imagination wild with indecency as he amused his companions by relating fantastic narratives best not committed to paper. More than once, Sparker reminded him that the time remaining before the exam was passing quickly, but Feng paid him no mind. Shortly after New Year's, he ran out of money.

For a while, he disguised the fact as best he could, selling Sparker's donkey and pawning his spare clothes, though it was still quite cold. When this money was gone, he sold his books, and finally borrowed what little he could from the youths who had professed to be his friends. But the bills mounted and finally the day came when he could put his creditors off no longer. He found Granny Squint supervising the installation of a new and elaborately carved front door and threw himself on her mercy.

"No money?!" the old madam cried. "And a goodly debt run up on my books, too, my lad. Well, you'll have to work off what you owe me, and then you'll have to leave."

Feng protested and then he wept and then he called for Willow but received no answer. He stormed toward the courtyard gate in a huff. Granny Squint shouted an order to the gatekeeper's grandson, a hulking carpenter, who leapt upon the unsuspecting Feng, beating him until his whole body throbbed with bruises and welts. The gatekeeper and his grandson dragged the young scholar to the servants' hall and dumped him on a thin mattress of woven reeds.

All during the beating Feng cried for help and tried to reason with the gatekeeper and the madam, telling them that after he passed the exam and received a post he would repay all his debts and more. But this did no good at all. Indeed, when he mentioned the examination, Granny Squint merely laughed and asked him if he thought he remembered enough even to try. Feng's best tools, his quick mind and his clever tongue, had failed him—they hadn't protected him from the beating, he thought as he lay weeping softly on the crude pallet. And he knew he'd forgotten so much of the classics that he had no chance of passing the exam.

Soon Sparker returned. Seeing his master, he let out a cry of woe. Feng told him all that had occurred, and asked Sparker if he'd managed to sell the roan horse in the Eastern Market that morning.

"I did, master," the manservant replied. "These hoity-toities in the capital dicker fiercely, but not as well as us Jia-jou folk. But alas"—and here he set aside the rag with which he had been cleansing his master's wounds—"from the marketplace I went straight to The Lucky Ivories to settle up with Old Yuan just as you ordered."

"Alas?" said Feng, who was trembling with cold and pain. He felt relieved that at least Old Yuan wouldn't be giving him another beating, but when Sparker told him that the gambling debt had taken every bit of the silver from selling the horse, his heart sank. What was he to do? The horse had been his last asset. Even if he ventured to write his parents for money, they had none to give. And besides, he felt that he would rather die than expose them to the shameful knowledge of his behavior.

Selling off his slave was out of the question: when Feng was five, Sparker had saved his life by pulling him out of a river, and the two had grown up close as brothers. Feng's adroit lies had rescued them from many a boyish scrape. Once Feng confessed to snatching a whole tray of persimmon cakes left on a window-sill to cool; the housekeeper hated Sparker and would have had him whipped had she known that it was he who took the cakes, but she dared not harm the Young Master. Now they were alone in a strange city, without friends or money.

The gatekeeper hobbled into the servants' hall. "Ah," he said, "the other rascal returns. Good. Your room and board have increased the bill of Lord Emptypockets here. No doubt you'll be accepting the mistress's kind invitation to stay on and work it out." He cackled at his own clumsy wit.

Sparker leapt up. "Ai, ai, ai!" he cried. He began to drool, twitching and jerking like a madman. All the while, he called out "bloodyblade" and "garrote" and "round the neck or up the back?"

The old gatekeeper froze, staring at him with amazement and more than a bit of fear. "Tzia!" sighed Feng. "My money gone, a terrible beating, and now my servant goes insane." He held his head in his hands.

Spinning like a dustdevil, Sparker came up to Feng. He bent low and grasped Feng's chin, pulling his master's face up close to his own. Only Feng could see the enormous wink that Sparker gave. He pulled back, blinking in surprise.

Whatever Sparker was up to, Feng decided, he'd better play along. He turned to the gatekeeper. "Stand back, you fool! He does dreadful things when these fits come over him."

"Yes!" shouted Sparker. "Ai! My hands are burning. Yes!"

So Feng hissed, "I'm warning you. I won't be held responsible if he strangles you. Stand back!"

The gatekeeper's eyes widened, and Sparker shrieked "throttle" and "twist it off." The old man scuttled away like a crab.

His grandson and Granny Squint rushed into the hall to see what the uproar was all about. They ran up to the gatekeeper, and as they did so, Sparker let out one last horrifying shriek and drooled and twitched and danced his way across the courtyard toward the gate. By the time the others realized what had happened, he was gone. The young scholar had been deserted by his childhood friend.

After that, things grew even worse for Feng. His dream of happiness and love had become a nightmare of forced labor. Granny Squint refused to show him her account books, and he suspected that she had cheated him by exaggerating the amount he owed her. Even so, the thought of appearing in court as a debtor and having his selfish waste of his parents' money exposed was too much for him to bear.

From the moment the dawn drum sounded, Feng labored in the courtyard, cultivating flower beds and transplanting shrubs in the cold dry air of winter's end. Then the time for the civil service exam came and went, and he was ordered to dig an elaborate winding pond and construct a system to bring water to it.

Each day, before any visitors arrived, he was hustled off to the back of the household, where he had to scrub floors and clean the chamber pots and do the worst of the kitchen chores. His clothes turned to rags. His soft scholar's hands grew calloused and ached with chilblains.

Worse by far was the pain in his heart. Granny Squint told Feng that Willow didn't wish to see him again. One day he snatched a word with the little maid Floss, begging her to plead with his beautiful mistress on his behalf, but Floss told him that it was true: Willow had taken up with the son of a wealthy magistrate, saying that Feng was a liar who had deceived her into thinking he could care for her when in fact he couldn't even support himself. Feng was greatly shocked to hear the story of their love told this way, though he admitted to himself that there was some truth in it.

Early one morning, as Feng carried a huge rock over to the winding pond, he heard a deep, angry voice outside the gate, demanding to be let in: ". . . or my sworn brother Judge Tsao himself will throw every person in this den of wickedness into prison to await a most earnest interrogation!" the voice boomed. Soon the expensive carved door swung open, and the gatekeeper backed up bowing into the courtyard.

A mighty general strode in after him, sweeping the old man aside as he turned to glare about the yard. His iron-black eyebrows scowled beneath a heavy helmet-mask shaped like an eagle's head, and the few gray hairs in his long beard glittered fiercely in the morning light. Feng crouched down in the dry pondbed and peeked around a rock.

The general's thunderous voice brought old Granny Squint out to meet him as quickly as if he'd been one of the divine Guardian Kings of the Four Directions. The old madam trembled and offered tea or wine, but the general stomped the thick soles of his high black boots and growled that he wanted none of her so-called hospitality. He wanted his nephew.

"At the personal request of my beloved younger sister, I have scoured the city for her son." The general proclaimed this as if he were vowing vengeance for a battle lost through treachery. "Though she has had no word from him for months, at last I have traced him *here*. And I will have him returned to me now."

Granny Squint anxiously denied any knowledge of his nephew, or anyone else's. But the general thumped the cuirass of rhinoceros hide that armored his chest and back, roaring, "If he is not here, then you have fleeced a young man from the provinces and killed him with your cruelty, and I will see that you are executed." His voice dropped and he added, "Slowly." With that, he threw back his helmeted head and called, "Nephew Feng! Feng Literary Victor! Your Uncle Huo is here."

Now, Feng had no Uncle Huo, so he crouched lower in the pondbed, confused.

"Nephew Feng!" the fearsome general boomed again. "My little nephew who always looked so keenly at the *reality* behind *illusion*, who always *trusted* his Uncle Huo! Do not be ashamed to reveal yourself in this time of trouble." And he stamped one heavy-booted foot.

What, Feng asked himself, did he have to lose? He drew in a great breath. "Uncle!" he called, leaping up from behind the great rock. "Dear Uncle Huo, you have come for me at last!"

It was a matter of few moments and many words—threats and curses and gruff demands to see the record books—before Granny Squint acknowledged that young Feng had doubtless worked long enough to repay what he owed her, and let him go. The two men stalked out through her gate with dignity, but when they reached the first turning, the general took Feng's arm and began to run.

"We'd best step lively now," Feng's rescuer said, wincing as he tore the horsehair beard from his chin.

Feng gasped, and his faithful servant chuckled. "When the old dame opens that 'purse of silver' I tossed her and discovers it contains only riverstones," Sparker continued, "she may send someone after us." They laughed and hurried away, never to be seen in that particular lane of the Pingkang Ward again.

Months later, Granny Squint overheard a guest, a well-known general, complaining of a runaway groom who'd cut off half the tail of his best mare and disappeared with his boots and helmet and rhinoceros-hide cuirass. But considering her own wrongdoing in falsifying Feng's account, and the hopelessness of catching up with the two, she let the whole matter drop.

As for Feng, he must have suffered for his foolishness: his name never appeared on the list of those who passed the national exam. Willow became the concubine of the magistrate's son, and after two years she died giving birth to a stillborn child. Decades later, during the An Lu-shan rebellion, I stayed some months with that same magistrate's son, now a prefect, when I was roaming south of the Yangzi. He told me this story more than once, not forgetting a single detail. I have since related it to friends whenever the subject of faithful and clever servants arises, and they have urged me to record it, that it might be preserved as a warning against foolish overindulgence and an example of loyalty to all who read it. And so I have dampened my writing brush and jotted down what I could.

The "transmitted marvels" stories of the Tang Dynasty may have arisen as a dodge around the famous Chinese civil service examination system. A man who came to the capital for the highly competitive national exam might write one of these tales as a showpiece of his skill in the concise, elegant language we call "literary Chinese." Dropped on the doorstep of a powerful literatus-official, the tale could impress a potential patron with its author's poetic sensibilities and high moral vision—and help him get a job.

Parrot Speaks: 13

When I first met Dreamdragon Feng and Sparker, I might have seen the subtle signs of each young man's discontent with his present place in life. But I noticed no more than the elegant airs of the one and the casual cheerfulness of the other. In truth, I wasn't noticing much about anyone; I'd been listless and withdrawn for months. All my thoughts were for what Ghalib had done, although by the time I met them, my feeling for him seemed only a kind of story I had spun for myself, no more substantial than my dreams of my mother astride her magnificent horse.

Arriving in the capital from Liang-jou, I had been joyful, eager, dazzled. With our two long stops and the bad weather, it was nearly the eleventh month, but something more than the cold had made me trade, some ten days or so before, the peacefulness of travel for impatience.

An autumn drizzle grayed the air as Ghalib's documents were checked and cleared and we entered the city proper. Even Khotan's walls had not stood as tall as these, more than three times Ghalib's height. We passed the food stalls and a swarm of hucksters, and rode into a side portal of one of the city's western gates, beneath its proud watchtower. My breath came quickly as we moved through the shadowy tunnel.

Our camels paced indifferently toward the Persian Hostel in the great Western Market. What would happen now I did not know; I could think only that somehow I would find my mother at last in the home city I was seeing for the first time.

It was past noon when we passed through the ward walls of the Western Market, so the shops and stands of every lane had opened. Wheelbarrows full of dried fruit or cabbages rolled past the gem bazaar and warehouses and cooked-meat stalls rich with the smells of pork broth and fried liver and roasted dog. I saw a sword juggler half naked despite the clammy cold of the air. Outside the hostel a remarkably tall woman, her hair the color of dirty copper, spun some wild tale for a crowd of yokels come into town for the day. As we passed, I noticed that her skin was virtually colorless; its freakish pallor revealed the blue web of a storyteller's forking veins. A shopcat yowled. Carriage wheels creaked through the crowds. Voices wheedled, shouted, swore. Then we went through the gate of the hostel and left all that, for the moment, behind.

But no sooner had we dried ourselves and taken the hot wine the hostel keeper offered than Ghalib bent close to my ear and murmured, "If the little mute really is your friend, you'd better make ready to say good-bye." Then he slapped Baby's hip and told her to run up to the room and change into her best.

Baby knew what was coming, I'm sure, but she only hung her head and walked upstairs, not even turning to catch my eye. I shouldn't have been surprised: on the journey, I'd tried again and again to have her speak to me in her old language of hand-

sign and glance. She refused. As long as I loved some other—
Ghalib or Nephrite, it didn't matter—and not her alone, she was
determined not to love me.

When she came back down to the dim main room of the
hostel, Baby's head was high, her face closed, and the pomegranate and leaf-green of her brocades shone even in the glow of the
charcoal fire. By then the rain had stopped. Wine-warmed and
rested, Ghalib wanted to take me up to the room; I could read
the subtle signs of his behavior well enough.

Ghalib drained his cup and ordered his nephew to take Baby
to the dancers' conservatory, in the Teaching Quarter of the Left.
"I'm tired of her sulking ways, Umar," he said. "Get the best
price you can for her, but take any, as long as there's a bit of
profit in it."

"And if there's no profit?" Umar stretched and grinned. He'd
made it clear that whatever his uncle's reasons for bringing the
two of us from Liang-jou, *he* had considered it foolish from the
start.

"Then find someone somewhere that offers one." Ghalib's
callousness surprised me; on the Road I had put aside my knowledge that he was above all else a trader.

Baby swept from the room before Umar could rise, as if impatient to be off. Perhaps she was. But I could not bear to see
her leave that way. Without looking to Ghalib for permission, I
ran after her to the entranceway and threw my arms around her
stiff torso. When Umar ambled up to us, I asked him to tell the
housemistress at the dancers' conservatory that Baby had a
cousin who would come to visit her someday. At an inn outside
Lan-jou I'd learned from a Chang-an singer headed west that female relatives were allowed to visit the *artistes* of the quarters
on the second and sixteenth days of the month. Somehow I
would manage it.

Umar reached out one lank arm, palm up. What did I have
to give him? Only the gilt earrings Nephrite had taken from her
hoard and pressed into my hand as I left Lutegarden House. Baby

had no way to tell the housemistress of her "cousin"; I needed him to vouch for me. I took one off and dropped it into his waiting palm.

"One's no good without the other, little honeytongue," he said.

"Give it back, then."

He just waited, smirking, till I yielded and gave him the last memento of my friend. "You may have spoken to me as a man speaks to his camel, but unlike a camel, I've remembered what you said." I'd picked up enough Persian to grasp his meaning, though I'd have understood the long-brooded anger in his laughter if he'd spoken in a language not yet born. Here was another sour fruit of my cleverness with words.

Baby knew who'd given me the earrings, and, no doubt, what it cost me to give them up. Hastily she returned my embrace and smiled at me, letting her eyes show sadness at last, as Umar pulled her after him into the courtyard. Then the hostel gate swung open and the hurly-burly of the market swallowed them up.

The rest of the day passed far too quickly, and not at all as in the tale I'd invented of how it would be in Chang-an. In the room, Ghalib said nothing, only stared at me with a measuring gaze and scratched his beard and shrugged. In a manner not quite playful, he pushed me to my hands and knees on the low bed. Then he knelt behind me, pulled his trousers down, and raised my skirts. Usually we undressed each other slowly, and he liked it when I teased him, prolonging his pleasure and my own even after a hard day of travel. But this time he was rough and hasty, as if bound to prove himself the master. On the stairway I had been eager for him, despite my unhappiness at seeing Baby go. Then my desire for him died. Perhaps he meant that to happen; I don't know.

"Umar says you are some spirit wrapped in flesh to enchant me," he said, standing and straightening his clothes. "And that I can't let go of you. But I know you're only a human woman,

Little Parrot, one of many human women along the Road." His words were cold; his deep-set eyes said that he was angry.

My own anger rose, and silenced me. That left only a muteness as sullen as Baby's, and a wash of sorrow. Later, there would be worse moments, when I believed that somehow I deserved what he had done.

"So we'll part, Little Parrot," Ghalib said, leaning back against the far wall with a forced ease that aped the civility I had loved in him, "and soonest is best. I'm sure the mamas who run the entertainment houses have sharp eyes for a pregnant girl." He gave the same considering, half-apologetic nod he had when he left me at Old Ma's, and went back downstairs.

I sat upright on that shabby hostel bed, counting in a dizzy rush the days and weeks of our journey from Liang-jou. Mama Chen had kept careful watch over us at Lutegarden House, though during my years there more than one courtesan in the other houses had given a child to a farmwoman to wet-nurse or to raise as her own. Collator Wu had never worried about the harmful effects of fleshly joy when drunk or gorged with food, but he had always stayed away from me on the days some said were ill-omened, the dark of the moon when my blood ran and again when it shone full.

What Ghalib had said was true. The weeks on the Road had hardened my body again, but in recent days my small nipples had swollen. It was not the rigors of travel that had stopped my blood's release, but the hunger of what would become a child. I tried to imagine my grandparents taking me in now and hated the body that had done this to me.

I rarely think of the next six weeks. Ghalib's luck, at least, held good, for after nearly a year away in the eastern capital of Lo-yang, the Brilliant Emperor and all his court would soon return to grace Chang-an. The city would fill with officials and hangers-on, and life would be busy again for the entertainers. This meant that Mama Lu of Felicity Hall was not the only one who sought out new talent: when Ghalib took me there and she heard me play my lute, she pulled her fur-lined jacket close with a money lover's pleasure. The transaction was concluded quickly, and as quickly and coolly, he left.

So I was registered as a musician and hostess at Felicity Hall. I tried telling myself that I had what I wanted—after journeying thousands of *li*, I was in Chang-an!—which was true enough. But somehow I could do only what Mama Lu ordered me to, and that as one no more than half awake. Even at the winter solstice, when people feast all night, exchanging merry wishes for good fortune with their companions, I only picked at the pork-and-ginger dumplings, and wished that I might leave our guests and slip away to bed.

My depression that winter set the tone of Mama Lu's opinion of me from the first: "What a waste of good silver *you* were!" she snapped one afternoon about ten days after my arrival, when she sailed into my tiny bedroom, bracelets ajangle, to slap me awake from yet another nap. Mama Chen back at Lutegarden had obviously never been especially good-looking; it was by means of her wit and her strength of will that she had made her way. But Mama Lu still had the well-rounded mouth and smooth skin of her youth, despite the shadows beneath her dissipated eyes, and a haughty beauty's airs. "That Persian trader cheated me—typical!—with his tales of your amusing ways. I thought the day he dragged you here that you showed some promise. Now I see I'm saddled with a pallid mope who can't do a thing on her own." She pursed her mouth, making it rounder and fuller than ever. "Your technique on the lute's not bad—someone took the trouble to teach you well enough out there in the barbarian western lands—but Lady Guan-yin bless me, there's not a spark when you perform. The men want some feeling to the music, girl! Surely you know that much."

Business grew lively with the court's return. Mama Lu kept me working chiefly as a wine server, tending to the drunkards and not the guests who appreciated the best in music. I liked to bring out the doll they called "the wine barbarian"; I'd set the roly-poly fellow on his rounded bottom in the center of the table, hoping he would fall in my direction, so I'd be the one required to drink a cup. The old men fell asleep and we made up beds for them, or their patient grooms took them home just before the curfew drum. Young men rode off to other parties, or stayed the night in someone's room, but not in mine.

The three older courtesans in the house—Mistmaid, who was rather clever and extremely idle, and gossipy Bouquet and gentle Amber—mostly ignored me. They looked down on the houses of the northernmost lane of Pingkang Ward as little more than brothels, but despite its more prestigious location, Felicity Hall was not quite one of the city's top entertainment houses. The women there had less reason to hope for a secure future as favored concubine or household entertainer than had Little Pink or Glory or the others back at Lutegarden. I didn't blame my new "sisters" for not wanting to be friends, for in those weeks I told myself that Ghalib would not have left me so easily if I had been worth staying with. And when a guest commented that the new girl was a fetching little beauty, or some such nonsense, Bouquet would murmur to Amber, or Mistmaid would purse her lips as Mama Lu did and draw her delicate eyebrows together. How could they see me as a friend when any attractiveness of mine might take away their one chance of a comfortable old age?

We had a full staff of maids—Mama Lu spent much more freely than Mama Chen ever had—but they took their cues from the senior entertainers and left me alone when they could. Only the gatekeeper, a bent old ex-soldier everyone called Walleye, seemed to like me; to pass the time when I couldn't sleep or drink, I'd listen, or half listen, to long stories about the days of his youth.

Finally winter folded itself around us. In the darkness of the third watch I would lie in bed, still half drunk and unable to sleep, and hear the steady hissing of falling snow. Mornings I woke with a dull throbbing in my ears and a queasy stomach.

Sometimes when I opened my gauze-covered window and leaned out on the carved sill to watch the slow growth of the icicles from the eaves, the cold wind braced me and I determined that I would soon take my rightful place as a general's daughter: I had only to seek out my mother in my father's house.

But how was I to accomplish that? I didn't have the freedom of the city, nor any idea where that house would be. I knew I should try to get some word of that particular Li family from our guests. But not just yet, I'd think, staring out at the white roofs. I'll do it soon, but not just yet.

One such morning not long before New Year's—I remember it was unusually sunny and still, and the east light clarified my icicles as unstrained wine clears when the lees settle—I roused myself early. Once again I checked to see if by some chance my blood had begun to flow in the night. Once again it hadn't, and again I started to put the thought of the future aside; it was surprisingly easy to forget, most of the time. But I knew the pregnancy would soon show beyond any hope of hiding it. So on this day I found a resolve within me, as if it had been waiting all along, the way the winter sunlight waits for the clouds to break.

It was time to find the family of my father. I corrected myself: my own family. Surely someone visiting Felicity Hall would know the whereabouts of the parents of the General Li who'd died on duty in Khotan. All I'd learned about managing a conversation was bound to serve me in good stead.

Just then Mama Lu, snug in her fur-lined jacket, bustled into the room, preceded by a strong smell of roses. "It's time, dear Bordermoon," she said to me, "that we took care of your little problem." Her round mouth set itself in an oily smile.

I hated the name she'd given me. Bordermoon. It had the vulgarly overblown air of the woman herself. She liked it because she thought it went nicely with the names of the two farmgirls she had recently taken into Felicity Hall as apprentices, dubbing them Luna and Crescent. She liked it, too, because it would appeal to men with a taste for the melancholic poems about the frontier lands that were all the rage. And, I had decided, she liked it because it made a virtue of my foreign appearance, which I supposed she looked down upon, though she'd never commented on it.

"You know, dear," she said, smiling again and holding out a cup, "I pay close attention to my girls' health, and I don't like it when they're careless. The moon has run its course and more since that Persian dumped you on me. Maybe when you're older you can indulge yourself in a child, though I shouldn't recommend it. Now drink this down."

I knew from stories at Lutegarden what kind of drink it was and knew that there was nothing I could do but swallow it. Some bitter oil with a leafy smell was mixed with the wine; I still taste it sometimes. Mama Lu turned and left. My stomach ached at once, and soon fire and icy winds raced by turns across my skin. I wanted to vomit but couldn't, so I sat weak-legged by the window and waited, watching the steady trickle of meltwater off the icicles. A thin needle seemed to stir deep in my belly. The pain at least was familiar at first, but after some hours it grew worse than any cramping I had felt before. I began to bleed, first slowly, then more heavily. My skin grew hotter and the cloths I used each month soaked through. At last the flow of blood sent me racing dizzily to the privy in the far corner of the courtyard. It wouldn't stop.

It was Crescent and wide-eyed Luna who found me hours later and washed me off and helped me back to bed. The stopped-up blood of three months had poured out between my legs, taking with it the thing that would have been a child, and leaving me too weak to walk.

I stayed in my room for twenty days, recovering from the poison and the lingering bleeding, then lost in feverish visions as my body suffered from the great imbalance of its vital forces. I hardly noticed the turning of the year. I wondered why Mama Lu had left me alone after she gave me the drink, until Amber told me that Mama Lu had lost a pregnant singer once to the herb, a sweet-faced thing called Charmeur whom she had loved like a real daughter. She had been afraid I too would die, and so refused to let herself care.

Yet all the time I was in bed, Mama Lu made sure the maids looked after me. She herself came to see me once the worst had passed, sometimes bringing me healthful powders mixed with broth, sometimes scolding me for a careless pregnancy and urging me to get well. This was not so different from the way I regarded myself then: unsure whether I was the helpless victim of someone else's actions or was responsible for all that had happened. It didn't seem that there might be any third way to understand things, so I lay there unresisting as she placed her plump hand on my forehead or shook her bracelets angrily.

I can remember, dimly, the sound of fireworks on the last night of the year, and how I wept because I felt so hot and weak. The fever left me for the last time on the day little Crescent skipped in with a toy oriole that Walleye had bought from a peddler and sent in for me. People played with them at the solar festival of Spring's Beginning, early in the first month; I could only look at the little bird and imagine its sweet song, but I did that many times.

The Lantern Festival ending the New Year's season was over the first day I was well enough to entertain a group of guests, but the late winter plum trees had not yet bloomed to herald spring. The remnants of a freak blizzard dusted the city with dry patches of white. Mama Lu hadn't forced me back to earning money right away, but now she scolded me and reminded me of all she'd spent on food and medicines while I lay ill. In fact, once I recovered, she kept her distance from me, and I never again saw the side of her that had lain a cool hand on my hot brow.

Despite this, I felt stronger and more sure of myself than I had since the day I entered Chang-an. Mama Lu cared little for most religion, but she kept a statue of Lady Guan-yin in a back room, and that morning I burned incense and set out a sweetpeel tangerine to thank her for my reborn health. I asked the Lady to watch over the soul of the child I might have had, when the Wheel of Birth and Rebirth next turned and brought it again to the world of dust. It would surely have a better life than if it had borne the burden of flesh with no family to protect it. Lady Guan-yin smiled, gracious and unmoving as ever. But as I stared at the strings of pearls looped down over the roundness of her torso, it seemed as if she'd nodded benevolently, or lifted a hand to gesture, *Set your heart at ease.*

Well before the guests arrived, I finished painting my cheeks and forehead, took up my lute, and played the first song I'd ever learned, when I was the daughter of the garrison commander in Khotan. The music ran more easily than it had for months, but the sound of it made me restless, so I put on my padded outer jacket and walked to the small room beside the gate where Wall-eye kept watch. Actually, he was too arthritic to dispose of a really nasty guest, but there was little need of that. Besides, he asked less salary than would a younger, stronger man, so Mama Lu let him stay.

"Nicely played, Miss Bordermoon!" he called as I slipped inside his door. "Your spirit has decided to remain on earth—I heard it in the music and now I see it in your face." His good eye sparkled as he caught the tangerine I tossed him and placed it on the ramshackle table beside him. "Ah, Mama Lu bought some of these two days ago from a peddler. Not cheap, they were, but good-looking. I thought perhaps a few might go your way, self-indulgent old vixen though she is. And now you've given one to me. Well, well." He shook his head, and his blind eye wandered from whatever unearthly objects usually held its gaze to fix itself on me. "You must peel it for me, and take a bite or two yourself, and I'll let you know all that's happened on the lane since you last crept out to keep an old man company."

I took a stool beside the tiny charcoal burner that warmed

his hands and feet. Carefully, I slipped the aromatic peel from the fruit in a single piece with petals like a flower, which made him chuckle.

"I knew a girl once who could do that every time," he began, and told me stories until Lotus, one of the maids, came running out to say it was time to meet the guests. Two manservants on their way to the warmth of the kitchen saw Lotus and me hurrying toward the reception room; the one with a slight potbelly called out something I chose not to hear. The sound of their laughter at their own cleverness hung behind us in the dry air.

One of the guests was an old friend of Bouquet's; she was leaning over his couch to whisper something in his ear. He'd brought with him two other minor officials, and a slim, slightly stooped young man with blue-black hair and the air of one who lives by his wits. I soon gathered from their conversation that this fellow, Dreamdragon Feng, was a scholar's son who had come to Chang-an several years ago to try to win a post in the government. Somehow he had lost his money and his hopes. Now he claimed to be a student, but evidently spent most of his time cultivating rich friends who were willing to pay his bills for the sake of his company, picking up cash by writing letters for some shopkeeper or doing a bit of tutoring for a merchant's doltish son.

Feng told an anecdote about a young man's tryst with one of the daughters of good families who stroll or ride their carriages about the gardens along the waters of the Serpentine in the southeast corner of the city. It was a springtime tale, and a bit improper, but it made the party laugh, though Bouquet pretended to be shocked. For a moment my heart twisted with love-longing, yet I had no idea for whom.

Later the conversation turned to poetry, and Bouquet, who had been born and raised only a few *li* from Chang-an, recited a poem someone had taught her, called "Moonlight on Jade Pass." It described the far northwest as a fearful lonely place, and I felt my cheeks flush with anger.

"It's not so!" I said, but Bouquet's friend was praising her with loud slurred words, so no one heard me except for Feng, and he said nothing. I retreated into the cool aloofness that I'd pulled close around myself when the slave girls at Old Ma's left me out of their games and during my early days at Mama Chen's. These others could not understand the desert lands for what they were, and clearly they couldn't understand me. Nor—I said to myself—did I want them to. Forced into this empty life, I would play the shallow courtesan, using them to my own advantage until a true friend came along, or I made my way to my rightful home.

Yet when I brought up subjects that might lead to information about my father's house, I was ignored. That night I went to bed hours before I slept. Feng didn't return (and I wondered why I noticed), but a day or so later one of the other young men invited me out to perform at a farewell banquet for a friend who had to leave Chang-an. Mama Lu saw that my reputation as a musician was on the rise and didn't pressure me to find a patron just yet.

Early one morning I sat by the window and let myself fall into remembering the desert. The wind blew cold: although I'd raised the blind for light, I left the gauze screen in place. The level sunrays threw the shadow of a bare branch onto the illuminated whiteness of the gauze. I thought of the winds in Khotan in the winter, and the clear dry air, and the eternal ice of Kunlun's peaks. Nephrite would listen to me talk of their beauty, if she were here, I thought, but no one else knew that land as anything but a place of exile; even Baby had forgotten it.

I'd taken up calligraphy again during my convalescence, though the brush Mama Lu had found for me was old and stiff. Nonetheless, it soothed me to put aside the little makeup boxes on my table, and grind the cheap ink, and begin to find a pattern of words to suit what I had to say.

Making the poems eased something inside me that had been knotted tight since I drank down the oily wine Mama Lu gave me, and those blood-releasing cramps began. But there was no one to show them to. Guests at Felicity Hall would laugh at the wine pourer who couldn't write a *proper* border poem. Baby at least would listen when I recited them because they were my words, yet how was I to get to visit Baby? The ink dried on the paper, and I rolled it up, and put it aside.

In Chang-an, Thinking of the Western Borderlands

I. Winter's moonlight frosts the city roofs,
    While colder rays fall clear beyond Jade Pass.
    The ice of home hangs down from gilded eaves:
    I dream of fires in far-off garrisons.

II. Signal beacons shine ten thousand miles
    Where Chinese troops subdue a barbarous land.
    Sand covers over pallid heaps of bone,
    Yet winds of longing chill this peaceful town.

III. I know the seasons of the distant west:
    The snow-fed rivers' surge, the great heat's end.
    There, subtle spring greens late down thin arroyos,
    But when, in Chang-an, do the pale plums bloom?

IV. A prince might pitch a tent on palace grounds,
    Desiring life where hoarfrost decks vast steppes.
    Though sand and gravel make a hard night's bed,
    Behind silk blinds, one tires of painted towers.

V. Well said! Chang-an's a winter paradise.
   The capital's canals have frozen hard.
   Yet cool gems gleam year-round on Kunlun's
       peaks:
   White metal ramparts of the Motherqueen.

VI. Here, the winter speaks a courtier's tongue,
    Slick and glassy as the Serpentine.
    The west has neither flatterers nor parks,
    Only arid skies where stars shine clean.

When Snowclouds
Block the Moon

A mother weeps for her daughter's loss. Sickened by strong herbs and loss of blood, the younger woman's body releases her spirit to roam unconscious through the turbulence between heaven and earth. Seagem catches sight of it in her mirror and knows: Greenpearl's bereft of her fatherly lover, alone in the city of her begetter, dispossessed of a child that might have been. The mother puts her new writing brush aside, remembers her own losses, and weeps.

The Hsiao River Princeling stands near his beloved and waves helpless hands in the air. Each time he touches her shoulders to comfort her—that beautiful flesh of creamy gold!—Seagem bursts out in tears anew: "Oh, what right do I have to be so happy, a faithless wife, the murderer of the man I was wed to, happy here in coral chambers while my daughter lies sick and despairs?" Unable to touch her and unable to force himself to leave, the Princeling strokes only air.

His uncle, the vermilion dragon, hears the wails that infuse with sorrow the mother-of-pearl corridors of the villa and disturb his slumbers. Again! He finds this mortal woman strangely upsetting: she's forever flicking her eyes at him, asking him to run some silly errand in the human realm, and for some reason he always agrees. But this weeping is too much for him. His head aches with last night's wine and he wants only sleep. Enraged, he flies up, away from Cavegarden, bearing with him a tumult of black blustering clouds. A fearsome storm sweeps over the sky, dropping great flakes of snow on the city of Chang-an and blocking the moon from human view.

This is not right. Tonight is the first full moon of the new year, the last night of the Lantern Festival. By agreement of all concerned deities and spirits, the Heavenly Almanac for this year decrees clear skies right through till dawn. Though Seagem's daughter lies ill, the other men and women of Tang wish to wander the streets admiring lanterns and the beautiful white disk hanging in the heavens. Yet the driving winds and stinging white gusts of the vermilion dragon's watch keep them huddled indoors, grumbling and stamping their feet.

High in the keep tower of her crystalline palace, in a luminous banquet hall, the Moon Lady celebrates the festival with her seven students. Their mood is merry at first, but an intangible pall settles over them: beings such as they require the nourishment of reverence and praise. Making some excuse, the moonmaid White Aureole drifts to the open window and looks down past gem-studded gardens to the human realm. And cannot see it. Dark roiling clouds block the delicate, powerful rays that even now should beam upon the earth. White Aureole's glistening gown of undyed silk flutters in agitation as she hurries back to the Lady's ivory banquet table and reports.

Little Oyster exclaims in shock, but the next youngest of the moonmaids, a gifted rhapsodist named Selena, hushes her, and signals with a frown that she should listen to the Moon Lady's quiet response. Having glanced over to the window and seen for herself the unlawful storm, the Lady instructs her students.

"We shan't go through the grievance procedures on this one, my dears," she says, pausing to sip from a goblet of opaline elixir. "They'd tie us up for weeks of depositions and hearings and written memorials. The point is to clear the sky right now. Selena, you seem to be keeping your head rather nicely. I think this would be a good time to put the Dragon Chant into practice. Will you do me the honor?" She glances over at White Aureole, who seems a bit put out, and pats her hand. "Let me know what you think of her performance, dear Aureole," she murmurs. "Your keen observation tonight tells me you're ready to help me judge the younger ones."

White Aureole swallows a quick triumphant smile and imitates one of the Moon Lady's gracious nods. Selena looks nervous, but she moves to the window, draws in a deep breath of the chilly air, and begins a resonant invocation. Her voice is rich, musical, authoritative, efficacious. In every depth and abyss of the cosmos, leviathans and krakens, wyverns and hydras and huge komodo lizards writhe and moan. Cave-riddled ridges tremble, lake waters swirl, spring tides hurl themselves high upon the shores. The vermilion dragon knows, however, that he is the one who's summoned; groaning in protest, he hurls his sinuous body through the void, coiling it about the Moon Lady's keep tower. He pokes his popeyed, bewhiskered head through the window so suddenly that Selena loses her composure for an instant, and hastily steps back.

"Nicely done, don't you think, White Aureole?" says the Moon Lady, motioning Selena to return to her couch. "Oyster, pour a bit of elixir to ease your elder sister's throat. I myself will serve our honored guest." Thus she distracts the youngest moonmaid—who appeared to be on the verge of disgracing herself with a fit of frightened tears—and soothes the ruffled pride of this creature of storm and stress.

The vermilion dragon gulps down the opaline liqueur and smacks his lips. "Ahh, better," he says, "better by far." As he exhales blissfully, a tracery of frostflowers settles on the pearl-sewn blind rolled above the window. Down in the human realm, the storm lets up a bit. "You've cured my headache, madam, and I'm much obliged, though I must say I don't think much of this little scholar's coercive methods of inviting guests." He glares at Selena, but she, proud that her first formal Dragon Chant has worked so well, lifts her chin with dignity and gazes coolly back.

Inquiring in tones of sweet concern into the source of the vermilion dragon's upset, the Moon Lady hears his blustery tale of Seagem's noisy woe. "I've heard of her, the unwilling runaway," she says. And: "You say she wants this girl from earth to join her in Cavegarden Lake?"

The vermilion dragon is not so sure that *he* likes that idea, but concedes that it will probably bring peace and quiet to the watery Mother-of-Pearl Villa, which is all he really wants. After offering her scaly guest another cup of opaline elixir, the Moon Lady rests her cheek on one pale, slender finger, and thinks for a moment. Then she calls White Aureole to her side and in low tones outlines a plan. Meanwhile, the dragon's red-gleaming eyelids begin to droop contentedly over eyeballs only slightly less red. A shaft of moonlight breaks through the tempestuous clouds to shine on snow-heaped roofs.

Soon the plan's explained to the dragon, who nods, agreeing to carry White Aureole down to negotiate in Seagem's coral chamber beneath the waters of Cavegarden Lake and to bring her back when her mission there's completed. He hints that another cup of the liqueur would speed him on the journey, but the Lady ensures her student's safe return by promising instead an entire flask for his trouble when he brings her back. Scarlet nostrils flare with anticipated pleasure, and tiny icicles spring into being on the nine-branched silver candelabrum closest to the window. The dragon grins. On earth, half the snowdrifts melt away as a sudden warm front sweeps in from the south, taking the last clouds from the sky. Revelers in Chang-an wipe their eyes in amazement, and laugh, and carry their festive lanterns out into the streets.

Bravely, White Aureole climbs to the carved windowsill and

straddles the dragon's thick neck, seating herself just behind the bony plates at the base of his skull. Oyster gasps, and Selena takes her hand. The other moonmaids wave farewell, trilling out wishes for White Aureole's success and—as tactfully as possible—for no ill fortune in her dealings with the erratic dragon. At Felicity Hall in the Pingkang Ward, a half-blind gatekeeper lights a candle, now that the gale has died, and places it within a lantern shaped like a monstrous head. Its beard hangs long, its silver horns display bright tassels, its eyes pop out all gold and red. Beneath the pure light of the moon's perfect disk, the lantern beams back an answering glow. The silk stretched over its bamboo frame tints that glow to a rich vermilion.

Parrot Speaks: 14

Oh yes, Empress Wu was a bad 'un, right enough." Walleye scooted his stool over a few inches, following the warm rays of springtime sun that struck the courtyard wall behind us. "Now, they do say that all the brightest and wisest men of the empire were eager to serve under her, and I've heard more than one poetical young gentleman pass through that gate praising her for making poetry writing so important in the big exams. But for a woman to declare her own dynasty! I was just past twenty the day that happened, and you could have rocked me back on my heels with a kingfisher plume, little miss. I'll tell you that."

I shifted on my own stool. I'd heard enough of the old man's descriptions of the fifteen years after the Empress Wu stopped running the country through her husband and son and reigned in her own right. Mama Lu usually looked disgusted when that empress's name came up; she had moved the capital to Lo-yang for most of her reign, which meant poor business for the entertainers of Chang-an during Mama Lu's first years in the profession. Yet even she conceded all "that woman" had done in building temples and schools and spoke enviously of the vitality and beauty that the empress had preserved into her seventies.

Walleye mostly liked to talk about the scandals. She had had our Brilliant Emperor's mother killed, and any number of other opponents. He said her lovers—a Buddhist monk, a Confucian physician, and finally a pair of beautifully painted and powdered brothers—made the palace a nest of wanton depravity. When he got onto this subject, I sometimes thought of the Brilliant Emperor's many children: I believe he already had around twenty sons at that time, with many more to come no doubt, but of course he was not a woman.

"Why, she even sent her grandnephew off to marry a barbarian woman, in order to seal the allegiance of a khan!" He clenched his arthritic fist, and I remembered the stern soldier within this kindly old man. I knew it didn't bother him that imperial princesses were regularly married off to Tibetans or to Turks, rarely returning home to civilization. I thought about going back inside, but I could hear Mama Lu in the front room scolding Mistmaid and Amber. A few petals fluttered from a tree in the neighbor's garden, catching the sunshine as they fell. Crescent and Luna were taking a nap, and I felt lonely. Surely I could get Walleye onto another subject.

". . . told me that back in the early days, when she was still trying to get her husband's chief consort out of the way—" Walleye had been staring at his knotted hands, held out before him in the warm sunlight as if the heat might ease the pain in his joints, but now his head snapped up. "Well, she killed her own daughter to frame her rival, and it worked!" The indignation left the old man's voice, and his good eye fixed itself on my face. "Of course," he rasped, "the shocking thing is that it was a living child she killed, one old enough to toddle about, not a sickly infant that might really be an evil spirit come to worm its way inside a family. It's not the same—"

The freshening breeze brought a flurry of petals over the wall. I knew old Walleye hadn't meant to speak ill of anything I'd done, and everyone knows not to care too much for babies in their early days—so many die—much less something not yet formed into a child. But my skin chilled just the same, and I stared at the design of the petals scattered over the swept earth at my feet.

The silence bothered me. "Tell me something else about Empress Wu," I said hastily. "Something new."

He rubbed one hand against the other. "Let me see now. Something new. Ah, here's something a talented young lady like yourself might want to know. They say that just before she proclaimed her new dynasty, she set herself up as equal to the very creator of writing." He glanced at me again. "Not that I mind women who write, you know. I'm admiring of anyone who can do more than scratch out a word or two, like me. But what she did was, she made new written words, you see. New forms for old words, that is, and said they showed the meaning better. I call that tampering with things that oughtn't be tampered with, myself." He massaged a knuckle too hard, and winced. "But maybe you can put some of that into a poem?"

I laughed. "Tell me another story instead," I said.

"Well, well. As long as I'm on about the women, has anyone ever told you that it was Empress Wu's daughter, the Peace Princess she was called, that really put our Brilliant Emperor on the throne?"

I shook my head, and he looked about us cautiously, but Mama Lu's scolding voice was the only sign of life around Felicity Hall.

"Well, you know his majesty discovered, oh, years ago, that this Peace Princess was plotting a coup against him. But his majesty let her kill herself quietly at home, instead of having her head chopped off for all the court to gawk at like most of the other traitors, and why do you think that was?"

"She was his aunt, wasn't she?"

"Ah, but those things don't count for much when the royalty's scrapping for power!" His good eye flashed, and I saw for a moment the idealistic, youthful soldier he'd once been, loyal to his code and contemptuous of those who'd break with right eousness for gain. But then he looked around again, afraid of being overheard, and became once more the gossipy old man, sitting in the sunshine and talking more than he should. "But our emperor did owe the Peace Princess something, so he let her die with dignity."

I picked up one of the flower petals and asked him why.

"Let me see now," he said in lower tones. "It all goes back to a power grab by some other women, when the Brilliant Emperor was still a young and unimportant prince. The Empress Wu died at last. Her son had been placed upon the throne. I must have been about thirty-five then. But it was the new emperor's wife, Empress *Wei*, and their daughter who ran things, you know, and there was no love lost between them and that emperor's sister, the Peace Princess.

"Anyway, after five years Empress Wei and the daughter killed the emperor by putting poison in his favorite cakes. At least, most folks think the story's true. The women set his last son, a boy no more than your age, young miss, on the throne. He was the Empress Wei's own son, you see, so she figured to rule through him as dowager. Two weeks later, though, our Brilliant Emperor and the Peace Princess's son rallied some of us Palace Guards and took the palace. The Empress Wei was killed trying to escape, and they got her daughter while she was putting on her fancy makeup." He chortled, and the gaze of both eyes, the good one and the dead, fixed far away. "There was another woman in the Wei clique, Shuang-guan Wan-er, who'd worked her way up from a palace slave and had been practically running the civil service exams. Wild for poetry they say that one was! She tried to change over to th'other side that night, but got herself killed for her pains."

So old Walleye had once been in the palace guard. I didn't want to hear any more, yet I couldn't stop listening: the sinuous history had me caught, as they say snakes in the faraway birthland of the Buddha catch birds with their eyes and dance before them the story of their deaths. Seeking some distraction, I reached into the pocket of my jacket and found a broken hemp-seed cake wrapped in a handkerchief. Walleye took half when I offered it, but his voice reeled out unstopped, describing that stifling summer night of the coup, the way the men's warrior shouts and the frantic voices of the women had rung through the long galleries of the inner palace.

I held my half of the cake uneaten. "How do you know it was the Peace Princess behind the move against the Empress Wei and the others?"

"I was there! Besides, who else had the connections and the money to make a coup on the palace itself succeed?" Again, his good eye went steely. "Remember, the Brilliant Emperor was only a concubine's son and had two elder brothers besides. He didn't have the standing to carry it off without her help."

"But I always heard he took the throne on his own, for his father's sake, and only ascended himself when heaven sent a comet to tell his father to abdicate."

"Oh, it's true about the comet. The government under the Brilliant Emperor's father was completely out of control. But don't you ever say that to anyone!" A tone of command leapt into his cracked voice for an instant, then faded as he continued. "The Peace Princess was running things—a woman in charge again!—through her brother, which was why she'd set him upon the throne in the first place. Things went her way for the next two years, you can be sure of that. Why, the Brilliant Emperor himself even got his father to recall his aunt from a banishment. But the comet came, the old emperor knew it was time to step down, and that was that. It was only a matter of time until the Peace Princess went. She'd already tried to poison her nephew once, but then she attempted that second coup and he couldn't let her stay around to make more trouble."

The story stopped at last. I crumbled a few seeds from a bit of the cake, and they fell among the petals.

"That's when I lost the sight of my eye." Walleye returned

from the maze of bygone days, though I don't think he knew, or cared much, whether I was listening now. "Not in the failed coup, but in the first one, against the Wei group. Some vixen of a lady-in-waiting nicked my eye with her dagger." He snorted. "Much good it did her! My own commander treated me well enough after that, but it was General Li who really helped me, got me a place when they mustered me out and all. Said it was a shame they wouldn't use a disfigured man in the palace of the Son of Heaven, considering how I'd come to be that way."

His voice trailed off, but mine burst forth, "General Li? Of the Palace Guard?"

"Oh yes." He smiled into the past. "Haven't I told you about him? He wasn't one of the three commanders they brought into the coup, but I'd been transferred over from his unit just a few months before, and he'd always had a liking for me. Said I was a real soldier's soldier. He wasn't a general yet in those days of course, but later he was and they sent him off to command a garrison out in the far west."

It seemed forever until I got him to confirm what my heart had known right away: this General Li was my own father. Some part of me still wanted to keep the secret of who I was, but when I described Baba's tiger tattoo and told Walleye how I'd been captured by the Tibetan raiders he struck his palm with his fist, then winced.

"Death-bound dogs of Tibet!" he muttered. After I mentioned those enemies of the empire, I needed add nothing else to win over the loyalty to my father he'd carried for years.

"The little daughter of my General Li!" he exclaimed with joy. "Well, well, Miss Bordermoon, now I know why I took to you. 'She has an air of quality about her,' I said to myself, first thing. A warrior's daughter, that's what you are, and it didn't escape this old soldier's eye."

Walleye was glad enough to talk about his hero. As the sunlight moved on, I found out where Baba's family home was, in a ward not far away. Then before we could talk further, Mama

Lu called me in, upbraiding me for sitting around in the court-yard when the first guests of the day might call at any moment.

"I've been thinking of how to handle your career, Miss Bor-dermoon," she said over her shoulder as her skirts swept before me through the reception room. "The reputation of Felicity Hall is on the rise, I'm sure of it, and now that you've come out of your shell, and the men are beginning to talk of your music and—" She turned to give me a look that made me cast my eyes down. "And your other charms, I think we'd do best if you stay a bit aloof. The Lady Guan-yin knows that suits your personal-ity, and with spring here the gentlemen will be ready to compete for a popular new beauty who seems unwilling to form an at-tachment. Yes, we'll be sure to have you circulate a bit, but don't seem too eager." She stopped and faced me, rubbing one of her green jade bracelets voluptuously with her thumb. "We have a good season before us, I feel sure."

Now that I'd found out where my mother lived, I was im-patient to put this life behind me. After several talks with Wall-eye, I came up with a plan. I was only allowed to leave Felicity House on the eighth, eighteenth, or twenty-eighth of each month, after paying Mama Lu a string of cash, and even then I was supposed to go no farther than a temple in the Pingkang Ward. But a certain friend of Amber's never left her room before midday when he stayed over. I would steal out before dawn and be ready to leave the ward when the morning drum sounded and the big gates were opened, riding the beautiful white mare that belonged to Amber's friend. That way I could travel quickly, and in a suitable style, without attracting attention by renting a se-dan chair.

I wanted to go alone, so I persuaded Walleye that it was far too risky for him to leave his post at Felicity Hall. "Right enough," the old soldier said. "I'll take care of things here for you."

So I dressed quietly in the darkness of my room, choosing a blue-green brocade dress, and a tight jacket with a higher neckline than most. I added a brightly patterned stole for modesty. The little "barbarian headdress" had already come into style for ladies of the upper classes, but instead I put on an old-fashioned broad-brimmed hat with a veil that came to my shoulders. I didn't want a chance meeting with some visitor to Felicity Hall to let my secret out, and besides, my mother and my grandparents might not approve of the new and more daring fashion, which displayed a lady's face. It could have occurred to me to wonder if they would not disapprove of other things, but it did not.

I felt strange, riding that horse down the lane away from Felicity Hall. I'd gone out to entertain at banquets, and once or twice a month Mama Lu took us to visit a temple. But now I was on my own, astride a beautiful horse with silken tassels hanging from her bridle. Her narrow, dished face revealed her descent from the big horses of the Arabs, perhaps one of those presented to the court in the days of Empress Wu; she stood taller than the stocky Mongol ponies I'd ridden before. The dawn drum sounded, and the ward gate creaked open. I hung back until a worried-looking scrubmaid, a few gentlemen with bleary eyes, and a sly-faced groom in the high boots and knee-length coat of the west had all gone on through. Then I rode out into the expansive avenue, happy and alone.

At first I wanted to toss my hat into the ditch beside me. I was the daughter of the heroic General Li, returning home to my mother's side at last! Why did I need to hide my face? Then there were moments, as the light rose and more people filled the streets, when I was glad for the veil and the distance it put between me and that multitude of strangers. I was not used to seeing so many new faces when I had no companion. Still, the white mare stepped proudly, as if she exulted in her exotic looks that set her apart from the common run of horses. And for once I felt the same.

That mood soon passed. I suppose I expected the Li family gatekeeper to summon my mother, who would sweep me in her arms, and crying tears of joy would lead me in to kowtow happily before my father's own father and mother. Then my grandfather would take me on his knee as Baba had, and my grandmother and mother would pet me, and listen to my stories, weeping and gasping by turns, and praising me for all I'd endured so well.

But our histories of the future have no more truth about them than our rehearsals of the past. I found the house with little difficulty. The crimson lacquer of its gateposts was badly chipped and cracked, yet the gatekeeper answered smartly enough. And closed the gate smartly, too, after I had given him my tale. "Be off!" he growled, squinting up at me. "What proof do you have for this reckless talk? We've trouble enough here without lying gold diggers like you. Go away before I call a bailiff and have you carted off for fraud."

Having no other choice, I left. I told Walleye what had happened—it took only a moment—and stayed on watch in his room by the gate while he quickly put the white mare away. When he returned, he wanted to talk of other plans, but I only shook my head and ran off to my room. The solitude I'd relished an hour before made a poor companion now.

Walleye thought of a new plan soon enough, but it was to be some time before we could put it into effect. That afternoon Mama Lu began preparations for our performances in the park along the Serpentine; the flower-viewing season was at its height, and she had managed to get one of the city magistrates to sponsor us in a recital in the Waterlily Garden there. She kept after us to practice every moment we weren't entertaining guests. The dressmaker came each morning. The whole house was in an uproar of music and cutting and stitching.

I was glad to have the distraction of the festivities to come. And glad, I must admit, that I would have the chance to play my lute and sing a set of lyrics of my own composing, though a nervous tightness gripped my chest.

The day dawned clear and spring-warm. Felicity House was

left in the cook's charge, and even Walleye came along to help with the arrangements. Our hired carriages left us near Purple-cloud Tower in the southwest corner of the park, and more than one head in the throng of strollers turned as Mama Lu led the six of us slowly north toward the Waterlily Garden at the far end of the park. It seemed that half the city had come to enjoy the springtime, and then it came to me that Baby too might be there, somewhere in the crowds.

I was uncomfortably conscious of the stares as we walked along an avenue of crab-apple trees in full bloom. Would I be able to play well before so many people? And yet the park was so beautiful that I soon regained my inner privacy. The shores of the Serpentine glinted green with new grasses and young willow leaves. I caught sight of a pair of half-tame teal leading their ducklings among the blossoms reflected, and fallen, on the clear water. The first of the redbuds were out, and the last of the white-petaled pear trees filled the air with flying foam.

Sparkling-eyed Bouquet and languid Mistmaid, as the two eldest, walked first behind Mama Lu, the kingfisher-feather ornaments in their hair wavering and glinting with every step. Crescent and Luna followed hand in hand, eyes downcast as suited little apprentice entertainers. But none of us could resist stealing a glance when a palace eunuch trotted by on a dainty horse, bearing a carry box of food toward the screens and canopies set up atop a little rise for the empress and her party.

Walleye, two hired bearers, and the four maids—fashionably dressed as Persian boys—lingered some distance to the rear. That left pretty, dark-skinned Amber to walk with me. I was a bit surprised when she took my arm, but pleased, too.

Amber seemed to sense my nervousness and did what she could to distract me from my thoughts. She whispered that the unusually snowy winter had dampened the emperor's New Year's entertainments in the park. But today, every pavilion was filled with picnicking courtiers, and many of the best families had pitched bright damask tents where they could drink with their friends.

Mistmaid began our first program with a solo piece on the classical stone chimes. Despite the glitter of the golden phoenixes embroidered on her robe, when she knelt on her cushion and began to play, I felt the austere beauty of the melody soaring above the scenery's springtime lures. Some of the tightness in me eased.

Then Amber played two songs on her harp of paulownia wood, one gentle, one rather lively, just as Amber herself could be gentle and lively by turns. After that, all of us finished off the first set of performances by singing together seasonal songs from the south. They went well, but my solo would open the second program. My chest grew tight again.

The crowd of watchers moved on. More people filled the walkways and lanes now, some already tired, some newly exhilarated by the weather or the wine. They stepped aside reluctantly for ladies and gentlemen on horseback or in flowery carriages with vines and leaves engraved on their sides. Mama Lu led us toward a pavilion and chose a little knoll some distance back where we could stand and watch. She plumped her lips and told us we were about to see the dancers of the Imperial Teaching Quarters.

This was my chance to learn if Baby was still at the Imperial Dancing School! *Good Lady Guan-yin*, I breathed, *let her be here today.* But a Kuchean drum fandango and then a saber dance blazed across the stage and I saw nothing of my friend.

I did see for the first time one of the tiny-footed palace ladies who were said to be setting a new fashion for feet no longer than a hand's width. Amber took my arm again and told me how the bones of the growing foot—held tightly by the wrapping-cloths— bend nearly double; the young girls it is done to weep with pain for months. I fell silent. Then a sprightly new tune swirled up and filled the space between us.

A troupe of perhaps forty young women clad in green came out to perform a "flower dance," turning their lithe bodies and forming the characters for "long life," "flower," and "wedded bliss." Their arms waved rhythmically and their long, fluttering sleeves cast their spell. It was several minutes before I noticed that one of them was Baby. At the end of the dance, she pattered quickly off the embroidered rugs atop the stage, before I had any chance of catching her eye.

A soloist appeared. Despite my mood, my attention was caught up by her spectacular performance. Four times she flung off a gauzy layer of her costume, transforming the colors of her dress each time the tempo of the music picked up speed.

Bouquet turned from her eager perusal of the audience and asked in condescending tones if I had ever seen the like of these dancers. I said I thought them splendid.

"But there are better to be seen, Bordermoon," she said, assuming the air of one introducing a dear but too-familiar garden to an outlander one knows will be impressed. "The best from the Teaching Quarters enter the Brilliant Emperor's own Pear Garden Academy. And I've heard that in her day the Empress Wu once choreographed a performance for nine hundred—now that must have been a sight indeed!"

Before I could answer, a pair of dancers burst forth, wearing Soghdian pantaloons and twirling atop great rolling balls. The one on my left was Baby. Without thinking, I left Bouquet and began to slip past the other watchers toward the stage. A gang of streetboys pointed toward me, and two noblewomen in pearl-trimmed capelets stared with annoyance—and curiosity—at the brazen courtesan brushing past them. But as Baby leapt high off the scarlet ball and threw herself forward in a stage bow, I broke through into a little clear space. Her face swung toward me and set itself afire with happy recognition.

Her partner took her hand. The two ran offstage, leaving me determined, now that I knew I could travel about the city on my own, to see Baby again immediately. I turned to hurry back to the others on the knoll before Mama Lu decided she should show the onlookers how carefully the entertainers of Felicity Hall were chaperoned. I nearly bumped into a young man I'd seen before, Dreamdragon Feng, the failed examination candidate. He must have been directly behind me when Baby looked our way.

The amused look he gave me implied that he had caught me out at something, but that there would be an agreement of silence between us. I drew myself up, finding it easy to let him see I thought he went too far. Easy too, after that, to fold my hands together in my soft sleeves and bow respectfully in his direction with an ironic but not inflexible courtesy. He bowed in return, and I walked off a bit more slowly for the knoll.

After one more number the dancers' performance ended. The six of us, led by Mama Lu, drifted back toward the Waterlily Garden. We made ready for our second program, and my other concerns dropped away as my solo neared.

I stood alone on the platform, swaying slightly, and played the first notes of the melody on my lute. There were more people listening than there had been earlier, yet they all fell quiet as the song spun itself through the warm air. Only ten days before, listening to those folk songs from lost southern dynasties that we had learned to sing, I'd felt a set of lyrics rise within me, and Mama Lu had said that I might perform them in the park. Bending one leg, I placed the sole of my foot against the other knee, curving my body to balance my stance as Bellring had taught me to do so long ago, and sang:

> In early spring I wander out,
>   I gather sameheart grass
> To tie a lover's knot and send
>   it off, to battlefields.
> But a soldier's posting takes him far,
>   and woven herbs are frail.
>
> When women dream of warriors,
> Bitter, thoughts of love.
> Bitter, thoughts of love:
> His hazy, distant face.

Though summer dries the river's banks,
this longing will not end.

Amber had said this year's flowers were unusually profuse because of the heavy autumn rains, but I think any spring in Chang-an would have dazzled me after the parched greening of Liang-jou. Yet something else struck me that day. Only during the dark weeks just after I came to Chang-an had making music failed to bring me pleasure. This was the first time I had played for so many, though, and I liked it. It was not the crowd's stares when I stepped out from behind the screen at the start of our performance. It was not the moment when I saw a gentleman turn his face toward another black-capped official and wave a wine cup in my direction, as if to say, "Oh, yes, she's fairly new in town, but I've been keeping an eye on her for some time now." What dazzled me were the moments when I became transparent, when all of us, players and listeners, were caught up as melody and lyric said what each of us thought they had to say.

My joy in the performance, and in Amber's new friendliness, was swept aside by Walleye's news the next morning. "The trip back from the Serpentine gave me my chance," he said. "I passed by the Li compound and had a quick word with an old comrade of mine who works as a gardener there now." His face was grave, as if he were making a report to my father, but he couldn't hide his satisfaction at his success. "He's agreed to persuade the gate-keeper to let you slip into the place and try your luck. I'm afraid he hasn't got the influence to arrange a proper audience for you with your grandfather, but this should do the trick."

After three long days, Amber's friend came again to stay the night, and again I rose early and borrowed his mare. I might have spared myself the risk of detection, and taken the time to walk, for of course the mare was put away by a surly stableboy at the

Lis' as soon as I arrived. I was left thin and childish, barely a woman at all despite my showy clothes, and so tongue-tied that I envied Baby's muteness.

The old gardener greeted me hastily in the great courtyard of the mansion. Looking past him, I saw that one wing of the house must have been empty for years. As I stared at those cobwebbed windows, the gardener told me what he hadn't had time to explain to Walleye: my father's mother—Grandfather's proper wife; he knew little of the long-gone Turkish concubine—had died only a few months earlier. "The master's grieving heavily, miss," he said, "and I can't say as I blame him when I remember my old woman. I'm sorry about your loss, and sorry to be the one to tell you of it." He hesitated. "Perhaps it will be your good fortune, though. Perhaps the master will be eager to take you in."

Unfilial though it was, I put the thought of this lost grandmother aside for later, so eager was I to see my mother. Then, when the gardener looked away and told me of her mysterious illness and disappearance, I went blank and stood in the deep morning shadows shivering.

"Go on now, miss," the gardener said, softening his old man's voice as best he could. "I'm terribly sorry for both losses. It's been so long since Mistress Seagem was spirited away that I thought you surely knew of it, or I'd have had a word with Walleye. Anyway, it's your grandfather that can care for you if he chooses. He's at his sharpest early in the day. You'd best go inside."

He led me along a corridor to a room where a dusty-legged table was laid with a morning meal for one. I followed absently. "This is the girl," he said to a tight-faced maid who brought in a steaming bowl and set it on the table. "How is the master this morning?"

The maid shook her head and bit her lips and sniffed at me. "Look at her!" she said to the gardener, as if she sensed that I was too far away to speak to her. "Iranian or some such, isn't she? Do you honestly think she looks like the late young master?"

Before I could hear the answer, one I wanted very much to hear, a thick voice called out from a back room. The maid ran off toward it, and the gardener bobbed his head nervously toward me and left. In a moment, my grandfather bore down on me in a querulous ferment, demanding to know who I was and why I had come to bother him.

"You're a little singer, aren't you, girl?" He broke off abruptly to pick a thread from the patched sleeve of his scholar's robe, then jerked his head back up. "Did some unfeeling acquaintance of mine send you as a gift? Has the corruption of this age taken over even the few righteous men left in the city? Well?"

I began to tell him that I was his granddaughter, though it was some time before I got enough of the story out for him to understand it. He kept interrupting me to expound peevishly on the fallen morals of modern times, when licentious camp followers strutted freely into good men's homes. Later, I realized that though he himself was a retired army officer of undistinguished origins, in his zeal to be accepted by the old aristocracy, he had taken on the ways of the strictest Confucian men of letters. Then, I was simply stunned. As soon as I managed to stammer out mention of my father, the old man's white beard set to wagging. He denounced him as a bad son, one who'd had the effrontery to die before his parents did.

"Bad enough when he insisted on that runaway slut of a vulgar merchant's get for his second wife instead of marrying a daughter of one of the great families as he should have. But then he let himself get killed. He still had the responsibility of caring for my spirit tablet after I leave this world! He's a wicked, unfilial son, and I'll hear no more about him." His face worked then as a little boy's might before he bursts into tears. I could see that grief and age had driven him into the renewed childhood that awaits a few who live that long.

More than that I could not think. A voice inside me chanted,

This is not real, not real, a lying fantasy, all of it, never real, so loudly that it was impossible to decide what to do next. I mumbled the one bit of proof I had, the thing that in my picturings of this day had put any doubt of my identity to rest. "He, Baba, he bore the image of a tiger on the skin of his left arm—here." I touched a spot on my own upper arm.

The old man leapt to his feet and shrieked with rage. "Unfilial! Unfilial! Do not remind me of this shame. He mutilated the body his father and his mother gave to him! If he were alive, I would beat him to death right here. If he were alive—"

Again he broke off abruptly, and returned to his seat to search his worn cuffs for another loose thread, as if we had been discussing something of no moment. "Have you anything else you wish to say, little sly-tongued foreign prostitute, before you go?"

I feared another burst of his anger, but I knew I had to speak. "Don't you see? I am his daughter, the daughter of your son. I know about the, the sign on his flesh. You say it was unfilial, but it was there and I saw it. Doesn't that tell you who I am?"

"Oh," he said, in an aged aristocrat's suave tones, "the tattooed tiger?" He chuckled. "Who can understand the rash whims of a young military man? Yet we need such fellows to keep the barbarian hordes in line." Then he leaned forward across the table and spat, "And any little slut who tempts a man away from duty might know of it. Be off!"

He bellowed for the gatekeeper, who must have been waiting just outside the door. The tight-faced maid poured my grandfather's tea as if I were already gone. "Go," the gatekeeper hissed, loosening his painful grip on my arm at the shabby front gate, "before he thinks to ask how you got in. Tell that friend of the gardener's not to bring us any more trouble, thank you. I'll not let him in this gate again. The boy has your horse ready. Go."

Still numb, I mounted the mare and started out, not thinking much about what I did. My mother had vanished into some supernatural captivity, my grandmother had died, and the father of my father had turned me out.

The white mare picked her way around a carriage where a fat man in well-to-do merchant's clothes submitted to the scoldings of his needle-thin, bejeweled wife. Whoever my mother's parents had been, I thought, they were only commoners like these two. And even if I knew their names or could find them in this great city, I was convinced now that they too would call me "fallen" and turn me out. I clucked to the mare to hurry and swore I'd go to visit Baby soon.

PART III

In a Shrine Cave
South of Chang-an

In a shrine cave south of Chang-an, among the foothills of blue mountains, a young musician sleeps through this delightful summer night. Far to the west, in a silver-walled palace atop a much higher range, her father's mother has come at last to serve as an attendant to the Western Motherqueen. Months ago, at the grandmother's funeral, the few women remaining in a declining household bade her farewell until they should meet her again after their own deaths, at the moon gate into the Amah's fastness, there in the heights of the Kunlun massif.

Now the grandmother tremblingly approaches the Western Motherqueen, who sits listening to music near a cluster of snowjewel shrubs in her garden. The goddess's leopard tail lashes idly. The air around her is adance with what you may call (in a pretty myth of *quarks* and *electron clouds* and *charm*) "electricity," or (if your mind is of another bent) with the numen of the place. Beside the nearby Malachite Pond, six jade maidens play for the Amah their unearthly instruments: a thundercall flute, a Kunlun-stone drum, a cloudbreath mouth organ, a magicbeast lithophone, a set of jade chimes, and a Cavegarden-limestone gong.

Still attached to the human world, the new attendant has learned of the plight of her granddaughter, her only living descendant, and wishes to see her protected. Though the young woman sleeping in the shrine cave has been barred from her paternal ancestral hall, she has paid homage to her grandmother's spirit, and the grandmother has been moved. But she is awed by the goddess and loath to disturb her.

Finally the music ends, and the musicians rest quietly. The jade maiden who was playing the thundercall flute unrolls a bundle of silk and takes out fifty yarrow stalks. She sets one of them aside.

Looking up, the Amah deigns to notice the tentative approach of the new attendant and bids her speak. The goddess's tiger teeth glint and her flower-wild ringlets wave free as she hears of the granddaughter's unjust treatment, of the denial of her paternity.

"So the old man fears his own lusts and calls her liar and whore?" the goddess asks with an eerie whistling of her breath. "But this granddaughter of yours—does she know me?"

A bit uncomfortably, the grandmother explains that although the young woman does not worship the goddess, certain friends of hers do, a novice Lady of the Tao named Nephrite, for one. Some of the musicians are listening in, but the graceful flutist bends over the yarrow stalks in her left hand, absorbed, counting them out. From them, she will learn the state of the forces of yin and yang at this point in their endless flux and reflux.

"Enough! For your sake I will help, but since she is no devotee, by no more than the sending of a dream for comfort. Or perhaps—" The Western Motherqueen stops as one of her blue-black birds alights on a nearby snowjewel branch, bearing a report. She reads it. The flutist rests her relaxed, attentive gaze briefly on the messenger bird, then divides the stalks and begins to count again. Soon she will know the moment's brief balancings and impending changes, and so something of the meaning behind synchronous events.

The report comes from the Moon Lady, who was herself an attendant on the goddess, before she married the archer Yi, stole from him the immortality herb, and ran off to live on the moon. "Yes," the Amah says thoughtfully, "a dream—or something like one—with a message of comfort and a job to do."

In response to a summons, a jade woman in dark red petticoats brings a little table with the goddess's writing things and starts to grind the inkstick on its stone. But before the preparations are done, the Western Motherqueen looks up, as if she hears some distant, startling noise. "The moment's not complete yet," she says, and tells her attendants that there is another event in resonance with these. "Perhaps that's word of it now," she adds in an abstracted voice.

The grandmother can hear nothing, but she dares not speak. The flutist, who has finished counting the yarrow stalks, nods once, with the satisfaction of an expectation fulfilled. Then a rapid chiaroscuro flicker of variable starlight blazes and dims near the Western Motherqueen, in a gaseous swirl of photons and interstellar dust focused about a gibbering voice: *—my jurisdiction— —I told you before, a brash interloper— —I've waited months now— —Amah, please, I beg you, something must be done—*

It is Dame Shamanka Star, come (not for the first time) to beg a judgment of punishment against the mute human dancer who spoke prophecy without initiation, in a fever in Liang-jou more than half a year ago. The Western Motherqueen listens for a moment, then stills the riot of torn shrieks by lifting a hand.

Would the presumptuous little sybil not be a good candidate to serve the Shamanka Star? she asks. Those who can restore, if only for a moment, human communication with the divine are rare finds, the Amah reminds the Star. But the starlight blazes more wildly and a voice moans that the dancer has not been tested, that she is no initiate. The grandmother shifts as quietly as possible from one foot to the other, torn between her awful misgivings about the volatile astral deity who has burst on the scene in the middle of her petitioning of the Amah and her desire that her granddaughter's case not be forgotten.

But the coincidence of events is meaningful: the lives of the granddaughter and the little dancer intermesh. "My daughters shall have their wishes granted," says the Motherqueen in her hissing voice. "The mute who would speak shall be tested, the woman barred from her father's house shall have companions on her quest, and if they succeed, the bargain that the Moon Lady tells me she has made shall be fulfilled."

Again the Shamanka Star burns and darkens, darkens and burns, anxious to know more, but the Amah stills her with a single vexed tap from the rhodochrosite sole of a phoenix-patterned shoe. Then she dismisses the Star, and the more self-controlled grandmother, simply by gazing beyond them toward the flourishing blossoms of her orchard, where the peaches of immortality grow. She picks up her writing brush to send her approval of the Moon Lady's plan. Dame Shamanka Star vanishes. The grandmother steps with cautious delight toward the jade woman who has beckoned her to take a turn at the thundercall flute. The opening rhythm of the next composition reverberates, struck upon a gong made of limestone from a grotto deep beneath Cavegarden Lake.

Bordermoon
Leaves Chang-an

The story has been told of the voyage the Brilliant Emperor of the bygone Tang Dynasty made near the end of his reign to the castle on the moon, bringing back the enchanting melody to which his Precious Consort Yang danced. It is told, too, how long before that, another dynasty's brilliant emperor—Mingdi of the Han—met a moonmaid in the hills south of the ancient capital. This beauty was one of the seven students of the Moon Lady herself.

And now, members of the audience, listen today while I recite the tale of a young woman of Tang named Bordermoon who lived in the time of the Brilliant Emperor. She herself traveled to the palace of the Moon Lady years before he did, guided by a bare-legged moonmaid in a white gown.

It was the seventh night of the seventh month, the Festival of the Weaver Woman Star and the Cattleherd. In households across the empire, women of good families made music and feasted on cool summer melons. In towns and villages, in palaces and country homes, they stitched in happy competitions, matching their skill at needlecraft in honor of the Weaver Woman. The Star herself—that bright beauty whom the inscrutable peoples of the Occident call *al-waqi'*, or *Vega*—left her dwelling on the bank of the Silver River, which flows like milk across the sky. This was the one night of the year when all the magpies of the world gather, piping their excited cries, to form of their long black tails and brilliant white breasts a bridge across the astral river. Crossing that chittering bridge, the Weaver Woman met with her lover, the rascally, yellowish Cattleherd Star.

Dear members of the audience, I need not tell you that in normal years in the Chang-an region, the seventh day of the seventh month comes at the end of the rainy season, when the plump grains of rice and millet and wheat begin to ripen toward harvest. Indeed, the skies clear then because the Weaver Woman, preparing for her meeting with her lover or consoling herself after its end, spins and shuttles every wisp of cloud into ethereal fabrics patterned with the heavenly designs of the constellations themselves. Yet in this year, the twenty-first of the Brilliant Emperor's reign, it was not so. Like the year before, it was marked by repeated downpours and great floods. The Son of Heaven, misguided perhaps by traitorous advisers, had not performed the ancient ritual of plowing the sacred field to ward off natural disasters. Moreover, the Brilliant Emperor revered Taoism above the teachings of The Compassionate One: sad to say, the pious Buddhist monks of the capital were not called upon to chant scriptures and thus bring a stop to the rains.

But enough of these digressions. The rain did let up for a while that night, though the skies remained patched here and there by foggy scraps. The light of a crescent moon broke through to shine on needle-threading competitions and on the less homely amusements of dashing officials and the singers and dancers who were their companions. In the foothills south of Chang-an, an outing to a country temple had been arranged for a member of the Imperial Chancellory by a young man-about-town named Dreamdragon Feng. This Feng had recently attached himself to the chancellor as a kind of unofficial social secretary. Feng created pleasant times for the venerable official and casually accepted little gifts of cloth or silver in return. The young man had the extravagant nature typical of people from Shu, and made an amusing companion.

The gathering was a success. Feng had invited several entertainers and the chancellor had found one of them, a singer named Bouquet, especially delightful. Let us not become too talkative, however, but tell instead about another of the women invited that evening, a young lute player with a standoffish air, who went by the name of Bordermoon.

How did she look, you say?

> Stepping lightly as a mist, she drifts in skirts of clouds.
> And dancing wayward as a rainbow, twists a slender waist.
> Eyebrows arched like moth antennae knit: she longs for one
> As distant as the Cattleherd, cut off by a stream of stars.

Now, this Bordermoon came from foreign lands, and though others found her oddly beautiful, she herself was certain that people looked down on her because of her barbarian eyes. Others mistook her shy withdrawal for excess pride. Just who it was she longed for, even she could not have said, but late that night, she slipped out through the temple gate (where a half-deaf monk slept in the guardroom) and onto the pathway that led farther up the mountain. The Nineglow lanterns that had been set out for the festival were darkened, and the other revelers had gone to sleep at last in the rooms provided for them by the monks.

The Moon Lady, who is sister to the Weaver Woman Star, sent cascades of silvery light down to the human realm, so delighted was she that the skies had cleared. In honor of the festival, this goddess sat at her own loom, working at a cloth of moonbeams. Bordermoon made her way uphill by a radiance that glanced off the damp hard-packed earth and illuminated her way.

In a short while, her restless wandering brought her to a clump of yellow bamboo. The deep resonant boom of a stone gong sounded somewhere in the distance; she turned her head and saw a deserted shrine to the Western Motherqueen, set back into a cave in the side of the mountain. Making her way past the guardian bamboo, she ran her hands over the pillars carved into the rock in half-relief at either side of the mouth of the cave. A long ray of moonlight fell over her shoulder, striking a mossy altar. She thought of her paternal grandmother, recently departed from this world and gone to live with the Amah at Malachite Pond. She prayed.

Bordermoon felt easier then, but the fatigue of the long day settled on her now that her restlessness was past. She spied a whitish carpet, scattered with a design of clouds and magic mushrooms in indigo, lying in an alcove near the altar. With a sigh, she sat down on it to rest.

Now keep your ears clean while I tell how, after some time, a moonmaid in a nacreous dress that trailed off into vapors around her bare calves came and bowed before Bordermoon. "Come with me, please," she said. "My mistress wishes to speak with you."

Bordermoon found herself rising naturally and walking behind the moonmaid, who said her name was Selena. Though they entered deeper and deeper into the winding cleft of the shrine cave, a diffuse light, like luminescent water, shone round them and lit their way. Soon, Bordermoon heard a sound like the tinkling of jade pendants, and felt the chilly air that hangs near an underground river. There, a sky raft waited for them. The two of them stepped easily aboard, and the raft moved itself out into the current.

The tinkling of the water faded and the raft carried them into a purple mist. Then it ascended among the milky iridescences of the Silver River, floating up to the sky.

Selena took a dark red tally from the bosom of her gown. "This," she said to Bordermoon, "was sent to my mistress by the Western Motherqueen herself, signifying her assent to the plan my mistress has for you. Should you succeed, you will attain your heart's great wish."

Before the human woman could think of what to say to this scholar from the sky, the raft bumped gently against a crystalline bank. Following Selena, Bordermoon stepped through a field of silvery dust. Then they entered a passageway leading underground; it twisted and turned like a great burrow. At last they came to a library full of scrolls that glowed, each with its own cool light. Among them stood a calm and stately woman, her smooth face beautified by wisdom. She bowed toward Bordermoon as a gracious lady bows toward an underling to whom she wishes to give honor.

"I greet you, Miss Bordermoon," she said, "and thank you for coming at my request. I trust the journey was not too wearying?"

Bordermoon, dazed already by the appearance of the moon-maid, and the magical raft, and all that she had seen, could only shake her head and try to return the bow with one as graceful. All her vague longings for some other life vanished like the puff of sparkling dust that Selena was brushing tactfully from the upturned toes of Bordermoon's slippers. She wished heartily that she could return that instant to Chang-an and see no more of supernatural wonders.

The Moon Lady—for indeed, dear listeners, it was she—waved a hand and the room's unearthly light warmed and softened, easing the tightness in Bordermoon's wide eyes. "I have left this night's weaving aside," the goddess said, "to ask your help in a certain matter. Only a human can fetch the thing I wish for, and I may receive it only if it is freely given." Her voice frosted. *"Do you understand that?"*

Again Bordermoon nodded mutely, and the Lady smiled, her remote appeal shining forth as brilliantly as before. "A hard time is coming for Chang-an," the Moon Lady said. "Many people will leave. You would do well to become one of them. In any case, there is nothing for you there that you cannot take with you. But of course things will be difficult for you if you choose to venture forth."

She paused. "A prized inkstone of mine has been, unfortunately, lost. If you will go from the earthly capital to Mothbrow Mountain and fetch a certain stone for me, I will then return for your gift another—my assistance in finding the person you seek."

At this, Bordermoon's tongue loosened, and she let forth a flood of questions. The fact was that the one she sought was none other than her mother, who had been carried off years earlier to be a dragon's bride. But how—Bordermoon asked—did the Lady know this, and where was the mother now, and was she well, and how was Bordermoon to reach her?

The goddess laughed. "I cannot simply tell you all those things, you know," she said. "Humans do best when they do not read ahead in the books of their lives. But your mother fares well, and awaits your coming anxiously. Let me tell you instead how you can find this stone, and who must go with you on the search, and what means you might employ. Remember, though, that the journey will be a difficult one, and dangerous, and that your success is not at all ensured. Perhaps you would rather live out your life some safer way?"

Bordermoon almost said yes, and almost said no, and lapsed again into silence while the two words struggled inside her. "In all fairness," added the Lady, "I must tell you one thing. If you refuse the journey, you will soon meet an old official who will buy out your courtesan contract and take you as his concubine. He is deaf, and prefers boys to women for pleasure, but he hopes to have a son, though he will not. Your life with him would be neither greatly happy nor excessively sad, and it would be safe.

And after some years, these longings of yours would fade. Tell me, is that your choice?"

The voice that would say yes rushed toward Bordermoon's lips and nearly forced itself out. But she thought of a lifetime in the inner apartments of a rich man's home, stirred no longer by the passions of her music, or love, or the vague restless searching that she had lived with for years, and blurted out, "No!"

After that, the goddess explained to Bordermoon what was required of her. More will be told of this later. Bordermoon listened carefully, but she was startled when the Lady suddenly asked if she had a bit of writing silk. Surely, the young woman thought, the goddess has silk of her own, and no need to beg of me. And when she looked up and saw a moonmaid bringing in a tray with writing brush and ink, Bordermoon was more puzzled than before.

But just as Bordermoon took a deep breath in order to say cautiously that she had neither paper nor cloth on which to write, she felt a hard lump pressing against her stomach. There, beneath the knot of her scarlet sash, was the little scroll she had found long ago. Bordermoon had no memory of placing it there when she dressed, yet as she drew it out, she recognized the tiny dragon's head carved at one end of the slender sandalwood roller about which the cloth was wound and the faded pattern of stars on the ribbons that tied it up.

"Ah, that will do nicely," the Moon Lady said as she took the scroll. Ignoring the writing already on the smooth cloth, she added a few words in the blank space at the beginning. "I have told you what you must do, my child," she said. "The Western Motherqueen has sent these words for you. Learn to understand them, and you will know what is to come." With that, she bowed farewell and left through the far door of the underground library.

And what, you ask, did the goddess write upon Bordermoon's scroll?

One shall speak, and one shall sink,
And one shall seek the Way,
And two shall wield their starswords
Till the shuttle goes astray.

Listen to what follows and then you shall understand all this. But now our story divides into two strands. Let us put one aside and tell more of this Dreamdragon Feng, a former scholar and unsuccessful examination candidate who had fallen into a life of knavery and hocus-pocus. In truth, he longed to return home to Shu but feared the grief that knowledge of his failure would bring to his aging parents. He was not a bad young man—he preferred to make his living by catering to the whims of well-to-do companions rather than by outright deception. But with the aid of a clever servant named Sparker, he had worked out several conjuring tricks that had gotten him through more than one tight spot. Using them, he would pass himself off as a heterodox wizard. Indeed, besides this servant, only the old woman who ran Feng's cheap lodgings knew that the failed Student Feng and the Wizard Mimesis were one.

Now, the Moon Lady realized the difficulties that awaited Bordermoon and had decided that this Dreamdragon Feng and his servant would be useful companions for the young woman on her quest for the stone. Accordingly, after guiding Bordermoon back to the shrine cave of the Western Motherqueen, the moonmaid Selena appeared to Feng in his sleep, and conveyed to him the Moon Lady's wishes: that he comply with any requests that Bordermoon might make of him, for only in that way could he escape his probable fate, a painful execution for chicanery and the proclamation of his misdeeds throughout the empire.

The young man bowed before the unearthly beauty. When he awoke, his teeth chattered with fear, for he had felt the cold breath of ill-fortune on the back of his neck more than once. To spare himself exposure, and to spare his parents the shame of hearing their son's name trumpeted in every marketplace, he decided he had best comply.

So in the morning, when the sleepy entertainers and their gentlemen friends began the return to Chang-an, he was quick to agree when Bordermoon took him aside and stammered out her strange request. Indeed, so eager was his response that Bordermoon flushed with surprise. But then he described to her his dream.

Eight days and nights passed like the clicking of fingers. The moon swelled and All Souls' Night arrived. Wraiths of mist trickled along city alleys; clammy breaths of air glided down paths between summer's fields. The Buddhist cloisters and monasteries of the empire prepared beautiful displays of candles and flower cakes and artificial fruit trees, set forth as offerings to the spirits of the departed. In the Taoist communities, too, public lectures were given on suitable scriptures. Those who stayed home made their own reverent sacrifices to the dead, fearing the ravenous ghosts who wander the earth because no living person cares for their needs.

In their lodgings, Dreamdragon Feng and his servant Sparker donned the robes of a great wizard and his assistant. Feng's was made from a length of crimson silk given him by the chancellor, trimmed with satin in black and white. Embroidered words of power, the swirling circle of yin and yang, and other mystic signs covered the front and back. The padded soles of his high black boots stood more than five inches thick, adding to his stature and granting him an imposing pace. Sparker, bent under a heavy load of sacks and poles and other strange accoutrements, followed him as they made their way to the dancers' conservatory, not far from the Imperial Palace itself.

When they reached the gateway to the quarter, Sparker began to emit a series of weird moans, punctuated by quick high yips. Now, this wily fellow was no more a true magician than was his master, but he had learned the art of casting his voice so that it seemed to emerge from some other place, while his own lips moved not at all. Accordingly, after Feng rapped on the gate with his thick black persimmon-wood staff, the gatekeeper who poked his head out thought the eerie noises came from the head of the staff itself.

"Stand back!" shouted Feng in a deep and terrible voice, quite unlike his usual rather pleasant one. "Can you not hear the cries of my Great Empyrean Factotum Staff? This is the night of wandering ghosts, and I have determined that there is dreadful trouble in this place. Stand back, I say! Stand back!"

The gatekeeper had no other choice, for the staff twitched and jerked in Feng's hand, and master and servant stepped quickly over the threshold and into the courtyard. Before the man could speak, Feng whirled on him and snapped. "The gate, fool! Close the gate. I refuse to be responsible for any evil spirits that have followed me here, be they mountain demons or valley shades, living cadavers or specters undead, ghouls or devils or hungry haunts. I, the Wizard Mimesis, Long-lived Grand Official of the Orthodox Covenant of the Great Unity, am come to help you in this accursed place on this most dangerous of nights. But I will not be responsible for the work of fools."

The gatekeeper's jaw dropped and his eyes widened. Swallowing hard, he scuttled over to close and bar the gate. Before he had finished, Feng—or the Wizard Mimesis—had stalked on with great rolling strides into the second courtyard of the quarter. Sparker tossed a contemptuous look over his own shoulder and hurried after his master.

The dancers were gathered in the courtyard, where a shiny roast pig formed the centerpiece of a great banquet offered up to the dead. Though the air was already heavy with incense smoke, the Wizard announced himself by shouting, "More incense! More incense! I am come to perform a hazardous exorcism, but however great the risks I am willing to take for your sakes, even I cannot succeed without cooperation."

All eyes peered through the haze toward the two strangers. Several of the dancers gasped, and the newest apprentice let out a tiny shriek. The staff twitched and yipped. "You!" the Wizard Mimesis shouted. "And you, and you, and you. Light more incense, quickly. Light every stick you can find, if you value your health. And you, girl. Snuff those candles over there. Now!"

Those he had pointed to rushed to do his bidding. Then one gimlet-eyed, wiry old dancing instructor stepped forward from the dumbstruck crowd. "Stop," she said. "Snuff no candles. Light no incense. Not until this interloper tells us who he is to barge in here and order us about."

Now it was Sparker's turn to gasp as if in fear. But before anyone could say anything, the Wizard's staff wrenched itself free and flew toward the old woman. The Wizard merely folded his arms across his chest, in the pose of one determined not to interfere with a just punishment, but as the staff screamed a terrible scream of rage, the servant dropped his bundles with an awful clatter and hurled himself forward to intercept the heavy stick in its flight. Catching it in both hands, he fell to the earth, interposing his body between the gleaming persimmon wood and the ground. He writhed and twisted like one engaged in a wrestling match with death itself. Except for an occasional wheeze of pain, Sparker was silent. The staff, however, yipped and cursed and vowed vengeance on all unbelievers.

At last, it was subdued. Servant and staff lay like exhausted lovers on the beaten earth of the courtyard. The new apprentice sniffled nervously in a corner. The Wizard Mimesis flicked a hand in the direction of the candles, and two Turkish dancers bustled over to snuff them as quickly as they could. Someone else stepped tentatively toward the offering table and began touching new sticks of incense to the glowing tips of those already burning. One by one, half a dozen others joined her. The wiry old woman shrugged and snorted and walked off toward her room in the farthest courtyard. No one else said a word.

"Let her go," the Wizard boomed, shaking his head in mournful resignation. "Let her go. Her soul will repay its debt to this brave green-clothed lad here sooner or later, in this life or another. It is all one to me." He turned a fierce glare on the staff. "You, Banished Immortal Undersecretary of the Jade Emperor's Heaven of Uppermost Purity, arise! You have done well to summon me to this ghost-ridden place. Now return yourself to me and hold your peace."

At that, the staff jerked an arm's length into the air above the servant's chest. He did not loosen his grip, but crawled and stumbled after it like a criminal being dragged behind an oxcart through the city streets. Only when the Wizard himself grasped the thing did Sparker let go, collapsing before his master's feet. The staff sent forth a final defiant scream and spoke no more.

"Now," said the Wizard in patient, wearied tones, "I will find the one my spirit-staff has brought me here to seek. It was told to me in a dream"—and here, dear listeners, he spoke the truth—"that you have here a young dancer who cannot speak." Eyes widened, and more than one face turned toward a slender-waisted, round-faced girl who stood near the doorway to the central hall. "Wait!" The Wizard's voice rang out harsh again. "The staff will find her." With that, he pressed one hand against his forehead and followed the staff as it twisted and jerked in his fist.

The crowd of dancers stepped aside to avoid the Wizard as he groped his way toward the round-faced mute, who stood straight and unmoving, half defiant, half paralyzed with fear. "This is the one!" he cried as he came to a stop before her, and again several people gasped. "A curse of silence has been laid upon her, poor thing, by—"

The Wizard paused for a moment, his face frozen in the wiped-clean look of an actor who has forgotten his lines. Then the staff spoke in quavering tones: "a curse from one who died by violence and cannot rest." A shade flickered deep in the mute dancer's eyes, and the Wizard nodded as if satisfied. In the gathering shadows, Sparker cleared his throat.

"More than that, I cannot say," the Wizard proclaimed. "But I can tell you this: on this festival of ghosts, one of three things will happen. The girl will be cured. Or she will die. Or she will bring death to those about her."

Now the other dancers stepped farther away, but the round-faced one only set her lips together and bit them hard. "Do not fear, little one," the Wizard said quietly. "For even should you chance to die this evening, I can bring you back to life, if I am allowed to have my will." Then he whirled on the crowd and his voice was loud and rough again. "But if another dies by incurring the wrath of the spirits, I can do nothing to help. Now let the ceremony begin!"

Sparker began to move among the assembled watchers, urging them to sit quietly on the benches that lined the walls of the courtyard and to join him in chanting a secret mantra of great power, which they were not, under any circumstances, to utter idly in the future. Next, taking up a handbell from his bundle of paraphernalia, he began to ring it gently in rhythm with the purifying chant. Through the swirling smoke, the dancers watched while the Wizard wrote magical words upon a sheet of splendid red paper and gave it to the mute girl to hold.

"Let the woman who is responsible for this poor creature step forward," he commanded, and a timid-looking beldame who looked after some ten or so of the younger dancers inched toward him. "Good," said the Wizard after staring for a long moment at her face. "Do not fear, good woman, but go light one of the candles and bring it here." She hurried to do so, and when she returned, he took her aside and spoke long and gravely to her, passing the candle's flame back and forth before her face and instructing her in low, even tones as to her role in the ritual to come. The others watched, continuing their chant, as the tension in the beldame's shoulders eased. She nodded her head in agreement to all the Wizard said. Then she walked without haste to a bench and sat staring like one who neither wakes nor sleeps.

Holding the candle beneath his face, which took on a terrible aspect in the smoky twilight, the Wizard began his conjuration:

I call on all the maidens of the moon,
I conjure up Shamanka Star herself:
Send your light to aid this spell of mine!
Bind up the evil spirit! Cast it out!

The mute girl quivered, but she did not speak. The Wizard gestured to his assistant, who drew from the larger of his sacks a leather wine flask. He gave it to the girl to drink. "Three sips, no more," Sparker hissed. "And remember, all shall go well with you."

For a moment, it seemed the girl would refuse, but Sparker resumed the ringing of the handbell, and the candle flickered, and the chanting of the mantra swirled amid the incense smoke, and she shrugged and drank. Sparker took the flask from her and squatted near her feet.

The Wizard now began to step with the dragging pace of one who dances a ritual dance among the stars, invoking the gods and goddesses of the astral realm. Finally, he raised his persimmon-wood staff high overhead, and addressing it again as Banished Immortal Undersecretary of the Jade Emperor's Heaven of Uppermost Purity, he bade it clasp the soul of the one who died by violence and carry it far away. Then he turned to the round-faced dancer and asked her if she could speak.

Her mouth opened. The chanting of the mantra died. Then her eyes rolled upward in her head, and she fainted clean away. One of the Turkish dancers rushed forward, but the Wizard held his palm up and ordered her to stop. He bent to check on the girl's condition. Sparker unrolled a length of heavy cloth between the two bamboo poles that had formed the bulk of his burden and carefully arranged the limp body upon it.

"Let the woman responsible for her step forth again," the Wizard said.

The old caretaker came up to him like one who walks about in sleep. Her face smiled and the other dancers took heart from her relaxed manner.

"It is not the worst," the Wizard said, as if to the beldame but loudly enough for all to hear. "But it is as I feared. The malicious ghost has disappeared. Yet as my spirit-staff wrenched it away, the ghost laid a final curse upon the girl. Now she is neither living nor dead, but if I do not take her off to the east at once and wash her in the waters of Tortoise Creek, she will die indeed. The rest of you need not fear. The talisman I have written out will keep you safe from harm, and in three days your sister will return full of happy chatter to resume her life among you once again." Bowing to the group, he gave the red paper talisman to the caretaker and bent to pick up the ends of the two bamboo poles. Sparker placed their other belongings beside the unconscious form of the mute and took up the other ends, that they might leave.

"Wait!" cried the gimlet-eyed woman who had doubted the Wizard before, emerging from the direction of her room. "Who grants you permission to carry off one of the dancers of the Imperial Teaching Quarters?"

The Wizard shrugged, and turning to face the caretaker, said to her, loudly and clearly, "Speak."

The caretaker blinked. "Let them go," she said in a dreamy voice. "Let them go, let them go. I am responsible for this girl, and I say let them go."

The gimlet-eyed old woman snorted and turned away. No one else said a word. The Wizard and his assistant, carrying their burden as casually as they could, walked from the second courtyard into the first, where the gatekeeper made haste to swing open the gate.

"You'd best hurry, sir," he made bold to say. "They'll be sounding the curfew drum soon."

"Hurry we shall," said the Wizard, never once breaking stride. Most of the dancers remained sitting half dazed on the benches, though a few of the bolder ones were peeking through the doorway of the second courtyard. "Gatekeeper," the Wizard said in low tones as he passed out into the street, "if perchance the beldame in charge of this poor girl doesn't awaken in the morning, someone must say to her, 'The Wizard Mimesis bids you wake,' and she shall be as she always was. Those exact words. Do you understand?"

The gatekeeper gobbled some words of assent, and the two rogues vanished, carrying with them the one they had come to fetch. They hurried to leave the city before nightfall and took her not to anyplace east of the city, but southward, to the deserted shrine cave of the Western Motherqueen. Bordermoon had arranged to meet them there the next day. The drug they had given the little mute in the wine wore off by morning, and when she heard the two claimed friendship with Bordermoon, she smiled, and waited for the lute player's arrival at the shrine.

Now, as to how the two young women had become acquainted . . .

The text ends thus. I have not left anything out.

This fragment was discovered in a hitherto unknown 1644 edition of the great Ming Dynasty redactor Meng Long-feng's fourth anthology of tales written in the form of marketplace storytellers' "promptbooks." The volume, found in a used-book shop in Shaoguan, Guangdong province, had been torn in half. The last two sentences are a comment by the copyist upon whose work this unauthorized edition was evidently based. They are one of many signs of corruption in this text.

All Souls' and the
Full Moon's Light

All Souls' and the full moon's silk-white light disturbs the sleep of the living and the dead. Perhaps you too have known something like this, sometime toward the end of a summer. This is how it might have been: You were awakened that morning far too early, by bright beams from a disk still slightly flattened on one side. You buried your face into the pillow (a soft lump, feather-filled, no cool white-glazed ceramic brick). But you could not return to sleep, so persistent were the rays angling into the room through your window (a window, remember, made not of gauze or wooden latticework, but—remarkable!—of clear glass). The familiar things around you, even the flesh of your restive hands, all were changed, their color drained away. Do ghosts, you may have wondered, see only tints and shades of gray? You moved through the day remotely troubled, found yourself humming the song your mother used to sing. Then the sun's light faded, and the full moon rose.

But whatever happened (or will have happened) to you, it is others who are disturbed on the full moon of the seventh lunar month of the year (you call it A.D. 733.) this story has led you to. The usual ghosts are out and about: weeping suicides lurk near wells; proud patriarchs accept offerings of food and flowers—no matter how great the cost to the living—as their due; neglected souls linger at country crossroads, hoping to feast on the life-force of the unwary. And one particular ghost is stirred up anew by a trickster's random words.

One who died by violence and cannot rest, said the glib servant of the Wizard Mimesis, unwittingly invoking this moaning, wild-haired creature. In fact, this ghost did not cause the little dancer's muteness, but it has been linked to her since that feverish morning in Liang-jou when it possessed her body and made her speak. So when the false wizard, prattling, invented for his staff (which was not rare ebony persimmon wood, but only painted poplar after all) the name Banished Immortal Undersecretary of the Jade Emperor's Heaven of Uppermost Purity, and ordered it to clasp this troubling ghost and carry it far away, his speechifying did more than he ever thought it would. For there is indeed (remember?) a banished Undersecretary, who occupies himself with keeping track of the ghost, the little dancer, and all who have to do with the corporeal form taken by that talkative pearl, the Luminous Emerald-Green Lunar Essence Sprite.

So now the Undersecretary, astride a yellow crane, hovers unseen by mortal eyes above the second courtyard of the Imperial Dancing School. Now he catches sight of the ghost's streaming hair and reads in its full breasts and knowledgeable hips the signs of his own desire. And now the ghost spies him and sees in him some promise of brief release from its own agonized attachments to the subcelestial realm. The crane swoops down, invisible. The ghost rises toward the great bird and mounts behind the Undersecretary, pressing a half-round belly and eager nipples against his back. The humans gawk at other things. The crane soars through smoke and shadow and ethereal clouds. And behind a bank of cumuli shaped like haystacks, in a far corner of one of the lower heavens, the couple clasp one another in that deep embrace, and the ghost is relieved, for now, on this night of restless death, of those unnamed fears that woke, or wake, or will have woken, you.

Parrot Speaks: 15

*S*he would have seen me die before she saw me bear a child. I thought this as I crept by the full moon's ghostly light into the tiny side-garden next to Mama Lu's own room. Kneeling, I dug behind the drooping stalks of the peonies for the chest of silver ingots buried beneath her window. All Souls' was the safest night for this, or so I hoped. The maids had joked about how Mama Lu would drink a great deal that evening. Though Felicity Hall was closed to guests, she had drunk heavily indeed, growing red-faced and shouting out coarse jokes, first cursing each of us, saying we should be dead, then weeping in repentance and, finally, collapsing into sodden sleep. I suppose that was how she mourned the sweet-faced entertainer called Charmeur, whom Mama Lu had killed with the same herbs she'd made me drink. Listening for any break in the rough snores from her bedroom, I made a shovel of a broken roof tile, and quickly dug.

Although it was forbidden to us, Amber took me into that garden once, some months before, when the crimson peonies hung their domed, heavy heads. She had laughed softly as she told me—thinking little of it—that Mama Lu's hoard was hidden there.

But Mama Lu had heard our voices, that late spring afternoon, and beat us both with a willow switch until we promised never to go into her garden again. It wasn't such a terrible beating. She didn't know that the secret of her treasure hoard was out. She was angry simply because we had presumed to go into the garden that was hers alone; I believe it had some association with dead Charmeur.

I'd have taken the silver even if she hadn't beaten me. There was no other way to leave, no other way to rescue my mother. But when I found the chest, I was careful to remove no more than one ounce out of ten from the trove; Felicity Hall might need the rest. Walleye had been talking daily of the famine he said was bound to come. "It will rain all fall, Miss Bordermoon," he'd say. "I can feel it in my left knee, here, where the Tibetan arrow struck. Months of rain to come yet, and there's already flooding in the lowest fields. More of the harvest'll be lost this year than last, you mark what I say." Then he'd tap his kneecap with surprising ferocity and talk of how rich they said the land around Chang-an had been long ago, before the fall of the Han Dynasty, before the centuries of chaos when the old drainage and irrigation system broke down.

It wasn't fear of the famine that determined me to try to escape. It was the dream I'd had. "Dream" was what I persisted in calling it in my thoughts, for all that I had proof it was no ordinary dream. Every morning I looked secretly at the puzzling words newly written on the little scroll of silk I kept beneath my bed and every morning saw that they were still there.

I had another reminder of the mysterious charge that the Moon Lady had given me. The bare-legged moonmaid had pressed it into my hand as she bid me farewell: a necklace, a plain silver chain from which hung a small, oddly colored pearl. That next morning, when I uncurled my fist and showed it to Feng, he'd touched it lightly with one finger and then stepped quickly back as if afraid. He told me not to worry about Baby, but to meet the two of them and his servant Sparker with all the money I could manage, the day after the festival of All Souls'.

So I wrapped the silver up and told old Walleye that the bundle was a gift of old skirts and leftover festival cakes for Baby to share with others in the Teaching Quarters. He did not question me: it was the sixteenth of the month, and he'd let me slip out twice before on that date to visit her, posing as her cousin. I planned to leave the city through one of the eastern gates, hiring donkeys there in hopes that anyone in pursuit would not suspect that I was heading south and west to Shu, where Mothbrow Mountain stands. Feng said he would manage the official travel documents, or something that resembled them.

In helping me, Walleye had simply repaid a soldier's obligation to my father, yet it was hard for me to say good-bye with no more warmth than usual. He eased the gate open in the dim light. "I'm taking my lute," I said as I stepped out, slipping the strap of its oiled-silk carrysack over one shoulder and struggling to carry my heavy bundle as if it were indeed no more than clothes and cakes. "My friend—I promised her I'd play for her today."

"Good-bye, Miss Bordermoon," his cracked voice whispered. He stood as nearly erect as he could manage, rubbing the knuckles of one hand inside the other palm. It was the last time I would answer to that name. The dawn drum sounded. As I walked down the lane, I wondered if Walleye knew I wasn't coming back.

My hair was arranged as simply as a scrubmaid's; under my silk skirt and jacket I wore a plain shirt of cheap kudzu cloth and trousers to match. The knees of the trousers were patched and, after the night's digging, so dirty that I hardly looked like one of the rising minor stars of the entertainment world. Near the head of the lane I slipped into the recessed doorway of a house called Coupled Joys, removed my silks, and wrapped them around the lute for extra padding. I wasn't sure when I would have the chance to use the instrument, but I couldn't bear to leave it behind.

Edging past the breakfasters in the night market, I left the Pingkang Ward. Two mounted soldiers from the night watch passed me, joking with each other as they headed back to their barracks. Had they seen the flash of guilt on my face they would surely have stopped to question me, but I looked downward before they drew too near. Or perhaps it was the lies my clothing told that saved me.

After hurrying past the entrance to the Eastern Market, I drew near the city wall. Already streams of people passed back and forth beneath the watchtower atop Springbright Gate. Soon I spied what I wanted: a train of bearers leaving the city. The group straggled, and I found it easy enough to avoid the city guards by trailing along as if I were the last of the servants following behind. And so I left Chang-an, and the grandfather who refused to listen to my words, behind.

Thinking of the hot sun and the rains that lay before me, I gave an old woman a few coins for one of the woven reed hats displayed before her doorway. Her face cracked as she smiled at me and wished me luck. I thought of her as I rented the donkeys—perhaps that kept me from showing signs of nervousness—and though the liveryman may have wondered why I should want them, he took my money eagerly enough.

I'll need luck, all right, I thought as I mounted the lead donkey and kicked my heels against its sides. I looked up at the blue mountains where the others waited for me in the hidden shrine cave, and wondered if I really was right to leave. Even with a famine coming, was that city of my fathers truly worse than whatever lay before me on my journey toward a mother I had seen only in dreams? A cloud passed before the sun, and a few drops spat tiny craters into the dust beneath my donkey's hooves.

A Decree Regarding the Temporary Removal of the Court from the Western Capital, Chang-an, to the Eastern Capital, Lo-yang

Drafted by Lin Jian on behalf of the Brilliant Emperor, this eleventh month of the twenty-first year of His reign

It is decreed: Whenever We from time to time do make a state journey through Our realm, We do so in accord with the current circumstances of all Under Heaven. Recently the harvest in the area around Our chief capital city has failed due to disastrous rains which fell without ceasing. The contents of the grain baskets are scanty and the people do not have enough to eat. This being the case, how can We not be constantly troubled on their behalf?

Supplying the needs of Our court has become a hardship for the farmers. Such bitterness is not in accord with the benevolence with which We are accustomed to treat them. Furthermore, the recent omens in the starry firmament attest that by manifesting Our heartfelt pity for the people, We shall win the goodwill of the spirits of Heaven and Earth and thus bring benefits to all humankind.

All this being so, We ought on the sixth day of the first month of next year make a state journey to Our eastern capital of Lo-yang, to remain in that more fortunate region until a timely return to Chang-an is possible, not giving a moment's thought to the comfort We must forgo, but caring only that We may thereby bring happiness to the people. Accordingly, We order the appropriate authorities to make preparations, that Our requirements while on the journey may be met without unduly burdening Our subjects along the way.

We permit Our ministers to promulgate this decree. Furthermore, though it is a trifling question better decided among themselves, We grant the request of some of them to send the various petitions of all Our counselors regarding this matter to the Office of the Historians.

When Famine Comes

The famine of the Chang-an region in 733–34 was a minor one, they say. Yet who can imagine famine who has not lived through one? We may have known hunger, may even have known it when we did not will it so. But our bodies soon fed themselves, soon reasserted their bond with the earth's fertile dust and so kept themselves apart from it. Maybe in those brief fasts we had some taste of hunger's deep demands. Maybe we knew airiness, a dizzied freedom, the gluttonous satisfaction of the will to control. We did not know despair.

That was not famine. Food was always somewhere near, or would be soon. And the hunger was only ours, only one mouth's or at most the mouths of a few. Who can imagine the hunger of a city, its suburbs, the great sweep of wearied farmlands farther than the anxious eye can see or the wasted legs walk? Just as the starved body consumes its own meat, the land in famine shrinks, trees stripped of their leaves and bark, roadsides of their grass blades, clay banks ravaged to still the stomach's twist.

Still, they say this famine was a minor one, no more than one of many that struck the overpopulated capital region in the first decades of the eighth century, before the rice transport system from the southland was improved. After three years of severe floods, too much rainfall killed the crops, but that disaster at least left the soil ready for another day: it did not blow off, as after a drought, in great light-headed clouds. The royal court did move in grand procession back to Lo-yang, amid the grain-rich plains farther east, for did not Master Kung himself say that a sufficiency of food is one of the three necessities for successful governance? Or as someone else might have put it, hunger breeds revolution. Those who died were, for the most part, only the very young or the aged, along with a scattering weakened by illness or by loss of hope.

Prices rose after the harvest failed, and the markets emptied early. The good folk of the city hurried home with their expensive purchases, pinch-bellied, safe for another day. Secret stores were broached, fortunes made, wedding feasts postponed or canceled, jewels sold off cheaply, and a few more weeping daughters left their fathers' homes at an early age. Life in the Entertainment Quarter dragged. Plump bodies grew slender and thin ones, thinner. Still, the government's relief granaries sold off their stores below the going price, and for most people there was enough. The land, the farmers, the glittering phantasmagorical city rising and spreading above its foundation of fine-grained loess, would recover and grow fat again.

Perhaps it is possible after all for us to imagine a minor famine. Walk into your kitchen, stare at an empty bowl. *Know* you have no way to fill it. Listen for the wailing of children, drifting across the courtyard wall. You have seen a Persian trader's caravan, heard speech in long-dead languages, tasted rice wine fermented centuries ago, felt the silk brush of a dancer's skirts. You have taken part in this construction of a world from documents and unearthed statues and notes on scattered slips of paper. See now if you can imagine a famine, a minor one.

Billow Talk

"And now you'll stay with me," the Undersecretary says, as if the question were already settled. He leans back on his pillow cloud and stretches. When he wanted the woman, the womanly ghost who lies at her ease beside him, he felt a bit uncertain: if he joined with her, who then would he be? But now he has a name for her, or names, *inamorata*, *leman*, *ladylove*. It was, after all, a pleasure; and he is still who he is. Satisfied, he smiles.

For the ghost, it was pleasure, too. Briefly, rolling there among a skyful of cirrocumuli, each face silvered over as the other's mirror. Each became the other one's desire, the very thing that each one most desired to be. There was no *he* or *she* then, only *I* and *thou* and *we*.

But now the Undersecretary senses something's lacking and seeks to fill the gap with words: *mistress! wanton!* He thinks the language that he knows is the only right one. She shifts her

277

legs and rubs her lips together and dreams of other tongues. Then she stands, and shakes her hasty skirts down, and prepares to leave. "No," she says. "No go, you know. I'll go."

Which snaps him bolt upright. Hysterical gibberish! How can the wench refuse his offer? He meant never to throw her past up to her; he meant to give her a place within his household. It is the kindest thing he knows how to do. The *trollop, chippy, strumpet, tart!*

The heavenly bureaucrat stands up, too, and shows himself the taller, and takes up from a nearby creamy billow the robe that marks him as the man he is: Acting Assistant Controller of the Ministry of Babble, though inside he knows he's something more. Still, its emblems reassure him. Its colors are the prescribed ones, not the proscribed; they are the legal indicators of his rank. The insignia of his office are blazoned on it, emblems assigned him by the Jade Emperor Himself, as a father bestows his name upon his legitimated son. Once it's on, the Undersecretary blusters. He has generously offered to regularize this unlawful union. She will be his concubine. She'll stay.

The ghost laughs. Long-lashed eyes blink at him, astonished. A red mouth blows a kiss. And with that nonword's smack, the ghost goes airy, goes.

Now the Undersecretary mounts his yellow crane and flies off in a rage. The *hussy, pussy, castrating bitch, cunt, crack, slut, whore!* In truth, he's never acted like this before; his anger's born of confusion and of pain. He's what they call "a nice guy," and "a thoughtful lover." He meant to treat her well. Only, her rebellion, her rejection, her mere departure takes from him the thing he thinks he needs in order to define *himself,* for what can *male* be if there is no *female* who is different?

Enough. He urges his magical bird off toward the ocean. Once he swore eternal brotherhood with the Spirit-Lord of the Eastern Sea. He'll ask of him just one fraternal favor. The Undersecretary knows who it is the ghost loves. Loves like a daughter. Oh, he'll keep the Jade Emperor's commandment, watch over that greenpearl girl all right, although in truth he has recently been so bogged down in celestial paperwork he's lost track of just what she's up to. But no one said he couldn't get a friend to bring down upon her rain, and floods, and famine. Wait till the ghost-wench sees her baby starving. He'll teach that woman just what the meaning of *regret* is, teach her new lyrics, teach her to sing them to another tune.

Parrot Speaks: 16

The donkeys ambled past the sodden fields and clustered houses of the suburbs outside Chang-an. Rain showers stopped and spattered, spattered and stopped. Part of me wanted to hurry to meet Baby and Feng and carefree Sparker in the shrine cave where they waited. Another part savored this moment alone.

I had long ago noticed that I thought about myself—observed my thoughts and feelings as one might observe a landscape before writing a poem—more than most of the people I knew. Now there appeared in my reverie not self-absorbed Little Pink or pained, grasping Mama Lu, but a gathering of women—Bellring, Saffron, pretty Amber—whose goodness I loved, even as I realized how differently they experienced their lives. None of them was likely ever to tell the story of herself. Why, I wondered as I rode, was I compelled to do so, even when I was my only audience?

The rain picked up. To the east, heavy banks of clouds were rolling in. I hunched forward and shook my head. My wet shirt clung to my shoulders and back. Then I caught sight of a farmer in a straw cape leaning on his hoe to stare at me. All I could do was ride on and hope that no one followed. From the corner of my eye, I saw him shrug and return to piling a wall of mud along a drainage ditch.

It struck me that with my hat covering my hair, he might easily have taken me for a boy. For once, I wore no makeup, and I hadn't regained the weight I lost during the winter: even if my shirt soaked through, an observer at a distance would be hard-pressed to see the signs of my sex.

Yet it was my fifteenth summer, two years and more since I'd become a woman. Had I grown up in my father's house I would surely have been leaving it soon for another man's. Instead of learning to make music, and write, and all the ways of artful conversation, I'd have sat beside my mother as she taught me how to weave and sew, how to manage the servants and the moneys of a noble household. Perhaps if that had happened I would have grown up without all this strange inwardness and would never have had occasion to wonder what or who I was, as the farmer might be wondering even now. I clucked to my donkey and soon found the pathway to the yellow bamboo before the cave mouth of the shrine.

Baby flew to greet me. Feng clasped his long-fingered hands and bowed his ironic bow, as if he held a post no lower than head of the Imperial Chancellory. Sparker ran his fingers through his sparse, shaggy hair and looked from me to Baby as if he knew something amusing that I did not. Though I felt we'd be safe waiting out the rain in the Western Motherqueen's cave, Feng—certain that the showers would stop soon—argued that we ought to set off right away. I preferred a soaking to a quarrel. Besides, there was bad weather enough before us, I knew, and good reason to depart. Mama Lu's silver, my contract price, and the reward for a dancer stolen from the Imperial Teaching Quarters might well spur a search.

Feng had taken the route we would travel when he came to the capital from his home in Jia-jou, so he knew the way. As we made our final preparations to leave the shrine cave, he showed me the travel papers he had forged. "Look here," he said, as a father might when instructing a child, "this mark is your new name. As a novice Lady of the Tao en route with me to study with a teacher in Shu, your name will be Skywhistle. That's what these words here mean." He looked up. "Perhaps you know the one for 'sky'?"

I knew them both, and almost all the other words as well, but only nodded. "A good name for a Taoist," I began. "But—"

"Oh yes." He waved one hand airily. "It's rather boyish, isn't it? But you see, a Taoist developing spiritual powers learns a secret whistle that can summon hosts of sylphs from the heavens. It won't hurt to have people think that you can do that. No need to worry about not knowing the right jargon. If we run into any tight spots, Sparker and I will do the talking." Sparker grinned in a half-crocked, abstracted way that made him look just like a wandering Taoist recluse, while Feng laughed as if he were a great deal older than he was. "You just follow Baby's example, and we'll muddle through."

Well, I thought, whatever the moonmaid may have told him, it's clear that he's the leader on this journey. I didn't care about that, but on my short ride alone I had made a decision. I would have to tell him about it now: I intended to travel as a boy.

First he chuckled, then he argued, then he shrugged a sulky shrug. "What will people think," he demanded, after I silently began to pack up the provisions they had brought along, "if only Baby travels as a little novice with two men and a boy?" Both of us looked over to where she knelt on the rug in the alcove, waiting impassively for the discussion to end. There would be no disguising her sweetly female form.

Another time that might have given me pause. But the headstrong spoiled daughter of a general answered for me that I didn't care. "You wouldn't be the only Taoist priest to journey with a little maid to keep your spirits up," I snapped. Sparker snickered. And from the corner of my eye, I caught a flicker of outrage pass over Baby's face. I realized she thought that I was trading her for greater freedom for myself and bit my lip and shook my head to tell her it wasn't so. But she turned away.

So I twisted my hair up in the rough knot of a youth who would be a Taoist, and tied an old sash tight across my small breasts. With Sparker's faded cotton jacket, and my new hat pulled down over my forehead, there would be no reason to think I was anything but a skinny boy whose voice had not yet broken. "Bordermoon" stayed behind us in the shrine cave, and I can't say I ever missed her much. I was Skywhistle now, and though I hadn't chosen that name either, it suited my taste far more.

The rains poured down on us all that afternoon. Cattle tracks had turned to creeks and creeks to torrents that the donkeys hated fording, and the River Wei roared foamy just beneath the Western Bridge as we crossed to the north bank, where travel was easier, and turned west. I wondered briefly what celestial vengeance was being wreaked upon the capital district, and why. But when I rode up to pose this question to Baby, who slumped in her saddle next to Feng, she still refused to meet my eye. I tried to comfort myself with the thought that for all the unspoken tensions twining among us, we four were a band united by the Moon Lady's bidding, off in search of a stone on Mothbrow Mountain.

At my last view of the walls of the Imperial City, I fell behind the others, staring and remembering Baba's old lessons: I was a daughter of Chang-an. But Chang-an had no proper place for me, and the mother that I sought was gone. I touched the secret pearl the bare-legged moonmaid had given me, nested safe within the sash that bound my breasts.

We arrived late, wet and exhausted, at a shabby inn—the sort where few questions are asked of those with cash to pay the reckoning—just outside of Hsian-yang, once the seat of the emperor who ordered the building of the draconic Great Wall. So began our six weeks' journey over the rugged road to Shu, a region famous for abundant crops, rhapsodic poets, and mountains veined by spiritual energy as if by high-grade ore.

Behold the Empires
of the World

Behold the empires of the world. In 733, the Toltec, Byzantine, and Dvaravatiera still have long to flourish. And in less than twenty years, death spasms will shake the Pallava, the Umayyad, the Merovinginan Franks. East of China, in the sacred islands where the sun is born, extraordinary temples are being erected in the new capital of Heijō-kyō. The Anglo-Saxons squabble with neighbors ferociously uncouth: their empire's rise and fall are yet to come, and most of its citizen-subjects will never hear these other names.

And what of Great Tang, and its glorious capital, the city of Everlasting Peace, largest on the earth? Look where it stands. The ghosts of other governing metropolises litter the plain around it, annihilated fortresses built perhaps as much as two millennia before. In ancient times a royal seat called Tai once stood somewhere along the banks of the Wei, and later Bin, and The Great King's Chi, and Feng, which afterward was known as

Hu, and mighty Hao. Just north and a little west of where Chang-an would lie, a book-burning, wall-building tyrant founded immortal Hsian-yang. Later, he buried ranks of pottery soldiers beneath that plain, to defend his soul's hegemony; his costly bier is still surrounded deep within its tumulus by a river of deadly mercury.

Then came the omnipotent Han Dynasty. Its early rulers raised the tawny walls of the first Chang-an just as Rome was winding down its second war with Carthage. This was Ptolemy's Sera Metropolis, his City of Silk. In time the dynasty, and the city, fell. Brief nomad capitals claimed one corner or another of the rich loess plain in the centuries that followed, but ruins from that former Chang-an still stood when—some fifteen decades before the moment you're observing—China stood united once again, and a new city was planned to rise and rule.

The advisers of the emperor counseled caution. Lay the city out in precise alignment with the cosmos, they urged. Observe the polar star by night and the gnomon-shadow of the sun at noon, that the central axis of the Son of Heaven's capital may run true. The grid of avenues must accord with earth's hidden lines of power, its vital breaths, as determined by the lay of waterways and the currents of the hills. Scrutinize the livers of sacrificial beasts to determine an auspicious day to start construction. And avoid the exact site of the old Han Dynasty Chang-an. Those acres where the crumbling corners of ancient buildings still held their peace had been corrupted, their spiritual energies fouled by ghosts as the water supply was fouled.

So the northern limit of the city was drawn south of the earlier Chang-an's ruins, though the private suburban park of the Tang imperial family embraces those tawny earthen monuments to what passes, or what lasts. Here ladies of the palace make their pleasure outings and royal huntsmen wrangle with the hunting cheetahs carried across their horses' rumps. How often does one of them gaze at those shards of grandeur and envision others yet to come?

You have seen the city now, perhaps have caught your breath

at its splendor or wrinkled your nose at its stench. There are still stories you have missed, of course: a half-blind scholar hanging a cage of fancy birds out in the fresh air, a woman weeping because she bore only another girl, a high official's steward reporting to the master on the welfare of great herds of oxen, horses, sheep. You could have stared at a solemn procession on the Buddha's birthday—majestic censers swaying, cymbals clashing out the pace—or might have winked at the down-home look of an Armenian or Jewish merchant among the quarter-million foreigners within or near the gates.

Still, you can say that you have traveled there, to the Chang-an of A.D. 733. And if you cast your gaze off toward northeast China, where brave armies defend the Tang against the encroaching Khitan horde, you'll see the gifted young officer who soon will rebel and sow the salty seeds of the city's lingering death. Barely thirty, he's already plagued by signs—dimming eyesight, pus-filled boils, remarkable obesity—of diabetes, but his end will come at his ill-treated attendant's own hands. The Chinese whom he serves, so far, with loyalty call him An Lu-shan, their version of his Soghdian name, Rokhshan. Odd, how this name's meaning ("light" or "bright") links him to the Brilliant Emperor whose reign he'll end. The Chinese historians will write that a certain magus saw a star of evil magic in the sky above his mother's tent that night, and that all around the infant the wild animals of the lawless wilderness howled.

Howled as someday the wolves will howl again where Chang-an once stood: but not for some time yet. Just after the fat general's murder, while the rebels hold the capital—*The state is smashed, yet hills and streams remain*—the greatest poet in all of Chinese history will wander by the waters of the Serpentine to ask for whom the willows and the rushes wear their spring-time green. Where sparkling ladies of the court once rode out with their hunting bows, the hooves of barbarian horses will kick up dust to sting his eyes. A few years later, Uighur troops brought in by the loyalists to take the city back will be rewarded with the freedom to loot and rape. Bodies by the tens of thousands will pile up in the marketplaces and the lanes. Temples and houses will smolder for weeks.

And after that? The city will serve as capital until the very end of this empire's long slow fall. In fifteen more decades, Chang-an will have suffered another dreadful occupation: tombs looted, the trees of the gardens cut down for fuel, sumptuous wall hangings ripped or burnt, silver filigree melted down for cash, bones of workers and dancers and bureaucrats lying among the weeds. Shortly before the last sparks of the Tang imperial line are snuffed, the order will go out: raze the remnants of Chang-an, and float whatever carved pillars or ornamental rafters can be reused to the would-be successor's own doomed capital in the east. The glimmering Serpentine will turn then to cracked yellow mud.

Return to your own century: a city called Xi'an now covers much of that land, proud of its vague memories, ashamed by its belatedness. You can climb restored pagodas, take a bus tour to see the heartbreaking willows around the hot springs where the Brilliant Emperor dallied with his last and greatest love, watch a movie about a wandering swordswoman not far from where Felicity Hall might once have stood. Archaeologists have determined that the ancient north-south axis was only sixteen minutes of arc west of what *we* take to be true north: that heap of rubble accorded with its orderly cosmos rather well. Ephemeral, eternal, Chang-an lives on in its inky midden-heap, a grand municipality now constructed chiefly of imagination, mortared together with electrons shot like nomads' arrows (the metaphors jumble as half-remembered dynasties do) at a video screen. Behold the empires of the world, lying at your feet. You have brought the city back. Go ahead and turn the page. Bring its brief walls down.

Parrot Speaks: 17

The road to Shu's a hard one, hard, it's said, as climbing to the bright blue sky. Much of the way we four travelers walked, for no donkey could carry a person up the irregular flights of stone steps that struggled past sheer escarpments and over the great folds of the Jin-ling range, easternmost outcrop of the Kun-lun Mountains themselves. But before we headed southward into that tortured landscape, we made our way in stages west, up the valley of the Wei. A new administrative system was sending a stream of fat officials and their retinues to the district capital of Shu—the Brocade City, people called it—through which we ourselves would pass before we got to Mothbrow Mountain. Hordes of shabby farmers from the north also took that route, flooded and starved out, or fleeing military service, or forced from their lands by the unlawful growth of private estates. The four of us clutched our forged travel papers and bobbed like flotsam on an uncontrollable river of people who'd turned their heels on whatever place they were officially registered to.

After Hsian-yang and Goldtown, we came to the Horsecrest Post Station, where once again we arranged to change our mounts for fresh ones. Dreamdragon Feng used a little sleight of hand to persuade the widow who ran the poorest of the nearby inns to put us up for free. In exchange, he gave her an amulet he swore would bring a long and wealthy life.

The woman treated all of us with deference, as disciples of the Wizard Mimesis. Still, although we had stopped early that day, she claimed she had no more to offer us than one tiny room. But who could blame her when there were so many paying guests along that difficult road to Shu?

Besides, the four of us had shared one room—and one wide platform bed—before. Baby always slept between me and the wall. She maintained the reserve she had fallen into in the shrine cave when she thought she heard me barter her for my freedom, though, and a slight wariness now replaced the delight she'd shown whenever I came to visit her at the Teaching Quarters back in Chang-an. Yet three or four times in those first days I'd caught a questioning smile sent to her from Feng, or a sidelong glance returned.

The day we stopped at Horsecrest, Sparker suggested that he and I walk over to the Buddhist temple beside the post station before our evening meal. He longed to follow the Tao, he said with a wink, but it never hurt to pay a little homage to the Teacher of the Middle Way. For once, it was neither raining nor too dusty, and our shadows stretched before us as we strolled. It pleased me that a man, even a servant, was showing me this special attention. After Lutegarden and Felicity Hall, those few days on my own had left me hungry for something I hadn't known I craved.

As the two of us approached the temple, a droning prayer drifted from the monks' chantry. In the outer courtyard, fugitive farmers and their children relaxed before the fall of night. A gang of young girls played a kind of football popular among the palace ladies in Chang-an, though they used a knot of rags. I wondered how they had the energy to play. Some of the other, thinner children already slept, or fretted over blistered feet, or simply sat and stared. Sparker squatted to watch two boys wrestling in a corner.

Inside an empty worship hall, I stopped before a stone statue of the Lady Guan-yin. She looked down at me as if the hubbub from the courtyard meant no more than the silence that would descend after dusk. Her stance undulated in smooth curves like those formed by the sand dunes of the Takla Makan, curves echoed by the draperies of her garments and her flowing scarves. Staring at the flask of sweet succoring nectar she wore suspended from her graceful neck, I tried to remember all that Nannie had told me of the Lady of Compassion.

I had no money with me to buy incense. On a sudden impulse I ducked into a dusky corner, reached inside my shirtfront, and pulled from its safe pocket in the folded sash that bound my breasts the tiny pearl necklace on its chain. Reaching up, I placed it in her outstretched palm and offered with it a prayer for Nannie's soul.

Then I went back out to Sparker. He grinned and said he thought that enough time had passed; we could go back to the inn. His words made no particular sense to me. But when I walked into our upstairs room to see Baby sitting flushed upon the bed while Feng stared out the tiny window, it all came clear. I can't say exactly what Baby's eyes told me when at last she looked up and into mine. Certainly I saw apology, and a kind of triumph, and something like happiness. So, it was done. She had chosen this attachment, and this time I was the one to be left alone.

After supper, because we had no cash to waste on oil or candles, and the landlady offered us none, we slept, crowded together in the little room. Baby lay down between me and Feng. I fell into a fitful sleep.

A sudden boom reverberated through the room. Baby rose up from the bed, drifting through the air before me, and danced—slowly at first, then flinging her arms in a frenzied sword dance. Sea-green and violet light washed over her. She called out feverish words, but Feng and Sparker slept. I wanted to reach out to her. I could not move.

Her face distorted. Her body softened. She—or was it some other woman now?—danced with a languid, bewitching grace, despite her plumpness, proud. She swayed and bent on a pavilion lacquered brilliant crimson, a curtain of delicate willow withes behind her, the clear, flower-spattered waters of a hot-springs pool spreading out in front. A dignified old man, an aging hero with an imperial air, devoured her with besotted eyes. Through the air between them, an unearthly melody twined. I hovered somewhere, unseen, watching, as if I were a disembodied traveler from the past.

Then I saw the old hero leaning on his cane inside the post station at Horsecrest, just where Feng had stood while he arranged for our next day's mounts. I understood that the lovers were resting there from the noontime sun and their wearying flight from a Chang-an torn by rebellion. Threatening shouts replaced the ethereal melody. The hero nodded his head, abruptly, sorrowfully, in response to the imprecations of a chubby, effeminate man.

The enchanting dancer was dragged out of the post station and through the temple courtyard where Sparker and I had watched the children play. The chubby man took her into the little chapel in which I'd prayed to Lady Guan-yin. There, he closed strong, pudgy fingers around the smooth flesh of her neck and strangled her. Angry soldiers cheered as if her death would cure an empire's ills.

I heard a moan of gut-wrenching remorse tear from the old hero's lips. I reached for a fragile bird of yellow gold that had fallen from the lovely dancer's chignon to the courtyard dust. But before I could pluck it up, Baby laid a hand upon my arm and woke me. The moan had been born of my own throat, and I knew as I lay waiting for the day to break that I would tell this story more than once.

I didn't understand what the dream prefigured, for Baby, or for that other dancer in the future. But I learned from it one thing: some tales must be told, and told again, in an everlasting rehearsal of love and betrayal and regret—or whatever it is they are taken to signify. Later I would see Baby dance possessed in that unworldly light, though I haven't yet learned who the murdered woman was, or will be. I knew, though, that what I saw would come to pass someday, as I know that someday even Great Tang must fall. I lay wakeful until the others rose.

On our journey the following afternoon, the plain rose steadily before us, and for the next few days we continued upstream and westward. The great range sprawled parallel to the road, on the far side of the River Wei. Soon we could see the last snows, a few shaded patches clinging even beyond midsummer, on the peak of Greatwhite Mountain. We turned our donkeys' heads toward that majestic summit. The ferry took us across the river with great difficulty. Currents swelled above sandbars normally exposed in that season, and we sighed with exhaustion when we reached our stopping place in Mei-hsian, on the southern bank.

We soon left the familiar rolling plateau, entering the foothills of the Jin-ling range by a rocky valley that narrowed to a gorge. Our donkeys' hooves rang against the cobbles of the trail, and Feng told us we'd have to walk. That was just as well, for our supply of silver would not have lasted had we hired mounts at each post station and stayed every night at inns.

Those north-facing, densely wooded slopes held the air's chill well into each day: I entered a lush, new world. The places I had known were grounded on sand, or loess, or grayish desert soils. Here, brown loam from an upland forest covered all but the sheerest outcroppings of sandy stone. Trees and plants grew thickly everywhere. One night we camped beneath a cliff magically stamped with the fragile shells of tiny snails and starry creatures Feng said lived beneath the waters of the sea. By our flickering cookfire, I traced one with my finger and wondered what watery deity had pressed its seal into the rock, and why.

We ascended by fertile ravines where tiny farmhouses huddled in the shadows, crossed the saddles of ridges, and climbed again, making for the high pass on the shoulder of Greatwhite Mountain. They say the trail is no more than a bird's track there, and what they say is true. Gasping for breath, we made our way up "sky ladders" and across "hanging bridges" of rough-hewn rock, craning our necks to see Sixdragon Peak. After the pass, more steps—some slippery with the spray of slender waterfalls—took us down a cliffside: every time I paused to rest the aching muscles of my thighs, my vision fell to the whirling torrent in the defile below.

Day after day, we descended by stages to the upper reaches of the River Han. The gohome birds cried gloomily about us, and from time to time a gibbon screamed. I saw mountain goats staring down at us, as if with contempt. Even the wind seemed to call out in an unorthodox poet's irregular meter, demanding, *Alas for you, who've gone a distant road, why, ah, whyever have you come?* I felt a vague urge to put some of this into words—song lyrics, perhaps, or even a formal poem. Yet nothing I could think of seemed adequate.

In the Han Valley, we came again to villages and could hire donkeys, riding once more upstream and to the west. One misty evening, we traveled late, hoping to stop the night at a settlement. Baby nearly rode off the narrow pathway into the wild river. After that, inn or no inn, we halted before the darkness fell. The gorge of the Han grew cramped then, and we left its gold-flecked sands behind (much to the regret of Sparker, who had kept a sharp and hopeful eye out as we rode), climbing over a low divide of broken hills green with paulownia trees.

We came to the Jia-ling River, which eventually flows southward to the great Yangzi itself. There we had a choice: to follow it a short way downstream to the city of Li-jou—whether expensively by donkey, or wearily on foot—on a path ledged into one cliff of the river's chasm, or to travel that distance in half the time, by boat. By now, I'd learned something of the ways Feng used when he was the Wizard Mimesis and asked if I might try to win us passage from one of the rivermen.

"You ought," he said, one eyebrow raised, "to be content with who you are. But I don't suppose you ever will be. Go ahead."

I conceded, silently, the justice of his remark. As Dragonfly and Bordermoon, I'd learned the language of accommodation, but Skywhistle—like that spoiled child, Greenpearl—inclined toward following the promptings of the will. "I'll get us a ride," I said.

I sidled up to one of the boatmen, an oily haired man of perhaps thirty years who lounged on the landing stairs, stroking his thin beard as he watched me approach. "I bring good news," I said, taking pains to make my voice and manner as boyish as I could. "The Wizard Mimesis has arrived!"

"Ho-la!" the boatman called, mockery heavy in his voice. "The Wizard Mimesis, eh?" He turned his head toward three other boatmen squatting on the bank. "Roundhead! Guo! Old Hsin! This young tendercheeks brings wondrous news indeed. Go on, boy. Tell me who this wizard is and why it is that I should care." He leaned back and fixed his gaze upon me.

Borrowing all I could remember from Feng and Sparker's patter, I spun the tale of the great Wizard's skills, the efficacy of his amulets, the awful power of his wrath. I could feel my companions' eyes resting on me from the shadows on the bluff above the landing stairs and wondered how much they could hear.

"In other words," the boatman said, "a grifter who wishes to ride downriver free. And bring his catamite with him. And whoever else can tag along. No, Young Master Tendercheeks, I've seen enough of his sort passing through here on the way to Shu. Boatman Wang doesn't give something for nothing, you know." Then he reached out one hand and placed it on my thigh. "But I can sometimes be persuaded to make a trade in kind."

I froze. One of the other boatmen hooted. Every word I'd learned, in every language, left me. Not because of his interest in the youth Skywhistle: I had no quarrel with men who went to bed with boys. But I found distasteful the idea of exchanging pleasure so directly for what I wanted. Neither Lutegarden nor Felicity Hall had been a brothel; the most boorish, drunken guest knew better than to violate the unwritten rules by openly presuming that a visit to my bedroom could be bought without attention to the niceties. Yet Nephrite, who remembered enough of the easy ways of Khotanese women to scoff at these Chinese distinctions, had once pointed out that had we been raised as daughters of good families of the Tang, we'd have made that same exchange just once, for life, and with even less say as to who the man would be.

My tongue failed me simply for one reason. Even if I forced myself to make the bargain, how likely would he be to keep it when he saw the ineradicable signs of my sex? And what would stop him from earning a few coins by turning us in to the local commandery as a party with something to hide?

Sparker strutted up to where I stood dumbfounded. I held my breath; what would he say?

Chez Wang

Will Sparker talk her out of there? Will the footsore party drag themselves along the cliffside trail to Li-jou, where the Wizard Mimesis can add to their dwindling store of cash by a bit of fortune-telling, some profitable verbal razzmatazz? The peasants of the narrow valleys through which the party passed have been too poor to do much good, but the people of the city will be quick enough to pay for the words that by their very presence mark the absence of the thing—a happy old age, success in business, an auspicious marriage—desired.

Or maybe Sparker will weave of Boatman Wang's lewd greed a badger game: lure him with promises of the supposed boy, or the boy and a shaggy-haired young man, or boy and young man and dancing girl all three. And then an angry wizard, storming into a shadowy room where an unspeakable drama of multiple secret lusts has just begun to unfold, will throw a bit of powder on the coals and terrorize the one for whom it's all enacted, and poor Wang will quickly, abashedly, grasp his boat pole and take them down.

Or will something go wrong with the con? Perhaps, as Sky-whistle fears, the boatman, eagerly tugging at the trousers that both hide and indicate the lad's round buttocks, will discover the reality behind that veil. What he's got here isn't what he thought it was. He's in the middle of a story not at all the one that he expected, not a manly tale where orderly causes—now this, now this, *unnh*, ahh, *unnh*, now *this* and *this*—give rise to—*sweet! final!* ahh, *predictable!*—effects. No, what he's found is this one lawless woman, disruptive, multiform, and floating free, outside the order of things as he's been told them.

Or—in this book it's certainly within the rules—will some god or goddess intervene? Perhaps a giant magical river turtle, sent by Lady Guan-yin or the Dragon Monarch, will suddenly emerge from the swift currents of the Jia-ling, a tortoise ex machina to bear the baffled foursome happily away, while poor Wang's jaw drops, and his audience of cronies stares.

The story's as the reader writes it. But what determines what the reader reads? Have it any way you want to, Boatman Wang.

Esoteric Transmitted Records of the Bizarre

by Lha Er-sun

A CUNNING ALCHEMIST

In the riverside city of Li-jou, a man called Miser Wang met a wandering alchemist, who traveled with two apprentices and a beautiful concubine. The alchemist casually mentioned that he could create pure gold from lead, along with a few taels of real gold, which were needed as a catalyst. After that, Wang invited the party to his home, where he treated them to a lavish feast. As they drank, the concubine danced, her delicate arms fluttering, her body free and sinuous, as if in dancing she achieved her heart's desire. Soon Wang was afire with lust for the woman and lust for wealth.

The alchemist had explained that his pursuit of spiritual purity prevented him from working the transformation for his own benefit, but he allowed Wang to persuade him; Wang needed only to provide the catalyst. The mixture had to remain overnight in a tightly covered pot, so after all was arranged, the party went off to bed. Shortly before dawn, the concubine crept silently into the bedroom used by Wang, who could scarcely believe his good fortune. But no sooner had he removed his trousers than one of the apprentices burst into the room and began shouting for the alchemist, who soon appeared.

Enraged by this betrayal, the alchemist gathered up his party, including the weeping concubine, and stormed out of the house. By the time the embarrassed and frightened Wang thought to look inside the smelting pot—which of course was empty—the four had left the city. They, and Wang's gold, were never seen in those parts again.

HUNTRESS IN DISGUISE

During the Kai-yuan reign period, a party of travelers made their way from Li-jou to the land of Shu, planning to enter that region by Swordgate Pass. These people—an impoverished scholar and two servants—were fleeing a famine which had struck the area around the Imperial Capital. But when they reached the checkpoint at the pass, a greedy officer pretended to find some irregularity in their travel documents. Since the scholar refused to encourage corruption by paying a bribe, they were turned back.

Trying to find another route into Shu, the party left the trail and struck off into the mountain forests. Up and down they scrambled, until they were thoroughly lost. The scholar's female servant sat on a large rock and began to weep silently with hunger and fatigue. The male servant set a snare and soon caught a strange variegated bird. In desperation he plunged his knife into its lovely breast. But as soon as the blade entered the bird's heart, its skin parted and a slim young woman stepped out.

"A Persian sorcerer spirited my mother away to be his bride," the mysterious woman said, "and cast a spell that sealed me in the form of a bird. Now you have rescued me, and at last I can continue my quest to rescue my mother. But tell me, what are you doing here, in these lonely wilds?"

Upon hearing the party's dilemma, the young woman, who had learned the language of the birds, summoned great flocks of her former companions. These birds wove of their feathers three soft nets. At her urging, the travelers stepped into the nets, and were swiftly carried over the rugged transverse valleys and ridges, into the great basin of Shu.

A FIT HOME FOR POETS

A certain young scholar of Jia-jou named Feng journeyed from his home some three hundred *li* northward to the Brocade City. Near Rinseflowers Stream, he found a rustic cottage where he might apply himself to his studies. To it, he gave the peculiar name of River Tortoise Lodge. Although Scholar Feng claimed to have no talent for poetry, a government clerk found some discarded poems beside Rinseflowers Stream just below the cottage. In simple but refined language, the poems praised the rural scenery: wild ducks and glimmering dragonflies, giant green bamboo and river shoals of jade-white sand. Word of the young man's genius quickly spread through the Brocade City, but he declared that the poems were the work of a reclusive young Taoist residing with him, whose name was Lunar Emerald. No one ever met this Taoist youth, but the poems became the talk of the town.

Shortly thereafter, Scholar Feng, his shy companion, and their two servants moved away, and the cottage fell into ruin. A generation later, the renowned Tu Fu built his Thatched Hut there, and some decades after that the witty and talented Xue Tao retired to the same area, planting fragrant loquat trees beside her doorway. Truly, this place was a fit home for poets!

TRAITOR OR TRUTH-TELLER?

During the reign of the Brilliant Emperor, a Soghdian fortune-teller named Skywhistle, who had learned his arcane arts in Persia and spoke that curious tongue, appeared in the central market of the Brocade City. It was said that the future was whispered to him by a magical pearl which he kept secreted upon his person, and many people came to him, seeking to know their fates. One day, he told a crowd that in two twelves of years, the emperor himself would be forced by a rebellion to travel the difficult road to Shu. A plump dancer who bewitched him would be strangled at the Horsecrest Post Station en route, and the fleeing monarch would set up his capital-in-exile in the Brocade City. All the townspeople reviled the fortune-teller as a traitorous liar, and he barely escaped the city with his life. Later, it all turned out as he had predicted.

THE CONSOLATIONS OF LITERATURE

In the years following his flight from the rebel forces that temporarily occupied Chang-an, the abdicated Brilliant Emperor lived in a back apartment of what was now his son's palace. There, his faithful chief eunuch used to tell him stories. These were not the finely wrought tales of the literati, nor was His former Majesty interested in elevated verse. Rather, when Gao Li-shi found him sighing for his enchanting, perished Precious Consort Yang, the eunuch would recite simple parables told by marketplace storytellers, and chanted monkish homilies on Buddhist sutras. In this way, he loyally attempted to cheer up the former emperor. Only one tale did Gao Li-shi refuse to tell: how he himself had quieted the fleeing emperor's mutinous military escort by murdering the Precious Consort in a temple to the Lady Guan-yin in the valley of the River Wei. Some say the death of that beautiful woman augured the downfall of Great Tang.

A GULLIBLE GOVERNOR

During the Tang Dynasty, a magician named Mimesis called on the military governor of Shu, and by a few showy tricks quickly won the governor's trust. "My assistant," he announced, "is a shamanka who has the power to interpret the very signs of nature, even when they have been altered by the work of human hands. Would you like to see this?" The governor assented, and the magician summoned the young woman in. "She is a mute," Mimesis explained, "but she is quite adept at making her meaning known. Do you have a mat of tortoiseshell bamboo?"

Of course, the governor had several such beautiful mats, upon which entertainers danced at his state banquets. The mute shamanka selected one, stared at its mottled markings, and began to sway. "Now she communes with the Lo River divinity herself," the magician said, "who once sent a giant turtle inscribed with vermilion script to the ancient sage-emperor Yao." Coming out of her trance, the sybil began to sign frantically with her hands. "Alas!" cried Mimesis. "Your Excellency is destined to be called soon to the netherworld by the fiery-eyed younger brother of the Dragon Monarch. She tells me that one thing only can save Your Excellency. There is a certain magic stone on Mothbrow Mountain, not far south of here. If you can provide us with the financial means to make the journey, she will lead me to it, and with it I will destroy this malevolent dragon before he can summon you."

The governor readily complied, giving the magician and his various assistants money and travel papers. So concerned was the frightened governor with the success of the mission that he insisted upon sending a military escort as well. The magician tried to convince him that his own powers were sufficient protection, but to no avail. The party disappeared somewhere in the mists of Mothbrow Mountain and were never heard from again. But the governor lived on for many years.

Hexagram 37:
The Moment Defined

Hexagram 37: *The Family* . . .
The Judgement: The perseverance of the woman furthers.
　　　　　　　　—I Ching, *Wilhelm/Baynes translation*

Early in the fourth lunar month of—you call it A.D. 734—in the Brocade City and southeastward through Shu to the Yangzi River gorges, the mulberry trees are putting forth their softly folded leaves. Life quiets—no tax collections, no social visits—for the duration of the Silkworm Month. The rapacious larvae must be warmed and fed both day and night.

In the Imperial Capital, a predecessor of Precious Consort Yang, Wu Hui-fei (who will be the Brilliant Emperor's First Lady for three more years, until she dies from the ghostly ill wishes of murdered princes who rivaled her own son), has already conducted the rites for worshiping the silkworm goddesses. In the private gardens of the palace, she made sacrifice at an altar set up on a terrace, while her ladies gathered round.

She has done this on behalf of all the women under heaven who stay awake nights in the fourth month to chop the mulberry leaves they've gathered, and sprinkle them on the trays of silkworms, and later must unwind a tender thread from each cocoon, to spin and weave the lustrous treasure which is coin of this mighty realm.

Outside dusty Dun-huang, twenty schoolboys in a monastery school bend their heads over their desks, copying their primers on clean scraps of paper from old scrolls. Their writing lines up cheek by jowl with wills and ballads, deeds and inventories, biographies, lost letters, contracts, the constitution of a social club: precious blank space fills with what's more precious, words.

A lay devotee on a retreat in a cell next door finishes his writing out of a sutra. *May I share the merit from this good deed with my father. May I share it with my brother the schoolmaster. With all beings may I share this merit and may I ripen them to supreme knowledge, which is enlightenment, beyond all words.*

Nearby, in a convent, the holy sisters stitch.

Head in hands, the Acting Assistant Controller of the Ministry of Babble tries to think how he can write down what he has to say. His August Highness, the Jade Emperor, awaits a report on the Luminous Emerald-Green Lunar Essence Sprite. The rains he summoned to Chang-an need not be mentioned; floods and famine have so often been that city's lot. But how (he presses his forehead harder into the heels of his hands, regretting his fit of vengeful pique, remembering his blissful communion with that mirror-image Other among the creamy cumuli), *how* is he to explain away the troublesome officer who, thanks to a tip from an anonymous celestial bureaucrat astride a yellow crane, questioned the green pearl's forged travel papers and tried to block her entry into Shu at Swordgate Pass?

East of Chang-an, the Silk-Weaving River Dragon, daughter of the Lo River Divinity, discourses on the nature of her kind. "Of the five elements, wood is the one for which dragons have an affinity," she says. "What surprise, then, to hear of a wooden weaving-shuttle that fell into a lake and transformed itself into one of my race."

Seagem's husband, the Hsiao River Princeling, knots his eyebrows in delicate concern. Is he doing the right thing? His vermilion uncle thinks he should, but then, among dragons, Uncle is something of a misfit. The Princeling eases over to his beloved wife. Pausing at a table in a corner of their bedchamber, he carelessly picks up a silver scissors, and begins to slap it gently against the palm of one hand.

The light slap-slap of flat metal on flesh, a sound like the lapping of moon-pulled wavelets on the shore of a great lake, breaks through Seagem's concentration. She lays her writing brush aside, and sighs, and looks up to see who stands so close behind her. Her husband. She blows him a vague kiss and turns back to her desk. Beneath Cavegarden Lake they reckon time by great hourglasses that drizzle seed pearls instead of sand, and hers says her calligraphy practice for that day is less than halfway done.

"Dear?" The Princeling's voice is hesitant, unobjectionable, only kind.

She looks up at him again, says nothing, brings a smile to her lips. At least the slap-slap-slapping has stopped.

"Dear," he continues, "I thought you might want me to comb your hair for you. Maybe try that new Towering Nebula style they're doing in the Eastern Sea, hmmm?" He looks at her expectantly. She always likes it when he does her hair.

Seagem thanks him. "Maybe later, darling," she says. "I'm copying Song Yu's rhapsody on the goddess of Shamanka Gorge.

I should be finished soon." Not quite true, but near enough, she thinks.

The Princeling's eyebrows knot again. Well then, he suggests, perhaps she could stop for just a couple of moments. He'd like to have a little talk. Surely the calligraphy can wait.

She doesn't sigh, but when she puts her brush down again, it seems as if she did. Then she swings her legs around, so that she faces him, still sitting on her stool. He stands so close that she has to tilt her head back to look up at him. "Yes?" is all she says.

After a good deal of stammering, the Princeling blurts out his problem. Since she's taken up this calligraphy, and reading, and now even memorizing poems, she's, well, to put it bluntly, she's been neglecting him. "Understand, dear love," he tells her, "I don't want to stop you from pursuing your new interests. Actually, I think they're quite nice, and I realize you never had the chance to do all this in the human world. But, don't you ever miss your embroidery and such? When we were still betrothed . . ." Here he pauses, blushing at his indelicacy in alluding, however indirectly, to her father's failure to keep his promise and to the years when she was the human general's wife. But Seagem has changed. No tears. She merely nods her head and, politely, waits.

"Your fame as a needlewoman preceded you here beneath the waves. Word of the smoothness of your weaving spread from Chang-an to the Yangzi Valley, and thence down here to us. I hate to see you give that up. Besides . . ." He stops and prepares to lay down the clincher. "When you did that sort of thing, I could sit somewhere nearby, and we could talk."

A pang strikes Seagem's heart. She does so love the Princeling. And she likes to be near him. It's just that she can hardly pour her full energies into the words she brushes on the page while carrying on a conversation; indeed, she likes it best when no one else is in the room at all. How selfish of her!

She hangs her head, and the Princeling pats her shoulder, and

stoops to kiss her glossy hair. Soon, the two have drifted over to
their silk-covered bed and give to one another joys laden with
the honey-sweetness of reconciliation. Then it's time to dress
for the family's evening banquet. Seagem practices no more that
day, and a carp-cousin come to visit from the Southern Ocean
watches them tenderly sharing morsels at the table and smiles
to see such a model of mutual devotion. But that night, Seagem
lies awake for hours, not quite certain what disturbs her. Tomorrow, she thinks, she'll gather up her courage and pay a call
on her mother-in-law, to ask for her advice.

Outside of Liang-jou, in the community of Taoist women
known as Darkdazzle Vista, the novice Jade Clarity—whose
name in the world was Nephrite—washes off her makeup, in
preparation for her ordination. Certain secret teachings have
been passed to her by women of the Vista. She has purified her
body by spiritual disciplines, has gathered essential energies
through intercourse with eager smooth-skinned youths, in hectic battles of pleasure and denial. She can now go nine days
without a bite of food, quite unaware of hunger.

Yet a longing remains in her. She yearns for a divine lover,
hopes to summon him by her careful pacing of a ritual dance,
tracing patterns on a greensward as the calligrapher traces signs
upon the page, as stars trace out their powerful constellations
in the sky. Her languid steps may bring her to a mystic consum-
mation. It is her one desire. Soon she'll be given tablets inscribed
with esoteric texts. Soon her soul will roam free to the palace
of the Western Motherqueen.

After wintering over in the Brocade City, four travelers and
their cumbersome military escort have made their way south by
riverboat to Jia-jou, and overland to the town of Mothbrow, at
the famous mountain's foot. They have come on a false quest

for the local governor, and a true one for the Lady in the Moon. Long before the spring came, three of them had grown impatient, but Dreamdragon Feng held back from making that last stage of the journey. And who could blame him? He failed to take the imperial examination and squandered all his parents' money besides. He may have the remote protection of the Moon Lady, but to a good Confucian scholar that goddess is little more than a runaway wife. Now he makes his living as an alchemist-magician of dubious honesty. No, he was hardly eager, when he came down to it, to move on to his old hometown.

And yet, they managed to pass quickly through the town, and no one from Jia-jou's thirty thousand households guessed that the proud Wizard Mimesis (who sports a beard as long and coarse as the hair from a horse's tail) has anything to do with the son of respectable old Tutor Feng. Now they've come to Mothbrow Town, and tomorrow they will enter the mountain's faerie realm.

But first, a final bit of business. The soldiers the military governor sent from the Brocade City for their protection in the wild mountain realm must be gotten rid of. A considerable inducement is needed, one that will make it worth their while to tell His Excellency that somewhere amid the cloudy ravines of Mothbrow Mountain, the foursome magically vanished. Yet the travelers' catch-as-catch-can earnings over the winter have left them little beyond expenses. Even today, in this country town, they're busy scraping up every bit they can. The two common soldiers can be fooled with a bit of razzle-dazzle and perhaps a cloud of colored smoke, but their sergeant (who has observed rather carefully the party's ways of making money) has let Mimesis know he's a hardheaded realist, with a taste for cash.

🁢 Meanwhile, just outside Mothbrow Town, the second daughter of a wealthy farmer of the Yin clan has been planning her future. She is perceptive, straightforward, skilled at the loom, and badly pockmarked. It's starting to look as if no one will send a go-between to compare the horoscopes and choose an auspicious wedding day. She has set her own eye on a neighbor who's reasonably intelligent, not unkind, relatively well-to-do. Unfortunately, the match would not be, for him, a particularly advantageous one. He'd only ask his parents—who quite dote upon him—to arrange a marriage with Second Daughter Yin if he were in love with her, but how is that to be when young men see pitted skin and not what lies within?

Second Daughter has decided to take matters into her own hands. A love charm—ah, a love charm would cure everything, bringing her security, and happiness, and a way out of her father's house, where remarks about her age are becoming rather pointed. So, weary though she is with caring for the silkworms, she has come on this day of their molting sleep to the inn on the edge of town. After a few minutes of thoughtful watching, she approaches the slender apprentice of the wizard who has lodged there these last two nights, waiting for the rainy spell to break.

"It's Master Skywhistle I want to speak to," she says with quiet boldness, and the two of them withdraw into a corner of the inn's main room. Once they are away from Sparker and the townsmen idling over their cups, her back straightens, her face loses its drawn look, and she smiles a reassuring smile. "I know you are no man," she whispers then. Skywhistle freezes. "But I'll tell no one. And I'll pay a fair price for what I'm asking. If you can arrange to fool so many, and travel about in freedom, I am certain that you can manage what I need." Skywhistle belatedly begins to feign outrage at the accusation of womanhood, but seeing amused intelligence gleaming in Second Daughter's eyes, desists, and asks her what she wants.

Soon the deal's concluded. Skywhistle hands her a twist of paper containing an occult mixture known as Scarlet Dust. Second Daughter is to find a sturdy box and place within it a snake, a centipede, a scorpion, a wombguard lizard, and a toad. She may give them no food or water. When only one of these antagonists remains alive, embodying the powers of all the others, she is to feed it the Scarlet Dust. When it dies, she must dry its body, grind it in an unused mortar by the full moon's light, and sprinkle a bit of the powder in a cup of wine, serving it with her own hands to her intended. No harm will come to him, Skywhistle assures her, but his heart—and so, a place in his household—will then be hers.

Second Daughter's gratitude is great. She tucks the twist of paper inside her sleeve and gives Skywhistle silver to the value of five strings of cash, or five bolts of high-grade silk. Small payment, she thinks, for escaping an old maid's doom of condescension and disdain. And so, she abstractedly hands the wizard's apprentice one thing more, a simple necklace with a single lumpy pearl. "My father gave me this," she says, with a wry, incisive smile. "He's never bought me jewelry. Says I'll just take it with me when I leave the family anyway. I think he got this in a swap of some kind, on the cheap. Perhaps you'll have some use for it."

At the sight of the pearl necklace, Skywhistle's eyes grow wide. Second Daughter stands, and with a grace and dignity unusual in a provincial farmer's daughter, turns and leaves.

Skywhistle holds the odd-shaped pearl with care and prays a silent prayer that the love charm will work. Surely an afternoon of wine and conversation will lead any young man to see Second Daughter's worth; she lacks only self-confidence to replace the apologetic hunch her shoulders take when she's with men.

Elsewhere, Lady Guan-yin lowers her eyes to the terrestrial realm, gazes at the little pearl, nods her elegant head, and calmly smiles.

A Geographical Guide to Jia-jou and Environs

(Yu Nuo-hu, ed.)

CHAPTER 13: MOTHBROW MOUNTAIN

Shu has many faerie mountains, but none of them compares with Mothbrow's magic realm. Its bold precipices thrust upward with the virility of a heroic man; its awesome crests arch like the eyebrows of a beautiful woman, delicate and resilient as a moth's feathery antennae. Yes, it harbors the dynamic interplay of the forces of yin and yang. In the remote gullies and coves of its winding ridges, fire demons roam. From its Golden Summit, travelers view mysterious spirit lamps gathered in the crevasses and actually see their own auras glowing on clouds spread out below them like hanks of soft silk floss!

Famous sites on Mothbrow Mountain: Among the numinous objects on this great mountain are the precipices known as Jade

Maiden and Skycleaver and wondrous stones such as The Flying Sword, Heavensdoor, and Chameleon Rock. Thousands of caves permeate the sacred mount. The people venerate them all, especially Nu Wa's Cavern, Fu Hsi's Grotto, the Three Immortals, and Dragongate.

Flora: Buddha pine, bodhisattva creeper, his-face trees dripping pollen, ragged-leaf plantains, golden chestnuts, parasol shrubs, banyans, redolent camphor trees, cypresses, desolate thickets of mountain laurel, giant ginkgos, mimosas whose leaves fold companionably together all night, and cassia trees that grow vigorously even when half their bark is gone. Climbing the high peaks, one sees the foliage change as if one journeyed many miles to the north: near the summit, all is windblown junipers and hardy rhododendrons.

In the foothills there are peaches, efficacious herbs, tea of surpassing flavor, and wild camellias filling the air with their haunting aroma. These last bloom rose and purple, pink and white amid early winter's snows.

Fauna: Mysterious phoenixes dance upon the branches of the tung trees, and from time to time a fortunate traveler may hear the sweetcry bird, trilling, "Buddha comes! Buddha, Buddha comes!"

Among animals there are wolves and tigers, giant pandas, bearded monkeys, enchanting choruses of frogs, and pythons a hundred feet long.

Sources of Spiritual Power: Those who study earthmagic instantly recognize a galvanic potency in the mountain's form.

Jade Nectar Spring, which lies partway up the main slope, is known to have its distant source in the mighty worldmountain.

Only here does it emerge into the human realm. A Dragon Maiden guards these pure and holy waters.

Buddhists interpret the halos shimmering around one's shadow cast on the clouds below Golden Summit to signify that the mountain has been granted special favor by The Enlightened One; seeing this "Buddha's Glory" round one's own head, one is as a blessed bodhisattva.

In tier after tier the skyward ranges, of which Mothbrow forms the easternmost promontory, run west to the Kunlun massif, reaching the icy fastness of the Western Motherqueen herself.

Parrot Speaks: 18

S top!"

The panting voice rang out behind us. "The soldiers!" Feng cried out. "They've come back!" He and Sparker vanished. Baby grabbed my wrist and pulled me after her into the crevice where the others hid. We pressed close together in the darkness, breathing as shallowly as panic would allow.

The months I'd spent as Skywhistle had quickened my tongue. Since the day I'd talked us past a dangerously cautious official at Swordgate Pass, I sometimes felt I could prattle my way out of nearly anything. Only the bright-eyed pockmarked farmer's daughter I'd met yesterday had seen through my disguise as a boy, and only when I'd forecast an unpleasant future for the Brilliant Emperor had my fortune-telling in the Brocade City gotten me into trouble.

But the sergeant we bribed must have betrayed us, I thought

when I heard that indistinct shout: we were being pursued. My new skill with the language of—call it double-dealing—would prove useless if they caught us. The crevice had no other exit. What were we to do?

I pressed myself harder against the rough rock wall and prayed to Lady Guan-yin to protect us. The scheme had seemed to go so well. Feng and the sergeant had come to an understanding, and we four had taken care to keep the troopers a bit off-balance: now a writing brush changed into a newt (Sparker had gotten very good at that one), now a pass of the hand and the flames of a cookfire burning eerie green.

We'd never wanted soldiers to escort us, but when Feng and Baby fooled the local governor to get the money for the last stage of our quest, he had insisted on sending along a military guard for our protection. They were still with us when we left Moth-brow Town that morning, peering up through the tender-leafed willow branches at massive, folded peaks.

Passing Chameleon Rock, I caught my breath. And before noon we reached the hundred-year-old Monastery of the Long-lived Sage, deep among a grove of hoary trees, where the monks gave us pickled vegetables and let us cook our rice. "Crossing the Bridge of Deliverance," the novice who waited upon us said, "you will escape the sordid attachments of earthly life. The swift waters carry all fatigue and woe away. Only, do not forget to cleanse your hands and mouths in the pool there, before you enter the bamboo grove and start your ascent." With this last, his eyes bulged like a spirit-general's. The troopers gasped.

We climbed more than a thousand feet on wooden steps, the ground around us slick and pale with a mat of dried bamboo leaves decades deep. The stems of the giant grasses creaked one against the other as they wavered overhead, a frost of gray dusted on their even green. Bamboo keep to themselves; no other plants grew within the huge grove. As we labored upward I reached out to run my fingers down a stalk, marveling at its smoothness and its constancy.

Behind me, Feng cleared his throat and softly laughed. I fixed my mind on the dispassionate emptiness at each bamboo's hollow heart. "Ah, you're a cool one," he murmured, but I still would not turn around.

The trail began to tack across the mountain. The third or fourth of its Ninety-nine Turns took us over a side ridge and into a small ravine thick with trees. Greening branches filled our vision with cheerless shadows. Feng turned to the sergeant and cocked an eyebrow. It was time. The sergeant called a halt.

Sparker gathered sticks and struck his flint to start a fire, while Baby shaved tea from a pressed brick. I took the pot from my pack and fetched water from a nearby spring. Silently, we waited until the water boiled, hissing in the stillness of the afternoon.

"Foolish to halt in this gloomy place," the shortest soldier muttered to his fattish friend. "Look how the shadows have started to grow longer. We'll have to stop for the night soon."

"Hope there's a monastery or a nunnery to take us in," the fat one replied. "Shouldn't like to camp out *here.*"

The sergeant's dark face glared in their direction, and the two soldiers—one plump, one stubby—stared down at their hands.

We sat in an uneasy silence. The ravine faced eastward, and I realized Feng had chosen it for its early afternoon shade. Just as great bubbles of air began to rustle upward from the bottom of the pot, I ambled by the three soldiers, loosening my trousers at the waist. We'd traveled together long enough that jokes about my boyish shyness in relieving myself had finally ceased, and they paid me little mind. The short soldier sat with his arms wrapped about his knees; he had foolishly chosen to sit on a stone rather than to squat, and in the coolness of the fourth month, the well-shaded stone was evidently drawing the heat from his body. As we'd arranged, Sparker kept a casual eye on me. When he saw me pass the soldiers, he reached out for the pot of water, spilled it, and ripped the still air with his scream.

Even I started at the sound of pain echoing through the silent ravine. All three soldiers jumped to their feet, though they were slow to draw their swords. It was easy for me to drop unnoticed the paper Feng had given me. It landed on the rock the short one had been sitting on.

Sparker trudged off, nursing his hand, to refill the pot with water. The rest of us laughed nervously and prepared to wait again.

"Hullo! What's this?" the short soldier cried. "Paper, eh?" He squinted at it. "Well, it's blank," he said and made as if to throw it away.

Another sharp sound, deeper and more commanding, set my heart beating fast again. "What are you doing, fool?" raged Feng (or perhaps I should call him Wizard Mimesis here). He drew himself up to his full height, putting forth an air of dignity and authority. "You find a mysterious paper on this mountain of python deities and fire demons and you'd toss it away? Bring it here, lad, bring it here!"

Feng wasn't much older than the troopers. But he'd struck the pose of one a generation older from the start, and by now the soldiers' deference to him was automatic, even without their superstitious awe of his supposed powers. The short soldier hustled over, bearing the small sheet of paper on two palms held flat and high before him like a tray of gold.

"Stand your ground!" Feng barked when the poor soldier, having delivered the paper to him, began to back away. "You're the one the spirits gave this to. Stay by me while I examine it." With that, he eased onto a log beside the cookfire as if onto a throne. The soldier squatted next to him.

No one but Feng knew exactly what would happen next. Faint brown writing began to form upon the paper as his long fingers held it near the fire, as if to see more clearly by its light. I gasped. The short soldier leapt up and stepped away, bumping into the other one, who'd run up behind him for a closer look.

"Read it!" Feng commanded, but the short one hung his head, and mumbled something, passing it to his plump—and literate— friend. The words stumbled from his lips:

> If men with swords should seek the stone,
> One word: and stones they'll be.
> If history's a story, then
> Which story's history?

"Well?" Feng demanded. "Tell me what you make of that."

"Can't say I understand the last half, sir," the fattish soldier declared. For an instant, Feng's eyebrows drew together as if he too were puzzled, but then his face grew stern again. He waved one hand dismissively, and the soldier hurried on. "The first part, well, sir, the first part's clear enough."

The swarthy sergeant snorted, but he wanted our money; he had a part to play. "What's that, private? Out with it!"

The soldier gulped, and looked down at his comrade, but no help was forthcoming. "Well, sir, begging your pardon, but I think 'men with swords' means us soldiers, sir. I mean, the Wizard and his, ah, his party, they're civilians and none of them carries a blade. At least I think not, sir." He turned half hopefully toward Feng, eager for any sign that all of us were in the paper's designs together.

"Do I seem to you to *require* so crude a weapon as a sword?" Feng asked, and Sparker, too, assumed a haughty look.

"No, sir. Not at all, sir." The soldier turned to the sergeant. "So I suppose it's only us that's going to turn to stones. Sir." The troopers stared anxiously at their leader. Sparker winked at me.

After that, the matter settled itself quickly, or so we'd thought. The sergeant allowed the privates to persuade him of the mission's dangers. Feng vowed that, though unfortunately he could not vouch for the soldiers' safety, he and the rest of us would never leave our quest. "You've protected us well, where mortal soldiers can protect us," he said at last. "Surely His Excellency the governor would not wish for you to throw away your lives. We are determined to find the stone and, ah, use it to slay the dragon that threatens His Excellency's life." His eyes narrowed. "And succeed we will. You may as well report the deed as done when you get back to the Brocade City."

Feng slipped a purse to the sergeant, who flashed one cynical grin behind the privates' backs. The soldiers marched a nervous quickstep back the way we'd come. Lighthearted, the four of us had climbed another hour before we heard that voice call out for us to stop. Now I huddled in the crevice with the others, certain that we'd be found.

Footsteps rattled over the planks of the bridge we'd crossed bare moments before. "Stop! Oh, stop, please. Skywhistle, do please stop for me!"

The sound of the voice, the words, the lightness of the footfalls: whoever it was that labored so to catch us, I realized, was not the greedy sergeant after all, not the soldiers angered at being played for fools. Though Baby caught my wrist again, I stepped out into the fading light. Farmer Yin's Second Daughter burst around the last curve of the trail.

I clasped her shoulders with my hands, and she leaned against them, gasping. Her pockmarked face glowed a peach-blossom color. Her eyes shone. By the time Baby, Sparker, and Feng stepped out of the crevice, Second Daughter had set down the bundle she carried and begun her tale.

The very afternoon—just the day before—that she bought the love charm from me and started looking for the creatures the recipe required, two callers arrived at her father's house. The visit was quite out of the ordinary, coming in the silkworm-feeding season as it did. But then, the man who showed up so unexpectedly was known for hotheaded impulses.

The woman with him, Mistress Bian, busied herself as a go-between for families of Mothbrow Town. Her companion was the father of the neighbor Second Daughter hoped would become her husband and so free her from her own father's contempt. That the prospective father-in-law should accompany the matchmaker struck Second Daughter as rather odd. But she was so used to scorn that she assumed he wanted to assure himself that the bride-to-be was not *too* disfigured by her pocks. And aware of the old man's reputation, she supposed he'd also seen in the call an opportunity to cadge a few drinks. Indeed, when Second Daughter answered her father's summons to bring more refreshments for the guests herself rather than send in the cook, the chief visitor's wine-reddened face had beamed.

" 'What matter a spotted peel, when the fruit is sweet?' " Second Daughter said, imitating the old man's croak. Her eyes dimmed as she continued. "And though Mother used to tell me something like that years ago, before she died, it sounded different coming from his slobbering lips, I can tell you." Second Daughter's strong shoulders twitched with surprising delicacy. "Father sent me off, but I listened from the hallway and heard the deal concluded. Only, it turned out that the old man intended me to be his concubine, not his daughter-in-law."

Her keen eyes swung toward Baby, who listened as avidly as any of us, half for the story's sake, half out of relief that no angry soldiers were marching us off toward some awful punishment. "Better a concubine than a despised old maid, they say, but not the concubine of that old wine sponge, living in the same house with the one man I ever thought would make a halfway decent husband!" She shrugged. "So, early this morning, I left my father's house."

"And now?" Feng stepped forward, assuming his place as chief among us, in charge of the situation at last.

Second Daughter lifted her chin. She was no common country girl. "And now, since my only sister died last year in childbirth, and I have no other relatives or friends, I've come to ask if you will take me in. Father worked me hard. I'm strong enough to be a useful servant, and—" She looked at me with gentle rue. "And I can learn quickly how to earn money selling people what they think they need."

I blushed, though I did believe the charm could have worked its magic, given a proper chance. Glancing away from Second Daughter, I saw a look of pity sweep across Feng's face. Then something he would have called discretion replaced it. Would the Moon Lady allow this? And what was to happen after we found the stone? He frowned.

Second Daughter must have seen the same thing. "And I've brought money," she said hastily. "No small amount. Whatever you're up to, I'll join you. This mountain is the only place I've ever traveled to, but I know it well. Mama used to bring us here on pilgrimage when we were girls. Surely you could use a guide."

This was no time to explain that we expected to be guided by the Moon Lady, and not until later did it occur to me Second Daughter might be the form that guidance would take. Feng put on the air of the stern yet merciful magistrate he longed to be and nodded curtly, yes. Soon we were all chatting and laughing somewhat giddily, even Feng, as the four of us described what we'd imagined when we pressed ourselves into the crevice.

In less than an hour the trail brought us to a run-down convent, and there our party spent the night. Frogs chanted antiphonal refrains well past evening, but I slept deeply, relieved to be rid of the soldiers. I often savored the freedom my boy's clothes gave me, yet I preferred to be known as a young woman: I understood that much at least about who I was.

We continued the next day past grotesque stones and through the unfathomable forest. Slick patches of laurel, their froth of tiny lantern buds preparing to bloom, caught wisps of low clouds that wrapped the trail in obscurity, then fell away as we broke through to clear vistas. Cliffs of bare rock rose like millstones some whimsical giant had upended, and gleaming ribbons of water rushed below us toward the faraway sea.

From certain points of land our ears caught reverberations from the hills. To me, it sounded like a great slide of sand down the face of an unbalanced dune. Second Daughter told us that the local people called it the Mountain Tide because travelers said it resembled the crash of ocean breakers whipped up by typhoons. From its sound, farmers in the foothills foretold rain and the fate of the harvest.

Eventually we came to the old monastery below Central Peak. After supper, we sat on its front terrace of beaten earth, and Second Daughter pointed out to us the nearby summits: White Cloud Peak and Echoing Hill. Just behind them, her mother had told her, was the cave called Three Immortals, after an ancient goddess and her two sisters, and next to it a famous square-shaped rock, ten feet across, known as the Chessboard Stone.

"All this sight-seeing's well enough," Feng interrupted, "but we have a job to do, you know, and no sign yet of where or how." At that, even Sparker stilled his jokes. Though the winter weather and lack of money had forced us to finish our journey from Chang-an slowly, we all had felt a growing urgency since we reached Mothbrow Town. I'd told Second Daughter of our quest for the stone—and earned a frown from Feng for doing so. Now she too was caught up in frustration: where on all this great uplift of layered rock were we to find the stone for which we hoped the Moon Lady would grant our various rewards?

Feng muttered something about angering the goddess by adding on a tagalong. Baby, Sparker, and I had learned not to take his attempts to play the austere official altogether seriously, but Second Daughter lowered her face and slipped off to bed. Soon darkness fell. The rest of us followed her to the damp-walled rooms the monks had given us, one for the women, one for the men; fortunately, they left us to sort ourselves. With only brief good-nights, we fell separately to sleep.

The droning of the monks at morning service woke us before dawn. Blinking, I rose and drifted out into the chilly incense-laden mist that filled the monastery courtyard. One by one the others came, stamping their feet and waving their arms in the pearly dimness, as eager as I for the warmth of the morning meal. Only Second Daughter did not appear. When a silent old monk with an apron tied over his robes bowed before us, indicating that we should follow him into the guests' dining room, I stepped back into the women's bedroom to waken her. She wasn't there. Nor was she in the privy.

I hurried to the dining room and told the others. Baby's round eyes grew wider. Sparker cracked a joke about fox spirits that appear and disappear and when no one laughed, looked sorry he'd said it. Feng knit his fingers thoughtfully.

At dinner the night before, we'd talked over our plans, deciding to seek guidance at the temple of Lady Guan-yin that lay some four-hundred-odd steep steps farther upward. Now Feng argued that we might as well proceed. "Second Daughter knows that's where we're going." His belligerence melted then. "And perhaps the Lady will intercede on her behalf if something's wrong."

And so his tender side revealed itself. Feng wasn't much for prayers, except the official observances performed by good Confucian scholars, despite the fine shows he put on as the Wizard Mimesis. Much as Sparker enjoyed our trickery, he seemed to be the one with genuine leanings toward realms beyond the human. But when we reached the temple, Feng lit incense with the rest of us.

We rested awhile. Sparker yelled her name, yet we saw no sign of Second Daughter. In the tones of a regretful but unyielding father, Feng told us it was time to go.

Sparker shouldered his pack and made ready to follow the master he'd served since boyhood. Baby got to her feet with none of her usual lithe vigor. To my own surprise, I continued squatting and said, "No."

Feng's head whipped round. "Come on, Parrot, don't be silly." He rarely called me that, insisting that he and I ought to be called by our assumed names at all times. "I *do* feel sorry for the girl, you know. But she's bound to turn up somewhere. Here, we'll leave a note on this pillar if you like."

I shook my head. It occurred to me to pretend I'd received some heavenly message, but I didn't want to lie. For months, Feng had led us, and I'd given it no thought: he was the eldest, and educated, and a man. But, I reminded myself now, the Moon Lady had charged *me* with finding the stone and Feng with assisting me. I'd wait for Second Daughter.

"Parrot." Feng's voice was softer now, something like Ghalib's or even Baba's when I had amused them, though that note rang false when young Feng took it on. "Parrot, we've a higher duty. We can't be distracted by one lost person. We've got to go."

I saw no point in answering. I didn't move. Then Baby's hands fluttered, though no one paid them notice until she stepped back and squatted down beside me. Sparker stood stock-still. Feng gave up his higher principles, and sullenly agreed to wait till midday.

The impasse broke before then. Second Daughter—again panting, a beautiful peach-blossom color again glowing on her cheeks—ran up the last steps to the temple porch where we four waited. Hesitation overlay her excitement, but she poured out her story, too absorbed in her own feelings to notice the tension in the air.

She'd gotten out of bed last night when the moon rose—it was just short of full—and shone through the open window. In a soft voice she claimed that the light had woken her. She stole from the room and out of the monastery and made her way in the flood of moonlight toward the cave called Three Immortals. "Mama used to tell us girls that she wanted to take us there," she said, "but there was always so much work waiting at home that we didn't have time for side pilgrimages. Still, it wasn't very hard to find the way. When I got there, I felt . . . easier." She looked away. "Maybe thinking of Mama helped. Anyway, I found a nook just inside the cave mouth. It was chilly, of course, but I made a nest of last fall's leaves, so I didn't mind much, and I fell right to sleep.

"After a while—maybe the cold woke me, or maybe I dreamed it, I don't know, really—I heard someone call my name outside the cave. For a moment I hoped it might be Mama's ghost, I'd felt so close to her there. But I saw a bare-legged woman in a shimmery white dress, who nodded her head with satisfaction when I came out to where she stood."

At the mention of the woman in the white dress, Feng caught my eye. The rift between us disappeared.

"The moon had crossed over to the western sky by then," Second Daughter continued, "but I still could see clearly. Most things looked gray, the way they do by moonlight, but next to the bare-legged woman—even though she looked young, she somehow made me think of a hermit who had been studying mystic arts in the hills for years—I saw a huge flat stone, bright yellow-green.

"The stone's color told me its name. People call it the Sulfur Flower Stone. I'd heard it lay somewhere near that cave. I could see another color too: a bright red design on the flat surface of the rock. The bare-legged woman handed me a writing brush, and ink and paper, telling me to copy what it said. I did the best I could."

"What did it say?" asked Sparker, his face merry with the thought of a messenger from heavenly realms.

Second Daughter hesitated. "Just a minute. I want to tell you the strangest part. Every word I copied disappeared from the stone the moment I brushed its duplicate on the paper. As soon as I finished, the woman waved me back toward the cave, and—I swear I'm not lying—walked up a moonbeam into the sky."

"Don't worry, Second Daughter." Feng leaned forward earnestly; clearly this sign of the Moon Lady's favor had convinced him we ought to keep this bold farmer's daughter with us. "We believe you. But we'd like to see the paper. Surely the message is important."

Now the hangdog pockmarked girl replaced the lively runaway. "I haven't got it. I *know* I took the paper with me back to my leaf nest in the cave. But in the morning it had vanished. Believe me, I looked everywhere. That's why I'm so late arriving here."

"The paper must have been made of moonlight," Sparker said in an uncharacteristically serious voice, "so it vanished when the moon set." His months of masquerade had had their effect: he'd become quick to offer theories about the ways of the suprahuman world.

"The copying-out may just have been to help you remember the message, Second Daughter," I added. "Tell us what it said."

The look she gave me mingled shame with an arched-browed amusement at the world's unfairness. "Do you suppose my father hired me a tutor? I don't think he would have done that for my brother, if I'd had one; surely he wasn't going to waste the money on my sister and me." Baby rested one graceful hand on Second Daughter's arm. I felt my cheeks burn. Sparker snorted.

"I've sometimes felt book learning got in the way of real knowledge," he said. "Begging your pardon, Master Mimesis. But now I've got to admit it can have its uses." He ducked his head, picked up a pebble, and began to practice making it vanish and reappear.

I felt too clumsy to say anything, but Feng echoed Baby's gentleness. "Never mind, Second Daughter. You're not to blame. Here, take this stick and write out what you remember in the dirt here. Don't rush. No doubt you can picture quite a lot of it."

A stroke here, a dash there, now a sudden flurry of her stick—Second Daughter squeezed her eyes, and opened them, and scratched out what she could in the dust. I knew what it was like for Second Daughter. Before my writing lessons began in

Liang-jou, words were just so many bird tracks to me. It was only after I'd learned a few that I could see the forms of the others more distinctly and noticed how certain shapes appear again and again in different words. The rest of us tried to keep ourselves from hanging over her. I sat near Baby and for the first time in months dared to fling a companionable arm around her shoulders.

"That's all," Second Daughter murmured at last.

It was precious little. She'd written one word as its mirror image, and I could recognize one or two others. But most were simply scribbles, and several were represented by a blank.

Feng appointed himself scribe and recopied, below the original, what he could make sense of. He wrote, "the stone . . . one word . . . a story," and then he wrote no more.

"Can you remember anything else about it?" he asked. "Was there—I don't know—a title, or a signature, or anything?"

Second Daughter frowned at first, hurt by his obvious disappointment. I vowed then that, if we remained together, I would teach her everything I knew about the art of written language. But her pluck sustained her. She closed her eyes again and thought, then picked up her stick.

"Yes!" she said. "Three more words. At the very end. I can see the last two clearly now. Look. The second's like a double doorway, sort of, don't you think? And the third—on the left three dots, like dripping water, and on the right a kind of archway around a short line like this one, and a little square." She looked up hopefully.

"Cave!" Feng and I shouted it together. "And the second one is *door* or *gate*. Well done," Feng added, while I began saying, "Something-gate Cave, Something-gate, Cave," in hopes of bringing the first word back to Second Daughter's recollection.

"Dragongate!" she cried out. "At least there's a Dragongate Cave near the foot of the mountain on the trail most pilgrims take down. Do you think that might be it?"

"Lots of caves with 'gate' in their names," Sparker muttered. But Feng, who had taken the stick from Second Daughter's hand, ignored him and scratched one more sign in the dust.

"Does that look right?" he asked her, and pursed his lips in satisfaction when she said it did. "Dragongate Cave it is, then. We'd best be on our way."

This time we set off eagerly together, and though the air was crisp at that altitude in the middle of the fourth month, the mountain's changeable weather had turned about again. Clear views greeted us the rest of the way. Up and down we traveled, across perilous bare ridges and along passageways squeezed through the underbrush. Coming down from one rocky spine known as Stone Tablet Ridge, we crossed a gorge on a bridge of stone. Nearby I saw the huge imprisoned bones of strange fish, flung up into the rock face, as if this whole vast terrain had risen from the ocean floor. I shook my head. There was magic enough in Mothbrow Mountain without my adding more.

Soon we passed a twisted lofty stone, its proportions the same as a human figure, but three times the height. This, said Second Daughter, was the Lady Guan-yin Crag. From her bundle she pulled her last sticks of incense and insisted that we pause to make a proper reverence. The simple bridge we came to shortly after was likewise named for the good Lady; even Feng admitted that the peaks towering above us and the clear waters roaring below created an air of mystery.

Descending, we made better time, and eventually came to a whole series of caves, including one called Windy Cavern, from which the wind blows without ceasing. That night we camped nearby, huddled against the damp cold, but pleased that we'd reach Dragongate the next day.

While Sparker cooked our supper, I put the others from my thoughts, tore a broad banana leaf from a tree, and settled down with Second Daughter to begin to keep my vow. A splint of bamboo from the frayed end of my walking staff would serve us as a pen.

"Here," I said. "You've already learned some words. I'll show you the proper order in which to make the strokes, so that the lines will flow correctly when you're able to write them more quickly. Watch."

Second Daughter started to beg off. Then the willful intelligence that set her running off from miserable respectability after a troupe of drifters gripped her. Her eyes brightened, and she bent to watch me as I scratched the words—clumsily—on the tough green leaf. Baby settled down on the other side of me to watch.

"The stone . . . one word . . . a story," I wrote, saying each one clearly as I formed it. Second Daughter took the bamboo splint and began to write. I was pleased. Writing down my own poems sometimes seemed presumptuous to me. But surely no harm lay in teaching a copyist's skill to someone else.

Suddenly Baby shook my arm and clapped her hands and began signing furiously. She must be jealous again, I thought, though she had never shown her jealousy this way before. "Baby," I said rather sharply, trying to temper my irritation by saying the name in Khotanese.

She snatched the leaf from under the tip of the bamboo splint. Then she squatted, holding the leaf up to the fire. Her free hand gestured wildly in the direction Feng had strolled off in.

By now Sparker, too, stared at Baby's antics in amazement. Just when she leapt up and backed away from the leaf as if terrified by what was written on it, he shouted out, "The poem! Don't you see? She's telling us that the words Second Daughter has remembered are from the poem Master wrote in secret ink to fool the soldiers. How did it go? 'One word and stones they'll be.' What was the rest of it?"

I ran and pulled a fresh leaf from the banana tree, then chanted the words aloud as I wrote them out:

> If men with swords should seek the stone,
> One word: and stones they'll be.

If history's a story, then
Which story's history?

Baby clapped her hands.

I added the name of the cave. "Does this look right?" I asked Second Daughter, and she nodded vigorously.

"I suppose I could be mistaken, but—" She broke the sentence off. "No, that has to be it. I'm sure of it."

While Sparker and Second Daughter talked excitedly, I thought about the second half of the poem, trying to make some sense of the gibberish. Surely it was just something Feng threw in to spook the soldiers. But it kept bothering me. "Those last two lines," I said. "They're nonsense in Chinese, at least as far as I can see. But in Soghdian . . ." Second Daughter blinked as she realized I actually spoke that language, but said nothing.

Soghdian, I explained, has words for things that Chinese doesn't. Sparker and Second Daughter didn't seem to like that idea much, but Baby nodded. I quickly added that sometimes it went the other way. "So in Soghdian, there's a word for when you tell about something that happened that means maybe it's sort of true and sort of isn't. You know, maybe it's real history, only changed, and maybe just rumors, or even something someone made up on purpose. Like what they tell in the marketplaces, to be amusing and teach a lesson, too."

"Or maybe like a lie," said Sparker, grinning.

"Well, yes," I admitted, *like* a lie. But you must have heard a wandering monk reciting in the markets in Chang-an, Sparker, and there are more of them out west. Or there's those books Feng has told us about—what are they called? *Transmitted Records of the Bizarre*? They report events from the past, but a lot of what's in them is just gossip."

Second Daughter interrupted. "You mean *educated* people read books they know are lies?"

Sparker started to pick at the frayed edge of one of the torn

banana leaves. Baby's fingers twitched slightly as they sometimes did when she was thinking deeply.

"Listen," I said. "Soghdian has another word for things like
that. The ones that aren't true but aren't lies either."

Sparker tucked his chin in skeptically. "That's what you
think the poem says history is? I used to listen to the Old Master, Tutor Feng, when Young Master and I were boys back in Jia-
jou, and the whole point of history is that it's absolutely true."
He grinned again. "Anything else is just a trick, like one of ours."

"Well," I said, "when I was a little girl in Khotan and a
monk's words gave me a bad dream, my Nannie told me it was
'just a story.' " The last I'd had to say in Soghdian. I said it again
for Baby in Khotanese. She knit her brows and gave one slow
nod. "I can't say it in Chinese. That's the point. But if you could
say it, then the poem means that history is—that there's more
than one way to look at it, or even that it's something we make
up. . . ."

I stopped talking. Baby remained deep inside her own
thoughts. Second Daughter's polite look had frozen over into
incomprehension. She may never have heard a traveling storyteller, in an out-of-the-way place like Mothbrow Town, I realized, nor a story not put forth as fact.

And Sparker grumbled to himself, "Can't say it in Chinese!
I never heard such rubbish!" He turned to lift the pot lid and
peek at the rice. "Nearly ready," he announced in a matter-of-
fact tone. "Master should be back soon."

In fact, Feng returned a moment later, just in time to be
served the first bowl of rice. Sparker gleefully began to relate
Baby's discovery of what Second Daughter had written in her
dream, not bothering to bring up my muddled thoughts about
the poem's meaning. "So perhaps, Master, it was the Moon
Lady's way of letting us know she approved of your trick with
heating the invisible ink by the fire. And she's named Dragongate Cave as the place we'll find the stone she wants. What do
you think?"

Feng stroked his chin. He'd removed the false beard of horse-hair shortly after the soldiers left, claiming he was glad to be rid of it. But he kept up the sagelike habit of rubbing his chin when he thought things over, even now, when only a few sparse whiskers grew there. "Makes sense," he said in his best magisterial tones. "Though one thing has been bothering me about that poem. I haven't mentioned it before, but I only wrote the first two lines."

In the Realm
of Transformations

Come. Enter the realm of transformations. Do not mind the pythons' slither. These scaly tutelary demons will not poison you, and surely you know how to evade their coils. Here on Mothbrow Mountain, they are known as Dragon Laymen, after the devout gentlemen pilgrims, the patrons of the serene temples scattered across its leafy slopes. In another country, another age, one of their number possessed the women of an oracular cult. And what harm lay in that? Only one warning: do not dismiss them as mere fiction. And do admit you know *that* word, though it hasn't yet been uttered on this fine spring eighth-century day. *Ficcioun* they'll say in English four hundred years beyond the great Tang's fall, harking back to an earlier tongue's *fingere*, "to feign, to mold, to form"—like clay squeezed breathless by undulating muscles. But, no, that simile's a mere invention. Leave your fears behind.

Climb to Golden Summit, on the eastern edge of the great central plateau. Unlike the eager travelers who've rushed on toward the next chapter in their tale, you're at leisure, you can choose your time. So: a sun-streaked day, here at the heights. Westward, Tibetan ranges float in midair. Eastward, a fabric of cloud coalesces below your feet. As the vaporous network weaves itself toward substantiality, it becomes a soft terrain they call the "silver world." Just at the right hour (some say the day's eighth watch, some the ninth), a sphere of light takes form, round as a mirror, seven-layered, prismatic at the edge. Should the cloudy web grow thick enough to catch it, your own shadow will appear, as if some odd design had been impressed upon the silvery textile. And glowing all about that shadow, the sphere of light becomes your rainbow halo, bright nimbus, aureola, *Heiligenschein,* your glory. Then the clouds unravel into hanks of silk floss, and the image disappears. The orb of light remains, reflecting this world's things in a giddying brightness of illusion that dazzles your aching eyes. Your retinas ring like clashing cymbals, bright bronze bells. It is too much. You look away.

Or come in the evening. Phosphorescent flecks drift up through the gorge below your feet. They glint and dapple like fireflies seeking out their mates. Right now, in the Tang, the people say these lights are the cleanest lanterns of the foothill villagers, come to pay respects to the temple of The Enlightened One. More and more lights gather, and if the ground were crisp with snow (but it is the year's fourth month, remember?), you would hear their quiet hissing as they extinguished themselves and fell. Try to grasp one—ah, impossible. Try, then (the monks will urge you to it; success is a sign of the heart's purity), to pull one toward you with a cedar branch. But wait. First invent a sturdy railing on the cliff's edge. And having done that, if you are certain you will pass the test, reach forward, out over the void. Draw in one of these wonders, and never mind if it is real or not.

Suppose now that you take the descending path to Windy

Cavern and beyond. You still will have to scramble upward from time to time, or trudge on piety's stairs. Some good while later, you'll arrive—cheeks blowing, winded—at Thunderdemon Shrine. Here it is always dank and sullen, however bright the sunbeams that paint the peaks. Hush. Not one word! Those superstitious soldiers were not entirely fools. Utter a single sound and the storm wyverns will hurl bolts of deadly lightning at your head.

Nearby, you'll pass a monastery already nearing its millennium. To its right—see that jagged escarpment there?—Nu Wa the Genetrix selected the stones with which she repaired the sky. All the caves of the mountain's honeycombed interior ooze draconic power.

Later, following Black Dragon River, stumbling with fatigue along the bank, mesmerized by its downpours and its eddies, you come to a foaming chute emerging from a spray-wet portal— inviting, fearsome—in a high wall of dark marbled jade. This is Dragongate Chasm. Enter in.

What's this? You've caught up with the other travelers. Damp and weary, they struggle across the rock face, up the pearl-foamed tributary. Be still and watch.

What light there is within the mossy chasm refracts off water-washed stone and tumbling waves. A rivulet hurls itself from far overhead. The five hide most of their belongings in a cranny, then proceed. They push past upthrust brushy clumps of thin bamboo. Seeking out shallow hand- and footholds, they angle some twenty feet up the green-shot cliff, and pull themselves at last inside Dragongate Cave. Why not follow after? It's easier for you.

At first, vision's dim and slippery. The travelers steady one another, catch their breaths, and look around. A few feet inward—inexplicable!—a diffused light irradiates the interior. Not sunrays sifted through some skyward crack. Not the blue glow of bioluminescent life-forms, though it sometimes wavers sea green, sometimes cool violet. Never mind: Second Daughter has heard of this phenomenon, and her recounting of what they see seems to reassure the party.

All around them sheets of flowstone hump and dish, now cataracts, now giant writhing claws. Stalagmites rise, every day a droplet or a ripple different, where stalactites in their myriad variations swell. Baby starts. A cave salamander, mutated into blindness, scuttles past her, avatar of metamorphosis. Wordless, the travelers accord; there's nothing for it but to plunge deeper in.

A sudden boom: a rumbling drum? a rainfrog's thundercall? The beating reverberates within the cavern, within the travelers' skulls, as Bronze Age rituals reverberate in devolved form through successive dynasties. The five stand close together in a pear-shaped chamber. The mute dancer steps away. Skywhistle (Parrot now to all around her) listens to the booming, blinks in the curious light, and trembles with a powerful sense of things *already seen*. At Horsecrest Post Station, once, she dreamed a dream. . . .

Baby begins her dance. In tempo with the pulsebeat rhythm, slow now, slow now, quick and quicker, hastening to hysteric frenzy, she flings her arms in a sword dance older than any written record, the ancient dance of women speaking for the sky. She moans, she shrieks, and the others know this time she cries out unfeigned: "Purple Thunder, Meteor, Damasktip"—it comes in gasps—"Iron-gloam, Liquidhues, Pure Filament, Steely Pleiades"—she sucks in air, she wheezes—"Flowerygraph, Rainbowwhite, Frostblade, Flying Constellation." The drumbeat stops. She finishes. She faints.

Parrot and Second Daughter rush to her. Feng looks on helpless. Sparker keeps his distance, grinning like a holy idiot. Parrot scoops water from a pool next to Baby in the cave floor and splashes the dancer's pallid face. She blinks and sits up, safely mute once more.

"We'll rest awhile," says Parrot, and Second Daughter nods. Feng removes his small carrysack and sits upon it. But Sparker's too uneasy to relax. That rapturous look, that seely-silly grin, has washed off his face.

He turns to his master in the unnatural light. "Those words. What did she mean?" he asked, taking the cup from his belt, giving Master Feng a drink of water before he can make an answer. Only then—devoted servant!—does he drink deep himself. Hushed echoes whisper hollow overhead.

After some consideration, Feng replies. Some of the dancer's cryptic words named swords renowned in history. The rest were suitable to be engraved on other blades. But as for why—

"And why here?" Second Daughter interrupts, forgetting in her excitement her maidenly modesty.

Sparker frowns at her, disapproving, and then resumes his usual perceptive look. "Because a sword—or swords—awaits us. Probably right in this dragon cave. I'm sure we're meant to find them before we can get the stone the goddess wants. Master! Tell us how we ought to make the search!"

This last he adds not because he himself lacks direction. You've seen that by now. Rather, it's because—though Parrot stays beside her friend, stroking her hair and murmuring restful words—Second Daughter has leapt up already and begun to look about. She grasps a dangling stalactite, as if considering whether to break it off and make of it a cutlass, but restrains herself from such defacement of the cave.

"First we'll need to map the place," says Feng. "Then analyze its components, dividing them among us so we cover them all thoroughly." He stops to stroke the beard that isn't there.

But meanwhile Parrot has quickly given Baby's hand a squeeze and leaned forward to gaze into the round, dark pool beside them. The strange light strikes its surface; it mirrors the bell curve of the dome above. "Look!" she cries out.

Feng comes quickly. To Parrot, it seems for an instant as if the refracted likeness of the would-be official has a chelonian look: outthrust neck gone leathery, jaw turned horny and toothless. Then someone knocks a pebble in the water, and concentric wavelets shatter the metamorphosed image, as the pebble's plunk shatters the brief silence. "No," says Parrot. "Look up!" She points overhead, to what she first saw in watery effigy.

Two quivering caskets. From them emanates the light that fills the cave. And to the musician's ears, a faint singing wells. All the travelers can make out the writing on the caskets. Second Daughter looks to Parrot, Sparker to his Master Feng. "Moonsaber," the two readers say with one breath, and then, "Dragonrill."

Time for action: Sparker scrambles up to the ledge and hands the caskets down to Feng, taking exquisite care. The Master lifts the lids, the unearthly singing rises, the servant clambers down. The swords match perfectly, strange talismanic figures chased on each twin blade. On Dragonrill, pearly inlaid stars of white jade inscribe a constellation; call it Draco. Moonsaber bears etched phases—bow, crescent, quarter, half, gibbous disk, round ringed silken fan.

"Perhaps we shouldn't—" says Parrot, but Sparker pays no mind. Kneeling before the caskets, he takes one hilt in each hand.

"Master," he says, preparing to offer them to the man he's always followed. Vision shimmers. Sparker turns into a small, flattish stone.

"Oh!" says Second Daughter sorrowfully. "Sparker."

The swords go silent. They hover in midair. The stone is translucent, fine-grained, oblong, no longer than a handspan.

Feng merely echoes, "Oh."

As if against her will, Parrot chants again the puzzling poem. " 'If men with swords should seek the stone . . .' Poor Sparker is to be the inkstone the Moon Lady sent us after! Why did I think only about that jabber in the poem's second half? Can the Moon Lady be so cruel?"

For of course, one glance at Sparker's transmogrification and all's clear: save for its cloudy crystalline look, the stone resembles the best of earthly inkstones; its glowing pallor marks it as suitable for the palace on the Moon. But Parrot errs in one thing, mistaking the goddess's detachment for cruelty.

The swords break the mournful tableau. They fly, Dragonrill to Parrot, Moonsaber to Second Daughter, and settle, one hilt easy in each young woman's hand.

Baby stares. "Say nothing!" Feng shouts out, stepping toward them, prepared to snatch the enchanted things away, prepared to risk his own fleshly form, eager even, as if the sacrifice might bring back his servant, his boyhood friend.

Yet Parrot knows they're safe. "If *men* with swords," she chants and stands unchanged. She's not sure she likes it, but she sees what's meant to be.

Second Daughter inhales deeply. "One word," she says and shows no visible alteration, though perhaps inside she moves another plucky step away from the farmer's browbeaten daughter that she used to be. Then she starts to laugh.

Soon the others join her, hoots and titters and wild guffaws rebounding off the bell-walls of the cavern, new laughter echoing with the old in an earsplitting clamor of relief, and grief. Baby, still weakened from her frantic dancing, is the first to weep. But not the last.

After that they turn back toward the cave's mouth. Second Daughter removes her linen headcloth and wraps the stone. Gently, Feng takes it from her then and carries it himself. No one says a word.

Evening has filled Dragongate Chasm. But the twin swords, thrust in knotted sashes, shed enough light to show the way. From the marbled cranny the four recover a lute and other belongings. When they reach Black Dragon River's wider valley, the swords dim again; the moon's full and floods the trail with light. The shrunken company gathers on a wide spot and considers what to do.

Parrot remembers Sparker's jokes and pranks, the struggle in him between his loyalty to Feng and his skeptical dismissal of society's rules. One moment he'd laugh madly at some pompous mark they'd cheated, the next urge Baby to behave like a proper concubine, and after that confide in Parrot his hope that in some grotto of Mothbrow Mountain he might find a rare mineral that promotes long life and the search for spiritual release from the human world. This last memory prompts another, of her lost friend Nephrite. Tears rise up again.

"Not now, my dear," says Second Daughter, who for years has swallowed her share of salt and more. "There's work we have to do." Parrot looks to her companion and, like her, draws her sword.

The moonlight fashions its transmutations. Or perhaps the gem-horned constellation—Chinese Draco, tail tipped by the Shamanka Star, Antares glowing red within its breast—works the change. Like the antique starswords of Feng-cheng, forged long ago in fallen Wu, Dragonrill and Moonsaber turn into dragonets.

Each sword wielder mounts, and draws a companion up behind. Like the double rainbow-dragon—portent of womanly power—that arced through the sky some tens of years before, when Empress Wei declared herself the regent, the twinned creatures climb the sky.

Opalescent dust puffs up. They've landed just outside the crystal lunar keep. Each dragonet turns sword again. Parrot leads the way.

A gate of ivory, hinged with silver, opens as they near it, and the party steps inside. A young woman gowned in undyed silk graciously bows before them. "Welcome," she says, "to you travelers from the crucible of changes. My teacher has been expecting you. Do please step inside."

All four draw in their breaths at the scintillating walls of the reception room, its argent furnishings. White Aureole bows to them again, offers round a tray with cups of pellucid nectar (but no one accepts), bows a third time and leaves to tell the Moon Lady that the guests have come.

Second Daughter, who has never even been as far from her

father's house as Jia-jou, stands uneasy, balanced on the balls of her feet, as silent now as Baby. Something in her heart calls her to sit and make herself at home here, but remembering Sparker she refuses it. Feng begins to question Parrot in an undertone, but she shrugs and he leaves off. Soon the goddess enters, waving them to white brocade cushions, and one by one the visitors bend their knees and sink.

"I thank you for your troubles," the Moon Lady says, in kindly, measured tones. "I've missed my Hyaline Cloud Inkstone and am certain that this new one will serve me well. Please do take a cup of nectar. It will refresh you. I'd like to talk with you about your rewards, my dears."

This time—not from greed, but from their several proportions of courtesy and awe—each one lifts a cup from White Aureole's tray. Maintaining anger toward one possessed of such charitable charm as the Moon Lady's isn't easy. But when the little cups are drained, Feng pulls the cloth-wrapped stone from the bundle by his side.

"Madam," he begins, summoning all the gravity he can. "I believe this is the stone you want." He unwraps it, revealing the smooth luster of the ink-grinding surface, the polished slope that runs down to its well.

She thanks them in her even, musical voice. But Feng has more to say.

"We do not give it freely, madam. So—I am correct, am I not?—I fear it cannot be yours."

Shocked, White Aureole springs to her feet with haste unseemly in a moonmaid. Even the goddess lets one hand fly up, uncontrolled. And yet, she only murmurs, "Ah? Do tell me more."

That's easily done: Feng has lots to say. Sparker saved his life in boyhood, saved him from brutish slavery in Chang-an, and though Feng respects the proper relationships between master and manservant (here, the Moon Lady allows herself a brief, dismissive gesture), he cannot, now that Sparker's gone, call him anything but "friend." A friend, moreover, to whom he owes a life. He will not leave him to this fate.

"Not even for an official position?" the goddess asks. "One of no little note?"

A longing passes through Feng's eyes. Yet it's soon replaced by firm determination. "No."

When the Moon Lady turns a questioning look to Parrot, the young woman bites her lip and silently shakes her head. She'll find her mother some other way, she thinks, not at such a price. Baby and Second Daughter cast their gazes to the carpet shimmering on the floor.

"But what . . ." the Moon Lady's voice grows sweeter, more persuasive. "What if I told you this transformation is his destiny? You know his heartfelt wishes. Long life. Release from passions. Transcendence of the body's appetites. Does not a stone have all these things?"

Feng begins to sputter in denial, but Parrot tells him quietly that what the goddess says is true. Sparker has confided these yearnings to her. The young man nods in acknowledgment, but still his jaw holds firm.

And, like Feng, Parrot insists that incarnation as a stone is not what Sparker sought. "Let him strive for these things in human form," she says, "as a mountain hermit, a seeker of the Way." A glance at Second Daughter somehow gives her courage, and she runs forward to throw herself in supplication at the Lady's feet.

The goddess is moved. "Come, child," she says tenderly. "You needn't do that. In truth, he would be best off as a stone, but I see the difficulty that notion causes humans. Let us try to come to an agreement. I really must have some replacement for my inkstone, though, and it seems you are the ones best suited to give it to me. Indeed, in your case—may I call you Greenpearl?—in your case, Greenpearl, what I may do is bound up by another bargain. White Aureole, will you be so good as to serve us all again?"

Parrot is silent, lost in wonder at the sound of her unknown name. Second Daughter watches White Aureole with a look of hunger. With her eyes still downcast, Baby's fingers twitch, following some inner discourse. Feng throws back his head and drains his cup. He makes to speak, but the goddess overrides him.

"Another rare stone, different but fully suitable for my needs, lies beneath the waters of the Yangzi River. You, Feng, shall fetch it for me. And shall pay a price—no small one—and be rewarded, too. Then your friend shall be restored to human form. Agreed?"

"Anything!" he says. The Lady nods.

"Dancer?" Baby looks up at the soft interrogation. "Your destiny is already fixed. My volatile starsister has taken you in hand. But in helping the others with their journey onward, I shall help you as well. Remember this: to speak in pain, as you did in the dragon cave, is nonetheless a kind of speaking. And someday you shall speak in joy. Do you understand?"

Baby signals that she does. Second Daughter makes as if to touch her with a motherly touch, but just then Baby shifts out of reach.

"Second Daughter." The young woman's attention turns entirely to the goddess. "It has been arranged that you'll continue with the others, for their good and your own. As for the recompense—tell me what it is you'd like."

Second Daughter tries to speak, but something blocks her. It seems a shyness freezes her tongue to her palate: The unlovely, unwanted daughter of a provincial farmer to speak aloud of her desires? And in this place? She hangs her head. Impossible.

The Moon Lady beckons, remote, sympathetic, irresistible. Cheeks ablaze with shame, the pockmarked peasant swordswoman stands up. She makes her way to the goddess, whispers her longings into one tilted ear.

"It shall happen," says the Lady. "Not now, and not so easily as you might wish, but—yes." Her smile warms just the merest

343

fraction, as the full moon warms in the hour of its setting, its light gone golden through a thicker sea of air.

Despite the years of practice, despite the vow she made once when confronted by her father's anger, tears wet Second Daughter's eyes. She blinks. They disappear.

"Now," says the goddess. "As to the journey. The dragon-swords will return you to Black Dragon River. I'm afraid you cannot travel that way through the human realm, however, for you would not learn the things you need to learn. But I can make sure you needn't beg and tell false fortunes and go on tired feet." In the middle of the river, she explains, there is a famous rock called Stoneboat. Second Daughter nods. She saw it once, before her mother's death. The flying dragonets will take them there, the Moon Lady tells the humans, and for as long as it's required, the rock will maintain the form of a wooden boat. On it, they can travel downstream to a tributary of the southward-flowing Min, joining it at Beyond-the-Clouds Mountain, where the monk Hai-tong devotes himself to chiseling a towering Buddha into a great bluff. The Lady looks at Parrot. "A woman named Xue Tao will write poems at the temple there someday. Think of her, and on this journey see that you improve your fluency in the languages of verse." Parrot's heart tightens, and she bows. If the goddess urges it, perhaps she is not overbold to make poems, after all.

"From there," the Moon Lady continues, "the waters will take you to the Yangzi, and eastward through the gorges to your various destinations. Stop and rest yourselves from time to time. The rice store in the boat will not diminish, and there are quilts and clothes and such aboard." She looks pityingly at the cheap garments that have been Second Daughter's lot and the stained near-rags the others wear. "The rest . . . will unfold when it unfolds. Now come, let us drink a farewell cup."

Her voice is a mother's good-night kiss, promising the rest of the bedtime story for another time. They savor the last drops of the pellucid nectar. But Parrot won't be content. "And my mother? Is she well?"

"Well enough," replies the goddess. "Though I cannot say free of sorrow. Her life changes, though she still awaits you. I will tell you only that your journey takes you toward her. Don't hurry it. You cannot reach her till the time is right, and you still have much to learn. But I think you have something else to ask?"

Parrot's eyes flick toward Baby and return. "I have a friend," she says, faltering. "Retired from life in the world of dust and devoted to the Motherqueen. As they say you have been. Can you tell me how she is? Has she achieved what she longs for?"

The Moon Lady rests her cheek upon her fingers. "There is a way you can find out. Think over what I've said to you. Now, I must send all of you off with a warning. I will treat this ink-stone like the treasure it is. But remember, nothing from the mortal realm, not stones or seas or mountains, lasts forever. Conduct yourselves with caution." She smiles in reassurance, though somewhere in the distance all can hear the steady sound of a mortar grinding in a pestle. "Now, I'm afraid it's time for you to go."

They leave, four of them, not five. White Aureole shows the party to the door. And you who need not mount a dragon-sword may fly with them to the river and observe the alteration of a foam-rinsed boulder to a boat: long sweeps for steering mounted aft as well as astern, arched cabin of woven reeds ready to be removed for shelter when they moor in sand-soft coves. Let the currents of change carry you with them. Dream of the three great gorges of the Yangzi yet to come, where the shores close in high and sheer, and the water runs swift and deep. Listen when the musician Greenpearl takes out her lute on the drifting boat, and—freed for once of an old reluctance—works another transformation, setting new words to a melody she knows.

Parrot Speaks: 19

Bearing my starsword and a new name, Heavenglaive, I learned many things on my journey. *Stoneboat* carried us downstream to the Yangzi and through the gorges toward the village where Dreamdragon Feng repaid his debt to Sparker and Baby found her true voice. Some of the lessons were simple: among them, how to give my words the regional lilt the people use in Shu and eastward, where the gorges rise. Proud though I was to speak in the tones of the capital—it was all I had left of my lost birthright—I saw the usefulness of talking as the country people did. After all, now I traveled not as a mysterious practitioner of magic arts, who gained face from a Chang-an accent, but as a roving swordswoman; wanderers like Second Daughter and I are rare, yet Shu is known to be a homeland of curiosities and knights-errant.

I learned, too, how little difference there was, at base, between Bordermoon's life as charming entertainer and Skywhistle's as apprentice charlatan. Both sought out others' needs in order to survive. But during those weeks as a swordswoman, I gathered up the bits of self-reliance scattered through my earlier lives and made of them a person quite unlike a contract-bound courtesan or Feng's follower.

Early in our travels, on Beyond-the-Clouds Mountain, Baby taught me again something of the power of words. We made our way from the Black Dragon River to a larger one, and then to the confluence of two rivers with the lovely Min. Near evening, we moored our boat at the base of Beyond-the-Clouds' grand stone bluff, where the Min curves out briefly toward the west on its southward flow. Scrambling up by means of a few scrubby bushes wedged into the rock, we paused a moment on a shelf above the waterline. Cut deep into the bluff were the huge feet of a seated image of the Buddha of the Future.

My neck ached as I looked up. We'd had a better view as we approached it. Now I couldn't see past the knees to the serene and mighty head three hundred feet or more above us.

We labored up steps devout monks had chiseled into the stone. Mists floated off the river, and we climbed through wisps of fog. Halfway up, as we paused to rest, the air trembled with the profound tones of a temple bell overhead. We passed the gigantic mouth with its smooth smile, the broad nose and the long-lobed ears, the heavy-lidded inward eyes, the skull's dome, and reached, at last, the top. There a monk with an Indian look about his face greeted us.

"Welcome, sseekers," the monk said in breathy accents. "Thiss one is called Nagadharma and will take you in his care. Thiss one sserves The Great Teacher of Illusion, but . . ." When he smiled I saw he had only his two front teeth. "No ssermon now, only resst and ssomething hot to eat."

So we followed him to a small hut, deep in a tangle of shrubs and wind-bent trees. "The evening bell has rung. The other monks make their final meditation and prepare to ssleep. The temple gate will sstay locked until the predawn prayers begin. Thiss lodge awaits late-arriving travelers. Here, you may find peace." Again, he smiled his gummy, otherworldly smile.

One by one, we ducked and entered the lodge, where a single oil-lamp flickered. The last one in, I turned a moment to gaze past a fretwork of pale pink petals on the branch of a mountain pear, toward the rising jade-white moon.

Second Daughter and I now wore the swordswomen's clothes that had awaited us on the enchanted boat: silver scabbards hanging from matched sashes of scarlet silk, knee-high boots into which we tucked our trousers—hers moon white and mine deepwater indigo—and round our heads plain turbans such as fisherwomen wear. Baby's new bodice flashed with lilac threads, and her skirts swirled darkest crimson. Like the rest of us, she had hung a pilgrim's bottle-gourd at her waist.

Only Feng, clad all in black, jade-handled dagger at his belt, dressed like a man. So when Nagadharma brought our supper in from some unseen kitchen, he offered the first bowl of steaming noodles, fragrant with pink peppercorns and sesame oil, to Feng. "Remember that thiss world'ss a phantassmagoria, good ssir, and eat," he said. Quickly then, he passed bowls round to the rest of us.

The favors life visits upon men do not arrive without a price. Feng was first to raise his chopsticks toward his mouth. One drop of the dripping noodles' broth upon his tongue, the good monks told us later, and he'd have changed within the hour to a serpent-demon, held thrall by the monstrous Nagadharma.

As we all would have, only Feng came closest. His lips parted, his neck thrust slightly forward—and Baby slapped chopsticks, noodles, bowl, and all out of his hand and onto the floor. Her round eyes rolled briefly up into her head. Her normally watchful, self-protecting face took on a look of authority and power I'd never seen before.

Feng sputtered, too shocked to say a word.

"Stay!" Baby shouted to Nagadharma, who'd whirled and stooped to pass through the single door. "Sire of the Rain, I command you by your rightful name. Assume your true shape, and reveal yourself to us." Then she slumped down in a corner, holding her head in her hands. The words had come, for the first time, easily from her lips, and something about her voice—was it only hearing the accents of Khotan about her Chinese words?—put me in mind of Nannie in one of her rare serious angers.

Nagadharma, barely outside the doorway, dropped to the ground at Baby's invocation. His body stretched out long behind him. White scales replaced his saffron robes. Horns like trees of coral sprouted from his snaky head and his tongue flickered past his two teeth. We hadn't seen a single snake on Mothbrow Mountain. Yet here on Beyond-the-Clouds we'd been taken in by a cobra monster, a malevolent breathy-voiced emanation in monkish guise.

A noxious odor filled the little lodge. With a piercing hiss, Nagadharma summoned other snakes, who crawled out from under rocks and fallen logs, heading for their master.

Alas, those who devote themselves to telling tales, composing lyrics, and contemplating the wonders of the written word are often slow to rise to action! For as I marveled at the power of Baby's words, as Feng rubbed his eyes in stupefied amazement, Second Daughter drew Moonsaber from its sheath and, rushing toward the monster, let loose a battle cry that rang among the stunted trees.

The giant cobra reared up, towering five times Second Daughter's height. Fiery red, sulfur yellow, pallid as a fish's belly, the smaller snakes slithered toward her, but fearlessly she fixed all her attention on her real foe. Moonsaber gleamed in the light from the Lady's crystalline sky palace. Second Daughter swung it as adroitly as one who'd walked the martial way since infancy. Again and again, the keen blade rang off the monster's colorless scales. Again and again, Nagadharma's head bobbed and weaved, seeking an opening through which he might sink his venomous fangs into Second Daughter's flesh.

I froze. Feng knelt beside Baby and stroked her hair. In that moment, I quietly named him coward. Now the memory gives me shame: evidence of his courage would come, and who can say it is not braver—and wiser—for a man to kneel and tend to a concubine perhaps endangered by some oracular spirit than it is for him to attack a monster with a dagger when others have been given swords?

I ran toward Second Daughter, who by now had fought Nagadharma to a spot some forty feet from the lodge. Dragonrill cut the head off several smaller snakes as I approached the battle. Then Second Daughter saw her moment, lunged directly toward the cobra's open mouth, and thrust her blade hilt-deep down his blood-dark throat. Her hand snatched itself free an instant before the fangs closed. She danced backward as drops of venom rained down, searing the underbrush.

The monster fell. Branches cracked. The noxious fumes swirled round us, thicker than ever, and the thrall-snakes turned and vanished into their hiding places. Second Daughter pulled Moonsaber free and wiped it clean on a tuft of grass. Then she who never cried buried her face in my shoulder and wept.

In the morning, the true monks listened to our story and rejoiced that the abomination had finally been slain. With blessings and promises of prayers on our behalf, they sent us on our way.

So the boat carried us down the Min to the great Yangzi River. Gliding easily, the enchanted boulder avoided treacherous sandspits and the combers running with the crosscurrents where submerged rocks hid. Hawks rode updrafts overhead; egrets waded in the shoals. We saw a small boat heading upriver under sail, caught in an upwelling, whirling helplessly, unable to leave until the Yangzi let it go. We passed terraced slopes and hilltop pagodas, passed sweating quarrymen and dreamers sifting for gold and families standing hip-deep in the water with their fishing nets.

We stopped where fancy took us, staying on a day if our blades proved to be of use to someone, though we accepted no payment but hot wine. The magic was upon us. We rode it like a river, or a storyteller's flow of words.

In larger towns, like Rong-jou, where we joined the Yangzi, we left our boat moored, giving some boy a few coppers for watching it. Then we'd seek out the comfort of an inn. Feng found men to bet with him on the fall of the bamboo sticks, though the compulsion of his wasted days in Chang-an did not return. In fact, he always seemed to win a bit more than he lost. I played my lute when the mood came on me, and Baby, who daily gained strength and pride, sometimes chose to dance. Dishes clattered in those smoky provincial inns, and the locals' approving shouts rang through warm smells of savory pork and frying chilies as she leapt and turned. The hostelers never minded the coins tossed in our direction, for they made as much or more in increased sales.

Baby was not the only one to change. As Second Daughter traveled farther from her father's house and the town where she'd been reckoned nearly worthless (not male, nor eldest, nor beautiful, though some conceded her a hard worker), her assurance grew. The pockmarks never left her face. Yet they became less noticeable, even though she'd left off using rouge. She learned—better than I, it seemed—how to balance friendship with reserve around Baby and quickly caught hold of the flying significations of the little dancer's hands. The two spent long hours at the rear sweep, though the boat nearly guided itself, pointing out to one another interesting objects in the panorama along the shore.

Feng's changes came with greater difficulty. His glance fell more often in my direction. He no longer assumed the airs of pater familias, or scholar-official, or wizard to apprentice. With Sparker gone and Second Daughter keeping Baby company—and me changing from the hesitant lad Skywhistle to the swordswoman Heavenglaive—the moods of the group were not the same. I think he viewed his actions at Beyond-the-Clouds as cowardice, for he stayed sunk into himself the next few days.

I felt a lonely jealousy of Second Daughter's casual camaraderie with Baby, but Feng seemed not to mind that, at least. He and Baby had slipped off for privacy less and less over the winter in the Brocade City, and hardly at all once we left there. Between him and her a distant concord had developed, a tenuous yet sympathetic bond, but little else.

I did make more poems, as the Moon Lady told me to, though I would have anyway, now that I had the chance. Travel by a boat that slips downstream is leisure to one who has walked the desert sands and the difficult road to Shu.

On the third day after Second Daughter killed the cobra monster, we stopped at a cove out of sight of any village, beaching our boat on brown river-laid silt. Baby kindled a cookfire—she'd taken a liking to that task—while Second Daughter brought out the cabbage and dried bean curd and began to wash the rice. Rather than stand uselessly watching, I asked Feng if I might join him on his stroll. Unexpectedly, he smiled broadly, the first time since Sparker's transformation. Now that he no longer knit them together in grandfatherly style, I saw again how long and fine his eyebrows were and the liveliness of the eyes beneath.

We walked into the bamboo grove feathering the shore. "I like it when you smile like that," I said. Then I blushed: to speak so directly to a man when it was not the coy boldness of a courtesan's flirtation! But he merely looked at me directly for a moment, then lowered his refined, thoughtful-looking face. A blue-gray bird called happysparrow banked past us, russet tail fanned out, to land in the shallows of a stream across the way.

We soon came to a grassy meadow. The air was valley-warm that late afternoon near the fourth month's end. Beside a glossy-leaved clump of clove-daphne bushes, I asked him to lie down with me. The pleasure, and the comfort against loneliness, that we gave to each other there weren't new to me, though I felt the joy of learning the lexicon of a new lover's body. But something else was new: without coquetry, or any aim of seduction, I had been the one who proposed what we did. I was not the waiting one some other stirred into desire. I was not the entertainer who needed a patron and so sent roundabout messages of receptivity. I wanted, and I asked.

Why we did not continue as lovers I can't quite say. It may have been the magic. Or it may have been the withdrawal we had for some time been making, separately, into our selves. In any case, the energies we might have spent in passion simply seemed to shift to different channels, as a river will.

An easy peace established itself between the two of us, though we never spoke of what had passed. I suppose it had to do with the new courses all our lives had taken since Dragongate Cave. We still lived in the human world. Yet the boat, my sword and Second Daughter's, even the jade-handled dagger the Moon Lady had given Feng—these things pulled us toward another realm. The way of chivalrous wanderers is not the way that Nephrite had chosen as Lady of the Tao, nor the hermit recluse's way that Sparker had longed for. But they are not without similarity.

And there was much for us to do. From Dun-huang to the capital, and from there to Shu, the suzerainty of Great Tang protected the people from lawlessness, even during famine. But the rugged mountain land above the gorges was not entirely pacified. The widespread, muddy Yangzi carried us to more than one adventure.

Just before reaching the perilous gorges, we stopped at a tiny riverside settlement—only three or four families—not far from Wan-jou. Feng and I took the path to the nearest house, to see if they had fresh vegetables to sell, while the other two began to cook the rice. Outside the compound's courtyard, I felt Dragonrill start to vibrate. Laying a hand on Feng's arm, I touched my finger to my lips. Alert now, all my senses open, I still saw nothing but the blue- and yellow-green of crops in the red-brown fields. Then I heard an infant's cry, sudden, as if someone had slapped it, and then the cry cut off.

We were too late to save that child. Bursting through the compound gate, we saw one of five bandits wiping blood from his sword. Shrieks and sobs from the farm family mingled with our shouts, the bandits', and the clash of blades. Almost before the bandits noticed us, Dragonrill dispatched the one who'd killed the baby, and Feng quickly sank his dagger into the heart of their stocky leader. I say Dragonrill did the killing, and that was how it seemed as I fought, though later I shuddered at the thought of ending any life, even a murderer's, and did not sleep well for nights.

Second Daughter never quite decided whether it was the sound of battle that drew her to our aid, or a trembling in Moon-saber that responded to its twin. But she joined us in time to kill the last bandit, the strongest, who'd cut my cheek, giving me the scar I wear today. I came to think of that thin white line as an emblem marking a part of me as always Heavenglaive. Back then, once the fight had ended and I had time to examine its gaping redness in Baby's little mirror, it seemed a sign of my mortality.

As for Feng, he'd slit the throat of one bandit, after the family's eldest son had valiantly knocked the man senseless with a hoe, then flung himself past the scimitar of the fourth, whom I had wounded, to administer the coup de grace. We both stared senseless as the grateful family crowded round us, and I saw his long-fingered scholar's hands begin to shake.

Baby must have been puzzled when Second Daughter dropped the rice pot and dashed off; certainly she was hampered, once she too heard the shouting, by her skirts. She arrived as the last two bandits released their final screams. Shock protected me from memory, but Baby must have traveled instantly to that spring day when the Tibetans raided the village outside Khotan and slaughtered all her family.

"Dead," she said. "All dead." I heard the words, and heard that they were not in the Chinese she'd always spoken when possessed by spirits, but in a childish-sounding Khotanese. Yet I hardly took notice of her then. The distorted bodies, the red-splashed courtyard, the sobbing of the dead child's mother, all seemed far away, as if I stared down at the scene from a lofty mountaintop, or a cloud. Later, I learned that Second Daughter had rushed to Baby's side, only to see that she seemed quite normal. As she was at last.

The old grandmother of the household insisted that we come inside, insisted on serving us tea herself. One of her daughters-in-law rushed around bringing out some food for us. The tea in fact smacked of its cheapness, yet only water in the desert was ever so delicious. I turned to Baby and asked her in Chinese if she was all right.

"Yes," she said. "I am." And smiled, startling me into laughter. Second Daughter laughed too, and even Feng broke from his daze to stare at her. In the giddiness of crisis past, she sprang to her feet and gave a dancer's fancy curtsy. Then she spied the mother of the slaughtered infant, mourning in a corner, and hastily sat back down. A salt-sweet metallic taste tainted my pleasure in the tea when I saw the mother's face, and I only shook my head when the grandmother, wishing to ease our sudden bleakness, touched my sleeve and offered another cup to "Kind Mistress Heavenglaive."

"No, thank you, madam," Baby said, when the grandmother turned to her, and again I was amazed. Baby's words shaped themselves oddly—as Ghalib's few phrases in Chinese had— when they left her lips. Over the next days, she spoke again from time to time, though her brief sentences never sounded fluent. She still used mostly gestures with our group, and in the larger world preferred silence, or a dance. No one pressed her to do otherwise. But that bloody scene at the farmhouse opened something in her.

Two days later we passed White Emperor City. The clean-cut shadows of the first gorge seemed to dispel the last sickening taste of blood that had clung to my lips and mouth since the battle. We stopped for the night just upstream from Goddess Mountain, at the beginning of the second gorge, Shamanka itself.

As we neared the river's great narrows, we had begun to see scattered groves of orange trees on the slopes and plumes of reddish grass taller than a full-grown man. Fewer bamboo grew there and no plantains. Desert-born, I still stared astounded at the constant expanse of water, and listened to it sliding by, and saw how it gave life all along its banks. Long flights of stairs ran down from towns perched above the floodline. Old women squatted on the lowest steps to do the wash, or to fill pails with water for their thatched-roof homes.

We might have climbed such a stairway, and stayed the night in the little town on the north bank that overlooked the upstream entrance to the gorge. But fearing the rip currents from the tributary river beside the town, we decided to cross to the south bank before nightfall and make camp on the last bit of easy incline before the cliffs. Besides, all of us seemed to feel a pull away from human habitation that night. We woke to see Goddess Mountain in dawn's stillness and made our cautious way among the twelve peaks of the gorge, accompanied by the eerie wails of long-armed gibbons concealed in the trees of the remotest slopes.

Turning to look back as the current pulled us past Goddess Mountain, I saw the weird pillarlike rock high in the shadows of its peak. The local people say the rock embodies the deity of the mountain and the gorge, protectress of the ships that thread their way through the walls cleft by the river. I remembered all I could from poems about the goddess that I'd heard recited by guests at Felicity Hall. Nearly everyone who came here composed some retelling of the famous tale: the shimmering beauty of the sacred woman when she coalesces from the vapors, her appearance to the king of ancient Chu, their one night of love, his lifelong yearning, the echoes of his woe.

Despite the loveliness of the place, being there was not at all like meeting face-to-face with the Moon Lady in her palace. Perhaps the primordial goddess of the mountain and the gorge had aged too far beneath the weight of history to show herself directly. It seemed to me that where she lived now was in all those poems. That afternoon, the water easing slick beneath the boat, I composed my own. I thought that nearing this elusive sacred woman had some connection with Baby's newfound speech—and with the words I'd said to Feng not long before, when in that valley meadow I asked him to lie down.

PASSING BY BOAT
THROUGH SHAMANKA GORGE

Up at dawn, where Goddess Mountain
  rises, veiled with mists,
And through the gorge: the narrowed river
  ripples, watered silk.

Rosy wisps of wavering vapors
  recall her gauzy dress.
Long-drawn wails of downstream winds
  cry her lover's cries.

The story's old. She's fragrant clouds,
  she's evening's shifting rain.
The gibbons howl for a long-dead king,
  after one night's love, bereft.

What speaks here? Iridescent haze,
  wild apes, and water's surge?
Or today's dream of that dream-reft ghost,
  old stories' musky flux?

Parrot Speaks: 20

Our boat took us on through the third gorge, where the river had found a broader way for itself, though whirlpools and submerged boulders lurked even there. On the bank above us stood the temple of drowned Chu Yuan, the ancient poet and statesman whose talents were neglected by his king. Feng knew quite a lot about it all. His delicate fingers clenched while he told the tale, as if he felt the story were his own. He'd heard that a giant fish swallowed the body and carried it off to Cavegarden Lake. Listening to this, I grew impatient, thinking that my mother waited for me not much farther downstream. Dragonrill hung heavy at my side, a reminder that the pace of my travel was not mine to decide.

Just past Chu Yuan's temple, Feng told us, on the north bank, a stream called Fragrant Creek carved through its own high-water depositions and entered the muddy Yangzi. Here, he said, the imperial concubine Wang Jao-jun had long ago dropped a pearl from her headdress into the water while washing her incomparable face. *A pearl in the water.* The yearning for my mother rose again.

And then the river fell from the last constricting close of rock. The floodplain opened wide around us, and we thought we'd stop awhile, to rest from our passage through those bewitching, formidable gorges. When we left the Moon Lady's palace, the moonmaid had murmured to Feng that he would fulfill his pledge to find a substitute stone just east of the third gorge. So when the little boat drifted to a village on the north bank and grounded itself on a shoal, we knew we'd reached a place where we had business. Thoughts of Sparker forced aside my longing to free my mother, and I stepped up with the others onto the bank.

The keeper of the little village inn split his greasy face with a grin when we four walked in. I'd gotten used to people's responses to our unconventionality, but his was different. He gave no sign of heeding our swords. He didn't ogle Baby, or cock an eyebrow at the sight of two roaming warrior women. He rushed over with a pitcher of warm wine—a gift for the noble strangers, he said—and made haste to acquaint himself with Feng.

"Well, sir, I see you are a man of learning as well as valor," he said, after some conversation. "I suppose you've studied the classics and such as that?" He spoke with the accents of the southland, giving his words a countrified twist I'd seldom heard.

While Feng described his education modestly, his eyes revealed his pleasure at being understood to be a scholar. His experience since we climbed Mothbrow Mountain had erased the bombast of the Wizard Mimesis; he wanted only what any educated young man of the Tang would want, the respect accorded a learned servant of the state.

"You know, sir," said the innkeeper, leaning forward across the table to refill Feng's cup, then waving a hand toward the rest of us to indicate that we might help ourselves, "our little village needs you."

Feng beamed. He made haste to explain that he traveled in fulfillment of a vow and could not accept a teaching post. Yet I saw how attractive the idea was to him. Tutor Feng, just like his father: a position more humble than the government official he had hoped to be but one far more suited to his true temperament than charlatan wizard, or arranger of entertainments for the rich and idle.

The innkeeper explained he had something else in mind. "It's only temporary, sir, and it would be a boon to us. The Dragonboat Festival's almost upon us, you know, and we need a headman for one of our boats." He shrugged in a worldly way; he'd heard enough travelers' talk to know the southland was regarded as half civilized, heathenish, not really quite Chinese. "The old folks say it's best if he's a stranger and an educated man. You'd bring joy to their hearts if you would honor us. And the good ladies, too." He quickly turned to the three of us with offers of a comfortable room until the festival day.

We were weary with our battles, and travel, and more than one good deed. True, courtesy required us to grant this request for aid, even though it was a bit out of a chivalrous wanderer's usual line. True, too, that we reckoned such an offer part of the Moon Lady's plans: the boat had brought us here. Yet our fatigue alone was enough to make us stay.

The next morning, before we ate, Second Daughter whispered to me of her pleasure at the prospect of a few days' rest and an interesting festival. "A friend of my father's once told him something of this Dragonboat affair—just tales he'd picked up in Jia-jou, he'd never seen it. They say the day's a potent one for making love charms." She glanced at me through lowered lashes. "And that a child born then will kill its father."

We had arrived on the third of the fifth month; the preparations for the festival, on the fifth, were already under way. Feng soon found himself out on the river at the head of fifty men in a slender boat called *Lunar Aqua*. The crew of a second, known as *Solar Fire*, paddled fiercely up and down nearby. Other boats practiced some way off, along the opposite shore. The villagers scanned the sky for rain clouds, and talked excitedly of how the race would bring the moisture needed for their paddy fields. I felt their difference from the people of the north; their very expressions, their ways of moving, sometimes puzzled me.

The morning of the fourth, the innkeeper's wife—a Mistress Hu—hesitantly invited Second Daughter, Baby, and me to join in the preparations. Her sentences bore heavy accents of the middle Yangzi and used more odd dialect words than her husband's. Most of the villagers' did; as host of an inn he must have learned how to tailor his speech for strangers passing through. I wondered at her shyness, then remembered how unusual we must have seemed to her: two women wearing swords, and one who spoke mostly with her hands.

Soon the three of us walked out with Mistress Hu, her daughter-in-law, and her unmarried daughter to the wetlands and the nearby hills. The day warmed us with the southland's heat. We gathered iris for the festival wine, marsh orchids to be brewed for special bath water, and artemisia to tie with multicolored threads to the doorway for keeping the spirits of war and malaria away. All afternoon we single women busied ourselves with fragrant blossoms, while Mistress Hu and her daughter-in-law steamed triangular cakes of sticky rice wrapped up in bamboo leaves. Near day's end, she gave us bright silk amulets to wear and painted the sign for "Monarch" in sulfur yellow on her little grandson's forehead, to protect him from poison and from snakes.

"Mind you don't rub that off tonight, Little Tiger," she said to the pudgy boy. "It's the start of summer, you know. The year will turn soon and the yin will rise." She clasped him to her soft bosom. "I want to keep my darling safe." He laughed smugly and ran off to show his maternal cousins in the house next door.

Supper was casual and hurried. No other travelers came to the inn. Feng and the innkeeper arrived sweaty but exuberant from their rowing. The young daughter, Sweetflag, turned her face down and said nothing; the contrast to her high-strung laughter while we picked the flowers impressed me. Then I decided it was no more than the presence of a strange man, for from time to time she stole a glance at Feng. The rest of us wore what we'd had on all day, but she had already bathed in the orchid water and put on a loose gown that must have been her best. Just before darkness fell her mother made a fuss of fixing honey clover in Sweetflag's damp, glossy hair.

Feng bathed next, laughing as he left to do so. He exclaimed that he'd catch a chill bathing in the open evening air, the way the innkeeper had insisted, even so close to the solstice. "Ah, but the good wine will keep me warm," he said as he stepped from the room where we had eaten, and I saw how red his face had gone.

Later, when the meaning of all this had been made clear to us, Second Daughter and I decided what must have happened. Though Second Daughter remained a virgin, she was the daughter of a farmer and spoke of such things more easily than I suppose gentlewomen do. I compared it to the wiles—the necessary wiles—of courtesans, and wondered once again if such things are trickery, or women's way of using the only power allowed them, or some force greater than either men or women. To the villagers it must have been a holy thing.

Feng had the best room in the inn; after bathing, he retired there for the night. Soon after, Sweetflag, all trembles and blushes, slipped past our door—Second Daughter saw her—with more wine, to wait upon him. Feng was the scholar-stranger who on the morrow would draw baleful influences away from the village. Sweetflag was the maiden who would send him to the river suffused with tender aching, as the priests of olden Chu had gone out in their half-forgotten rituals, to tryst with a fickle deity. I think she had been carefully instructed how to excite him to an ardor he would carry with him through the ceremony to come. "Touch him so," the village women would have said. "Allow your skirt to fall a little open. Say this, or this, brush your nipples unseen against his back, let him glimpse your body's heat. Then quickly leave."

Certainly, in the morning the three of us saw the strength of his new feeling for her, though none of this was spoken of. Baby was remote, turned inward, as she hadn't been since that night on Beyond-the-Clouds when Second Daughter killed the monster Nagadharma. Feng too kept silent. The innkeeper's face shone jovially, while Mistress Hu seemed ready to burst with excitement, for all her protectiveness toward Little Tiger. The boy ran about shouting and waving a magnolia branch, a glutinous rice grain stuck to one of his chubby cheeks.

The day warmed before we arrived at the riverbank. The villagers had put up reed mats as awnings, and sat beneath them to eat and drink, or strolled about to talk with friends. Scarlet banners and garlands of pomegranate blossoms decked the long boats and their dragonheaded prows. Soon some kind of singing contest began. Then, forming a procession, we marched with the hundred boatmen—all the young men of the village, and the strongest of the middle-aged—to the sound of gongs. Feng came last of all, striding side by side with a curly haired outlander who'd been staying in the village elder's house. Like Feng, he looked eager, and a little dazed.

The boatmen took their places, stepping carefully to sit in pairs in the narrow boats. *Lunar Aqua* veered and dipped as Feng took his single seat behind the prow, and the drummer in the stern struck his first rhythmic beats. Many of the people waved flower wands like Little Tiger's. Finally, the village elder was rowed out in a small boat almost to midriver, where he dropped bamboo-wrapped rice cakes into the water, offering them to drowned Chu Yuan. The boats put out from shore.

Feng nodded his head toward me in a farewell reminiscent of his earlier bows. But he was touched now with a new, abstracted air of dedication. Earlier, at the inn, he had taken Baby's hand for one instant and murmured something that sounded like a request for her forgiveness. That made little sense to me: what gentleman begs pardon for neglecting an unofficial concubine? Now, as the drumbeats quickened and the oars flashed, he fixed a lingering, entranced gaze on Sweetflag. She hung her head. Then the boat carried him so far I could no longer see his face.

Solar Fire and *Lunar Aqua* joined six other dragonboats from two villages across the wide river. The day grew hotter, though a fresh breeze had sprung up. The boats paired off as if at random, vying feverishly for a while, then dropping off when no one gained an obvious victory. The races had no clear beginning, no marked finish line. "My father's friend heard it was like this," Second Daughter whispered, as we stood in the crowd admiring the distant, gleaming backs of the boatmen. "They'll paddle back and forth and back again. The boats look unstable, don't they? Maybe no one wants to take a chance of spilling."

Iris wine passed among us, groups of unmarried girls and boys challenged one another in song, and a sense of anticipation grew. Or perhaps it was just the steamy air, so different from the arid northwest, or Chang-an, or the high basin of Shu.

To distract myself, I began a conversation with Mistress Hu. She was curious about Baby, who had wandered off toward the singing, and began to ask about her, where she'd come from, how she got her peculiar name.

The name, I explained, was a Chinese substitute for what she'd once been called in another language; *Bao-bei*—Baby— she'd been dubbed west of Dun-huang, "Precious" if you took it literally, but the fond nickname of ten thousand babies. "Do you know the words?" I asked her, a bit bored, headachy, and no doubt showing off. "*Bao* meaning 'jewel,' and *bei* like 'cowrie shell.' " And then I added, feigning more interest than I felt just then, "Do you use the same nickname down here in the south?"

" 'Cowrie shell,' " mused Mistress Hu. She caught her breath.

"Sweetflag!" she called, and her daughter came closer, careful to keep her mother between us, as if she feared me. "Sweetflag, give me that purple treasure Granny Gu lent you for, ah, last night."

Blushing, Sweetflag took from her bosom a tiny jade-white seashell, a polished purplish tinge edging its single slitlike opening, like heavy lips suffused with blood. Reluctant though she seemed at first to display it to a stranger, she held it out on her palm with an air of newfound pride. Shells like this one circulated as money in the wild lands farther south, I knew, and they were said to stud the gateways of underwater palaces.

"That's right," I said in polite tones. "So you call it 'purple treasure'?"

Sweetflag drew back.

"Ah," said Mistress Hu. "Yes. It's wonderful what peculiar names you travelers come up with for ordinary things."

I might have called my own names ordinary and hers peculiar, I thought a little sourly, but I made some empty pleasantry instead of saying this. The gray thunderheads piling up beyond the farther shore seemed to be pressing against my temples.

Baby returned, and now, in the height of the afternoon, I could see that the suppressed agitation of the crowd animated her round eyes. She seemed to sense my mood, for she stared down into her wine cup.

One swift shriek: she sprang to her feet and ran, the cup grasped still in both hands, to the riverbank before us. "He sinks!" she cried out, and dashed the fragrant spirits into the Yangzi.

Heads jerked round. Voices hushed. My eyes met Second Daughter's, and we rushed to Baby.

Ten pairs of hands stopped each of us. We might have drawn our starswords, but how could we, against defenseless villagers who did her no harm?

Then there was something else to think of. The hands dropped. All of us on shore stood unmoving, staring out across the river. A dragonboat had overturned.

Men flailed in the water. The other boats kept away. No one, we learned later, dared attempt to rescue a drowning boatman, for the gods of the river might take the rescuer as their sacrifice instead. One by one, the drummer and forty-eight oarsmen made their way to us—our shore was the nearer—but I knew before I heard it said that it was *Lunar Aqua* that had tipped over, and I felt it in my heart that Feng had drowned.

PART IV

On the Fifth Day
of the Fifth Month

The fifth day of the fifth month: for intercourse, inauspicious. For casting mirrors out of bronze, most puissant. For love charms, excellent; a good charm may be made with earthworms one has caused to copulate this day. Cut a magpie's tongue out on this festival and the bird will speak. An official appointed in the fifth month never loses his position—good news if he likes the post. Long ago, on Doublefiveday, the body of a royal minister in the delta lands was wrapped in a sack of fishskin and thrown into the Yangzi.

Seagem paces slowly through nacreous corridors, enjoying her solitude, thinking about these things. More lore, something Seagem's only lately learned in one of her talks with her mother-in-law: at noon on the fifth of the fifth, one may make a solarfollow, the reflector-mirror that takes fire from the sun, companion to the squarepearl, a shell cup for collecting the waters of the moon. Once more she sees the necessary, beautiful equilibrium of yin and yang.

She thinks of her beloved princeling and frowns a pretty frown. She can't conceive of the interchange of yin and yang as a struggle, though up in the human realm the country people think it so. She walks out through a gateway trimmed with white-and-purplish shells, into a garden of shadowy waterweeds drifting higher than her head, growing toward the light that filters down from the distant surface.

Someone else wanders those sun-dappled pathways. The vermilion dragon, the Monarch's younger brother, celebrates today. The fuss the farmers are making throughout the southland stirs up something deep in him. Despite his nostalgia for the more splendid masques of bygone times, he's unusually at ease. "Ah, niece!" he says, careful for once to modulate his voice. "Well met! Well met this glorious day."

Seagem represses a half-gasp, inclines her head, and raises it to meet his bulging eyes. Her years of virtuous tremulousness have ended, she tells herself. She has seen how seriously the women—or females, one might say—are taken here. Her mother-in-law admires the tensile strength of her calligraphy, has told her she's a clever learner and that her husband's fretful demands for her attention are something he'll outgrow. Besides, in spite of his impetuosity, her uncle has a kindly side. She thinks of the times he has assumed the guise of a red-gold carp to see how her daughter fared; perhaps it was no more than a lark for him, but she is grateful nonetheless.

"Dear niece," says the vermilion dragon, "in human lands did you ever wade through the waters on the Doublefifth? Or partake of iris wine and holy hemp? Ah, a beauty such as you might have been sent on a cassia-wood raft out into a river to be wedded to its deity. In the old days—did you know that in the old days young women were dropped like belt ornaments of tinkling jade into this lake?" He, who has recently indulged in both hemp and wine, blinks then, and catches a strained expression on Seagem's face. "No offense meant." His toothy smile is foolish, almost winning. "The women knew it was an honor, and I treated them"—he sighs reminiscently—"quite well."

"But wait," he says. "I'm being rude." And changes into manly form. "Come sit with me awhile." One red-sleeved arm waves her to a coral bench, and he joins her there.

At least I'm not blubbering, Seagem thinks, or struck dumb with terror. She regards his new appearance with some pleasure. Nice of him to take on such an attractive aspect, just for her. But she'd best keep the conversation going. "We don't do that where I come from, in the north," she says, ignoring a little internal shudder at his nearness. "Tell me about the old days, please. What was it the folk of the southland used to do?"

The vermilion dragon describes it all: the holy music, the flower wand passed from one dancer to the next, the appearance to the fortunate priest or priestess of a divine lover in a dragon-chariot. The wide pupils of his eyes radiate dark light. Almost (but not quite) imperceptibly, he slides closer to Seagem on the bench.

What now? Shall she strike his newly handsome face with a stinging slap? Certainly a chaste wife should. And yet, she thinks of her first, and hardest lesson here: that she did not belong to the general who picked her out and wed her. What's more, to her surprise, she wants the dragon-man. The summer solstice nears and the libidinous yin prepares to rise.

How much easier life seemed when she knew her place in it! Surely he can see her nipples erect beneath her bodice. Does he despise her, think her body stridently outspoken? She remembers the Hsiao River Princeling's sulky withdrawal last night when she put out the moonpearl lamp on her writing table and came at last to bed. He is still the one she loves, despite their present disagreements, but perhaps there is a difference between love and desire? Awash in the romance he brought into her life, she's never thought of this before. With General Li, she learned of sex as a slightly unpleasant duty. With the Princeling, she came to think of it as physical love. Might there be another lesson, might a woman (didn't that disturbing ghost once speak to her of this?) enjoy pure lust? Unwilled, a mental image rises: her legs wrapped round the dragon-man's broad back, her heels dug into his muscular buttocks, a quick exhausting rutting among the waterweeds.

Whatever he's thinking, the dragon in man's form certainly has caught something of her mood. With what for him is great restraint, he bends his head to brush his lips above the gold-cream of her breasts.

"No!" Seagem's cry is half smothered, since a heartbeat later she throws herself against him, and meets his mouth with hers.

It nearly happens. The intercourse prohibition on this day applies to mundane couples; to such rules the dragon realm pays little heed.

Footfalls on the pathway interrupt them. Seagem jerks away, and to her feet. "Yes?" she snaps at the crawfish-runner who bows before her.

"Your pardon, madam, sir," the runner says. No telling from his bulging eyes what he might have seen. "We've received a message in the guardhouse from the Moon Lady, for Mistress Seagem."

The vermilion dragon snorts, but Seagem draws herself up tall and takes a calming breath. "Yes?" she says again. This time her impatience is for the message.

"The Moon Lady wishes you to know ..." The runner's antennae thrash and one claw clicks anxiously until he retrieves the memory. "Ah. She wishes you to know that your daughter and the other candidates have passed through ... through an examination? I think that's it. In any case, the main point was that one of them is about to find some stone beneath the Yangzi, and the humans need help in transporting it. She says she knows that was no part of your agreement, but it seems your daughter has tied herself in some way to the stone and won't go on until it's dealt with. That's all." His antennae twitch, and he bows again.

Seagem dismisses him and considers. The plan has moved on nicely since she made her secret agreement with the Moon Lady's student, that nice White Aureole. And some months ago, when Seagem had slipped into despair at the slowness of its working out, Guan-yin the Compassionate gave her a certain necklace as a sign of Greenpearl's well-being. But recently her daughter's made a bit of trouble, dawdling about as a swordswoman instead of hurrying along, as her mother would have her do. Seagem shakes her head at the willfulness, not thinking how much it resembles her newfound own.

"So?" The handsome man clothed all in red steps toward her, now that they're alone again. He assumes an authoritative air.

A mistake. Seagem still feels herself pulled to him. And she needs his help now. But she's had enough of commanding men. She turns her face away.

"All I can think of is my daughter," she says. That's close enough to true. After all this time Seagem still yearns for her. "Perhaps you and I will meet out here again someday," she adds. She wonders at the touch of wistful longing in her voice but decides it's purely innocent; she has put manipulation aside.

The sound of promise is not without effect. The vermilion dragon snorts again. He shakes violently and resumes his natural sinuous form. He turns to leave and then turns back again. He wants to strike a bargain with this woman, but something tells him that she cannot be had that way. With every bit of indifference he can muster, he says, "Perhaps." After all, he has his pride.

Seagem stands her ground, despite the transformation. The unspoken notion of exchange still lies between them. He has already done so much spying for her—what could she offer for his further aid? If only she weren't bound to stay at the Mother-of-Pearl Villa, except for that one wild journey of her spirit to the Western Motherqueen! Then she remembers the last time she saw the dragon so mild-mannered, when he brought White Aureole down from the moon, mellowed by the opaline elixir he'd been served.

She resolves to take things into her own hands, as she once would not have done. "Dear Uncle," she says. "Might I ask of you one more favor?" She starts to cock her head winsomely, as she used to do when she wanted something from her father or the general. Then she stiffens into an unusual awkwardness. "Not because of—this," she mumbles, her determination not to be charming covering over half her charm.

Half's enough. But the canny dragon merely says urbanely, "Quite. Of course." He's getting restless, though. If in these modern times nothing else comes to him for the festival save iris wine and such, that will have to be enough. But he thinks he'd like a bit more.

She makes her proposition. If her dear uncle will fetch from the Yangzi bottom the stone the Moon Lady wants and carry it up to her—no more than that—Seagem will arrange for him to be given a flask of that supremely pleasing opaline elixir. "The Lady and I have an arrangement," she declares. "I guarantee it. Will you, Uncle, please?"

In fact, though they are in league, Seagem is by no means so certain of the Moon Lady's cooperation. A mere year ago, she'd not have dared such boldness, yet she thinks the gamble will work out. She'll write a quick note for the dragon to take with him, assuring the goddess of some favor in return.

Shortly, the vermilion dragon whirls from Cavegarden Lake, churning the waters of the Yangzi as he makes his way with supernatural speed to a village below the gorges. Upstream folded rockbeds rise up rich with thunder-lizard bones. Downstream Cavegarden empties into the river from its great bed of alluvial soil. Just here, two women stare unspeaking toward the spot where a man has sunk beneath the surface currents, while another woman howls and gibbers in her trance.

The vermilion dragon cares for none of this. His mind's on opaline elixir, and to get it he must find a silly stone. There. The man clutches an unnaturally heavy, inkstone-sized chatoyant, holds on to it as determinedly as he holds on to his last breath.

The man has just now realized the precise nature of the bargain he made with the Moon Lady: he said that he was willing to pay any price for the friend who saved him once from drowning, long ago when they were boys. Pay he shall. This self-promoting son of doting parents has come to true nobility. Seeing the fearsome, bewhiskered dragon heading for him, he knows there will be no reprieve. His last hope vanishes, but not his will to see the thing through. So long selfish and unfilial, he wishes only that his father and his mother might know of his valor. A few bubbles seep from his lips. Blackness overtakes him.

The dragon barely notices the man. Snatching up the stone, he bursts upward through the river to the air. The crowd on shore erupts in one collective gasp. The dragon hurtles on, through concentric seas of rarefied vapors someday to be named troposphere, stratosphere, mesosphere, ionosphere. He lands among the glimmering dusts of the moon.

Brave Selena greets him at the palace gate. She takes the chatoyant stone and Seagem's letter to the Moon Lady, and soon returns with the flask the vermilion dragon wants. The goddess, admiring the human woman's uncharacteristically daring move, has consented; the dragon quickly takes his leave.

Up in the crystalline keep tower, the Moon Lady gathers with her seven students for an impromptu celebration of the beautiful new inkstone. With a respectful bow, and a flick of her graceful wrist, the goddess herself hurls the old stone from a lofty window. It falls meteor-bright to earth, a flash in the sky of the planet's dark side: the few bronze-rimmed human eyes watching there just now recognize its mantic power. Spiraling downward, it lands not far from Chang-an, on hallowed Flower Mountain, westernmost of the five peaks that marked off and sustained the realm of the primordial emperors along the lower reaches of the River Huang; the present empire is a far larger one, but the five mountains' spiritual energies still protect the order it maintains.

The stone shakes. It crumbles. Sparker emerges from it, scratching his belly, rubbing his eyes. Back in Dragongate Cave, the vanity of human aspirations flashed upon him as his very hemoglobin crystallized. He's free now, far from the society that called him slave. He picks up a stick to serve him as a staff. He laughs and walks away.

The little moonmaid Oyster has arranged fragrant cinnamon branches upon the Moon Lady's banquet table. The underground storehouse-burrows of the moon hold opaline elixir to spare. Having brought up one flask for the dragon, Selena suggests opening another, and soon the party's making merry jokes about the new inkstone and what fine things might be written with it. The Moon Lady observes White Aureole's self-possessed demeanor, her quietly displayed understanding of her arcane studies. It is nearly time, the goddess thinks, to send this oldest of the moonmaids off to the position for which she's been preparing, as jade-white damosel guardian of an esoteric archive.

Sister! A variable flickering surges through the room. From a vortex of photons and unstable hydrogen, an erratic voice shoots out. *It is as the Amah told me! Ah, why do I ever doubt? Oh, but first my greetings. And to the lady students, too. Now: that little human chit—chit, I called her, but I will no longer do so—the dancer has proved herself a seer. She spoke the mystic names of starswords, spoke the true name of a demon, foresaw some man's riverine plunge. Sister! Are you not glad?*

In tranquil tones, the Moon Lady indicates her pleasure at the news. The seven moonmaids follow suit, though Oyster, wide-eyed at Dame Shamanka Star's fluctuations, grasps Selena's hand beneath the table.

Oh, she was wrong, in her presumption! Long-held resentment briefly overwhelms the Star's tones of joy. *But I've forgiven her. She's found her linking spirit, did I tell you? An unquiet ghost who's finally had her fill of fleshly things! Oh, sister, forgive my rudeness. Forgive me, lady moonmaids. I must run off. There's much for me to do.*

She vanishes. But down on earth, new power rushes into the little round-eyed dancer shrieking on the riverbank. With the Shamanka Star's blessing upon them at last, a wild-haired, proud-breasted ghost achieves full union with the medium.

The villagers remain astounded by their vision of the vermilion dragon soaring skyward. They knew, of course, that the sacrifice of the stranger-scholar would bring fertility to their fields, but they never expected so much. Those clustered around the little dancer put aside the terror that the distorted sounds torn from her lips provoked in them; she speaks clearly now, decisive, free of pain.

"There's much to say," the dancer tells them. She no longer twitches. Only the far-off focus of her gaze indicates her unworldly state. Her eyes have double pupils now. The villagers know this marks her as a true seer.

"Greenpearl! You've been shown my name has another meaning. Do you still think all others invisible pointing sticks?" These words flow from her in Soghdian, the language of Greenpearl's nannie. The rest she speaks in unhesitant Chinese, touched slightly with the accents of the southland. "Second Daughter, listen to the poem on the scroll. But when you come to write, it will be another way. Let neither of you mourn Dreamdragon Feng. He chose rightly."

A cloudbank dims the sunlight, like dark banners carried by the foreguard of a spirit army. A maiden known as Sweetflag takes a small shell from her bosom and presses it in the medium's hand. "Purple Treasure, this is yours," she murmurs. "Use it as you will." She steps back, and her mother comes forward to place a wreath of pomegranate flowers in the dancer's hair. A chubby boy darts forward to lay a magnolia branch at her feet.

At that, Baby sighs once, long and shuddering, as if she cast off the old pain of abuse and years of conflict and denial. The ghost joined with her shudders, too. The wind picks up, whipping whitecaps on the broad expanse of muddy river. A rumbling, as of distant hoofbeats or the great wheels of mighty chariots, sounds.

"Now this village is my home," the dancer cries. "I am shamanka now, not entertainer, and no man's concubine. For this village, I call down the rain!"

In the sudden coolness, hairs on more than one neck rise.

The storm breaks, first of the summer rains. A sheet of silver races from the south shore toward the village and the needful paddy fields. A few people dash for the reed-mat awnings, but most laugh and cut capers and talk excitedly, making plans for the sustenance of the maga come to live among them. Several couples who took part in the singing contests earlier slip off unnoticed, hand in hand, Sweetflag among them. From a time-worn shrine on the edge of the village, a temple raven calls.

FROM *Biographies of Chivalrous Wanderers*

compiled by
Mi Tu (fl. after 1066)

Yin *Er-jie* was a virtuous maiden of Mothbrow Town. She was frank and brave by nature. Stolen from her father's house by four roving brigands, she escaped from them, taking with her a precious sword and what she had learned of their arts.

She traveled widely, defending the helpless and righting wrongs. Once she killed an outlaw from India who had slaughtered a monk. She won the admiration of both the upper classes and the common people.

Later she grew tired of such things, and shut herself away to study. Her only amusement was calligraphy.

Feng Sheng-wen, known to his friends as Meng-long, was a native of Jia-jou. As a child, he showed himself to be intelligent and generous with others.

He traveled to Chang-an, where he made friends with many of the most dashing youths of the empire, hunting or watching cockfights, and raising many a cup. His nature was free and easy, and he loved to gamble, thinking nothing of selling a priceless charger to pay a debt or provide more wine for his host. Yet he had great ambitions.

He was eager to aid victims of injustice. With only his frost-bright dagger, he single-handedly slew fifteen bandits who were terrorizing a country town. Another time, he helped a young woman named Purple Treasure join with her true mate.

In the end, he was seduced by an evil female kraken called Sweetflag, disguised as a dancer from the far west. This she-demon made him drunk on wine that was really human blood, then pulled him into the Hsiao River. Some say this never happened, that he gave his life in a battle on the riverbank to save a friend. In any case, he was never seen again. Of him it may be said, as the poet Li Bo wrote of two earlier knights-errant, "sweet the scent of chivalrous bones!"

Tao Jia-huo came from Shu. He was a potbellied man with tousled hair. Born into poverty, he indulged in chivalrous deeds and followed the Taoist way. It is said that his mother was impregnated by a meteor. Once he saw a boy drowning and jumped into the river to rescue him, with no thought of his own life.

He spent some years with his hair let down, as pilgrims do, walking barefoot among the mountains. On Mothbrow Mountain, he saw a jade-white hare making a potion of immortality with a mortar and pestle. Then he retired utterly from the world and received secret instruction from a Purified Teacher named Jade Clarity.

Li Tian-jian, swordswoman, poet, and musician, was a native of the capital district. She lost her mother at birth. Originally a man, she transformed herself into a woman. She cared little for conventional behavior but cultivated her personal integrity.

One day, she met a young woman weeping beside the road. "I have no money to bury the bones of my mother," the young woman sobbed. Hearing this, Li quietly gave her fifty ounces of gold belonging to her own paternal grandfather. She never asked the other woman's name. When word of this reached the grandfather he was astounded. But Li regretted acquiring a reputation for generosity at her grandfather's expense. So she took a job as a serving girl in the Chen family hall, to earn the money back, although she was a gentlewoman.

Later, she roamed the realm under heaven for many years, performing deeds of chivalry. Afterward, she vanished. Some say she went to Mount Mao, on the lower Yangzi, where she studied the alchemy of the body and nourished within herself an immortal embryo.

Parrot Speaks: 21

Now, how was I to reach my mother? The question thrummed in my ears as the boat carried me through the great oxbows the Yangzi makes downstream from the gorges. I should have been excited and happy, nearing Cavegarden Lake at last. But I found it hard to imagine the end of my travels.

I'd caught sight of a glittering stone in the claws of the monster who soared skyward from the spot where Feng sank beneath the waters. So I could comfort myself with the thought that Sparker must have been released by the Moon Lady. But Second Daughter and I both grieved for Feng. Had that terrible vermilion dragon devoured him? Imagining it, I shuddered.

Baby refused to leave the village with us. She set her lips and shook her head, a last return to her old silences. I saw her joy, heard her fluent speech at last, and told myself I should be happy for her sake.

So the morning after the festival, Second Daughter and I packed our few things in the enchanted boat and settled on board. It nearly leapt out toward midstream. Bamboo, trees, and scattered houses on the riverbank sparkled, washed clean by hours of rain. Nothing for it but to go on, I thought, and brought out my lute.

I couldn't play it. With one finger, I traced a mother-of-pearl parrot inlaid on the glossy surface of the wood. Second Daughter placed her hand on my shoulder when I closed the instrument back in its carrysack. I stared blankly at the swallows skimming for insects above the river.

I lost count of the nights we stopped, though I know it was only a few. One morning Second Daughter briskly announced that she figured we were only a short way upstream from the town of Yue-jou, which overlooks Cavegarden Lake. Our conversation turned to Sparker. Was he really free of his stony form and living a hermit's life? Where had he gone? After days of keeping silence, Second Daughter asked me to take out the scroll and read to her the poem Baby had spoken of. I unrolled the white silk and chanted out the words the Moon Lady had added at the beginning:

> One shall speak, and one shall sink,
> And one shall seek the Way,
> And two shall wield their starswords
> Till the shuttle goes astray.

Only the last line left us wondering now. Second Daughter must have seen my look of miserable guilt—I could read, and write besides; surely it was my job to understand—for she placed her palm on my arm and said, "Never mind."

Soon the boat drew up to the Yangzi's south shore and halted. We climbed onto the bank. I was looking around for the most likely pathway through the green young rice when Second Daughter called out, "Sister, look!"

The boat had vanished; a great rock split the current in its place, the boulder Stoneboat from the Black Dragon River now holding fast in thc Yangzi's waters. Only our few coins sat atop it, barely safe from the water spraying up against the rock.

"So the Moon Lady's done with us," I muttered. "She has what she wanted, and we're left here on our own."

Second Daughter, again calling me her elder sister, began a gentle demurral. Then Dragonrill and Moonsaber broke free from their silver scabbards, assumed once more the shape of dragonets, and flew off into the heavens. The scabbards melted away, droplets of quicksilver flowing down into the river. No place for swordswomen in this world, I thought, biting my lower lip—and now no aid for us.

Second Daughter knew more than I did of enduring. "We'll walk to the lake from here," she said. "It's not far." She picked up my lute in its bag and slipped the strap over her own shoulder.

I wiped my eyes and tried to make a joke. We laughed more than it merited, picked up our bundles, and walked off, choosing the southward paths in the foot-packed web between the paddy fields.

My spirits lifted: my mother waited for me beneath that huge stretch of water, repository of the Nine Rivers and gateway to underground passages permeating the earth. In less than two hours' time, its wavelets lapped near the toes of our boots, mirror-bright.

I could not see the far shore. I could not see into the depths. But I could feel my mother as close to me as square-shouldered Second Daughter standing by my side.

Squeezing my eyes shut, I called on Lady Guan-yin, the Western Motherqueen, and every other god or goddess I could think of, even the inconstant Moon Lady. I'd heard the stories; only with divine aid could a mortal pass through the heavy, ordinary waters of the lake to the dragon realm. Smiling assurance at Second Daughter—I would return for her—I stepped into the lake.

Three times, six times, nine times I entered those broad waters, and each time my feet floated from the bottom as I bobbed and floundered. I breathed in water, I coughed, I choked. The last time, Second Daughter plunged out to where I could grasp her extended arm; otherwise I might have sunk into the lake for good. After that we tried plunging in together, hand in hand. I prayed aloud and invoked my mother's name. Nothing worked.

Exhausted, I looked to Second Daughter.

"There's one thing you might try," she said. "A gift."

I exhaled slowly, trying to still the petulance that threatened to rise in me.

"A sacrifice. Something for the dragons." Her gaze rested on my lute.

Well enough, I thought. All else had failed. If I had to make my own way in the world, I would not become an entertainer again, caged up like a gaudy parrot. True, the instrument was precious to me, but so much the better. It would be my mother's ransom.

One last time I stood knee-deep in the lake. With each step forward, I called on my mother's otherworldly captors to let me come to her. When only my head and shoulders remained above the water, I raised the lute high with both hands and hurled it as far as I could.

The mother-of-pearl glinted peach and blue and curiously green as the awkward thing arced out and down. It floated. Then water filled it and it sank. I stepped forward, certain that this time my feet would remain on the bottom and I would breathe the airy waters that my mother breathed.

Instead, I felt myself buoyed up again. Useless. I turned back and lay facedown on the sun-warmed rock where Second Daughter sat waiting.

She stroked my hair. Some while later—our clothes had nearly dried—I sat up. "Let's go," I said. "You choose the way, please. Anywhere." I felt too tired for tears or anger. I followed her, head down.

Silently, she led me toward a prosperous village we had

skirted perhaps half an hour before arriving at the lake. As we neared the first house, a young woman with a pinched face rushed toward us, quivering with eagerness for strangers' news. In moments, she had learned something—a story that would suffice, at least—of the two orphaned sisters whose papa and mama had fled a crop failure in the hills of Shu, only to die of fever just downstream from the Yangzi gorges. I was giving up my old hopes but not my glib tongue.

"We left their bones at a monastery there, and traveled on disguised in these odd clothes to find a place to live," I told her, thinking as quickly as I could. "This was their last command." Easy then to look downward and blink away the moisture from my lashes.

Pinch-faced Tussah pressed her lips into an expression that radiated understanding, though I noticed deep in her eyes a look of calculation. "Splendid luck!" she said. "Not, of course— My condolences on your terrible loss. Naturally your good parents would not wish their daughters to linger on at a monastery un-protected. The tales I could tell you of nasty-minded monks!" She clicked her tongue. "The spirits of your loving parents have obviously guided you here." She shook her head as a pious woman would. "Come with me."

We followed her into the village. I cared little what we did just then, but Second Daughter seemed glad to be so near Cave-garden Lake.

Tussah asked our family name. "Li," I told her hastily. Even here, Second Daughter's might bring pursuit upon her. Yet I could hardly call myself Heavenglaive or Skywhistle, or even a courtesan's decorative Dragonfly or Parrot or Bordermoon. So I took my other name from my sister's, and became First Daugh-ter Li: the only one of all my many names I've given to myself.

As we walked through the village, I caught Tussah staring curiously at my eyes. Amazed that I'd forgotten even briefly about my looks, more exotic here than in the north, I spun out some story about our father's first wife, an outlander who had died in giving birth to me, and the second wife, who bore my sister and raised us both. It seemed to satisfy her.

She led us toward her mother-in-law's house, the largest compound in the village. As we walked, Second Daughter and I learned all that Tussah deemed important about the family she'd married into. Their storerooms bulged with rice. Just now, they also held huge stoppered jars filled with silk cocoons waiting to be processed. One hired girl had disappeared last week ("pregnant, no doubt, the filthy trollop!"); the other had been dismissed just that morning for losing a shuttle that had been the widow's grandmother's.

"A small crime, you may think," Tussah confided, doubtless observing an odd mingling of consternation and understanding on our faces as we remembered the poem's prediction about our vanished starswords. "But the girl lost or broke everything she touched! So we need two good workers right away." She clicked her tongue in admiration. "An excellent businesswoman, my mother-in-law! Rather than make do with the shoddy silk reelers and quilling wheels one rents so dearly out here in the countryside during the peak season, she's patient. 'I'll wait a few weeks,' she likes to say to me, 'and hold my cocoons until the better equipment's available.' "

She stopped short outside the household gate. "No need to chatter where one might be overheard," she said. The thin scar on my cheek evidently caught the measuring gaze she turned toward us then, but she merely pursed her lips and shrugged. "You girls look bright enough to know quality when you meet with it. Come on."

Widow Chian greeted us complacently. Her skin retained a youthful smoothness, though gray streaked the hair she pulled back in a simple bun. She bore the look of one who knew life would bring her what she needed. Later, I came to see her composure differently.

Second Daughter and I settled quickly into life in the Chian household. When my old longing for my mother rose up, I'd remember my hopeless attempts to enter Cavegarden Lake and tell myself I had to put the past aside. Once or twice we did ask about the lake but received only vague—or evasive—answers. The villagers regarded it with awe, and they kept their distance.

Just how the widow dealt with our unregistered status, I never knew. Surely her brother's position as village headman helped; she held a good deal more land than a widow's allotment of thirty *mou*, plus the standard hundred *mou* in her two sons' names. Did a husband twelve years dead live on in the official roll of village citizens? Were Second Daughter and I legally listed under the names of the last two hired girls? I didn't care. Widow Chian gave us each a set of simple work clothes against our future wages, and she never meant to be unkind.

She did expect us to work as hard as she did. First she taught us how to find the loose end of a cocoon's single fiber and pass it through the tiny guiding eyes of the silk reeler to make up a thread. Later, she showed us her own way of taking those threads from the reeler and stretching them out on a wooden frame, to be rewound onto smaller reels and spun together on a peach-wood quilling wheel. Finally, we learned how to finish preparing the threads for weaving and how to dress and operate the looms.

Sometimes I smiled silently to think how Mama Chen had disparaged the women she called "thread-and-needle stay-at-homes." The world of Lutegarden House and Felicity Hall favored the refined and beautiful, but what was more refined than the filaments unwound from the cocoons, what more beautiful than the lustrous threads stretched on the wooden frame?

I told myself I didn't miss my lute. The household was too busy for music anyway. Besides, they might have thought I put on airs; I needed badly to be liked, if I was going to stay on here.

Only in one thing did the Widow Chian indulge herself. She owned two cats, extraordinary breeds of the far northwest that her sons had brought her from great trading cities. Their exoticism gave them value, which pleased me. The lively half-grown kitten, whose fur resembled the color of the darkest oranges, she called Redsteed; the older one, blue-gray and cranky, was known as Grizzle.

A strict ban kept them from the workrooms, but young Redsteed played with whoever sat in the courtyard between the end of the workday and sleep. One sultry evening toward the close of the fifth month, he skittered over to where I chatted with Second Daughter and Springgauze, the younger of the widow's two daughters-in-law. The cat had found a scrap of crumpled paper somewhere. It made a fine rattling noise on the packed earth of the courtyard, and Redsteed batted it about while we fanned ourselves and laughed.

Soon, he hit it into the crevice behind a doorstep, and couldn't get it out. I walked over to pluck the bit of paper free. Preparing to roll it into a tighter ball, I noticed a word written upon it. Three horizontal strokes joined by a vertical, a single dot placed at the lower right: odd, I thought, to see that particular word the very evening after I'd dreamed away the hours at the quilling wheel with memories of Nephrite and her jade-white hands. She'd taught it to me, the first word I knew how to read or write, long ago in Dun-huang, when she stitched her name inside the collar of the tunic she had sewn for me.

I unfolded the battered scrap, idly curious as to what else it said. In crabbed characters a tiny poem staggered down the paper's whiteness:

> When the ice horse plunges to the river,
> The silent shell shall spread its lips and speak.
> When pearl and jade have met beneath the waves,
> The child of wood shall weave a heavenly web.

By now, the other two had lifted themselves from their stools and come over to see what I was looking at. They moved lazily, for even at day's end, we felt the sticky heat. Then Springgauze's hand shot out.

"You can't see this!" she said, grabbing the paper from me.

"It's written in women's words!" She perused it for a moment, then grimaced and shook her head.

"Oh," said Springgauze then. "I'm sorry. I've made a mistake. It's just some foolishness, isn't it? Here." She handed it back to me and hurried off to wish her little nephew good-night.

Second Daughter caught my eye. "Women's words?"

I shook my head and told her that the words were perfectly normal. But the peculiar incident did remind me of my often-postponed promise to teach her to read. I showed my friend how to scratch out the word for "jade" or "nephrite" in the courtyard dirt.

She asked me to teach her the rest of the poem. I concentrated on writing each word just so, explaining all I could about their forms. Second Daughter pulled her high-arched eyebrows down in concentration, then cried out, "Baby! The second line is Baby! Remember how the villagers made so much of her name meaning 'cowrie shell'? And Feng plunged into the river. He *must* be the ice horse, though I don't see how or why."

I thought a moment. Then I wrote the name Feng: a short dot and an elongated one on the left, signifying "ice," and then the pictograph for "horse." I'd never known why it was written that way, but clearly, "Feng" was what the word-riddle meant.

"What does it mean to put 'pearl' and 'jade' together?" Second Daughter asked quickly, once I had explained.

I shook my head. "The word for 'pearl' already has a small 'jade' on one side—to show it means something precious. But look," I said. "If we write 'wood,' like this, and 'child' under it—see?—it makes the name Li!"

We tried to make sense of the rest, until the shadows lengthened and the Widow Chian herself sent us off rather sharply to get the sleep we needed for the next day's work. When she saw what we'd been doing, she said nothing, but her black brows eased back to their usual calmness. A few days later our lessons in the women's words began.

Many women south of the central Yangzi, we discovered,

know a written language not used by men. No fuss is made if a husband or a brother picks up a word or two, but—to judge from what I heard Widow Chian's second son say to his wife Spring-gauze—the men mostly scoff or shy away. "Women's business" they call it, and in that phrase who can distinguish disdain from reverence? In any case, I noticed that the women kept it rather quiet when there were men around.

In form, the words resemble the oldest Chinese writing, not the Soghdian or Indic scripts I'd seen along the Silk Road. Spring-gauze once whispered to me that she'd heard some of them had been preserved long ago when an emperor forbade any written symbols save those he chose as standard; many of the outlawed variant forms became women's words. Even the order of the words in a sentence, and their relationships to one another, are not like the language these women speak to their menfolk every day. But perhaps I tell more than I ought.

Springgauze clapped her hands, delighted, when she heard that Widow Chian wanted us to learn the women's writing. "I felt terrible, trying to keep it from you," she confided the day the widow started teaching us. She and I were stringing the warp thread on the largest loom. "But you surely understand I had to wait for Mother Chian's approval."

Perhaps two days after our studies began, Tussah sniffed into the workroom, her son—whom everyone called Little Monkey— resting on one bony hip. Springgauze was leading Second Daughter and me in chanting a weaving song written in the women's language.

"Younger Brother's Wife!" Tussah gasped. "Whatever are you doing?" Before Springgauze could answer, Tussah grabbed the text and whirled off, looking for her mother-in-law.

Springgauze smiled at us apologetically. "So that's what I looked like when I snatched that scrap of paper from you, First Daughter Li." She screwed up her mouth and narrowed her eyes, to make herself look like Tussah. We all laughed.

Tussah may have heard us; or she may have blamed us for

the face she lost when she ran to inform Widow Chian, only to learn that the lessons had been authorized by the widow herself. In any case, she ignored us at mealtimes for the next few days and kept herself too busy with Little Monkey to help out in the workroom—not that that was so unusual.

Soon her husband returned from a journey of some months. Tussah fluttered around him, assuming girlish airs that suited her far less than her mother-in-law's gravity would have. Her chief goal seemed to be to get herself pregnant with another grandson for the widow, and so ensure her ascendancy over Springgauze.

She was successful. By the year's eighth month, she was spending most of her afternoons in the coolest corner of the courtyard with a neighbor woman, discussing suitable names for the next son of the house of Chian.

Unfortunately, they also talked of other things. "Good news, dear mother," Tussah announced at supper one day toward the end of summer. "Auntie Ren has suggested a possible husband for the pockmarked hired girl!"

Second Daughter's face paled, and all light left her eyes. But what could she say? Certainly it was suitable for an employer to arrange a wedding for an orphan servant. Yet I knew that ever since she'd found another way to leave her father's house, Second Daughter had put the necessity of marriage quite happily from her mind.

"And you'll never guess who," Tussah continued, oblivious to the silence in the room. "Old Man Tuo! Can you believe the toothless gaffer's hankering for young flesh? And he's hard up enough that we should come off rather nicely in the exchange of family presents. None of our local girls will have him, of course." She let loose a flat imitation of Springgauze's merry laugh. "Think of it! He's so blind he'll hardly be able to make out those craters in her skin."

Unseen beneath the table, my hands reached out to rest on Second Daughter's knee. We'll run away, I tried to make the pressure say. And when she looked at me, I saw that if we didn't, someone would find her body in the well.

Then Widow Chian drew her straight spine straighter. "I thank my daughter-in-law for her concern," she said. "But I can manage these affairs myself. The girl's just gotten trained and shows no sign of misbehavior. We won't bring the matter up with him right now." Tussah's narrow mouth snapped shut, and soon she carried Little Monkey off to bed.

"She won't forget, you know," Springgauze whispered later to Second Daughter and me. But for some months it seemed as if she had.

Near the Malachite Pond

Her hands pale as the purest jade from the fabulous riverbed of the Yurung Kash, the devotee approaches the Western Motherqueen. She has paced out the ritual steps on the sacred meadow, its precincts defined by brilliant feather banners. She has abstained from mortal food until her flesh achieved the lightness of a bird. She has united with a divine lover, summoning him by her longing and her disciplines, learning from him the last of the teachings that led her to this state of power and grace. She has called forth, through meditation and techniques of the breath, spirits that swell within the body, as one might recover a mother submerged within the self. Now she can fly across the great desert to Kunlun's peaks, to the argent ramparts of the Western Halls of Jade.

Within those high walls, in a garden of white willows and pallid coral trees near the Malachite Pond, the Motherqueen listens to her musicians play. The devotee steps forward, makes deep and reverent obeisance. A jade maiden offers her a chilled dish of herbs and mushrooms, a refreshing drink from the Glassy Alabaster Spring. She accepts. And waits.

The limpid music ends. The leopard tail of the goddess sways gracefully, once, twice, a third time. She turns to the devotee, nods permission to speak. As she nods, her starry loom-crown shines in her disordered, snowy hair.

On behalf of a certain wandering hermit who made his way from holy Flower Mountain to the Taoist vista where the devotee dwells, she would like to have one of the Amah's blue-black ravens carry a message—a brief poem—to the young woman in the southland.

"You would, eh?" the Motherqueen asks. Her tiger teeth glint. "But has she not already been sent some scrap of poetry?"

The devotee's lovely eyes widen. She shakes her head. "I know nothing of that, Amah," she says. "I would take the message to her myself, if I could travel freely. Indeed, I long to see her."

The leopard tail curls itself neatly across the feet of the goddess. She remains silent. Perhaps she listens.

"As I always long to see you, Amah," the devotee adds, hasty and sincere. "Remember, please, that the request is made for a man who journeyed far to seek out wisdom, a man to whom I am transmitting sacred teachings. As you would wish me to do."

The tiger teeth glint again, but this time in a smile. "Well said. I shall consider the request. But I do know something of this case. I'm certain that a poem has already . . ." She gazes far off: considering? listening? "Ah!"

The jade maiden's head whirls round. The goddess meets her knowing eyes, then looks back to her devotee. *"That* poem was sent down by the Moon Lady. Yesss. To remind your little friend—I must tell you, she's let herself stray from her quest—to remind her where things stood. I'll give you a copy if you like. Well, perhaps this second poem will jar her loose. Let me have it, and I'll have a messenger bird sent off soon. Now stay and rest a bit. Listen to this next melody."

Parrot Speaks: 22

Another poem, less cryptic than the one Redsteed had found, brought me trouble from poor, malicious Tussah. It arrived in the tenth month; all the women of the household were gathered in the courtyard folding lengths of silk. I glanced up to see a blue-black raven flying toward us from the west, a slender roll of rice-paper dangling from its beak.

The raven's feathers glowed like no mortal bird's. Tussah shrieked. The bird perched, undisturbed, on my shoulder. Everyone stared as it hopped down to my hand, dropped the roll of paper, and flew away.

"A demon!" yelled Tussah. "The girl's a demon in disguise, come to spoil next year's silkworm hatching. I had a feeling she'd cause trouble." She bobbed her head toward her mother-in-law. "Your pardon, good mother. But I knew! I knew!"

"That will do," said the widow. "First Daughter Li, I believe you'd best see what the bird has brought."

"Yes, ma'am." Unrolling the slip of paper, I read it to the group:

POEM SENT TO SOMEONE FAR AWAY

I climb the stony path to Flower Mountain.
White clouds wrap the Flower Mountain peak.

The falling waters' spray paints dry moss green,
Then moonlight turns the gaudy hillsides gray.

A locust casts its hollow shell aside;
A yellow crane's born from the Primal Egg.

Who will sit alone on rocky outcrops
And, whistling, summon up ten thousand spirits?

I read every word aloud, except the signature at the end.

"Interesting," was Widow Chian's only comment. "I suppose it's from one of those silly hermit fellows, run off from his family responsibilities to traipse about after sylphs." *Practical* best describes her attitude toward the spirit world. Maintaining the house of Chian, in which her own strength lay, was the force that drove her life.

"A poem from a hermit?" exclaimed Tussah, narrowing her eyes. " 'Run-off fellow' hits the mark, I'd say. Good mother, if the girl's lover is so audacious, she'll bring disgrace down on our house for sure."

"I don't have a lover!" I said with enough heat to make a lesser person doubt me. But Widow Chian only nodded, as if to say, I know you don't.

"We'll accept this as a good omen," she said. "And"—she paused just long enough to rest her gaze on Tussah—"we'll say nothing of it to anyone outside the house."

Second Daughter had guessed immediately who sent the poem. We talked late in low voices that night, puzzling out the implications of the words and wondering how Sparker had managed to have the thing delivered by a messenger from the Western Motherqueen.

Shortly before cockcrow, the sound of pecking on our little wooden shutters woke us. I opened them and the blue-black raven flew in to perch on the rush mat where I slept. It cocked its head at me, expectant.

"What answer will you send?" asked Second Daughter. "Lucky you're a poet! Imagine if I'd been here alone." She smiled.

I fought a sudden dryness in my mouth. "I can't just write a poem because you want me to."

Hurt spread across her face. But before Second Daughter could answer, Tussah's sharp tones in the courtyard let us know we were late to start the fire and prepare the morning rice. We ran out to the kitchen and made certain that the widow saw how hard we worked that day. I felt my friend's dissatisfaction, her certainty that the poem must be written, and from time to time a suitable phrase glimmered in the back of my mind. Yet how could I make a poem out of our failure to enter the lake?

The next morning the glowing bird pecked at the window again, though I ignored it. That evening I wrote out a simple letter, telling Sparker that all went well with us, and the news of Baby and Feng. I felt better when I'd finished, as if the telling had eased something, and looked forward to the morning, when I could send it off and have the whole thing done with. Life at Widow Chian's had lulled me with its orderliness; I wanted no disruptions.

But when the raven came to our window and I offered it the rolled-up paper, it tapped its beak against it once, then flew away.

"Sister," Second Daughter said. "Feng told me that poem you composed in Shamanka Gorge fit a tricky verse form. He was impressed by your talent. Besides . . ." She paused to place her folded quilt on the foot of her bed. "The poem will make Sparker happy. It may even win us the favor of the Motherqueen." She stepped closer. "And that might bring us to your mother at last."

Widow Chian bought only the cheapest paper and brushes

for our writing lessons; the refinements of the calligrapher were not for her. Still, I found one sheet thinner than the rest and, by the shaded light of a candle Second Daughter smuggled to our bedroom, wrote out eight lines in the same rhyme and meter as Sparker's poem. Once I set thoughts of failure aside and made up my mind to begin, the words came easily after all:

THINKING OF THE FLOWER MOUNTAIN HERMIT

From a southern village, I watch the Yangzi's moon
And think of you, a wanderer in the hills.

Swathed in silks, I dip my writing brush.
In rags and vines, you climb that stony path.

Your shack is bare, the doorsill banked with leaves,
Yet meditation bell-sounds cleave the thickets.

Now I know: true landscape's not on scrolls;
The best poem is a hermit's fishing song.

In the morning, the bird took the thread-bound poem in its beak and flew off westward at last.

Winter came and life passed quietly. Tussah grew more irritable as her body swelled, so we avoided her as best we could. Sometimes Second Daughter spoke of going to Cavegarden Lake again. But what could we do, I'd argue, now that the Moon Lady had withdrawn her aid? In truth, I was not anxious to leave the household: my place there was lowly, but it was comfortable, and mine. Though I worked long hours, I loved the rhythmic clinking of the looms, the pure colors of the thread come back from the dyer, and most of all the shimmer of the undyed hanks.

Toward year's end, both of us caught colds, and our dry coughs lingered with us into spring.

Late the first morning of the third month, Tussah started labor. By evening, there was still no end in sight. Widow Chian stayed by her daughter-in-law through the night, wiping her forehead with damp cloths and murmuring encouragement.

When day broke, the widow set us three childless ones to our weaving, saying there was nothing we could do for Tussah. Her friend Auntie Ren had come over from next door to help; she would be company enough. Widow Chian instructed Springgauze to get things ready for spreading the silkworm eggs on the warming trays to hatch. We'd start them off the day after tomorrow, she said, after the birth and the festival on the third.

Tussah's daughter arrived just as evening fell. The mother loosed one last exhausted shriek, the weak-lunged baby spat out a feeble wail, and Auntie Ren shouted out in tones heavy with false joy. "A young lady! A precious little lady for the house of Chian." Running to the bedroom with Springgauze and Second Daughter, I heard Tussah groan.

When I saw her, her face was turned away. Widow Chian sat beside her, stroking her sweaty hair. Auntie Ren held the baby out to us, her arms stiff, her tongue unmoving for once. The poor child's forehead puffed out unnaturally, and even as Auntie Ren held her, I could see the twist of her spine.

Springgauze began to weep at once, her delicate back shaking, violent with pity. Second Daughter smoothed one finger down the baby's soft cheek. I pressed my hand against my own mouth, then followed Second Daughter to stand looking at the little girl. I could not speak.

Tussah hissed something too faint to be heard. In a spiteful whisper, she began to scold her sister-in-law for crying, but broke off when Widow Chian held a cup of fruit juice to her lips. "It's them, isn't it?" she said flatly a moment later. "My first baby was healthy, and then those two arrived. See what they've done—cursed me with a girl, an ugly, monstrous girl." In a weak and toneless voice she began to rail against us and her own evil fate.

Even the widow had been taken aback by Tussah's attack on Second Daughter and me. When she recovered, she curtly waved the three of us out of the room. Standing stupidly in the courtyard while Second Daughter calmed Springgauze, I heard the widow order Auntie Ren to go to the kitchen and make a tonic for Tussah. We three still stood there, shocked and aimless, when Auntie Ren returned with a steaming bowl. Passing us, she quickly sketched a gesture with one hand, a sign the country people use to ward off evil.

The events of the next hour blurred even as they took place. Springgauze stopped crying and sat with Second Daughter and me in a dark corner of the courtyard, near the bedroom window. The old cat Grizzle stalked moodily past us more than once. The baby's thin, hungry wailing rose and fell. Tussah muttered angry words. Then Widow Chian slapped her, and she fell into quiet tears of exhaustion and, I think, self-loathing.

Finally, the wretched baby's wailing stopped. "Poor Tussah's given it the nipple at last," said Springgauze. But before any of us could say another word, the Widow Chian came out into the courtyard, holding a candle. We three drew together, facing her.

"The child is dead," she said. "It is a blessing. She would have hurt this family. But—hush now, Springgauze—there is something else: Tussah still says the hired girls cursed her baby and swears she will not share a roof with them." She paused. "First and Second Daughter Li, you'll have to go."

Faced with the imperturbable candlelit countenance, neither of us dared speak. Dryness seized my throat. This, then, was the end of my attempts to live as a proper daughter of Great Tang. Springgauze began to argue with her mother-in-law, but the widow cut her off.

"No, I don't suppose the two are demons. I rather doubt such creatures trouble themselves very often with human affairs, to tell the truth. And many a malformed baby dies early"—she shifted her gaze to stare at the candle's flame—"one way or another. But my first son's wife has an active tongue. She'll bring down the real curse of idle gossip and slander upon the house of Chian. I won't have that."

Springgauze argued further. The silkworm-rearing season would soon be upon us, those frantic days and nights of gathering leaves and feeding. Moreover, she added, finding and training new workers to reel and weave the thread would be impractical.

"Indeed," Widow Chian replied. "But more impractical to lose trade because we're thought to be a house beneath a curse. We cannot lose our good name. The two may stay till morning. Good night." She turned back to Tussah's room. Second Daughter listened to Springgauze awhile longer. Then we packed up our belongings and got what rest we could.

Shortly after dawn we took our leave. At the gate, Springgauze wept, then brushed away her tears. Widow Chian pressed a bit of cash into my hand. "I know it's an odd thing," she said, "to want a girl before one has half a dozen boys at least." I saw in the fresh daylight how tightly her unwrinkled face was drawn. "But I should have liked a girl, a healthy one, who was as quick to learn as either one of you." The widow caught herself then and ended with a grave and brief farewell.

Without discussing it, Second Daughter and I had put on, for the first time since our arrival in the village, our swordswomen's clothes. I suppose we thought they'd offer us some defense. This was, after all, my first journey without a guardian—Nannie or Ghalib or the goddess of the moon.

Where else to go but to Cavegarden Lake? I'd failed to enter the dragonrealm beneath it, but I felt that it would be a comfort to see those broad waters again before we wandered on. If there was no place for us in the home of the wise and careful Widow Chian, what chance was there we'd find one—free of spite, or the threat of unwanted marriage—in some other household? If only we could rescue my mother. *She* would know where we might make our home.

Second Daughter and I had had our fill of the Yangzi. We chose paths tending southward and so kept the great river at our backs. Since it was the third day of the third month, people were gathering on its banks for the holiday, wearing spring clothes and sprigs of shepherd's purse on their heads. Let others dance and make sacrifice to river women, I thought bitterly. I had been turned out into the world with only one companion, to make a search with no direction and an uncertain end. A deep breath filled my lungs.

We struck the lake's great springtime mud flats at a point a little east of where we'd been before. I insisted that we rest a while under the maple trees on a low knoll. The tiny red flowers at the branches' tips fit the festive day but not my mood.

"Now what?" I asked Second Daughter, as if it were her responsibility to form a plan. She shook her head, and seeing the sorrow in her fine eyes I regretted my childishly demanding tone.

I stared out at the lake. "If we turn east," I said, "we'll reach the lake's outlet to the Yangzi and have to pay someone to ferry us across to Yue-jou. I know there's a town westward on the lakeshore—Springgauze's husband goes there to buy silk." I drew in another lungful of the lake-moist air and set my lips into a smile. "Surely sooner or later we'll find whatever it is that will let us reach my mother and carry her away. Shall we try our luck to the west?" Now I'd adopted the false cheer of a nursemaid encouraging a fussy charge. That too suited my friend poorly.

"Or," she murmured, "we might go straight ahead."

On Flower Mountain

Dawn: the third day of the third month. Festival of Drowned Women. Birthday of the Western Motherqueen. Bearing the emblem of her authority—a moonbright mirror inscribed with a cinnamon tree, a toad, a riddle-poem that's answered by the thing itself—the moonmaid White Aureole arrives on sacred Flower Mountain.

To a traveler from the direction of Chang-an, Flower Mountain, a great upthrust of Precambrian granite veined by erosion, resembles last year's dried lotus leaf rising above the cracked mud in a ruined pleasure garden. Its stone stands so unyielding that the southbound River Huang, striking it, veers acutely eastward toward the sea. Five peaks linked by knife-edge ridges manifest the sinuous spine of an enormous dragon sleeping in the earth. Cool moss and early sprouts of columbine and springstark oaks and pine trees bearing huge cones all cling to the gray-mauve rocks. From the West Peak one sees the village-dotted plain spread out as if it mapped itself. Sees, too, the waters of the River Wei, rich with all they have carried out of Chang-an, pouring themselves into the mighty Huang. Soon, the crucial pass at Flower Mountain's foot will flash red with the disastrous failure to halt the rebel general An Lu-shan's advance toward the Brilliant Emperor's capital. But you know how that story ends.

White Aureole's not concerned with an empire's fall. Her education completed, she comes to take up new responsibilities on the holy mountain, as archivist and teacher to seekers of astral lore. She already knows the first human to whom she must reveal herself.

Feet calloused, calf muscles knotted, belly rounded and relaxed, the Flower Mountain Hermit wanders down the narrow trail leading from the cave that is his home. After his long journey to Liang-jou and Darkdazzle Vista—where he received instruction from a certain Lady of the Tao his old friend Parrot once told him all about—he walked back to Flower Mountain, returning to the spot where he broke forth from his stony form. Today he's out looking, in a casual way, for the rare white fungus said to grow here, an edible fungus that transforms a mortal into a sylph. Actually, he doesn't care much if he finds it; after a life of servitude, he's finally happy as he is.

The hermit pauses to scratch an itch on his left shoulder blade. He ambles on, around a head-high boulder. He stops short and stares.

Austere, serene, and gracious, White Aureole nods her head. The hermit can't remember their earlier meeting in the lunar palace, when he was senseless stone. But at Darkdazzle Vista, his lovely teacher passed on to him the secret signs by which he recognizes an unearthly guardian of the mountain's hidden library of esoteric texts. Perhaps, he thinks, she will grant the one thing he still craves. Released from the desire for action, the hermit nonetheless still holds within himself one attachment to the world. Some months ago, Nephrite arranged for him an exchange of poetic messages with his mortal friends. All, he thinks, is well with them, and he is very nearly right. But growing up in the properly Confucian household of Old Tutor Feng, the hermit soaked in a bone-deep sense of the student's binding obligation to the teacher. And what has he done to repay Nephrite's assistance in the matter of the poem exchange, or all her kind instructions?

Nothing. That is, nothing yet. But this meeting may be his opportunity. He laughs a belly laugh, delighted by this splendid working-out of cosmic chance. Then he pauses, as the demon of uncertainty rises up within him: will the heavenly damozel grant his wish?

White Aureole allows herself a pleasant, close-lipped smile. She delivers a message transmitted to the Moon Lady from King Yama's tribunal down in hell. Some years from now, when the hermit's aged joints begin to ache, an ignorant, fiery-eyed lad from a nondescript village on the plain will stumble across his path. This lad will have been reborn early, excused from further years of purgatorial pain as recompense for an unscheduled early death in his previous existence.

In that life just past, White Aureole continues, the lad was a mighty general from Chang-an, slain in Khotan by a vermilion dragon. In this new one, he'll be given the chance to become the Flower Mountain Hermit's disciple. "And," she says with delicate majesty, "may he seize this spiritual opportunity as well as he once gripped his sword!"

The hermit indicates his willingness to take the general-disciple on. Then he gathers up his nerve—something wandering Taoists seldom need to do—and makes his request. His former teacher, whose name in the world was Nephrite, has achieved the spiritual power necessary to let her soul fly to the Western Motherqueen. But she cannot travel anywhere she wants. And where she wants to travel is to the side of their mutual friend, variously known as Parrot and Skywhistle and so forth. Could the unearthly maiden now before him somehow make this possible? It would bring great joy to the heart of a devoted lady of the Tao, and—the hermit must admit—it would ease his own.

White Aureole pauses to consider. Perhaps, with the aid of her lunar mistress, such a thing can be arranged.

Meanwhile, down in the reeking, torturous depths of hell, the hermit's agreement to accept as his disciple the reincarnation of one General Li is jotted down in King Yama's Book of Life and Death. But what, the infernal recorder idly wonders, of the vacancy White Aureole's departure has created for a seventh student in the palace on the moon?

Parrot Speaks: 23

I was giddy on the breeze blowing off the lake, giddy and light as clouds. Each lap of water on Cavegarden's shore echoed those before it, and Second Daughter's murmured words—*we might go straight ahead*—rang inside my head. Sunlight glanced off the waves in glittering designs; the brilliance struck dark spots on my field of vision. Squinting, I made out a steep-sided island, the tip of a submerged mountain really, still wrapped in morning's mist.

Startled, I blinked. It seemed like somewhere I'd lived a long time ago, and yet like no place my eyes had ever seen.

Second Daughter jumped to her feet.

"What is that—" I began, then let the question drop. A rare energy swelled inside me, born of that day—the Amah's birthday—and that remarkable place. The island's name meant nothing in the face of its compelling beauty. Tell me the place means risk of death, I thought, or that it means the silent time before awareness. We can get ourselves there, somehow. I stared at the bright-dark dragonpatterns on the water, and caught my breath.

Second Daughter was tearing wildly through her bundle, looking for something. "Cavegarden Isle," she said, her voice faraway and certain. "Remember? In one of the weaving songs that Springgauze taught us to read last winter—a huge rock from the Kunlun Mountains. It flew here." She snatched the knife she'd taken from her father's kitchen and waved it overhead. "Get something," she said. "Those sewing scissors Springgauze gave you this morning."

I laughed, and understood precisely what to do, as when I suddenly saw the right words to finish off a poem. An old temple to the Hsiang River Ladies stands on Cavegarden Isle: I'd copied out a poem about it for calligraphy practice, years ago in Liangjou. "Maybe the Ladies of the Hsiang will tell us how to reach my mother." I snatched up the scissors and added, "Once we're there."

Second Daughter dulled her knife as she sawed through four great bamboo from a nearby grove. I ruined the pretty sewing scissors hacking the slim branches off those large bamboo and two smaller ones that would serve as poles. Everything we did seemed part of an elaborate dance, rehearsed time and time again.

We worked steadily but with more than natural haste, tearing our spare clothing into strips and braiding ropes to lash the four bamboo together. My body felt fully alive—for the first time, I realized, since we'd settled into the confines of the Chian courtyard and the throat-catching security I'd clung to.

The sun slid westward as Second Daughter and I finished. Our eyes met and we laughed. The long, narrow raft looked so preposterous, the lake so large. "The currents—" I began.

"Not so bad this season," Second Daughter said, and grinned. "Our biggest worry is the mud." Our laughter burst out again; for a moment, I thought it might carry me up into the air. We threw our boots off and rolled our pant legs to our knees. Whether the lake opened to us was beyond our doing. And until that point, we could not rely on starswords or on human protectors. All we had were things we'd learned—a bit from a weaving song in the women's language, a bit from an old poem—brought together within ourselves.

We discarded the knife and scissors. Our few coins we placed beneath a flat stone, our cups and flint and cooking pot deep in a clump of bushes. I tucked the little scroll I'd carried for so long snugly into my sash and kept one thing more: "Remember this?" I held a small pearl on a chain up to Second Daughter. "The day we met? It reminded me of one I used to have, so I didn't add it to the sergeant's bribe."

"Wear it, then," she said. "We're bound to get soaked, but at least that way you won't lose it." We cackled like happy madwomen once again. I put it around my neck and realized it was the first time I'd ever worn the thing properly, since it had seemed too elegant for a swordswoman or a hired girl at Widow Chian's.

We put out west of the island, hoping to angle across the lake's eastward currents. The hollow sections of the bamboo rode low but buoyantly. Waves soaked our clothes and skin. I nearly tipped the raft trying to guide it with my pole, which proved completely useless as we moved out into deeper waters.

My self-assurance faded. I began to imagine drowning in that enigmatic lake, as I had nearly done the other time I tried to enter it. Wasn't this day the festival of drowned women of antiquity? Poor Feng had met his fate on the Doublefifth, the day dedicated to the drowned official Chu Yuan. I began to wish for some water spirit to rescue us, a giant tortoise, say, that would rise beneath the flimsy raft and carry us safely on its back to the island.

The bamboo clattered against unseen stones that would have bashed a hole in the bottom of a proper boat. Now the poles showed their worth as we wedged them between the smooth stones and pushed ourselves close to the island. We scrambled onto shore.

A faint path wound up the steep hill before us. We took it at a run, still moving with the haste of the possessed. Beneath a flowering citrus tree, we stopped to catch our breath.

"Listen!" Second Daughter hissed. "There's a spring here. And I'm thirsty." She stepped around a rocky shelf and called out for me to join her. The water had a faint sweet taste of wine. I'd heard the stories: this *was* the island where the Hsiang River Ladies' temple stands. Rapt, panting, we resumed our climb.

The roof of the shrine had vanished long ago. Lichens splayed their unreadable messages on the walls. Within the dimness we could just see the forms of the two archaic sisters carved into the stone wall above the altar. We sank to our knees on prayer cushions of moss. I heard Second Daughter sigh and felt my own breath ease.

At last we slipped outside, into the twilight. "We should make an offering," I whispered. "My necklace? The little scroll?"

She shook her head and looked around. "I don't think so," she said. "Those would be out of place here. It should be something one of us has made, don't you think? You'll have to compose a poem."

"No paper."

"You can write it on the wall, as temple visitors do."

"No ink."

"Scratch it with a stone, then. In the women's words."

And so I did.

LOOKING FOR THE GODDESS
ON CAVEGARDEN ISLE

Spring: a maple shore
  tinged red with flowers.
Glossy waters spread
  out to sky's edge.

Uncertain currents sweep
  a bamboo raft;
Wild waves carry it
  to misty shores.

The rocky isle's brushed green
  by sourpeel-orange trees.
Travelers laugh, gone high
  on sweet wine springs.

Now spotted bamboo trace
  an uphill trail,
And pepperwort inscribes
  the mossy altar.

We breathe here, where the empty
   sanctum stands—
Unroofed, untouched—and waits
   a poet's words.

Around the Go Board

The Guardian of the Celestial Stores lights the camellia-scented oil in his ruby-sunset lamp and sets it on a nearby puff of cloud. He tugs one earlobe thoughtfully and looks around: everything's prepared for the visit of his friend, now a subaltern in the ministry of Babble but formerly the Assistant Undersecretary of Baubles, and—who knows?—perhaps soon to rise again.

The Guardian's a bit nervous. At the former Undersecretary's request, he has slipped a certain precious set for playing Go out of the Jade Emperor's treasure vaults. The Go board's squares of inlaid rhinocerous horn form a grid of nineteen horizontal lines, and nineteen vertical. Two bowls hold the stones to be placed upon the intersections: perfectly matched black pearls fill one; the pale pearls in the other bowl glimmer in a lovely multitude of tints. In fact, His Heavenly Highness has lost all interest in the precious geegaw. Nevertheless the Guardian doubts the wisdom of conceding to his crony's desire to see that marvelous set again. No question about it, since his demotion, the former Undersecretary has been obsessed with the thing. But the obligations of friendship cannot be ignored.

With a flurry of splendid robes and elegant bows, the former Undersecretary arrives. The game begins. The Guardian would like for them to linger over their cups of Jade Sap and chat a bit before they start to play, but that's obviously impossible. He tugs at his earlobe again. Naturally, the story of the Undersecretary's demotion flashed through the ranks of courtiers and bureaucrats in Taoist heaven at once. Yet little has been said recently; the Guardian would like an update on the whole affair.

After several cups of delightful elixir, when chains of pearls have begun to weave and twine across the board, he brings the subject up. The former Undersecretary grunts, describing bits of what has happened.

In a desultory way, the fragmentary story of a certain pearl necklace begins to come out—not the banished Luminous Emerald-Green Lunar Essence Sprite itself, but something somehow like it. This odd gem, presented by the Dragon Monarch to a greedy merchant upon the betrothal of the merchant's daughter to the dragon's son, fell into a trunk with her possessions, and so went with her when she was wed to another man.

The Undersecretary drains his cup and goes on talking. When a vermilion dragon went in doctor's guise to the human realm to fetch the mortal woman to Cavegarden Lake, he fetched the necklace back as well. The woman gave it to the Moon Lady, with whom she is in league, and the Lady to the woman's roving daughter, incarnation of the green pearl sprite.

"You know how, ah, *assertive* that particular goddess can be," the former Undersecretary grouses, cocking one grayed bushy eyebrow and rolling a sky-colored pearl between his forefinger and his thumb. "His Divine Majesty charged me personally with overseeing the case of the banished pearl—the one born as a woman—so of course I had to keep an eye on this necklace-pearl too. But when I called on the Moon Lady to inquire about it, she just smiled her smug, frosty smile and said, 'Every mother gives a pearl to her girlchild,' or some such thing. Next thing I know, the human—the green pearl sprite, that is—has given it"—he drains his cup—"to the Lady Guan-yin."

The Guardian gives a knowing grimace.

"Guan-yin's no more forthcoming than any Buddhist deity," the former Undersecretary continues. "Did I ever tell you how she sent me once to muck about in a sand dune, rescuing some monk who was vaguely involved in this case? Well—he's rather famous, that monk, or will be when enough tales have accumulated around him—after I did it, I heard he was in the wrong place at the wrong time, headed in the wrong direction. At least if you believe his record of his travels." His eyebrows perform a kind of jig. "History!" he snorts. "At its best it's full of loops and loopholes."

In tones of sympathy and interest, the Guardian offers more Jade Sap. And is accepted.

The former Undersecretary places the sky-colored pearl in a position that completes the encirclement of three of the Guardian's black ones; he removes them from the board and piles them with the others he has won. "I needn't bore you with the details of all the rest of it, but in short, the mother gets worried and Lady Guan-yin gives the necklace back to her as a sign of comfort, *but* the mother takes it into her head to send it to the human realm by that vermilion dragon, who somehow gets it to a companion of the daughter, a runaway who returns it to the foolish girl at last. Still with me?"

The Guardian nods. He finds the story's convolutions, its criss- and double-crossings, as bizarre as those of the lives that humans lead. For that very reason, it's curiously fascinating to this dweller in the clouds.

"You'd think by now the sprite-girl would figure out the necklace is important," the former Undersecretary goes on. "But, no, she'd practically forgotten she had it, last time I checked. The silly female seems to think she wants to spend her life in one courtyard, spinning and weaving. How's she ever going to finish doing what she set out to do that way?" He shakes his head and grunts again.

The Guardian selects a fine black pearl and holds it closer to the lamp's alpen-glow light. "But what does the whole thing *mean?*" he inquires in pettish tones.

The former Undersecretary's developing a headache. He stares at the forkings and the conjugations of the chains of pearls upon the Go board. His eyes begin to lose their focus. In truth, he prefers the straightforward look of the empty board's neat grid to these twisting fragments of a web. "You wanted the story," he says. "Why don't you tell me?"

Beneath the Waters

And when the last word of the poem is written, the lake opens wide to take the two young women in. A dry path appears between the waves, leading from the island's shore toward unknown depths. Greenpearl and Second Daughter run downhill from the shrine and stand at lake's edge, bemused.

Let Cavegarden spread its watery gates for you as well. Don't be afraid of that pull to go beneath the waters, where the mother waits. Suspend your disbelief and enter in.

A thunderworker swims up, gestures toward the pathway along the lake bottom, and indicates to Greenpearl and Second Daughter that they must close their eyes and step forward. The humans obey. Their feet seem to float from the unseen path, yet the two breathe easily. Soon, they find themselves in a light-dappled garden of waterweeds outside a glimmering mother-of-pearl villa. The thunderworker waves them inside and bows farewell.

They enter a great audience hall, raftered with sea amber and walled with brilliant living corals. Upon a throne of nacre, the Dragon Monarch sits, scales aglitter in the light of paired moon-pearl lamps. A few carp-courtiers linger in an alcove, and a brace of eel dancers awaits the Monarch's pleasure. The mortal women kowtow. The Monarch greets them with a courteous nod.

"Second Daughter, someone will come with news for you," the Monarch says. And then: "Greenpearl, you should know I gave that pearl you wear now to your mother, Seagem, who passed it on to you. You may as well address me as Grand-mama."

For yes, the Dragon Monarch is a queen, you know. But a mistake—if indeed you made one—is understandable. Even the good people of the Tang lost sight of the gender of many of the ancient womanly deities of the watery deeps, letting it be leached out, or covered over in fatherly Confucian guise. And yet, archaic truths remain; here, you've read a history of what has been submerged.

As for Greenpearl, she's pleased at the Monarch's kindliness. But she will no longer be distracted from her goal; she's learned the danger of falling into her old traps of self-doubt and despair. "With all due respect, Your Majesty," she begins in formal tones, "I've come to set my mother free." She stands like a proper swordswoman, balance easy, legs firm. And though Second Daughter feels a great reluctance to quarrel with the Monarch, she's loyal to her sworn sister and takes a solid stance beside her.

"Ahh." The Dragon Monarch responds with what later generations will call mandarin irony. "That's well enough. If she chooses to be freed." Before Greenpearl can respond to that last puzzling comment, the Monarch adds, "First, however, I fear I must inform you of one rule. Uninvited humans are welcome here for a night, but then you must return to your own realm."

Greenpearl finds the prohibition pointless. She's not one to lose her sense of courtesy, however, despite her newly strength-ened purpose. She makes a silent bow to indicate compliance, relieved to learn that she too won't be captured. Why would she want to stay?

To send one's soul soaring among the Kunlun Mountains to the Western Motherqueen is no easy thing, even for a spiritually advanced Lady of the Tao. Far more difficult to send one's body, too, and to choose some other destination. But aided by White Aureole's teachings, Jade Clarity has arrived at Sparker's cave on Flower Mountain. The tousle-haired hermit sees her exquisite form descending through the morning fog, breaks into a belly laugh, and runs to greet her.

The two converse in tones that are not quite the dispassionate ones you might expect of holy recluses. She thanks him for his assistance; he expresses his gratitude for all she taught him when he came to Darkdazzle Vista. Then Sparker winks at her and jerks his head.

"Back there," he says, "beyond that bend in the cave, I recently discovered a tunnel leading downward. I've never stepped inside it—seems to me my place is here. But perhaps you ought to have a look at it."

Jade Clarity's eyes widen, but she says nothing. This reunion has been pleasant, but Flower Mountain is not the place she was trying to go to. What, she wonders, is the meaning behind Sparker's teasing smile?

He guides her to the tunnel's mouth. A dim, silvery light seeps out, spilling itself in an irregular pool at their feet. A soft roaring sound trickles into their ears. Jade Clarity cocks an eyebrow. Sparker grins and nods to tell her *yes*.

From the depths of Cavegarden Lake, such tunnels branch throughout the porous earth, linking sites of spiritual power, providing access for a few lucky mortals to immortal realms. Jade Clarity's pale hands grasp each other. She bids farewell to Sparker and begins her descent. At the first bend, she looks back. Sparker ducks his head and grins again. Farewell.

There she sits, the longed-for mother. Her brow is smooth. Her bearing's proud. Her eyes shine, moist with love. "First Daughter!" Seagem cries, choosing from all the young woman's many names the one she herself gave her.

For long moments Seagem embraces this child she has cherished from afar. Without the daughter's difficult journey, without the mother's painful lessons, this union could not be the joyful thing it is: could the Seagem who kept to her father-in-law's house in Chang-an have loved a concubine's child in this same unfettered way? And how would that spoiled, uncultured hoyden have turned out, suddenly confined to the women's quarters of a good family's house? But here, and now, such happiness is possible.

Seagem has kind words too for Second Daughter; the farmer's runaway child soon curls beside Greenpearl at the mother's feet. Then looking up, Greenpearl finally notices who sits on the dais with Seagem. She backs off, surprised and shocked.

Seagem's right hand tenderly holds that of her dear husband, the Hsiao River Princeling, while her left palm presses lovingly against the inner thigh of a vermilion-clad gentleman, her new Second Consort, on her other side. For just as the nameless mother who gave Greenpearl birth—her father's Iranian concubine, dead in Khotan when the daughter first drew breath—was reborn to a new life as a peasant girl, was captured, and became first a mute dancer and finally a shamanka (yes!); just as Greenpearl's second mother, who gave mild and loving scoldings and praise for childish songs, was finally redeemed from her attachment to the flesh, redeemed by the blissful oceanic union of ghost and medium, of Nannie and Baby (yes); so this third mother, the mother of Greenpearl's heart, having cast off the old restraints, has been released into her own desires. Yes.

Hasty introductions are made. Uncle and nephew beam agreeably toward their stepdaughter: the Hsiao River Princeling has learned to be less possessive, the vermilion dragon, more genteel. The Princeling sends a serving fish to fetch hot towels with which the weary travelers may refresh themselves. The vermilion dragon calls for wine all round.

Greenpearl forces herself to review her own past, struggles to accept the dragon realm's free and easy ways. That's not terribly difficult, in fact; but there is another, harder thing. She has come so far to rescue her mother, and now Seagem seems quite happy. Is it possible that she will not want to leave?

Soon, mother and daughter sit together, alone in the little study where Seagem's writing desk now stands. Greenpearl bites her lower lip.

". . . But all that's gotten better now," Seagem concludes. "There are moments, of course, when he feels neglected, or when my Second Consort gets too boisterous." She shrugs. Faced with the child she dreamed of—no, not child, but nearly grown-up woman—she feels the old constraints. What *would* they think of her in Chang-an, not just twice married but with a lover at her side?

Greenpearl tries to display a look of understanding, remembering how Baby's jealousy set the two of them apart. And with that tolerance gives her mother the greatest gift she could. Yet she's still bothered. "You truly want to stay here, don't you?" Greenpearl asks.

When Greenpearl first asked that question, handing her empty wine cup to a serving fish, the gentleman in vermilion roared—literally—with laughter. The Princeling smiled a smile of wan delight. Even Seagem shook her head, as if afraid that she too would shame her daughter with an escaped laugh, then hushed her with the promise of this private talk. Now the mother looks at Greenpearl, heartsick at what she knows she has to do. "Yes," she says, "I do."

The old Greenpearl would have retreated into depression, or at best into dreams. But she has gripped a starsword and has left the safety of a weaver's life. "It's really what you want?" she asks; then, reading Seagem's face, says, "So. At least I know you're happy. When morning comes, I'll go."

Thus, quietly, she declares her break. The mother can do nothing, only nod when Greenpearl adds, "Of course, I have to. The Dragon Monarch made that clear." Both fall silent, brooding on the one word not spoken: *where?*

A carp-courtier summons mother and daughter to an impromptu banquet arranged by the Dragon Monarch. At first, they feel rather stiff, each determined in her course, each regretting that those courses will carry them apart. Greenpearl sits close to Second Daughter, and they start to tell the tale of their adventures. The atmosphere eases a bit.

Seagem breaks an awkward stillness with a question. "That scroll the Western Motherqueen sent you, daughter, years ago. The Amah gave me her word that it was what you needed. Whatever happened to it?"

The scroll! Greenpearl hasn't looked at it for almost a year. Perhaps the meaning is finally to be revealed. Second Daughter meets her glance, eyes alive with anticipation.

Greenpearl draws the little roll of cloth from the folded pocket of her sash. She loosens the strings that hold the scroll closed and unwinds a length. Alas, a grayish ink wash stains her fingers: the water here in the dragon realm cannot be distinguished from the purest air, but during the raft ride to the island, mundane waves on the surface of Cavegarden Lake rinsed away the writing. Only a few faint signs can still be discerned.

And Greenpearl sees that she can read them now. "Look, sister!" she cries. "It's in the women's script. See? This one's 'mother' and, look, here's 'jade,' and 'pearl' I think, and . . ." Her voice trails off. Whatever words once made their way along that road of silk, Greenpearl decides, they're gone forever now. Seagem is aghast. She looks over toward the Monarch's throne.

"*I* think," the Dragon Monarch says, her voice brisk and sensible, "we'd best do something about that dripping mess." She picks up a mallet of silver and strikes a limestone gong. "His Excellency, my Minister of Fictive Histories, will help you out."

An instant later, the Minister, a huge river tortoise, enters. He bears an ornate basin on his back. "Rinse the scroll in that," the Monarch says. Greenpearl obeys. Then she and Second Daughter stretch the blank length of heavy silk between them, as they did so many times at Widow Chian's. They shake it, hard, and snap it smooth. No one in the Mother-of-Pearl Villa objects to a few flying drops of dense water from the terrestrial realm; indeed, one of the eel dancers come to entertain them titters sybaritically at a cool splash on his skin.

The Monarch strikes the gong again, and two carp-courtiers bring in a drying frame. The human women drape the cloth upon it. Finally, Greenpearl collects herself and turns to the Minister of Fictive Histories to offer thanks.

"So, Parrot," the Minister says, stretching out his long leathery neck and fixing his beadlike eyes upon her. "Is that all you have to say to your old friend? I thought you'd be happy to see I have an official position at last."

"Feng!" cries Greenpearl, recognizing the light, cultivated voice if not the face. She throws her arms around that long neck, and in an instant Second Daughter's there beside her. Tears of joy fall from six eyes.

"I have your lady mother, Seagem, to thank for my rescue," Feng says. "Her magic mirror showed me helpless on the Yangzi's floor. She pitied me and ran to beseech her gracious mother-in-law to save me with a spell. After my transformation, the Monarch was pleased to grant me office in her court." He pauses to bow toward the throne as only a stately river tortoise can, then turns back to the two women.

"And look!" He wriggles and shimmers and stands before them, handsome, smiling, a man again. "I can return to human form when I want to, but I'm fond of both." At that, the two nearby eel dancers break out in chuckles—one high-pitched, one low—and Feng tilts an eyebrow in their direction as ironically as any courtier in Chang-an. Then he rests one hand lightly on Greenpearl's shoulder. "I hope, dear Parrot, you'll be staying on? I think you'll find life better here than in the human realm."

Poor Greenpearl feels a decided pang. She remembers, as clearly as if she smelled the sweet spice of clove daphne blooming along the upper Yangzi, the afternoon when she lay down with Feng. She breathes out slowly and looks at her feet.

A dainty cough: Nephrite's slender figure steps out from behind a cockleshell screen. Greenpearl gasps, and the two embrace. All those around them murmur happily, though Feng looks a bit put out. But perhaps he thinks of his frolics with the eel dancers, for he puts that look aside.

Nephrite's tale tumbles out, interrupted now and then by introductions and questions and explanations from the others. Feng beams when he hears of Sparker's new freedom as a hermit. "Without the request the Flower Mountain Hermit made to that moonmaid," Nephrite says, facing Parrot, eyes aglow, "I might never have seen you again!"

"Ah, loyal Sparker." Feng sighs like a sage, or nearly so.

Amid sounds of general agreement, Nephrite gestures toward Second Daughter with a cool white hand. "And for you, the Moon Lady's message is this: you will obtain your heart's desire."

The face of the farmer's runaway daughter is faintly hopeful, guarded. The Lady of the Tao smiles a delicate smile. In exchange for the goddess's aid to Greenpearl, Nephrite explains, Seagem promised to select and help train a human to take the place of the seventh moonmaid when White Aureole moved on to her new position. "The Moon Lady felt a human woman should make the choice, you see—a matter of perspective, I suppose. At any rate, one night Seagem's mirror showed her your face. So she found out all she could about you, and sent you the pearl necklace that started you off adventuring as companion to her daughter."

Second Daughter fixes her gaze upon the mother, willing what she thinks Nephrite is about to tell her to be so. Seagem nods.

As the two watched over one another on their travels, Nephrite continues, Second Daughter learned the skills—the perseverance, the faith in her own strengths, the love of what the writing brush can do upon the page—she needs to become a pupil of the Lady on the moon. "I believe you'd find that pleasant?" Nephrite concludes, and smiles again.

Second Daughter's face is beautiful in this moment, with a beauty beyond that of the smooth complexion she doesn't have, or the high-arched brows she does. In her audience with the Moon Lady, she asked only to be allowed to learn to read and write. Later she told herself to be content with what she'd been taught at Widow Chian's. Now, she knows, a great library lies open to her, reams of the finest paper, and all the time she needs. She nods her quick assent.

Only Greenpearl fails to feel unmitigated delight at this turn of events. "I'll miss you, sister," she says, and wonders how she'll manage alone.

In her gleaming fastness, upon a throne of purple ice, the Western Motherqueen strokes the brilliant feathers of a blue-black raven. The bird croaks, hopping up and down the Amah's arm. It cocks its head and fixes one beady eye upon a slip of paper lying on the silver table at the goddess's side, beside a plate of beautifully rounded, blush-pink peaches.

The paper holds birthday greetings sent by the Dragon Monarch to the Western Motherqueen this very morning. "Ten thousand natal felicitations to the Metal Mother, embodiment of the occult nebulae of the western enigma, origin of the ultimate yin!" it begins.

Now, her celebrations having abated with the fall of evening, the goddess has prepared a return message for the Dragon Monarch. She ties to the bird's leg an even smaller slip of paper, rolled to the fineness of a straw. It bears merely six lines, piled on one another: a yielding, two firm, another yielding, two more firm. This ancient hexagram will help the ruler of the dragon realm understand the proper course of action in the present situation.

In the Mother-of-Pearl Villa beneath Cavegarden Lake, when the paper is unrolled, the Dragon Monarch looks about her at the others come together by the light of moonpearl lamps for tonight's banquet. Her son is whispering something to Seagem. Feng and Nephrite are making rather strained conversation with the vermilion dragon, who has just finished off a plate of scallops and is filling their cups with wine. Second Daughter stares at one of the serving starfish, though her thoughts appear to be fixed quite happily upon the moon. Greenpearl is looking down at her slightly ink-stained fingers. She hasn't eaten much.

"Hexagram 57," the Dragon Monarch announces. "A message from the Amah." She pauses to reflect. *Hsun, The Penetrating*, it is," she tells them. "Or some might say, *The Gentle*. Its element is wood, of course, It means changeableness and scents wafted by the wind. In the family of Dark and Light, it represents the eldest daughter." She stops. "It is the hexagram of homecoming." Her eye meets Seagem's. Seagem turns to Greenpearl and squeezes her daughter's hand.

🔲 Two late-night talks: In a coral chamber, Seagem speaks urgently. The Hsiao River Princeling smiles with doleful compassion and shakes his head.

Seagem's vermilion lover growls something in her ear; the woman frowns prettily. "No, he's right," Seagem replies, soft-voiced. "You know what *she* is like about uninvited guests." Her fine-haired husband begins to speak, then sets his lips, and sighs.

"But," Seagem continues slowly, "there's one thing that might work. We'll let it rest till morning, while I think about whether it can be done." The vermilion dragon shrugs. The Princeling blinks, surprised but far from optimistic.

Meanwhile, out among the waterweeds, Greenpearl and Second Daughter stroll by the flickering light of distant stars, strangely augmented here in the dragon realm. Second Daughter says she'll give up going to the lunar palace, that she'll travel on with Greenpearl, that surely somewhere in the human realm, they can find a home. Greenpearl refuses. She insists her friend cannot ignore this celestial calling. Both know it to be true.

Off in his own sleeping quarters, Feng tosses restlessly, remembering a certain delicious look that passed to him from Greenpearl. No enchanted journey calls on their bodily energies now. If only she could stay!

And Nephrite, behind a guest-room door that shines with purple cowrie shells, lies as sleepless as the others. As a mortal who's acquired some transcendent powers, she's welcome to return to the Mother-of-Pearl Villa anytime she wants to. The Dragon Monarch took her aside to tell her this, pointing out that Nephrite now can fly to Flower Mountain and that from there she knows the way. A kind of invitation, surely, but all that Nephrite thinks of is the look *she* got from Greenpearl at the banquet's close: indefinably different, perhaps, but surely just as sweet.

Later still, the new moon climbs the sky. In a village on the neck of land between the Yangzi and Cavegarden Lake, a widow woman squeezes her tired eyes, then checks the warmth of the tiny silkworm eggs spread out on their trays. The work goes on, though her daughters-in-law still nurse their sorrows. They will heal, the widow thinks, glad that it's still some weeks before the voracious larvae hatch. Back in her own room, she falls into forgetful peace at last.

Off to the northwest, high windborne loess drifts through the air. Stars and moon, tinged auspicious yellow, shine down on the garden of an entertainment house in Liang-jou. Within, the aging proprietress mutters and rolls over in her curtained bed. Bathed in fortune's light, she sighs. Then the corners of her mouth slide upward, and she rejoins the throngs of sleepers—men and women, barbarians and Chinese—who fill the valleys and the fertile uplands of Great Tang.

In another Yangzi River village, just downstream from the gorges, a shamanka wakes. She steps outside and sees in the cloudless sky the rarefied light of earthshine reflected in the dark space embraced by the thin crescent moon. Like mist or ash, the faint glow manifests some powerful force in subtle form. She knows it signals a great good, returns contented to her bed and dreams of swimming easily beneath slow silver waters.

Did Seagem sleep at all last night? In any case, she rose early, and returns now from a predawn conference with her mother-in-law to join Greenpearl and her three friends at a gloomy farewell breakfast. Her husband and her vermilion consort chat drowsily in a corner. Feng says nothing, hunched moodily within his stately robes—except to mutter "Turtle's egg!" when he scalds his tongue on his third cup of tea. Only Second Daughter reveals a hint of suppressed happiness as Nephrite tells her White Aureole will meet them in the cave on Flower Mountain; she'll guide the new scholar to the cinnamon-shaded garden on the moon.

As for Greenpearl, she has gathered her determination. After all, she has seen her mother at last and knows she is content. The quest is over, and if that leaves her with no place to go, she'll simply have to find one on her own.

Second Daughter turns to her with reassurances of regular letters. She puts her mouth to her friend's ear. "Nephrite will come to you again, if she can manage, and Feng as well. Just look at him!"

Greenpearl's smile twists wryly. Yes, if only she could stay here, she'd have friends and lovers enough, and never worry about distinctions between the two. But she doubts that a river tortoise or a Lady of the Tao still bound by human flesh will really be able to make their ways to whatever place she'll stumble into once she's forced back to the human realm. Perhaps she'll simply wander all her life.

"And something else," says Second Daughter, louder now, so that all can hear. "That poem the cat Redsteed brought you?" Nephrite looks interested but holds her peace. "I was thinking about it late last night. Remember, we figured out about Feng and Baby in the first two lines. And you, daughter of the house of Li and daughter of dragons, whose element is wood, are surely 'the child of wood.' I think—" She frowns in recollection. "How did the last couplet go?"

" 'When pearl and jade have met beneath the waves,' " says Greenpearl automatically. She starts then, and looks from her mother Seagem to Nephrite's jade-white hands.

Second Daughter joins Greenpearl in chanting the last line: " 'The child of wood shall weave a heavenly web'!"

Seagem smiles benignly. Nephrite looks as if she sensed the misty, ashen light of hope. Feng drains another cup of tea. Greenpearl's irritated; she has said she's through with weaving, and she's certainly through with garbled rhymes.

Greenpearl cuts Second Daughter off before she can say more and begs leave to depart. But Seagem bids her listen.

The mother describes how she too believed the arts of needle and loom to be a trap, trivial beside the arts of brush and ink. "But consider this, daughter," she adds. "You learned those words in women's script in the house of the silk weavers and nowhere else. With them, you could have read what was written on your scroll. And would that scroll of yours exist at all without some woman's weaving of the cloth? I believe the Dragon Monarch means for you to understand that, to weigh the value of what was given you—and weave upon it your own web."

Greenpearl looks up, puzzled.

"Daughter. You've put words together in song lyrics, and in poems. Are you willing to do that again?"

Yes, Greenpearl says, she's more than willing. A part of her would like to leave immediately, to get the misery over with. But if reciting poems can help them stay together a few hours longer, she'll stay on. Besides (she puts away her old doubts for the last time; Second Daughter's right, the opening of the waters proved it: she *is* a poet), the making, and her mother's praise of it, would bring her pleasure.

"Then, daughter, I will have your lute returned to you." Seagem holds up a hand to signal that no questions need be asked. "Yes, it came to me when you cast it into Cavegarden. But you weren't ready yet to enter in yourself. Now let me ask you this."

Seagem leans forward, staring into eyes where the wish to stay has replaced the defiant assertion of the will to leave. "The Monarch loves nothing so much as a good story," she says. "Ask Feng." The Minister of Fictive Histories nods. "So I spoke with her this morning. She has thought over the message from the Amah and has decreed that if you'll read to her what's written on this scroll, a bit each afternoon perhaps, you may stay on here, as her Minister of Verisimilar Romances. Are you willing?" The mother holds out the fine-spun roll of writing silk, given her so long ago by the Western Motherqueen.

Greenpearl opens her mouth to protest. She's willing indeed, but the scroll is blank! She pulls it—dry now, yet washed white all the same—from her sash to show her mother.

"Daughter, if the Monarch commands you to read her what's written on the scroll," Seagem continues, "and there is nothing written on it, what must you do?"

Now Greenpearl claps her hands and bursts out laughing. Second Daughter, Feng, Nephrite, and the others follow. Soon, even the vermilion dragon sees the answer and roars for a catfish-in-waiting to bring a brush and ink.

"But what," Greenpearl says a moment later, carefully grinding the inkstick on its stone, "should I write? The scroll is small when it's rolled up, but it's much too long to fill with poetry or songs. Look at it." She gazes at its magical emptiness, silent now, great with potentiality.

"Take up your brush, child," says the mother. "Write the story of yourself."

So Greenpearl dips the fine fur of the writing brush into her ink's dark pool, and writes: *Once above a time, deep within the rosy cloudbanks of the morning sky . . .*

Epilogue:
Nu Wa's Grotto Again

The small waterdragon nudges Nu Wa's hand again. Fu Hsi stretches and yawns. "Excellent, dear sister. Told as only you can do it. Those yellow-mud creatures are indeed amusing." He slides his tail around hers sensuously. "I don't suppose . . ." he begins.

"We ought to get some sleep," says Nu Wa, though her lips slide into a faint, considering smile.

"I'm not sleepy," Fu Hsi says, his eyelids heavy. And the waterdragon looses a tiny plaintive *prrt* deep within its throat.

"Hush," Nu Wa answers. "Rest now, and when you wake up, I'll tell another story. Or maybe . . ." The smile grows wider. "Maybe then we'll play." She rolls over on her side and, with determination, shuts her eyes. The other two sigh and do the same.

Lying there, sliding toward the uncarved silence of sleep, Nu Wa considers how the next tale might begin. *My name is, for the moment, Parrot*, she thinks. And wonders how it will all come out this time around.